THE LAST BALLAD

Also by Helen Cannam
A High and Lonely Road

THE
LAST
BALLAD

Helen Cannam

St. Martin's Press
New York

Library of Congress Cataloging-in-Publication Data

Cannam, Helen.
    The last ballad / Helen Cannam.
        p.   cm.
    ISBN 0-312-06388-1
    I. Title.
PR6053.A58L37   1991
823'.914—dc20   91-20640
                                                                      CIP

First published in Great Britain by Macdonald & Company (Publishers) Limited.

First U.S. Edition: November 1991
10 9 8 7 6 5 4 3 2 1

For my daughter Mary,
with love

AUTHOR'S NOTE

Although this book is fiction and not history, and the central characters are all imaginary, many of the events did in fact take place much as they are described.

I would like to thank the Killhope Leadmining Centre, Weardale Minerals Ltd., the Weardale Museum of High House Chapel and the staff of libraries and records offices in Newcastle, Gosforth, Durham, Crook, Darlington and London, for all their help with my researches.

Sadly there is no space to list all those many other individuals, in Weardale and beyond, who so kindly gave their time to help me in so many different ways. All I can do is express my warm gratitude for that help and emphasize that any errors in the book are mine and not theirs.

PEOPLE IN THE STORY

Individuals who had some existence in history are marked with an asterisk.

The Emerson family:

Jane Emerson, known as Jenny.
Tommy, her younger brother.
Joseph (Joe), the older brother.
William, their father.
Ralph Emerson, William's brother.
Ann, Ralph's wife.
'Ralph's Joe' Emerson, their eldest son.
Luke Emerson, his younger brother.

Other members of the mining partnership:

George Lowes, old friend of William Emerson.
Isaac Lowes, his brother, masterman washer.

Other miners:

*Thomas Thompson.
*John Peart.
*George Robinson.
*Thomas Stephenson.
*Anthony Coulthard.
Jock Wilson.

Joe's friends:

*Charles Siddle.
*Anthony Siddle, his older brother.
*John Kidd.
*James Craggs.
*Thomas Low.
*John (Jock) Currah.

Representatives of the Church:

*Joseph Dawson, the Bishop's gamekeeper, also publican of
  the Black Bull, St John's Chapel.
Revd Edward Selby, deacon and temporary curate.
Georgiana, his sister.
Peggy Gibson, maid at the parsonage.
*Revd William Wilson, JP and rector of Wolsingham.

Mine officials:

*George Crawhall of Newhouse, Weardale agent for the
  Beaumont mines.
*Martin Morrison, head mining agent.
Joshua Bowman, inspector of washing.

Other residents of St John's Chapel:

*Thomas Walton, publican of the King's Head.
*Frank Johnson, constable.
Eve Todd, Joe Emerson's girlfriend.
Jacob Todd, her father, grocer.
Lancelot Hall, blacksmith.
Tabitha Hall, his mother.
Rowland Peart, her nephew.
*John Scott, surgeon.
Hannah Milburn, devout Methodist widow.

THE LAST BALLAD

1

Two weeks after his father took to his bed for the last time, Tommy Emerson started work as a washer lad at Level Gate mine.

He was nine years old, wearing clogs a little too large that clattered satisfactorily on the stony road, and a coat cut down from his brother Joe's, and he was bursting with pride to be a man at last. He strutted at Joe's side out of the house (swerving with a giggle to avoid a kiss from his sister), down the track and on to the road that ran gently downhill along the northern slope of the dale. As if he knew the importance of the occasion, Spot, their dog, followed them for a little way, until Joe turned and ordered him home.

Jenny stood at the door and watched her brothers until they were out of sight, the elder trying to slow his long strides to allow the small proud figure beside him to keep pace. She smiled, full of love for them both, and then found herself overcome by a sudden rush of tears to the eyes. She rubbed the back of her hand angrily across them and went inside and shut the door firmly on the fine April dawn. She cleared the remains of breakfast off the table and then went to plump up her father's pillows, saying nothing, but pummelling them in an explosion of bitter rage.

'Did Tommy take my bait bag, lass?' The faint gasping voice forced its way through her angry abstraction. Jenny straightened, pushing back a wisp of unruly brown hair from her forehead.

'He's got his bait in his pocket today, father. He'd nowt else to take.' But that had not been the main reason, of course. Tommy would have been proud to carry his small portion of rye bread and cheese, and the leather flask of ale,

1

in the grimy and ragged bag that had served his father on and off through nearly thirty years of leadmining; a lifetime, though none of them wanted yet to admit that William Emerson was at the end, that he would not be working the lead again, ever.

A sudden paroxysm of coughing seized the sick man. Jenny held him in her arms, and when he was quiet again wiped the blood from his mouth, telling herself it was foolish, stupid, pointless, trying to pretend things were any different. They knew the truth well enough; just as they knew, but would none of them ever speak of it, that in time, almost inevitably, Joe and then Tommy would come to show the unmistakable signs of the miner's disease: the painful breathing, the black spittle, the lack of appetite and the wrenching cough, all the other steadily increasing symptoms of the sickness that now had William Emerson in its last pitiless stranglehold.

Jenny propped her father more securely against the pillows – lying down, he could no longer get his breath at all – and went out to see to the animals, the same anger giving vigour to her movements as she unbarred the byre door to let out the geese, and milked the cows and then brought hay down from the loft for them and for the shaggy, long-maned black galloways, mare and foal.

The mines had taken them all – her father, Joe, now Tommy; and just over a year ago, not slowly and relentlessly, but in one sudden violent moment, Billy Hall, in all the vigour of his youth. Most lead miners had a pallid and sickly look, if not to begin with, then very soon after they went underground; but not her Billy. That was what had first attracted her, she thought, when she had seen him that hot day at the wrestling. He had been taller than most, broad, his hair a fiery red above his bright face, a great ox of a man in the pride of his youth and strength. That all that strength could be so suddenly extinguished, leaving nothing behind, had seemed impossible, unthinkable ... if only there could have been a bairn ... But there was no point in thinking of that.

She filled the basket with peats and carried them into the house to make up the fire for the day. At one side of the

2

wide hearth stood stones like those in many a lead miner's cottage, rough chunks of crystalline rock, dazzling with a thousand fiery sparks of light; pearly white, purple, green and palest yellow. One of them, a large piece of violet fluorspar mixed with quartz, Billy had given her at their first meeting, down by Harthope burn falls. *Finer than any rich man's jewels*, he had said, and though she knew little of jewels she had been sure he was right. She paused now and looked down at it, wondering from what black and perilous void it had come. Strange to think so much loveliness could lie hidden for centuries undiscovered in the bowels of the earth. What was the point of it, what purpose did it serve? Only to provide a love token for a miner to give to his girl, so that she could keep it by the hearth where the firelight might catch it and remind her (if she needed reminding) of the man who had given it? Better to have Billy still, rather than this bright and useless thing.

She flung the peats on to the fire, and sparks shot out into the chimney space, fierce as her anger.

Just out of sight of their home at White Lea, Joe and Tommy passed through the hamlet of Side Head, where they were joined by their uncle Ralph Emerson and his sons Joseph ('Ralph's Joe' to the neighbourhood, to distinguish him from his cousin, who at twenty-four was his senior by a year) and Luke, who was fourteen. Half a mile further on, George Lowes, old friend of their father, came panting up the steep path from St John's Chapel to fall into step beside them. He clapped Tommy on the shoulder.

'Why, we've another man to the partnership today, I see.' He glanced at Joe. 'Maybe now washing's started up again they'll get round to making the Pay at last.' Then he grinned, and shot a glance back the way he had come. A week ago Tommy would have left them there and scampered down the hill to the primitive little school in the village below. 'Wishing you was at school then?' George asked him. The boy shook his head vigorously. He had liked school well enough. He liked sums and reading, enjoyed watching the marks his pencil made on the slate, stringing words together. But that was child's work, and he could read and write and reckon up

3

well enough. He was a man, or nearly a man – no more school now until winter again closed the washing floors.

Tommy looked up at his cousin Luke, who was lankier and paler than he had been a year ago, when he had left school for good. Luke had been underground this winter, as the older washer lads were allowed to do, labouring for the fully grown men who toiled at the dangerous, exciting, skilled work, deep in the earth. In Tommy's eyes, Luke was a kind of hero; in his own eyes too, perhaps, for he marched along at the side of the men with scarcely a glance at Tommy and none of the chatter they had once enjoyed together. Tommy felt more than a little in awe of him.

The sun was rising as they came to where a small burn rushed down the dale side, hidden in a deep tree-lined cleft. The noise of the water filling their ears, they turned up beside it and followed a track that led to the entrance to the mine. Under the trees there were primroses and wood anemones, and the blackthorn was snowy with blossom; overhead curlews called, and a lark sang. But where the wood ended there was no sign of spring, no grass, no trees, no flowers, only great heaps of waste rock tipped either side of the black arched entrance that led into the hillside. There was a rough stone stable, heather thatched; a series of marked off sections, each walled on three sides, which made up the bousestead, where each partnership had a place for the untreated ore (the bouse) that it had dug from the earth; and a level muddy area just below and to one side of the mine entrance, straddling the burn, from which a number of channels had been diverted to serve the different functions of the washing floor.

It was there that the washer lads were gathering, their voices sharp with excitement, for many of them were, like Tommy, beginning work for the first time, now that the coming of spring allowed washing to start up again; and those who had worked on the washing floor before were happy to return after the constraints of schooling or idleness. Only the older boys, like Luke, reduced once more to the juvenile status from which they had temporarily escaped, resented the reopening of the washing floors. Better, they thought, the dust and darkness and danger underground with

4

the men, than the company of children out of doors. Besides, washer lads, with their long hours, had no time to join the men after work to hunt and talk and tend their plots of land.

'That's the washing floor,' said Luke, in case Tommy was in any doubt, jerking his head towards it. And then, after a moment, he added, 'I'll show you what to do.' Tommy, who was beginning to feel just a little apprehensive, cheered up at once and quickened his pace to keep up with his cousin. He scarcely felt the gentle pressure on his shoulder that was Joe's parting good wish to him, before the older men went on their separate way towards the mine.

Each mining partnership had its own area on the washing floor for cleaning the lead ore it brought up from underground. There were several other boys, and even one girl, employed by Uncle Ralph's partnership, most of whom Tommy knew, at least slightly, though he was the only complete newcomer among them. He grinned at them shyly as Luke led him across to them, and was glad that they seemed to accept him with no more than a nod or a grin in return. Three of them – amazingly strong, Tommy thought – were already busy with massive flat mallets of iron and wood, smashing the bouse into small pieces within a boarded area set aside for the purpose. 'They're bucking. When you're bigger you'll do that,' promised Luke.

'Quaker Company's got machines to do it,' one of the lads said, pausing for a moment. The Quaker-owned London Lead Company, as Tommy knew, worked rival mines to their own over the border in Cumberland, and also the other side of Stanhope; even one not far from their house at White Lea, newly started. But most of the Weardale mines were on land owned (like most of the dale) by the Bishop of Durham, and leased, through his wife's inheritance, to Colonel Beaumont.

'So have our masters, up at Breckonsike,' Luke corrected the lad, with lofty superiority, before leading his cousin away.

Tommy quickly found himself faced with a great number of new words, which he relished, murmuring them over and over to himself as he listened to Luke, eager to put them to use as soon as possible, with all the casual assurance that would indicate that he now belonged to this new world. The untreated ore was *bouse*, which had to be smashed with a *bucker*, before being shaken in a sieve – a *hotch* – in a large tub of water. The tiny particles of ore that fell through to the bottom of the tub were *smiddum*, and had to be *buddled* in a specially constructed area in the diverted burn, a little like a shallow man-made waterfall, raked over again and again until all the ore had separated.

There was a sudden shout from somewhere, and Tommy dodged to one side only just in time to escape being sent flying by his new workmates, as they grabbed tools, filled pails, flung themselves into their work with formidable energy, all talk silenced. Only Luke stayed where he was, one hand on Tommy's shoulder. 'That's Mr Bowman,' he said, gesturing with his head towards the cause of the commotion, a little sharp-eyed man making his way towards the washing floor. 'He's the washing inspector. Be sure you're busy when he's by ... Howay now,' he urged, as Tommy looked round with alarm, in search of something to do, 'let's seek Isaac.'

Isaac Lowes, brother to George, was the partnership's masterman washer, who, once found, looked Tommy up and down and then said, 'I'll set you on hotching, lad. See what you can do with that.'

It was easy enough, simply a matter of shaking the sieve filled with bouse – broken by the bucker – in a tub of water, until the smiddum fell through and the larger fragments separated out; the lightest, worthless stone, at the top; ore that needed further crushing in the middle (*chats*, Tommy had learned) and pure lead ore, grey and heavy and shining, at the bottom. The stone had to be pushed off with an iron tool called a *limp*, to add to the growing waste pile close by. The chats were sent back to the bucker for further crushing, the purest ore placed in a *kibble* – a large wooden pail – and taken to be weighed. The amount was always carefully recorded, since each partnership was paid by the bing of dressed ore weighed out at the end of washing, a *bing* being, as Tommy well knew (his teacher had liked to use local examples for his arithmetic exercises), eight hundredweight. After weighing, the ore was carried to the bingstead, from whence, packed on the saddle of a galloway, it would be carried over Scarsike Head to the smelt mill at Rookhope.

Isaac soon felt sure enough of Tommy to leave him to

work alone. At first he enjoyed it, conscious that this was real work, proud to be even the smallest member of the partnership's workforce. He listened with awe to the talk of the other boys. He had never in his life before heard such exotic swear words, or such colourful stories, even from his father's friends, or Joe's, gathered at White Lea on winter evenings. Some of the lads even smoked pipes as they worked, and drank spirits from flasks and spat like grown men. He watched and listened, eager to learn their ways. This was a different world indeed, even from the rough and tumble of school.

But soon his arms began to ache, and his legs too, with standing still so long, and the water was icy cold, so that his hands quickly grew red and sore, and then white and wrinkled and without feeling. At first the sun had felt warm on his back, but after a while it might as well have gone in for the good it did. He began to shiver, even with the thickness of Joe's old coat about him. He felt as if he had been standing by the tub shaking the sieve for hours, but they had not yet stopped for their bait, and he knew they would not finish until seven at night at the earliest, perhaps later with so much bouse wanting dressing. He began to feel very sorry for himself, and hoped no one would speak directly to him, for fear he would disgrace himself by bursting into tears. It was at that moment that Mr Bowman came his way and paused to watch what he was doing. Tommy held his breath, conscious of an increased tremor in his chilled hands. He took the limp and swept the top layer of stones aside, glancing at the inspector as he did so. He was relieved to see that there was a glimmer of approval in the man's expression.

'Neatly done,' he said with a nod, and Tommy relaxed a little, expecting him to move on somewhere else. Instead, the inspector asked suddenly, 'You're Thomas Emerson, White Lea?'

Tommy nodded. 'Aye, Mr Bowman.'

The man looked at him for a moment longer, then half turned away, and then apparently (to Tommy's alarm) thought better of it and swung round on him again. 'Your sister bringing your bait up to you?' He spoke casually, but his eyes, on Tommy's face, had an odd expression, at once

7

eager and sharp; the boy did not like it much.

He said, 'Why no, Mr Bowman. I've got it here.' And he patted the capacious pocket of his cut-down coat, bulging with the food Jenny had packed into it this morning, before they left the house.

A momentary disappointment was evident on the inspector's face. 'Oh – I see.' This time he did turn away, stopping very soon to shout at one of the other boys for some misdemeanour.

The lad who came to carry away the kibble of finished ore paused to shrug sympathetically. 'He's in a bad mood today,' he said. 'Gets like that sometimes. When he is, watch out.'

A flurry of snow, sharp and sudden and stinging, greeted the Reverend Edward Selby as he left the little town of Stanhope behind him. In Bishop Auckland this morning it had been a fine spring day, the improbable warmth of the sun even hinting at summer. Expecting these northerly lands to be bitter in every sense, he had been agreeably surprised, as he had been too by the sumptuous comfort of the Castle, re-sidence of Bishop Barrington, where he had spent last night. He knew of course that Durham was the principal Bishopric of England, and the Bishop, by long tradition, a powerful ruler of this remote corner of the country; but he had not quite expected the Bishop's palace to conform so closely to the splendour of its name. His small acquaintance with such places had led him to anticipate something closer to the more ordinary comforts of his home, if perhaps on a somewhat grander scale; something, in fact, like the rectory at Wolsingham, where he had paused today to lunch with the Reverend William Wilson.

But now he was a long way from any comforts, whether of home or elsewhere, riding along a rutted track towards the grim snow-swathed hills – mountains, almost – in which he was to pass who knew how many months of his life.

Admittedly, he was here of his own free will, as far as he could be said to have had any willpower left, once Made-moiselle de Mortain, that bewitching daughter of a French *émigré*, had so effectively broken his heart, and his spirit with it. It had seemed a good idea to come as far away as possible from any place remotely associated with her, to bury himself in the depths of an unknown tract of untamed countryside where he could nurse his misery unobserved and undisturbed.

The suggestion had come from Mrs Diana Beaumont, a family friend who loved to boast of the wealth of her Pennine leadmines, which produced silver too, as she was never tired of saying. Edward had met her a month ago not far from her estate near Wakefield, at some tedious country assembly (try as he might, he could find no gathering interesting without Mademoiselle de Mortain, though he knew her presence would only have brought him pain). He did not remember that he had mentioned his recent troubles, but Mrs Beaumont seemed to have heard of them somehow, and she had a suggestion to make. She understood that the curate in charge of St John's Chapel, at the western end of the wealthy parish of Stanhope in Weardale, one Mr Whitelock, had lately been in poor health. A period of rest in a less rigorous climate had been suggested, so he and his young family were to spend some months away from the dale. The rector of the parish was, by tradition, an aristocratic absentee, and there would be no one left to minister to the souls of the people in that large and remote district. Edward himself, still only a deacon, serving a desultory curacy in his home parish and with no immediate prospect of a living of his own to occupy his time, could surely make himself useful in the dale during its incumbent's absence. 'If nought else, the Durham air'll put some colour in your cheeks,' Mrs Beaumont had added in her vulgar way, and offered to see what she could do.

So it had all been arranged, and he had even found himself looking forward to it and making plans, in a way that was already proving a wonderful salve for his broken heart. He had received a kind letter from Mr Whitelock, full of his affection for the dale and its people, but telling him little that was of any use to him. From other sources, he had learned that Mr Whitelock, though a respectable enough man, was at best inactive. Ill health gave him some excuse perhaps, plus the inadequacy of the tiny salary grudgingly allowed him from the rector's vast income. But, in any case, one did not expect a man who was apparently content with the curacy of

9

an isolated upland parish to amount to very much. For
Edward, the months ahead were simply a starting point,
offering him a challenge that, if met, might one day stand
him in good stead. Not for him a life of impoverished retire-
ment in some remote backwater; he wanted to make his
mark upon the Church (though not, of course, in any crude
or worldly sense) – and what better way to begin than by
making his mark upon the western portion of the parish of
Stanhope?

Not that he had been under any illusions about what lay
ahead, even before today. There would be no comfortable
social life to lighten his days, no mixing with people of his
own class, for there were few resident landowners and only
one other curate, in Stanhope itself, a man who was, like Mr
Whitelock, scarcely even a gentleman. Furthermore, he had
been warned that Methodism had begun to gain an unwelcome hold on the unruly dalesmen. It was for him to try
and counter its claims, to win the people for the Established
Church, above all to do his best during his weeks or months
in their service to tame their wildness, their lechery and
drunkenness, to bring them some measure of civilization and
respect for authority and true religion. He thought he might
even undertake to try some schoolmastering. He understood
there were few schools of any kind in the dale, and what
there were offered little even to the unlettered lead miners'
children who dwelt among these hills.

He knew little of mines, though there were coal mines not
so very far from his father's estate in Nottinghamshire, and
on his way here he had passed through a number of colliery
settlements, where a wild population lived more as animals
than men. Lead miners, he had been told, were wilder even
than colliers, more inward looking, more remote from any
contact with civilization. In spite of his resolve to bring
enlightenment to the people he was to serve, he had to admit
to a measure of apprehension. Already, east of Stanhope,
he had seen signs of lead mining; quarries too, and the
chimneys of a smelt mill belching stinking blue fumes into
the air, so that not so much as a blade of grass grew
for many yards around it. But at least in that part of the
dale it had still been spring. He had seen celandines and

wood anenomes in flower, and even, here and there, a few
primroses.

West of the town, as the snow swirled ever faster, there
was no sign of spring on what little he could see, with his
head bent, of the banks that edged the road. The grass, still
dry and crushed from the frosts and snows of winter, would
soon be covered again, he thought, shivering inside his thick
coat and wondering how far he still had to go. All his good
intentions, all his high ideals, began to shrivel in the bitter
wind. Why on earth had he not travelled in the chaise with
his luggage, instead of transferring to horseback at
Stanhope? The chaise might be uncomfortable, but this was
surely worse.

After a time, not quite believing his ears, he thought he
heard, through the roar of the wind, a faint tinkling sound;
and a little afterwards saw, emerging without warning from
the snow before him, a pony, shaggy, slowly plodding, its
head bent, its back laden with sacks laid over a heavy
wooden saddle, its collar edged with bells. Behind it plodded
another, and another, in a long mournful line, and behind
them, the only thing perhaps that kept them going, a man
and a black and white dog. The man, head bent like the
ponies (only the dog seemed alert), looked up briefly, sharp
eyes scanning the figure on the horse with what seemed a
hostile curiosity, and then, without any hint of a greeting or
the least sign of respectful acknowledgement of the rider's
gentlemanly appearance, bent his head again and trudged on
behind the ponies.

Edward was a little annoyed that his presence should win
none of the customary courtesy he met with in other places;
in the villages near his home, no passer-by would fail to
touch his hat, or his forelock if he had no hat, and would
often accompany the gesture with a friendly smile and a
warm greeting – 'Good morning, Master Edward,' for
example. Of course, these people could not be expected to
know who he was, but that did not excuse discourtesy.

But worse than his sense of annoyance was the feeling of
loneliness that swamped him suddenly, the more overwhelming because he had not quite expected it. All the talk
of the remoteness of the dale, of the lack of people of his

11

own class and kind, about which he had been warned, now took on a reality, and he did not like it, not at all. He tried hard not to think of what he had left behind, the warm and comfortable house where his father read by the fire, while his mother sewed, his brother dozed, his sister and sister-in-law played duets at the piano, all graciousness and comfort, wrapping him round with affection. He had thought he would welcome solitude, but at the moment he dreaded it and wished himself anywhere but here.

He came to some houses at last, solid enough (unlike the colliery houses, which had been built of raw red brick, ugly and flimsy, shoved up higgledy piggledy around the coal mines), made of pale sandstone, many with small fields near them in which cattle or sheep huddled together against the driving snow. A small boy stared at him and shouted something that (fortunately perhaps) he did not catch, a woman peered out of a window at his passing, a girl coming from a well with a wooden pail in her hand glanced his way with what he took to be something of the same hostility he had seen in the eyes of the carrier, though he could not be sure at this distance, through the veiling snow. Perhaps he was simply being fanciful, even self pitying; though he had reason enough to feel sorry for himself, with the cold setting him shivering, and so far still to go (he supposed) before he reached his destination.

This should be Eastgate, he calculated (*so called*, the Bishop's chaplain had said, *because in medieval times it formed the easternmost border of the Bishop's hunting park; Westgate has a similar origin*), but he wanted to have it confirmed. It was no day to risk losing one's way. He came on a man, wrapped in a plaid like a Scotsman, walking slowly towards him, and he drew rein and enquired if this was the right road. But the answer he was given, through frequent coughing, was quite useless; he could not understand a word of it. He asked the man to repeat what he said, but still could not make it out. Reluctant to keep him standing in the cold any longer and, doubtful if he would ever understand him, Edward thanked him politely, feeling more depressed than ever. Would everyone in Weardale be so incomprehensible to his southerner's ears? How could he hope to

12

minister to a people whose language or accent made them unintelligible to him? He rode on, realizing soon that he had left the houses behind him. But he must be on the right road; no need to fear otherwise. He had been assured that it was impossible to lose one's way, that the road was clear and obvious. But then he did not imagine that anyone had expected snow.

It seemed a very long time before he came to the next village, if such it was. Would this be Westgate, or was there somewhere else on the way there? Had he in fact come through other settlements after leaving Eastgate? Now and then he had passed buildings of various kinds, often with an unappealing wasteland of spoil heaps surrounding them, but whether or not they stood alone he could not be sure in this weather. Before he could find anyone to ask, the road forked. He must continue going westward, but which way was westward? He could not tell. He had almost decided to take the left fork, not from any conviction that it was the one he wanted, but simply to end the uncertainty, when, to his relief, three children came into view, laughing together, unaffected by the snow, though they fell silent as soon as they saw him, and studied him with enquiring eyes. He assumed a benevolent and (he hoped) paternal smile. 'Good afternoon to you, my little ones! I wonder, can you tell me which is the right road for St John's Chapel?'

It was hardly, he thought, a question calculated to cause amusement, but the children glanced at one another and began to giggle. Then the elder, a boy, having paused a moment in silent communication with his companions, stepped forward with assurance. 'That way, sir,' he said, quite distinctly and with gratifying courtesy. He pointed to the right.

'And how far have I to go now?'

'Three mile, about,' said the boy.

Edward pressed a coin into the child's hand – to his utter astonishment, it was clear – thanked them all, and turned his horse towards the indicated road. As he rounded the corner past the high wall of a house, he thought he heard the sound of laughter, but he could not be sure.

The road began to rise a little, going steadily uphill, and

then more steeply, winding to the right; and then took a turn once more to the left, in what must surely have been a westerly direction. The wind had freshened, and was blowing now straight into his face, and he could see little around him. But the thought that he had almost reached his destination cheered him and set him on his way with renewed energy, though his horse was tiring, slowing on the now steep hill, panting painfully.

After a time the road levelled and the snow showed signs of easing; just as well, for he did not think he had ever felt so cold. His cheerfulness had subsided again, and he began to wonder how much longer he had to ride. Surely by now he must have covered three miles? But then in this winter landscape it was easy to lose all sense of time, and what seemed like hours might indeed simply be minutes. He reached inside his coat and pulled out his watch and peered at it: half past five – surely it could not be that time already? Perhaps it had taken him longer than he thought to reach the place where he had asked the way. He knew it had only been three when he left Stanhope, with no more than eight miles of his journey still to go. But then it was not easy, riding in these conditions. He drew rein and looked about him.

The snow was indeed easing now, dwindling to a slow, silent fall, and the wind had dropped too. Somewhere a faint sun was beginning to shine. And he saw with a sense of shock that he was not, as he had thought, riding along the bottom of the dale, but high in the hills, wild, snow-covered hills, travelling on an open moorland road with no sign of human habitation – no tree or house or hedgerow or wall – as far as the eye could see, except, distantly, a scarring of barren heaps on a hillside, which he supposed must mark a lead mine. *Take the road along the bottom of the dale. There's no mistaking it. You can't go wrong.* So he had been told. And yet here he was, quite clearly very far from where he ought to be.

He realized with a sharp sense of anger (and more than a twinge of embarrassment) that those apparently innocent little children had deliberately sent him the wrong way. Surely there could be no other explanation, in view of the looks exchanged, the laughter (no doubt now that he had

14

heard it). And to think he had given them money; worse, that they had accepted it, knowingly, without any sign of shame. That was corruption indeed!

As he sat there, the snow ceased altogether and the sun, high and clear, shone out with a surprising warmth. The soft, thick layer of snow that the shower had left was already melting from the fells, restoring colour and depth to the landscape. Overhead, in a sky of piercing blue, a lark began to sing as if it knew nothing of snow or wind, like a child whistling its innocence of wrongdoing. He began to feel better in himself, but angrier and more impatient than ever. What should he do now? Turn round and retrace his steps? It seemed at first the most sensible course. But even if he were to find his way back without mishap (astonishing how different the landscape looked now), there were the children. What if they were to see him passing again? He imagined their laughter, the way they might call after him. He ought perhaps to face the humiliation and take the opportunity to administer a stern rebuke to them for their behaviour. But quite clearly they had no respect for authority, not even in the shape of a respectably dressed man of obvious breeding. Perhaps when they had time to learn who he was, and he had been able to establish himself, then such a rebuke might be more effective.

But what to do now? If he went on, would he not find himself ever further from his destination?

He rode a short distance, into a shallow valley, across a stream and up again, and there came to another fork in the road. This time he turned to the left. For a little while there was nothing to tell him whether he had made the right choice. But then, all at once, reaching the brow of a hill, he saw that the land sloped down, undulating a little, into the hidden depths of a valley, from which, facing him, two great hills – no, mountains – rose steeply at the far side, lowering over the wintry landscape. Surely this must be the dale! He drew a deep breath and urged his horse on.

A little further, and the road turned to run westward (he hoped) along the slope of the valley. Then he saw to his right a long, low, two-storeyed stone house set just below the brow of the hill, a little distance from the road, facing across the

15

dale. A belt of trees – Scots pines and hawthorn and rowan and birch and ash – sheltered it on the western side, straggling down the edge of the field that fronted it to cross the road a little further on. As he sat looking at it, a young woman came round the side of the house, a splash of vivid colour against the pale grey-gold walls. She wore a neat white apron over bright blue skirts, tucked up to reveal a scarlet petticoat (all rather old-fashioned in style), and a shawl of a darker blue flung over head and shoulders, which fell back a little from light brown hair that even at this distance seemed to gleam in the sunlight. Why the sight should be so unexpected, or so striking, he did not know, but for some reason it made him catch his breath. For a moment he quite forgot how cold and tired and miserable he was, and simply stared at her. Then she opened the front door of the house and disappeared inside, closing it behind her. Edward continued to look at the house for a time, and then, on impulse, he turned his weary animal up the stony track towards it. He might well find her as unhelpful as the rest of the population in this inhospitable wilderness, but he had to take his chance. All she had to do was to direct him to the right road.

At the eastern end of the house was a small walled garden, free of weeds but with little in it except a few ragged gooseberry bushes. The western portion of the building evidently consisted of housing for animals, with a hay loft above, for it had few windows and no chimneys, and a midden adjoined it. On the other hand, the flagged area before the house door, and the doorstep itself, had a scrubbed and cared-for look, which was relatively encouraging. Edward dismounted and rattled on the door with his whip.

A dog barked somewhere inside, and then the woman opened the door, and he found himself for quite some time unable to do anything but stare at her. She was more of a girl than a woman, a little younger than he was, he thought – about twenty perhaps, a small person with a trim figure and brown hair looped back from a wide fair-skinned face, from which a pair of candid grey eyes looked back at him. Not that there was any hostility in her expression; there was even a hint of friendly interest which was quite without imperti-

16

nence. A line of poetry came suddenly into his head: *A violet by a mossy stone, half hidden from the eye* ... Untouched, unspoiled, she appeared there before him, the embodiment of healthy innocent girlhood. Charming, he thought; and as different in her fresh prettiness as anyone could possibly be from Mademoiselle de Mortain, with her wiles and deceptions. Then he saw that she was growing troubled at his silence, and recollected himself, and began to explain that he had lost his way (though not how) and asked if she could direct him to the right path. 'I think I must have been going the wrong way for hours now,' he concluded.

She smiled a little, a sweet warm smile that once again drove all thought of his predicament out of his head. 'Why, it's not ᴊo far now,' she said. Her voice was as warm as her smile, and this time he did not find the strong accent offensive to his ears. 'You're not so much out of the way –'

'Jenny! Who's there?' Another voice, calling from the dark interior behind her, was weak with sickness or age, and ended in a frenzy of coughing.

'A gentleman, father, lost his way,' she called over her shoulder, and then turned back to Edward. 'You'd best come in, have a bit sit. Then I'll set you on your way.' He found himself following her into the dark stuffy warmth of a large kitchen. She led him to a settle by a glowing peat fire and he sank down, suddenly realizing how very weary he was. He thought perhaps he would not have been able to continue his journey at once, even had she not invited him to rest.

She disappeared somewhere into the shadows of the room, beyond his sight, presumably to see to the needs of her father, whose coughing had not lessened at all, the painful exhausted coughing of a man who was certainly very ill. Edward felt too tired, too warm and relaxed, to bother to look round. He let his eyes wander instead over what lay directly in front of him, gradually becoming accustomed to the dark after the brilliance of the day outside. There was something charming in the simplicity of the place, he decided; the wide hearth, with its cooking pots and fire irons, and pretty stones by way of ornament, the fresh peats stacked nearby, the sparse and simple furnishings – wooden bowls laid on the table, horn spoons beside them, a bench

17

and two stools for seating, bright pegged rugs on the floor, a grandfather clock in the corner and a chest against the far wall. Above the chest, at eye level for a man of average height, was the one thing that he found astonishing in this poor place: a bookshelf, on which stood a row of clearly well-used books. Curiosity overcoming his exhaustion, he stood up and went to see what they were. There was the Bible of course – that was not very surprising – and a *Pilgrim's Progress*; but also several heavy-looking volumes on geological subjects, and others on history, geography and flowers. There was also a newspaper. He screwed his head round to see it better: the *Durham County Advertiser* for 4 April 1818. Little over a week old then, suggesting that not all the Weardale population was as inward-looking as he had been led to believe.

He turned to the girl, who had come quietly up behind him. 'You like to read?' Beyond her, he could now see the box bed in the wall, in which an old man sat propped in a sitting position against a rampart of pillows.

'Sometimes,' she said. 'Father started a book club, him and other four. My brother keeps it up now. They pay two pence a week each – or they do when they have it to spare. They buy what they can from that, and pass the books round. They have a canny few between them.'

'That is very commendable,' said Edward carefully, more than a little surprised that anyone living in this poor place could even read, let alone put that ability to constructive use, but he felt he could not quite say that. 'You keep house for your family then?' he asked instead. A quick glance at her hand told him she wore no wedding ring, but who knew what was customary in this wild part of the world?

'There's only my two brothers – and father.' It sounded as though she regarded him as scarcely counting as a member of the family; as soon, very likely, he would not be, if that cough was anything to go by, or the painful and raucous breathing that had succeeded it.

'Your father is very ill,' said Edward gently, his voice full of compassion.

'Aye,' she said softly. 'He's dying.' She spoke simply, without much sign of grief, as if it was only to be expected, a

18

matter of fact, on which there was no point in wasting regret. Perhaps, he thought, these wild hill people did not feel with the same sensitivity as the more tenderly bred. He thought how his sister would have wept had she had to give such news, even to a stranger. This young woman showed little emotion of any kind.

He studied her in the soft light of the fire. She was bending over it now to stir something in a pot, moving with a pretty grace, as natural and unaffected as that of a young animal.

'Will you have owt to eat?'

He was hungry, but he was conscious of the time, and that he was already very late. The brief rest had taken the worst edge from his exhaustion and he was anxious to reach the end of his journey. He was wondering how best to extricate himself, when the door suddenly opened, letting in a great rectangle of dazzling light that framed the square figure of a man, who stepped inside and stamped his clogged feet on the flagged floor.

'Joe,' said the girl; then, at her brother's questioning glance (he could only be her brother, with that same build, on a rather larger scale, and those same direct grey eyes), she turned to Edward. 'My brother, home from work.'

Edward stepped forward, hand outstretched. 'The Reverend Edward Selby,' he introduced himself.

The young man made no move to take his hand, but simply nodded. 'You'll be in place of Mr Whitelock then.'

'Yes – yes indeed,' said Edward, looking at the rejected hand as if he wondered what it was doing there, and then letting it fall rather hastily.

'I'll say one thing for him,' Joe continued. 'He's never stuck his neb in where it's not wanted.' He perched his hat on the end of the settle and went to warm his hands at the fire. Edward was not entirely sure what the young man was saying, but its tone made him feel an intruder, his presence unwelcome. In his manner at least Joe was nothing like his sister. Clearly his small experience of education had not civilized him to any great extent. But then learning – especially of the wrong kind – could be a mixed blessing for the poor.

19

'Mr Selby lost his way, and came in for a bit rest,' Jenny explained.

'Then you'd best get on before dark,' Joe advised. Edward, who had been seeking an excuse to take his leave, now felt offended that one should be so unceremoniously offered to him. But he had no choice; he stood up, thanked the girl warmly for her hospitality, and followed her to the door, where she pointed him in the right direction. He was not sure if he imagined it, or if her manner had indeed cooled, taking a lead from her brother. He hoped not, for she had already made a very favourable impression upon him. A charming little thing.

As he rode west along the valley, coming (at last!) within sight of St John's Chapel and the road that led down to its straggle of houses, Edward had an uneasy sense of inadequacy, of missed opportunities, even of failure. Surely he should have shown his compassion for the troubled household more effectively, ministered somehow to the sick man (who was after all one of the parishoners for whom he was to be responsible), offered some suitable words of comfort and support to the girl and her brother? He had done none of these things. But then, he told himself, it was the end of a long and trying day and he was tired, and not yet quite resident in the place. Once he was settled here it would be different.

Joe closed the door, glad that the stranger had gone, and then went upstairs to change out of his damp and muddy working clothes, so that Jenny could hang them before the fire to dry. 'Billy's mother called today,' she said, when he came down again.

'How is she?' Joe asked.

'Why, she's canny,' said Jenny. She went to the settle and took something from it, handing it to her brother. 'Here.'

He gave her a sharp questioning glance, but when she simply continued to look at him he turned his attention to the object in his hands. It was obvious enough what it was – a roughly made bag of coarse cloth, in which lay a number of tools, a hammer and a chisel-like implement among them. That they were not new was evident, for though kept carefully free of rust they were stained and notched with use. Joe saw such tools every day, used them too, as did every lead miner. But all the same he knew at once that these were different, knew whose hands had last used them, those strong freckled hands that had turned the chisel – the jumper – against the rock as he himself hammered its end to drill a hole for the gunpowder ... the powerful hands of the finest wrestler in Weardale.

'They're Billy's,' he said quietly.

'Aye,' said Jenny, her eyes on his. 'Tabitha Hall said you should have them, save getting new when your own are worn. No sense in keeping them put by, she said. She said ...' and here Jenny's voice cracked a little, and there was a pause before she ended: 'she said Billy would have wanted it.'

They neither of them spoke or moved for a long time then. Joe gazed down at the tools, his hands slowly fingering them, clearly absorbed in some old memory of his own; as Jenny was too, and this time (thank God!) a gentler one than the nightmare that had haunted her, waking and sleeping, since the dreadful accident a year ago.

She wondered sometimes if Joe felt Billy's loss more even than she did, if that were possible. There was a special comradeship linking the men in a partnership, and in particular the two shoulder fellows who, day after day, worked together in the depths of the earth, depending upon one another for their safety. Joe and Billy had been friends from boyhood, at school, as washer boys, working the lead; they had passed their leisure hours together too, fighting, dancing, drinking, singing, poaching, pursuing the same girls, with amicable rivalry on occasions. When Billy had found Jenny, with that odd kind of inevitability with which a young man discovers a girl he has known all his life, and yet never known until one particular day, that had only bound them closer, brothers now as well as friends. Since Billy's death, Joe had been quieter, more serious, given to long moody silences, with a bitter edge to his former casual attitude to life. A natural rebel, that loss had turned him into an angry man with the fire of revolt in his belly.

Now, as if emphasizing the fact, he said, 'We went to

Newhouse today, three of us, to see Mr Crawhall.' He began carefully to pack the tools away, and then went to put the bag in the chest. Jenny ladled potato broth from the pot into his bowl and he ate in silence for a time, then went on, 'Mind, Uncle Ralph was right; it got us nowhere.'

'About the Pay, was that?'

'Aye. To say we can wait no longer. We told him, there's hardly one of us has credit left in Chapel now.'

'And he said he was sorry, but it was out of his hands and there was nowt he could do just yet.'

Joe looked surprised. 'How did you know that?'

'Why, it's not the first time the Pay's been late, now is it? That's what they always say.' Lead miners were only paid in full once a year, living until that time on an advance of thirty shillings a month, which would later be deducted from what was due to them for the year's ore they had raised.

'Then we'll just have to see what the Bishop can let us have till pay day,' Joe said, with a grin at his sister. He finished his supper and went to the door, whistling to the dog to follow him.

She returned the smile, but a trace of anxiety creased her brow. 'Joe, do you think you should? You know they'll be watching. There was that notice –'

'His Grace the Lord Bishop of Durham ...' with sweeping gestures of the arms, Joe made a mocking bow, '... commands that all shall refrain from poaching upon his land.' There was derision in his smile now. '*His* land! His, when he never sets foot on it, when the only use he ever has for it is to grab all he can from the mines and the fells. It's we live here. It's we have to eat. What's a grouse to him, but a bit fancy food now and then, something to tempt his palate, set before him on special days? To us, many a time, it's all we have between us and starvation. Joseph Dawson knows what he can do with his game laws.'

'Joseph Dawson has the law and the Bishop behind him.'

'Do you think I fear him for that? A year or so gone he was poaching with the best of us, and had not a thought of the law.'

'That's why he's to fear. He knows your ways. How else did he lay hands on Charlie Siddle?'

'Much good it did him!'

'But he's been turned out of work. Did you not know? Billy's mother told me. Just think of it, Joe – no work, with a five-pound fine to pay.'

'Just let them try and make him pay it, that's all.' Then he relaxed and laid a hand on Jenny's shoulder. 'Don't fret, our Jenny. I was having you on. I'm not going on the fell. Not yet anyway. Take a look behind the settle when I'm gone – you'll see my fowling piece still there. It's Monday, remember.'

Eve then; that was where he was going, Jenny thought, not greatly cheered by the reflection. But this time she said nothing. Joe paused in the doorway. 'Tommy'll be tired when he comes in. Be sure and tempt him with something good to eat.'

'You know well enough how I look after a washer lad at the end of his first day,' Jenny reminded him; and he remembered his own first homecoming, when he was little older than Tommy and she only seven, already caring for the household during one of her mother's painful stillbirths, as if in preparation for the time when she would have to take that place for good. He grinned at her with warm affection.

'You'll be home before Tommy's in bed then?' It was rather more of a request than a question, but Joe only said, 'Like enough,' and set out into the bright evening.

Jenny told herself she feared for him, that Jacob Todd's anger would be terrible if he were ever to find out Joe was still meeting his daughter. But she recognized with a small part of her mind that it was not fear for Joe, or for Eve, that made her disapprove of what her brother was doing. In fact, if she were honest, what she felt was not disapproval at all, but something much more painful. That they should be meeting, that they should seize a few sweet hours together in a byre somewhere, or out on the fell – the very thought hurt her, because it brought so starkly before her that she was now shut out from those same delights. If she had been ignorant of them, then it might have been different. But once, little over a year ago, it had been she who stole out at dusk to secret meetings (secret because that was the way of Weardale, not from any fear of discovery), she who lay in the arms of the person she loved most in all the world, she who

23

felt that world shake and explode into joy; and she who now could scarcely remember what it felt like, only knew that the brightness had gone from her life and left a hungry ache in her, along with the simpler, devastating pain of her loss. But she would never let Joe see what she felt, because envy was a poisonous thing, of which she was ashamed.

Joe slowed as he came within sight of the tiny cottage at the western end of St John's Chapel where Hannah Milburn, widow and devout Methodist, held her class meeting every Monday night. He was a little early, so he stood with his back against a tree across the lane, the dog at his feet, and watched the cottage for Eve to come out to him. She always told Hannah that her father wanted her home early, and as yet Hannah had not thought to check the truth of the claim with Jacob Todd. It was the one occasion in the week when Eve could evade his vigilance and spend a little time with Joe.

She came at last, slipping round the side of the cottage into the lane. She kept her eyes modestly lowered, as if nothing was further from her maidenly thoughts than a meeting with her sweetheart, and Joe had time to study her while he waited for her to see him. He knew the appearance of modesty was deceptive, and the high colour in her cheeks belied it too. If she was not looking up, it was because she was teasing him a little, pretending she did not expect him, that she did not care very much whether he was there or not. The colour suited her, adding to the vividness of her appearance: black hair, dark eyes sparkling through long lashes, mouth warm and rosy, a little mole beside it, drawing the eye there − and not just the eye, as he knew well. He smiled a little to himself and stepped out into the lane, putting a hand on the neck of the dog to keep it silent. She *must* have seen him; there was a sweet self-consciousness in her bearing, a hint of laughter in the curve of her lips, just visible in spite of the bent head.

She reached him and collided, very gently, with him. Then she did look up, swiftly, as if startled, though she was clearly laughing now. She did not draw back, just stood there, lightly touching him, as he reached out and put his arms about her. Then she laughed again, breathlessly, teasing, but also just a little fearful. He knew that, in spite of her pretty coquettishness, the fear was real. The wonder was that the lightness remained in her nature, and the laughter. She had little enough to laugh about when she was not with him, which made him long all the more to make her happy when they were together.

They drew apart and walked quickly, side by side, round the corner, where they stopped in the doorway of a byre. He held her again, urgently this time, suddenly impatient of all the furtiveness, the scarcity of their meetings, the apparent hopelessness of it all. He kissed her very thoroughly, then he whispered, 'Come in, out of the cold.'

She looked up at him, not hesitant exactly, but trying to judge his intentions; and her own too, perhaps. Then she nodded, and they slipped into the byre, leaving the dog to keep watch outside. There was a little hay in the loft, enough for them to lie on, and he drew her down there beside him, and knew that for both of them the time had come to end the waiting.

Eve's colour was higher still by the time she returned home. She was thoroughly warm now, glowing with the sweet aftermath of love, her thoughts full of Joe's kisses, of the touch of his hands on her body, of everything they had done together. She could bear anything after this.

But she had been gone over an hour and the class meeting would have ended some time ago, so there was a good deal to bear when she crept softly into the house by the back door. Her father was standing in the kitchen waiting for her, his sternest expression on his face.

'Where have you been, girl?'

Eve knew only too well what was coming, though she made some excuse for her absence and she did not think her father suspected the truth. He beat her even so, until she sobbed in harsh painful gulps, as silently as she could, because weeping only made him angrier, in his cold way. Then she was sent to bed without supper. She did not ask herself whether it was worth meeting Joe, if this was the result. She knew quite well that her father would very likely have found some excuse to beat her anyway, even if she had never met Joe or stayed out late. 'You have a proud and corrupt spirit, girl,' he often said. 'It must be broken, or you will be utterly cast away.' And, in spite of everything, even he knew he had not broken it yet.

Rowland Peart came into the dale, not, like the curate, from the prosperous east, but on foot from the south, from the barrenness of Teesdale, reaching the hills above Chapel just as dusk fell. He was later than he had intended and anxious to reach his journey's end, but he halted all the same and gazed down into the valley with feelings so intense that tears sprang to his eyes. 'I thank thee, Lord!' he whispered.

He had come in love, but even so the strength of that love, now he was within sight of his destination, took him by surprise. His eyes scoured the landscape. Small stone houses scattered it everywhere he looked, right to the very edge of the fells, wherever a living of some kind could be scratched from the land. Immediately below him clustered the roofs of Harthope, Burnfoot and St John's Chapel itself – all hamlets that made up the village – stone slabbed or with dark untidy heather hatch, like the unkempt mops of hair of poor children, and as full of wildlife, the fragrant peatsmoke curling lazily up from their chimneys to add to the gentle evening haze of the air. Among them, yet not of them, stood the solid stone church that gave the place its name, with the neat parsonage house, a disapproving matron amidst unruly gipsies, half hidden in trees just beyond it.

The hills were dun and brown, spotted with grazing sheep, the depths below shadowed and soft in the dusk. The air was full of the constant lovely long-unheard sound of the waters of his home country, made up of every sike and burn that chattered down the sides of the dale, the great rush of the river, the splashing of Harthope Burn Falls just out of sight. And then there were the human and animal sounds, amongst which, seven years ago, his own noisy youth had roared its way: the sounds of ponies whinnying, sheep bleating, cows mooing, children laughing and calling, men singing or arguing, a woman shouting an angry command; and the raucous reedy notes of the church band thumping out an ancient psalm tune – Monday night had always been practice night. He almost thought he heard his father's clarinet clear above the other instruments, and for a fraction of a second his heart seemed to miss a beat, his breath caught in his throat. But his father lay in the churchyard, had done for four years now, and they would not meet again this side of the grave. Down there remained only the neighbours and friends to whom he had come with a message of love and hope.

A wild, unbiddable, drunken, licentious people they were, as he had been once, but he loved them, loved them with a deep and passionate – a divine – love that burned in his heart at the very thought of them. There was no trace of apprehension in him. How should there be, when he knew the Lord was with him, had sent him here, with a command as clear as any he had ever known? Once he had told them all that had happened to him, and what it meant – that great, amazing, breath-stopping truth that had so transformed his life – there would be no doubt of his welcome. He was swept suddenly by a longing to waste no time, to wait no longer, but to be once more down there among them, feeling again their warmth, hearing their laughter, seeking out old friends, long abandoned.

He wiped the back of his hand over eyes misted with tears, took a deep breath, murmured a brief prayer – *Lord, give me strength to do thy work!* – and set off at a brisk pace down the hill, across the burn, to the smithy on its further side, where he banged on the house door. It opened at last, and a man stood there, staring at him, saying nothing; a big man with gingery hair. Behind him, an old woman looked enquiringly up from her chair by the fire. There was no recognition on their faces, only suspicion of the stranger who had come knocking on their door so late in the day.

'Do you not know me, Lancelot Hall?' said the newcomer after a moment.

There was a faint glimmer of recognition on the other man's face, but if anything his expression hardened. 'Aye – aye, I believe I do. So you've come back at last.' Then he stood aside to let the young man pass. 'You'd best come in.'

2

Joe Emerson came off Harthope Moor about seven o'clock, in the company of the Siddle brothers, Ralph's Joe, James Craggs and half a dozen other young men, fowling pieces on their arms, their various dogs running at their heels. They had done well this morning and their bags were bulging with grouse, but they walked softly, saying nothing until they were safely through the back door of the King's Head, the bolts slid home behind them. They stowed the birds carefully in the usual hiding place, an empty barrel in the inn's cellars. Later today one of three carriers known to them would call, discreetly, and take the birds on his cart by a devious route to the kitchen doors of one or other of the great houses of Cumberland, Northumberland or County Durham. By next weekend each man hoped to find himself with a sizable sum of money to augment his dwindling resources; since several of them were out of work, that was no small consideration.

Once, only a few months ago, they would have been more open about it all, taking their catch to the Black Bull a few doors away, where their contact would have met them over a drink, agreed a price and gone on his way, leaving their pockets full. But the landlord of the Black Bull was Joseph Dawson, and Joseph Dawson had defected to the side of the law – or the Bishop, rather, for he had become one of the Bishopric's gamekeepers, lured by the prospect of fat fees. As a result, everything had to be more carefully planned, taking into account that whatever they thought of had probably already been considered by Joseph Dawson, or soon would be. 'Well, now we've a friend in the right place,' Anthony Siddle had said, when they first heard of Dawson's appointment. After all, he was a close and trusted companion. But they had soon learned their mistake, even before the night when Charlie, temporarily separated from the rest of them up on the fell, had been arrested and hauled before the Reverend William Wilson, the magistrate at Wolsingham; for which misfortune he had also lost his job. Now Dawson was the enemy, as much as the Bishop and all who had anything to do with him.

Once the birds were safely disposed of, Tom Walton, the landlord, brought tankards of ale, and their hatred of Joseph Dawson spiced their talk.

'Five pounds he got for taking Charlie in,' said Anthony bitterly. 'And we know where that five pounds came from.' He thought the rumoured reward was abnormally large, but like them all he would have believed anything of Joseph Dawson, so long as it was bad enough.

'Have you paid it then?' Joe asked in surprise of the younger brother. Charlie, a lad of few words, shook his head.

'Why, where would he get five pounds?' Anthony demanded. 'Where would *I* get five pounds, and I'm still in work! No, he'll not pay, and I'll thump any man who tries to make him.'

They drank to that, noisily, and then moved on less happily to consider the prospects of Charlie finding other work.

The drinks disposed of, they left the King's Head by the front door and, once out in the rain, broke into song, not very tunefully, but with vigour, their voices deliberately raised as they passed the shuttered front of the Black Bull.

'Thirty pieces of silver old Judas did take,
But Chapel's Joe Dawson five gold pounds did make...'

The words were Joe's, but they all sang them with enthusiasm, watching the inn as they did so, waiting expectantly for some sign of life. Sure enough, a second or two of their singing brought an irate red face to an upper window, tasselled nightcap falling forward over its brow. 'Damn the lot of you, hold your tongues! What time is this to wake a man from his bed?'

'Why some of us still have work to go to, Joseph Dawson!'

29

returned Anthony Siddle. 'No thanks to you!'

'Aye, the devil's work!'

Anthony flung an arm about his brother. 'We'll be by tonight, to taste your hospitality, Joseph Dawson.'

The window slammed shut, its noise snuffing out the man's last inarticulate curse. Below in the market place his tormentors laughed and cheered. 'That's agreed then?' Anthony Siddle looked round at his companions.

'We meet here tonight? Aye.' They parted then, the brothers going along the lane to the cottage, tucked behind the King's Head, which they shared with their widowed mother, the others making their way to the bridge over the river, from where Joe and his cousin and James Craggs took the steep hill path towards Side Head and White Lea. As usual, Joe had kept a pair of grouse for his sister, and she in her turn had his breakfast ready, a bowl of crowdy – oatmeal steeped in milk – which she set on the table as he came through the door. 'Tommy left an hour since,' she told him, her tone faintly disapproving. But she sat down at once to pluck and draw one of the birds.

Watching her as he ate, Joe grinned. 'Now tell me I should not hunt.'

She shook her head. 'It's you I fear for, not the law. And it sticks in my throat we must do this to live.'

Joe followed a natural train of thought. 'Charlie Siddle says the Quaker Company's paying forty shillings a month subsistence.'

'How should he know?'

'They've a cousin Nenthead way. He went there seeking work – not that he got owt, of course.'

'Maybe Colonel Beaumont will raise the lent money then.'

'He should by rights. It only went down to thirty shillings because lead fell so low. Or so we were told. But prices are up a bit now.'

'But I thought ... What was it that man said, the one who came in January – the one who put steam engines in the Derwent mines?'

'Aye, him.' Joe's expression was derisive. 'Mr Hall. A friend to lead miners, he called himself. But why then was Mr Crawhall all over him the way he was, I'd like to know?'

30

'He said lead prices were kept low on purpose. He wanted them raised.'

'Why aye, so he did. But it'll be his pocket he had in mind, not ours. There's not much finds its way down to us without a fight, not even when prices are right up. Anyhow, we'll soon know what Mr Hall had in mind. There was a notice for some book he's written about it, in last week's *Durham Advertiser*. We're going to get a copy, if we can; see what he has to say for himself. But that doesn't alter the fact prices are up a bit on what they were. I heard Mr Crawhall say so, just last week.' He glanced at the clock, then threw down his spoon and got quickly to his feet. 'We're meeting at half past eight. Can I make it to Level Gate in five minutes?'

'With wings, maybe!' Jenny called after him as he grabbed tools and bait and ran from the house.

There was no sign of his partners when Joe reached the mine, but then he was half an hour late and they would long since have given him up and gone in to begin work. He entered the level by the arched entrance, lined with unmortared stone, which was just high and wide enough to admit a galloway pulling a waggon; that made it too low for a tall man, but then galloways required more consideration than men, being more costly to the masters and thus less dispensable. Besides, few lead miners were above average height, Billy having been one of the exceptions.

Joe picked his way along the wooden rails of the waggonway, trying to keep out of the water that ran in a little stream towards the level mouth – the level was designed for drainage as well as access. Further in, the tunnel, rising slightly as it went, was simply cut from the solid limestone, without need of other support. Here, as the darkness grew, Joe halted at last to get his breath and then lit a candle from those that hung on a string about his neck, before going on again.

A little further on he heard waggons rattling behind him, and glanced round. The man leading the galloway that pulled the waggons peered at him in the dim light. 'Take a ride along, Joe. I'm drawing your deads today.' Joe had forgotten that; it had been another reason for coming to work in good

31

time, for the waste rock left by the partnership had to be carted in barrows to where the waggons waited, a laborious business. It meant leaving off working the ore, but then the deads had piled up so much that there was now little room to get at the vein. They would have left it and managed as best they could, but Mr Crawhall was particular about such things.

He clambered into the first waggon and they rumbled on along the level. Here and there, his candle flame, augmented now by that of the waggoner, caught a gleam of water running down the rock face, or a bright orange seepage of iron, or even the sparkle of some mineral breaking its dark monotony; everywhere water splashed down, sometimes from above, like raindrops, sometimes in a trickle over the walls. Once, reverberating beneath the rumble of the waggons and the jingle of the pony's harness, a deep muffled roar reached them, from some far place where a partnership fired a shot for blasting; it was some time before its echoes subsided. Now and then they passed the foot of a rise, a shaft reaching up from beside the level to give access to workings above, and to allow bouse and deads to be dropped down close to the waggonway. After some time, they saw ahead of them the glow of a candle, bobbing and dipping towards them, to an accompanying rumble. Its hesitant flame lit the face of another waggoner, and the shine of his pony's eyes at shoulder height. Joe's companion halted where the level widened and the rails doubled to allow a passing place. The men exchanged greetings as the little train of waggons rumbled by, this one laden with bouse on its way out to the day; the light caught the silver gleam of lead among the dust and rock in the waggons, the sparkle of fluorspar and iron pyrites and quartz.

They came at last to where the level widened at the end of the rails, and there halted. Now that the rumble of the waggons had ceased, other noises flowed in on them: the constant sound of water, not only from the rock around them, but further off too, splashing down long narrow shafts in many parts of the mine as a means of keeping the air flowing; and the rhythmic sound of the water-driven pump that drained the lower levels, and the echoing voices of miners, and the clash and thud of picks on rock, all muffled and distorted by distance and the angles of the levels and shafts.

Just beyond the horse's head and to one side, a stone-lined shaft, a sump, descended into the darkness below. From a windlass at its mouth a rope fell into it, out of sight. Joe scrambled out of the waggon, thanked the man and called into the shaft, 'I'm coming down!' Then he wound up the rope, until a kibble full of deads reached the surface. He left the waggoner to tip its contents into the first waggon and then lowered himself into the sump, his candle still clutched in his hand. 'I'll tell them you're here,' he said.

The sump was lined, on either side, with stemples, wooden rungs set into the walls at regular intervals, though not very close together, to provide foot and hand holds for the descending miners. Joe let himself down by that means for several feet, swaying from one side to the other with the easy rhythm of long experience, and at last came to another level, much narrower than the first, and lower, so that once in it he could not stand upright. Here the layer of rock was softer, more friable, requiring timbering to support the roof and line the walls. He peered along it and could make out a distant glimmer of light held in the hand of a bent figure coming his way with a barrow; after a moment, he saw that it was Ralph Emerson, who halted beside him, looking him up and down with some sharpness. 'What kept you? We're held up for want of you.'

'I got behind – I'll make it up somehow.'

'Aye, and we all know how you got behind,' Ralph said drily. Ralph's Joe came into sight, pushing another barrow, also piled high with deads. He must have heard his father's last remark, but there was nothing in his expression, all innocence, to suggest that he thought any of it might have anything to do with him. Joe supposed he had managed to creep back into the house before his parents were awake, by the same window through which he had escaped some hours before.

'Well, now you're here, let's get on.' That was one thing in his uncle's favour; he was never ill-humoured for long.

They waited for the man above to let down the kibble

33

again, and then refilled it, tugging the rope to indicate when it was ready. As soon as one of the barrows was empty, Ralph turned to his son. 'You stay here and see to filling the kibbles. We'll get back along and give George a hand.' Then he and Joe set out, one behind the other, Joe pushing the barrow. 'Maybe,' said Ralph as they went, 'if you gave up poaching, then Jacob Todd would think more kindly of you.'

Joe had never said anything to his uncle of his courtship of Eve, but these things were generally pretty well known, however discreetly carried on. He shrugged. 'Why then, how would we eat, I'd like to know? It's all right for Jacob Todd. He's not a miner, and besides he never gives credit, so he never wants for owt.'

'We don't live by poaching either, and we get by. A bit knitting to bring in a few pence, and your aunt's spinning – it's enough.'

Joe muttered some kind of agreement, but did not add that they knitted and spun at White Lea too, only he would not choose to live as his uncle did, always anxious, often hungry, never able to afford even the most trivial of luxuries, like tea or rum, or spices to flavour cakes for special days, or more than the most basic homespun clothes. It was from that the poaching spared him, and from seeing in the faces of Jenny and Tommy the pinched greyness that so often marred the faces of his uncle's family.

They came very soon to yet another sump served by another windlass. Ralph wound up the full kibble that had been waiting at its foot, and then Joe descended to the next level down, where George Lowes, impatient at the inevitable delays, was standing with the deads piled all around him, unable to do more for want of help. 'About time,' he grunted, when Joe appeared, but then, like Ralph, he let the matter rest.

Joe spent the next few hours shovelling deads from the forehead of their workings to the foot of the sump, so that George could fill the kibbles. It was a lengthy and tedious process, for there was little space to work freely, no room to stand upright, and to make matters worse the air in their ground was poor at the best of times. After a few minutes Joe, like George, had a ferocious headache and felt drowsy and heavy limbed, unable to breathe deeply or think clearly, an irritating condition because it slowed them both down. 'You can tell it's raining up there,' George said. 'The air's worse than ever today. Maybe a good thing we're just drawing deads.'

But by the end of the morning the bulk of the deads had been cleared away, and the partners sat down together at the top of the lower sump to have their bait before getting back to work.

'What say we knock off early?' suggested Ralph's Joe, casually, but without any great hope. 'We'll not get much done with the air so bad.'

His father shook his head. 'If you want to clear the masters' books at the year's end, lad, then you can't knock off just for want of good air.'

'Maybe we should be looking for a better ground next quarter,' Joe suggested. 'What with the air, and now there's that bit twitch –'

'More than a bit,' said George. 'Mind, it's what's beyond the twitch I want to know. It could be nowt or – well.'

He did not need to say any more; the others understood him at once, and Ralph, as usual, was set off on a train of reminiscence. 'Do you recall, George, when we were up at Breckonsike? It would be the year I was first underground, I think. I came in for the winter, and William – he would be seventeen then – he'd just been taken on as a full partner ...'

'That would be about 1790, not long before my father died. Now the last grove he ever worked, that had a devil of a twitch in it.'

'Aye, I know, but that's not what I had in mind. I was thinking of the first one I saw worked. We thought she wasn't worth going on with, so the next quarter we took a bargain down here, and what happened then but another partnership – the one Jack Kidd was with, I think it was – they had a second look at our grove and got themselves placed just beyond it, on good terms ...'

George nodded. 'And five fathoms on they found a great belly of the finest ore ... Aye, I recall that well enough.'

'I learned from that, I can tell you,' said Ralph. 'I swore if ever I had a say in it I'd never give up, not unless I knew for

35

sure she wasn't worth the working.'

'That's just it, you can never be sure with a twitch. Besides, that grove was in the Great Limestone, as I recall ...'

Ralph's Joe nudged his cousin and gestured with his head towards the sump. Joe grinned and got to his feet. 'We're off to make our fortune. You old grovers can stay and dream your time away.'

'Less of your cheek, lad!' George called after him, but Joe was already well down the sump, his cousin close behind.

The two older men followed more slowly, but nearing the forehead Ralph Emerson was so short of breath that Joe said, 'You and George get back up and wait. We'll fire the shot, then you can come back for just as long as we need to clear the ore.' Ralph only hesitated a moment before retreating to the slightly fresher spot where they had eaten.

Through the winter months they had cut a rise into the vein from the base of the lower shaft, working upwards by means of a series of platforms until they reached the upper limit of their ground. The vein was narrow and hard and well mixed with other minerals, so that blasting was needed all the way, but they had got out enough ore to feel it was worth the effort. Now, working their way in a westerly direction, they had found that the cheeks of the vein had unexpectedly closed in, until the thin silvery thread in the rock had dwindled away to nothing. The twitch might be a short lived thing, or it might last for several fathoms, beyond the western boundary of their ground; no amount of skill or knowledge could tell them which. There was one last fragment of the vein still remaining at the uppermost limit of their workings, but today would bring them to the end of it. After that, there was only barren rock, for who knew what distance. They could only work on through it and hope that they would soon find the vein again, and on much the same course as before. They had, in any case, bargained to work this ground until the end of June.

Joe and his cousin clambered on to the wooden platform at the top of their rise, on which they had been working last. Here, in a space only just high and wide enough for the two of them, the air was so thick and foul that the candles, stuck to the rock face with clay, had to be tilted downwards so that the wax ran on to the flame, because otherwise they would not burn at all.

Joe did not quite know why, but he had brought Billy's tools with him today. It gave him an odd feeling to be handling the jumper and hammer, knowing that it was Billy's hands that had last used them underground, holding the jumper as he was holding it now, against the edge of that last narrow, silvery line of lead, slowly rotating it as Ralph's Joe hammered on its end, just as Joe used to do for Billy, with a careful, steady rhythm.

Once a large enough hole had been bored in the rock, Joe, watched by his cousin, very carefully spooned the gunpowder into it. Then he took the pricker, a thin iron rod. He thought how often he had stood as Ralph's Joe stood now, watching Billy insert the pricker with great care into the gunpowder, to the very end of the hole. When it was in place, clay and small pieces of shale were packed round it and rammed home, and then the pricker was gently pulled out again; gently, with extreme caution, for an iron pricker can strike sparks from sandstone, and the gunpowder was very near.

This time, as usual, there was no spark, and Joe fitted the paper fuse, rolled in a long tube, into the space where the pricker had been. Then: 'Get back, man,' he said quietly to his cousin, as Billy had said to him that last day. And as Billy had done then, he waited until his partner had jumped down from the platform and stepped back into the base of the shaft; and then he lit the match and applied it to the fuse. Then he ran.

He and Ralph's Joe crouched down together, hands over ears, eyes tight closed. There was one tense moment; and then another ... *Damn, it's gone out*, Billy had said. *I'll go and light it again.* Joe had watched him climb back on to the platform, the tiny glow of his candle flickering on the sparkling, sparry walls; he could see him now, as clearly as he had then, just seconds before the blast.

As now, there had come a great rush of air, a muffled boom, dying away with a last spattering of stones falling to the platform; and then into the silence had broken the sound of moaning. Somehow – he still did not quite know how –

Joe had found himself on the platform, peering through the dust and smoke, scrabbling helplessly at the rubble of ore and rock that scattered the blackened and mutilated body of his friend. The noise of that moaning had echoed and echoed in his head ...

He rubbed his eyes, swallowed hard. Today nothing had gone wrong. The shot was fired, the way into the rise blotted out by the fog of the blast, and he and his cousin sat back to wait for the air to clear enough for them to see what they were doing; to pass the time, Ralph's Joe lit up his pipe. Then it was back on to the platform, to work with picks at the ore loosened by the blast, pieces so few and so meagre as to be scarcely worth the effort. Just another shot fired, a small part of another day's work ...

The older men, hearing the blast, came to wait at the foot of the rise, ready to shovel the ore into the kibble, as Joe and his cousin sent it down to them. It took little doing, but after a short while Ralph grew so dizzy and breathless that he was forced to sit down and watch.

Two more shots were fired off, by which time the forehead was so thick with smoke that they were unable to see what they were doing at all, and in any case they had come to the end of the ore. 'That's it,' gasped Ralph, to everyone's relief. 'Let's get home.' They gathered up their tools and made their way back through the sumps and levels to the day.

Early in the afternoon, Aunt Ann Emerson came up to White Lea to sit a while with William while Jenny went down to the village. Jenny had already put the grouse to cook slowly in a pot over the fire, with herbs and onions to flavour it, and made her father as comfortable as possible. Now she pulled a shawl over her head against the rain and set off down the road, feeling the strain and weariness fall from her with every step. On her arm was a basket in which, hidden beneath a white cloth, lay the second grouse Joe had brought home. She had known better than to offer it to her aunt; Ann Emerson would rather have starved than accept such a tainted gift.

Tabitha Hall, on the other hand, was impervious to her son's disapproval and partial to a plump grouse. On her way to the smithy, Jenny glanced across at the Black Bull and smiled with more warmth than usual at the scowling figure of Joseph Dawson, standing in the doorway of his inn – enough to repel any would-be guests, Jenny thought. He did force some kind of smile in return, however, and then turned to go inside. Jenny, conscious of what lay in her basket, relished her sense of triumph.

The fire glowed in the dark recesses of the smithy, and the air rang with the clash of hammer on anvil, over which Lancelot Hall's voice boomed as he exchanged opinions with a customer. Jenny slipped by unobserved and went to the house door, pushing it open. She was sure of her welcome here, and never knocked.

The room looked out over the Harthope Burn, and was filled with the sound of rushing water. Tabitha Hall, tiny, black eyed, heavy browed, with a fuzz of black hair on her upper lip, sat by the window where the light was best, mending a coat of her son's. She looked up and smiled, but Jenny saw at once that something was wrong. She loved Billy's mother, loved her indomitable spirit, her invariable cheerfulness and courage, her bright observant eyes. But today their brightness was dulled and suspiciously rimmed with red, and her face had a grey look. Jenny put the basket on the table, knowing better than to make any comment. 'I've something for you.'

Tabitha laid her sewing aside and went to look in the basket. 'A bonny moor hen!' She grinned. 'Joe's been out then?'

Jenny nodded, and went to help her prepare the bird for the pot.

'It'll be the more welcome,' Tabitha said, in the careful tones of someone not quite able to sound as casual as she would have liked, 'that I've company to feed.' She paused for effect before adding, 'Rowland came back last night.'

Jenny's eyes widened. 'Rowland Peart?'

'Aye. My sister Mary's lad. God rest her soul.'

'But why? What has he come back for after all this time?'

The old woman shrugged. The tears were brimming in her eyes, as clearly they had been for much of the night since that unexpected return. She sniffed loudly before replying. 'Oh, he has his reasons. Not that they're owt to do with Mary, or with his father, not as they should be. I don't understand it, not rightly.'

'What does Lancelot say?'

'He was angry at first. But then – ' She shrugged again. 'He took it all in. Rowland always did have a way with him, when he chose. He's not changed in that, whatever else may be different. That's what made it worse for Mary, I'd say. If she could have hated him for what he did, for what he was, then it wouldn't have hit her so hard. But there we are.'

'Billy always said they'd been close once, as lads.'

'He was just a bit lad when he went, in years anyway, no more than seventeen. But old in sin, so Mary used to say … But aye, you're right; he and Billy were close. Even after he went, Billy would never have a word said against him. I never knew why.' She seemed to have regained some control over herself, enough to speak more soberly of what had happened. 'He's come back to preach.' She smiled then, a thin bitter little smile. 'Rowland Peart, preach to us – why, just think of that, Jenny my lass! That's the world turned upside down. He's out somewhere now, seeking a place to preach in. I can't see anyone wanting to give him houseroom, can you?'

Rowland Peart: a name from the lost past, before Billy's death. Jenny had not known him, except as a shadowy figure spoken of in scandalized gossip, and, later, as someone whom Billy remembered with an affection that had surprised her, used as she was to the village's condemnation. She could not even bring to mind what he had looked like, though she supposed she must have seen him about. But then she could not have been more than thirteen when he went away, with Tommy a lively toddler in her sole care. Her mother's death less than two years before that loomed much larger in her memory.

'Did he know about Billy?' she asked quietly.

'He does now,' said Tabitha. 'Not that he said much.' She shook her head. 'I used to envy Mary, when my man died. Up to then, I'd thought, being wed to a blacksmith, we'd grow old together, and poor Mary would be a widow long before me.' She gave a faint wry smile. 'In the end I wouldn't have swapped places with Mary for anything. Even after

40

Billy ... Well, Billy was a good son, a good man.'

'The best,' said Jenny, holding the old woman's hand in her own. It was not the first time she had felt very close to Billy's mother, united not simply by their shared loss, but by a real kinship of spirit.

Later, making her way, clogs slithering, through the churned up mud of the market place, her shopping done, Jenny thought of the man from Billy's past who had returned so unexpectedly. What had he found, out there beyond the hills that sheltered the dale? To her the outside world was a remote and dream-like place, hard to imagine yet infinitely desirable; a place where men did not toil in the earth for lead until they died of it, where children were not left fatherless and women could hope to see their husbands grow old, to share a lifetime with them, a long lifetime. Why should anyone, once away, want to come back to this place of heart-break? She looked around her, at the grey sky and the grey houses and the squalid streets, and the endless miserable rain that blotted out all sight of the hills, and could see nothing remotely enticing in any of it. Today there were not even any human beings about to relieve the bleakness, except Jacob Todd, short and thickset and assertive, standing in the doorway of his grocer's shop confronting a slight young man – a stranger to Jenny – who was stepping out into the street, encouraged none too kindly by the grocer himself.

'Over my dead body, young man – over my dead body!' Jacob was exclaiming. 'And if you know what's best you'll pack your bags and leave this very hour, that's all I can say!' His eye was caught by Jenny. 'You hear that, Jane Emerson? Take note, for I'll have everyone hear it. This – this reprobate shall never defile God's house with his blasphemings!' At which he stepped back into the shop and slammed the door. The young man looked round at Jenny, and she saw his expression was no more than a little rueful. She was surprised. People did not usually take Jacob Todd's strictures so lightly.

Then his gaze sharpened, and he said in quite a different tone, 'Jane Emerson, did he say? Then you're my cousin Billy's girl.'

41

She knew who he was then. She studied him, a mild curiosity stirring beneath the dread of what he might say next. He did not look very terrible, a small man with worn clothes and untidy dark curls, on whom the only marks that hinted at an evil past were the deep lines that ran from nose to mouth, ageing the bony young face more perhaps than the years would have done, if he had lived as other men. There was, she realized, a family resemblance, for he had Tabitha Hall's strong brows and dark colouring.

'You're Rowland Peart.'

He did not waste time acknowledging it, as if his purpose was far too serious to be deflected by stating the obvious. He said quietly, his voice very gentle, 'Will you tell me what happened?' It was what she had most dreaded, yet if he had known Billy and loved him it was understandable that he should want to know what had become of him.

'Did Lancelot not tell you?'

'A bit. Aunt Tabitha would not talk ... I know you were to be married.'

'Aye.' Instinctively her eyes slid over his head, over the shop roof in the direction of East Blackdene, a little way up the hill beyond the river. It could not be seen from here, even in good weather, but in a sheltered corner among the cluster-ed houses of the hamlet stood the half-built walls of the house that should have been theirs. The day before the accident, a Sunday, Billy had worked on the house, and she had come to bring him food and drink and they had lain together in the March sunlight, hidden within the man-high walls. The last time ...

'Lancelot said there was an explosion.'

'Aye.'

'It was what we always feared, that and a roof fall.'

So Rowland must have been in the mines before he went away, which was unsurprising, since his father too had been a miner. Had he, alone among lead miners, felt the need to escape from his fate? But why return, if that were so?

'Aye.' She found after all that it was not difficult to talk, at least not while it was simply a matter of recounting facts, bare and mundane. 'He thought the fuse had gone out, so he went back to see. Only it hadn't. Joe was with him. My

42

brother,' she added, in case Rowland did not remember. 'He was Billy's partner. He was there, but not close enough to be hurt.' And had never forgiven himself that he had been safe when the explosion came; but she did not say that. To bring Joe's feelings into it would be to risk touching her own, and she knew that would end all her calmness. 'They thought they had a good ground. The lead was easy to get. They didn't need to fire many shots. Afterwards, they got Billy out and took him home. He died the next week.' A sad tale, but a simple one, which left out the burns and the mangled body and the days of agony while she and his mother, Lancelot and Joe sat at Billy's bedside and watched, and knew there was nothing they could do but pray for his sake that it would soon be over. It was the things she had left out that had stayed with her through all the months since, polluting her sweet and happy memories, so that she could not remember Billy without thinking of his end.

Rowland was silent for a time, his eyes steady on her face, though whether it was compassion or grief she saw in them Jenny did not know; both perhaps. She wondered if he would talk of Billy, tell her of things he remembered, things that might help her for a little while to forget what had come after.

Then he said, very softly, 'Sometimes the Lord's ways seem strange.'

Jenny caught her breath. 'What has the Lord to do with it?' she demanded, enraged by the platitude, like so many she had heard since Billy's death, always from those who could have no possible idea how she felt, nor what it had been like to watch Billy die.

'He has to do with all things,' Rowland returned, as if that was beyond argument. He was apparently quite oblivious of the effect his words were having, for this second remark was worse than the first.

'Then I want none of your Lord, Rowland Peart – not if he had owt to do with Billy's death.'

'He suffered too ...'

'Not as Billy did!' she retorted with a sob, and turned from him and ran without stopping down the lane to the river and over the bridge and on up the hill, not pausing to draw breath until she reached the road that ran along the dale side.

There, standing still, her breath coming in long harsh gulps, she became aware of a pony clopping steadily towards her from the west; and did not realize until it was too late that the rider was Joshua Bowman, on his way to inspect the washing floor at Slitt mine, in the valley beyond White Lea. The rain had stopped at last, or he might have continued on his way, not wanting to linger. As it was, just as Jenny turned to go on, he halted beside her and dismounted. 'What a lucky chance!' he said, coming uncomfortably close to her. When he spoke, the pungent odour of his breath choked her, along with other smells; she doubted if he washed very much.

'I've left my father – I must get back,' she said, quickening her pace, wishing she was not so far still from Side Head and the watching eyes of her neighbours. Unperturbed, the inspector kept up with her, leading his pony.

'Why then I'll make sure you get safe home,' he said.

'Thank you, I don't need your company.' She wished someone would come, anyone. It was a long time since she had seen Joshua Bowman. Once they had met often, for she used to take Joe's bait to the mine each day, so long as he was not working too far underground; it had been an excuse to see Billy, sometimes to take him some little morsel she had baked. While Billy was alive, Joshua Bowman had been no more than a minor irritation, given to making remarks she did not much care for, breathing over her if she did not make her escape in time. Once Billy was dead he seemed to regard her as anyone's property, and with increasing frequency the advances became gestures and not simply words, a pat on the arm, a stroke, a hug, a kiss, and latterly several of these at once, if no one was by at the time. Fearful of telling Joe (she knew his temper), she had made some excuse and stopped going to the mine any more. She had thought that was that, for they never seemed to meet by chance – until today.

'It's been a long time. You're almost a stranger.'

'Then we can have nowt to say to one another,' she returned. He was breathing hard with the effort to keep up, but his pace did not slacken.

'Why, there you're wrong. You're a bonny lass, Jane

44

Emerson. Oh, I know you've had your troubles, but that was a long time ago now –'

She turned furious, anguished eyes upon him. 'That shows you know nowt of such things!'

For a moment (to her satisfaction) he looked a little taken aback; but not for long. He was not the sort of man to let inconvenient facts or emotions get in the way of what he wanted. 'Time to put the past behind you. Time to think of the future – a lass of your age shouldn't be lying alone at night.'

'I've a sick father to care for and no time for owt else,' she retorted.

'Then the more need you have of a strong arm at your side,' he said. As if to illustrate the point, his arm slid about her waist, pulling her closer to him. She struggled, trying to free herself, conscious that he had one hand on the rein, which must hamper him. 'Try this!' he said then; and he looped the rein over his wrist, put his other arm about her, pulled her to him and kissed her. His mouth was hot and wet and smelled horrible, but his grasp was too strong for her, though she struggled fiercely. In the end, without thinking, she reached out and slapped the pony, hard, on whatever part of it was nearest.

The trick worked. The pony, already made uneasy by sounds and movements it could not place, was startled into activity. It leapt forward, jerking the inspector by the arm, pulling him along some way on the mud and stones before he could free himself from the rein. Rubbing her mouth to remove all traces of his kiss, Jenny watched with satisfaction as he fell on his hands and knees on the ground, his breeches torn, his hat blown some way off, across a field. But she feared his anger and began to run, before he could regain his footing and come after her.

Another rider, ahead on the road, turned his horse and came back her way. Between the two, she halted, hesitating, fearful of worse to come. But Joshua Bowman was already on his feet, shouting as he came after her, and she resumed her running, her breath rasping in her throat. She reached the horse, grasped the bridle and stood there, leaning on the smooth brown flank of the animal, trying to bring the face of its rider into focus above her, through vision spotted and hazy.

'Miss Emerson, pray what has happened?'

He took shape at last, a young man of dazzling elegance, tall and upright on his fine-boned horse, his boots gleaming, his breeches tight over muscular thighs, his coat fitting his slim strong figure to perfection, slender gloved hands firm on the reins. The face looking down at her had fair clear-cut features, bright blue eyes under fine, blond, arching brows; his hair, when he removed his hat out of respect for her, was a rich gold colour, waving thickly over his head. He was, she thought, gazing at him in astonishment, like some creature from another world, suddenly set down in the dale to right wrongs and punish the evildoer ... But how did he know her name? She had not dreamed he had said it, surely?

Then she realized that she had seen him before, and he was merely a man, though it was hard to recognize yesterday's exhausted and bedraggled traveller as this elegant being gazing down at her with well-bred concern. He swung himself out of the saddle, but even standing beside her, reduced to more normal stature (though he was tall, almost as tall as Billy had been), he still seemed like some alien creature, as far removed from her fellow dalesmen as a high-bred Arab horse from the shaggy galloways that served them so well.

'Something is wrong, Miss Emerson –'

She only remembered then why she had been running; the young man's appearance had so startled her that all thought of her fright had momentarily left her. Now, a little lessened, her anxiety returned. She glanced behind her, and saw to her relief that Mr Bowman had come to a halt and was standing watching her from a safe distance. The next moment he turned round and began slowly to walk back to where his pony had paused to crop the grass beside the road.

The curate followed her gaze. 'That man, was he ...?'

She smiled, suddenly feeling quite different; not only no longer frightened, but unreal, taken out of herself, as if she were a little intoxicated, as if indeed some godlike creature had suddenly deigned to set foot in the dale and walk at her side. 'He's going now. It doesn't matter.' She wondered how

46

she could ever have been frightened of so insignificant a figure.

'Permit me to see you safely home,' said Edward, in his clipped educated voice, full of a decisiveness and courtesy she had not noticed yesterday. 'I was in any case making my way to call and ask after your father.' He glanced down at her. 'Pray let me carry your basket.'

Glad that it now contained only innocent items of shopping, she let him take it, exhilarated by an unaccustomed sense of being cared for. Even Billy had not treated her so, as if carrying a basket might somehow prove too much for her. She felt an almost irresistible urge to giggle, she did not quite know why. She was not generally given to giggling, certainly not lately.

With a sense that she must somehow try to keep a hold on reality, even bring herself firmly down to earth, she said after a moment, 'It's kind of you, but we don't go to church, you know, except for – well, the things everyone goes for.'

He smiled down at her, and the enchantment only seemed to deepen. 'You are still my parishioner, in my care.' The thought of being in his care, of prolonging this sense of being protected and watched over, set her heart beating faster, and only the forefront of her mind took his words in any more prosaic sense. Then he said, 'I heard something of your tragedy.'

That brought her up short, touching her in the dangerous, vulnerable part of herself, reminding her who she was and by what difficult paths she had reached the present moment. It reminded her, too, that he was simply a man doing a job of work, even if it was not the kind of work she would readily recognize as such. He had scarcely been in the dale one day, yet he had already begin to inform himself about its people, so as to do that work more effectively. 'Aye, they would tell you,' she said, a little drily. 'It's not that old news yet.' She waited, braced, for the religious platitudes, the consolations that did not console, only further irritated the wound.

'This past year must have been very hard.' He said no more, simply looked at her with compassionate blue eyes that somehow made her think of quite other things than her own grief. It was an odd sensation, as if she no longer had

47

control over her mind or even her body, as if something outside herself was directing her.

'I hope you will find that time heals, but I do not know if that is indeed so. I have never had the misfortune to lose someone dear to me.' That was a relief too. She found it unbearable when people said, *I know how you feel.* It was something that those who did know never said.

Edward, conscious only that he was not talking to her as a man of the cloth should, and thus failing entirely to offer her the proper consolations of religion, wondered how he could remedy the situation, and searched his mind in vain for some more appropriate words. Since hearing her story from Peggy Gibson, the parsonage servant, he no longer thought Jane Emerson cold and unfeeling. It was natural dignity that kept her from complaining, or from making much of her grief. If, the other day, speaking of her father's illness, she had seemed uncaring, that was rather because she had already suffered so much, than because she did not suffer. He felt ashamed of his own relative impunity, as if it made him somehow less of a man, less fit to minister to those who daily faced real anguish and grief. The loss of a favourite dog in childhood, though painful enough even at this distance, could hardly be set in the scale against what life (or whatever it was) had done to this girl. On first seeing her, he had thought of Wordsworth's poem about the untouched child of nature. Now he thought of other verses by the same poet, concerning simple country people who endured with a patience of which their betters were incapable.

Try as he might, he could think of nothing very suitable to say to Jenny, and in the end retreated into more mundane talk, asking her, with a genuine interest that touched her very much, about the ordinary things of her daily life. She told him about the animals, and Joe and his work, and how Tommy had just started work too. At that the curate gave her a long look, and then said, 'I think you regret that step. You do not want to think of him growing up perhaps?'

She shook her head. 'It's not that. I ...' How could she begin to put into words all that she felt, all her bitter resentment at what life did to those she loved? How could someone who was not Weardale born ever understand?

'What then?' he prompted gently, when she had been silent for some time.

She looked up at him, and he was startled by the angry light in her eyes. 'Bairns should have time to be bairns, time to be happy.'

'Time to get into mischief?' he added, with a smile and a raised eyebrow. He remembered the children who had misled him yesterday. Was that the kind of life she wanted for her brother?

'Tell me,' she asked abruptly. 'What were you doing at nine years old?'

The question surprised him, since he could not quite see what bearing it had on her or her brother. Memories flitted through his head – riding his pony, with Ben the groom for company; lessons with gentle old Parson Williams at the rectory, enlivened each day by a tiny glass of sherry and several of Miss Williams's exquisite almond biscuits; picnics in the harvest field, with the harvesters singing around them and the sweet smell of the cut corn in his nostrils ... But then he had, very properly, been prepared for a very different kind of life from the one that this girl's brother could look forward to. One did not expect the children of the poor to live as he had done, nor was it desirable that they should. Give them expectations beyond their station, and they would only be miserable. Give them too much leisure, and they were only too likely to use it to ill effect. That they should work hard was only to be desired – within reasonable bounds, of course. But he said none of this to the girl at his side, though he was not particularly conscious of deliberately choosing concealment. He smiled and said, 'Ah, many things I should not have done, I suppose ... But perhaps you want for your brother what he would not choose for himself.'

Jenny knew he was right. For months now Tommy had looked forward to starting work on the washing floor. Once there, his greatest ambition was to be old enough to go underground like Joe. The lead took hold of the men of Weardale long before they were old enough to make any conscious choice, that Jenny knew full well, filling their heads with dreams that would never be realized.

At the house, she led the curate inside, and made him

49

known to her aunt, who returned his greeting with a distant chilliness. But then Edward quickly gathered that Mrs Emerson was a Methodist (as it seemed the White Lea family were not), and at least she was polite, or more so than Joe had been. To his relief, she left almost at once, promising Jenny that she would return that evening, with her daughters, to keep Jenny company for an hour or two. 'We'll have a bit knit and talk,' she said, which sounded pleasantly cosy to Edward, faced with the prospect of a second solitary evening at the parsonage.

Once her aunt had gone, Jenny ushered him to the settle while she put the shopping away and saw to her father, who was wakeful now and in need of soothing. After a time, she invited the curate to come and talk to him. Feeling very nervous, for he had little experience of the sick, still less the dying, Edward sat down on a stool near the bedside and took William Emerson's hand in his own. It was thin and cold and claw-like, with no feeling of life in it. The face from which blank grey eyes watched him was bathed in sweat and had a bluish pallor, the mouth fixed open in a constant, hopeless struggle for breath. He looked as if death had already laid hold on him. Jenny went away somewhere, presumably to attend to some domestic task, leaving Edward alone with her father. He sat there talking softly to the sick man, without quite knowing what he said, though he tried to find some suitably consoling words from the Bible or Prayer Book. He felt he was floundering, for there was no response on the haggard face, no movement in the thin fingers. He could only hope that the poor man did not positively object to his presence there. He was greatly relieved when William Emerson fell into a noisy slumber, freeing him to return to the settle by the fireside. Jenny saw that his expression was grave and rather sad, as if he felt for her father's plight. Combined with the beauty of his features, its effect on her was curious. It was not simply that she felt comforted by his sympathy, but she was moved too, and excited, an odd and contradictory mingling of sensations.

'Has the surgeon seen him lately, Miss Emerson?' This morning, Edward had called on Mr John Scott, the St John's Chapel surgeon, and found him an honest, overworked man, whose enthusiasm for strong drink was only too understandable. He had told Edward, in a voice harsh with suppressed rage, that the one great enemy he fought, ceaselessly but without avail, was what they called the miner's disease, an affliction that blighted a population in other respects rather healthier than most, and ensured that few lead miners lived much beyond their forties. William Emerson was just one of many patients dying in what should have been the prime of life, for whom he had been able to do nothing.

Echoing all Edward had been told, Jenny said, 'There's no point him coming. There's nowt he could do.'

Edward wished he had not asked the question. He felt more conscious than ever of the bitterness of this girl's life and its uncomfortable contrast with his own, and he was unused to sensations so disturbing. He was relieved when she said, 'I'll make some tea,' and at once put a kettle to boil and set cups on the table. The easy domesticity of it all was somehow soothing to his troubled spirit.

Yesterday he had found the room agreeable in its simplicity. Now, after the shabby solitude of the parsonage, it looked positively welcoming; warm, the fire glowing in the hearth, a good smell of cooking (something rather more savoury than yesterday's fare) coming from the pot over the fire.

'That smells delicious,' he said kindly. He was surprised that Jenny's eyes took on a faintly defensive look.

'Just a stew for supper, when they get in.'

She turned away then, hastily shuffling the cups around, rather as if she hoped he would be distracted by the move. Troubled, he pondered the matter for a moment, and then said with apparent casualness, 'I understand that there is a great deal of poaching in this district.' He wondered if she would see a connection between the two remarks. If she did, he supposed it could only indicate an uneasy conscience, so he rather hoped she would not.

Her reply should have been innocent enough. 'Who told you that?'

'I was warned of it before I came to Weardale. And this morning I found myself in conversation with one Joseph Dawson, who is, I gather, retained as a gamekeeper by the Bishop.'

51

'Aye, he would tell you, right enough.' There was a dry note in her voice that was not encouraging to someone wanting to believe in her innocence – or at least her ignorance – of these nefarious matters.

'I fear he claims that there are few miners who have not been engaged in poaching at some time or another.'

She came and stood before him, her gaze very direct. 'What would you do, with pay low and prices high: starve, or go out and shoot a moor hen?'

'The moors and the game are the Bishop's property,' said Edward, very gravely, alarmed that this charming girl should speak of crime so lightly.

That she frowned now was only briefly a reassurance. 'Do you think that just or right?'

'Of course. It is the law.'

'That poor men should go hungry, so that the Bishop may have entertainment for his friends whenever he has a mind to it? Why, if that's the law, then the law's unjust.'

'I don't think you know what you are saying,' Edward told her, with growing distress. Clearly that sullen brother of hers had been poisoning her with his pernicious ideas, which in her simplicity and innocence she could only repeat parrot fashion. 'You have a natural partiality for your brother's point of view. But he was one of those named by Joseph Dawson, I am afraid. You must know that he runs a considerable risk if he is caught – and Dawson has instructions to enforce the law with greater rigour than hitherto.' Then all at once his voice lost its calmly authoritative note, and he said, 'I should not like to think of someone close to you finding himself before the magistrates.'

She was not quite sure, for there was not a great deal of light in the room, but she thought he had coloured a little. She herself had certainly done so, moved by the note of concern in his voice, which she sensed was real enough. He was not, then, so loftily removed from her as she had thought. 'Joe won't do that,' she reassured him, leaving him to decide whether her brother's immunity would be due to innocence or cunning. 'In any case, no one will be after game any more now, not till summer. It's the breeding season.' Digesting that last observation, Edward realized that it indicated at the very least an intimate knowledge of the habits of both poachers and game birds.

'Nevertheless, perhaps you would tell your brother what I said,' he went on after a moment. 'I would far rather a man stepped back from the brink, than that he made the fatal leap and was forced to face the consequences.'

'I suppose that's what you're here for,' said Jenny thoughtfully.

He looked startled. 'For what?'

'To stop folk falling into wrongdoing. Mind, I don't think you'll get far. Weardale folk have no love for the Church.' She saw his startled look, and added, 'We never minded Mr Whitelock, because he lets us alone. Besides, his wife's people are from Weardale. But you're from a long way off and – well, you're not like him.' She coloured, very faintly.

He was not sure how to take that. 'What could anyone possibly have against the Church? Is it because so many of you are of the Methodist persuasion?'

She stared at him, as if amazed that anyone should need to ask such a question. 'Why no, there aren't so many Methodists,' she said. 'It's because of the Bishop, of course. He owns everything, but he does nowt for us in return, except take the profits from the lead and forbid us to shoot the game. If the masters didn't have to pay so much to the Bishop, and the rector too, then maybe the miners would be better paid. The Quaker Company hasn't got the Bishop on its back, and it pays better. How can he preach that we should love our neighbours, or love God, while he lives like that?'

It was an awkward question, and one to which Edward could think of no immediate answer, not least because it had never occurred to him to view the Bishop in any but a most reverential light.

He smiled faintly. 'I can see I have a great deal still to learn about Weardale ways,' he said, careful not to commit himself to any point of view. Then he found himself adding, 'Perhaps you will be my teacher in that.' She looked at him with clear astonishment, and he enlarged, 'You have been kind, you welcomed me, yet you share the prejudices of your own people.'

She was not quite sure how to take that, and from another man might have thought it insulting; but somehow she knew it was not. 'You've only to ask, and I'll answer your questions, if I can,' she assured him. She wondered if that meant he would often ride up to White Lea, to sit here by the fire and talk. The thought brought an odd tightness to her chest, as if excitement stopped her breathing freely.

A little later, when he had gone, she tried to give her attention to the things she had to do, but her thoughts were beyond her control. She burned her fingers at the fire, broke a cup (they only had four to begin with), and all the time she went over and over in her mind the meeting on the road – the rescue, as she saw it – the walk at his side, the talk with him here in her own house place. Something new and different and exciting had come into her life, and she wanted it to remain, to free her for a little time from the hard reality in which she passed each day.

That night, Joe and his friends met with an obstacle to their evening's entertainment at the Black Bull; Anthony Siddle was not able to join them. 'His cough's bad,' said Charlie, 'and you know how mother frets. He'd to stop in to keep her quiet.' There seemed little point in going into the Black Bull without him (apart from anything else, he would hate to miss the fun), and so they went instead to the King's Head and cheered themselves with Tom Walton's good ale.

'Have you heard who's back?' James Craggs asked, once they were comfortably seated.

'Aye,' said Joe quietly. 'I heard.' Jenny, in a strange mood tonight, had told him the news, almost as an afterthought, just as he was leaving the house.

'They say he's changed,' said Charlie Siddle.

'I'll believe that when I see it,' Tom put in. 'Mind, I'll grant you he's not been in here yet. Once he'd not have let the grass grow under his feet so long. I remember when never a day passed but he was in causing trouble. I was for ever chucking him out. You'd have thought every night was Mischief Night with him around. Can't say I was sorry when he went.'

'Father says he used to swear and shout at them coming

out of High House chapel, him and his mates,' said Ralph's Joe, with a sideways glance at his cousin.

'Don't look at me,' said Joe. 'I never did that.' But he had a faint reminiscent smile all the same. The swearing had been imaginative, even witty, and could still make him laugh, though he no longer thought of it quite so lightly. They had been wild days, when Billy's cousin had led his devoted group of friends into ever more reckless mischief. They had all been hard drinkers – still were – but Rowland had beaten them for drinking and fighting, for malicious inventiveness, in charming the girls (even Billy had taken second place to him in that). A neat dancer too, a tuneful singer, a fast lively talker – none could better him, even if sometimes it was Billy, steadier and stronger, who had to get him out of some scrape he had led them into so impulsively. Yes, Joe remembered those days well enough; but he knew there were few who shared precisely his memories, or looked on them so tolerantly, especially not considering the manner of Rowland's going. He would not easily be forgiven for that.

Later, their thirst thoroughly quenched, the young men decided to go back to Charlie's house, to keep the housebound Anthony company. It was very late when the party broke up, well after midnight, but passing the smithy Joe saw there was a light still burning at the house end. Letting the others go on ahead, he stood still, gazing at it, wondering whether to go and knock on the door. Once he and Rowland had been close enough to cause great disquiet to William Emerson, who had refused to have someone so turbulent at White Lea. When he went away, he had, for good or ill, left a great gap in all their lives. Would he remember the old days, and the friends who once had meant so much to him? It would be good, Joe thought, to talk of those times, to remember Billy with someone else who had known him and loved him well.

But Rowland had changed, so they all said. Perhaps he was now ashamed of his past, as Joe was in a way, for all its disreputable excitements. He liked to remember, but he would not wish those days back again, except to bring Billy back, of course. There was another thing, too. Joe knew quite well how Rowland would be received by nearly everyone in the district; there would be no kindness for him, no friendly welcome. Anyone foolish enough to take his part would share his rejection, and Joe could see no good reason to put himself in that position. After all, Rowland had done things even the Joe of seven years ago could not condone. Besides, it would hardly help his cause with Jacob Todd.

He began slowly to walk on, across the market place, glancing towards the grocer's shop on the corner. In its small dark rooms, Eve, the brightness of his life, was held a prisoner, and his dearest wish was somehow to free her from that place, to bring her out to light and happiness. He would not jeopardize any hope he had of achieving that end by taking a step back into a past that was better forgotten. No, he would not seek out Rowland Peart, tonight or any other night.

He hurried to catch up with his friends.

3

Jacob Todd, gathered with other Methodist leaders in High House chapel to consider Rowland Peart's request to speak there, at the earliest opportunity, to whoever wished to hear him, was quite sure of his own position, which he had been expounding at length: '... I told him, and I tell you now, that he will not speak in God's house while I have it in my power to stop it.'

Pleased with himself, he looked round at the assembled local preachers and class leaders, but before he could resume the minister quickly intervened. 'I think our brother Jacob forgets that others have a voice in who shall preach to us.'

Jacob coloured, with anger not embarrassment, that being a sensation entirely foreign to him. 'Why then, you'd let that vicious and unprincipled young man tell us what we must do to be saved, is that it?' he retorted indignantly.

The minister remained calm. 'That is not what I said. But I think we should keep it in mind that no human soul is without hope of salvation. Rowland Peart is no exception. Should we not hear him and judge for ourselves?'

'We only have his word for it that anything's changed. What other evidence is there?'

'Why, he's been back three days and Chapel is still quiet,' put in Ralph Emerson with a little smile. 'That's worth something.'

Jacob, who disapproved of lightness on serious matters, pursed his small lips. 'It's not enough for me. Not when I consider what he said to me. It's my belief, if he has changed, then he's turned Ranter, and we don't want their kind here. The dale's been free of them up to now.'

57

'He says he's a Ranter then, does he?' Hannah Milburn enquired, though with a hint of scepticism in her voice. One of the select band of Weardale Methodists who had been converted by John Wesley himself, she was greatly respected.

'In as many words. He said they had the Spirit with them. I said what did he have to say to the charge that they were opposing the rulings of Conference.'

'What was his answer?'

'He said he accepted the guidance of the Holy Spirit and no other. Naturally I asked did that mean he denied that the Spirit moves Conference. And do you know what he said to that?' Jacob paused dramatically, though not long enough to allow anyone else to intervene before he could reach his scandalous conclusion. 'He said, "Does the Spirit guide Conference, or has Conference set itself to bind the Spirit, tell me that?" Now you see!'

There was a murmur of dismay, before Jacob resumed, his voice smug with satisfaction, 'In any case he's not licensed to preach, not by any authority. He admitted as much.'

It was that in the end that decided them. Some of the Methodists shared Jacob Todd's view that Rowland Peart's conversion was at best suspect and tainted with leanings towards the breakaway Primitive Methodist sect that had begun to cause such sad divisions in their church. But even those, like Ralph Emerson, who were willing to give the young man the benefit of the doubt, felt unable to offer him the use of the pulpit at High House chapel, the very same where John Wesley himself had preached, without the due formalities of official recognition.

'Then I'll do as John Wesley did, and speak in the market place,' declared Rowland, when the decision was conveyed to him at the grocer's shop by a gratified Jacob Todd. The young man stepped back a few paces into the street and raised his voice. 'Here, on market day, I shall tell you why I've come back.' Several heads turned to look at him, expressions varying from curiosity to outrage. A group of small boys jeered, and when he walked away, back to his aunt's house, hurled a few small stones casually after him.

'That's just a taste of what he has coming to him,' predicted Jacob Todd, with satisfaction.

Eve, overhearing Rowland's announcement, felt a shiver of pleasurable excitement. Market day promised to be lively.

She was not alone in her happy expectation. There were more people than usual in the market place the following Saturday, and a distinctly holiday atmosphere, in spite of intermittent rain and a bitter wind and the fact that many of the usual stall holders had decided not to come. But then who wanted to waste time shopping, when there was the prospect instead of a rare and highly diverting entertainment? It was likely to beat cock fighting or bull baiting any day. Eve was sorry that Joe was not there (or not that she could see), but she would enjoy telling him all about it later.

It was not until early in the afternoon that Rowland at last made his appearance, walking along the lane from the smithy, singing as he came. Behind him strode his cousin Lancelot, who had shut up shop and come to give his support, his face rather red and his deep voice booming out the hymn, sure as to melody, but very unsure as to words.

Eve, watching from the shop doorway (her father was with her mother and her sister in the parlour, praying noisily), thought what an unimpressive figure Rowland was. A small, slight man, bareheaded, the long curls of his hair clinging damply to his head and neck, his worn coat and breeches faded to some indeterminate colour, he would be no match at all for the men and women, their tempers soured by the long wait, already starting to jeer. She felt sorry for his inevitable humiliation (that was the very least he could expect), but also rather cheated, because there would not be much sport or entertainment in so unequal a contest. It was hard to imagine that he had once been the evil-living young man of her father's tirades. He did not look as if he had ever had the spirit for that.

Edward was standing by the parsonage gate, as he had been for about an hour now, putting off his lunch so as to be sure not to miss the preacher's arrival. He had received a visit at breakfast time from one of the churchwardens, full of indignation at the impending event, so close to the very walls of the church itself. Forewarned, Edward was ready to take whatever steps might prove to be necessary. Here already, within a week of his arrival in this place, was a chance to take a stand on behalf of the Established Church. He felt a little nervous, but excited too, almost exalted at the possibilities offered to him.

He waited until the young man had taken up his position on a stool conveniently placed beside the market cross, just outside the shelter of its arches (why? wondered Edward; did he think allowing himself to get wet would demonstrate humility?). Then, as the jeering grew louder and Rowland simply stood there, quite still, head bent as if in prayer, Edward pushed his way forward. He called out, 'Young man, have you a licence to preach?' Even to his ears his voice sounded high, clipped, precise, carrying clearly through the impenetrable thicket of dialect around him. It had quite the opposite effect from what he had hoped or intended. In an instant the mood of the crowd swung in Rowland's favour, forming a sudden temporary alliance against the outsider who had dared to intervene, and speak, what was more, for the Law and the Church. Several people even jeered Edward, and a burly miner bawled at him, 'Hold your tongue and let him speak! You can have your say in there tomorrow!' He gestured towards the church.

Conscious of hostility all around him, Edward could think of nothing else to say. In truth, it was quite clear that anything he could do or say would only make matters worse, particularly for himself. With as much dignity as possible he retreated to the parsonage, where Peggy Gibson was sympathetic but blunt. 'They've no time for Rowland Peart,' she said, 'with reason. But at least he's one of their own. You'll never be that, sir.'

It was not an encouraging beginning, but Edward did have one consolation: once he was safely back in the parsonage, the jeers and shouts resumed as loudly as ever out there in the market place. He even found himself pitying the preacher.

In fact Edward's intervention had given Rowland a brief respite. A moment before, there had been a real danger that the people would stone him out of the village. Now they stayed to jeer, but the dangerous edge had been taken from their hostility, for the time being at least. There were even some, like Eve, who were silent, hoping that Rowland might somehow make himself heard.

At last, he threw back his head and raised one hand (the gesture achieved nothing, for the jeering only grew louder), and called out, 'Brothers and sisters!' His voice was surprisingly strong for someone so slight, carrying clearly to where Eve stood, but almost at once drowned in the rising jeers. She expected him to turn pale and crawl away, or perhaps to gesticulate in helpless rage. He did neither. He simply stood there for a moment, very still and quiet, and then all at once, when the noise died down just a little, while they wondered what he would do next, he threw both arms dramatically into the air and cried, 'Here am I, the most wretched of sinners!'

Surprise silenced them, and he seized his chance. 'That's what you say, isn't it? – and you are right, my friends, indeed you are right! If there is any justice, then I shall be pitched first into Hell!'

His hearers growled their assent, but quietened again as he lowered his hands and stretched them out before him; his voice fell too, still resonant, carrying clearly, vibrating with a scorn that none of them could have equalled.

'You know what I was, my friends, none better: drunkard, lecher, brawler, thief, I was all that, and more!' Then, a hoarse undertone: 'You knew my father, George Peart, and Mary, his wife. You knew them, all of you, knew them as good neighbours and good friends, righteous and God fearing. You know how I repaid them. It is not hidden from you; my shame has been on all your lips. When I left this place I had my father's life's savings beneath my coat. To my mother, to gentle Mary Peart, I did worse; I returned her tenderness with cruelty, I left her with my curses ringing in her ears.' He gestured towards the churchyard. 'There they lie now, together, in one grave. I sent them to that grave. I broke their hearts. I made their last days bitter with grief. I can hear yet the words I spoke to them as I turned to go; they burn in my heart to this day. "I hate you! I despise you! I shall be free of you!"'

A great anguished groan was torn from him. 'Those were the words that rang in my mother's ears till death closed them for ever – the last cruel words of her only son!' The

61

crowd's anger roared out again, prolonged this time, and Eve shivered at the hate that was in it. Why did he go on like this? He must know that he was in danger of goading them to tear him to pieces; especially at this time on a Saturday, when many of the men were already pretty drunk. Yet he went on shouting through the increasing fury of the crowd, his words full of an anger that sounded as fierce as theirs.

'I know why you've come today. Some of you were once my friends, many I wronged, many I betrayed. You come to jeer, to hound me from the dale. Your hands are closing on the stones you'd hoy at me!' He was right, Eve saw, for around her several people had picked up stones, and now one or two others stooped to do the same. In a moment he would have to run or risk serious injury.

'Stay your hands! Hear me a moment more!' His arms were up again. In the tiny instant of near-quiet that followed, while only a subdued anger growled on, he cried, 'Hear what I did with the freedom so cruelly bought!'

Silence fell, a cold silence, sprung only of curiosity to know what had happened next. All those who had asked, over the years, *What became of Rowland Peart, I wonder?* were to have their answer. If he had told them they must be converted, they would have hurled their stones and roared the louder. Now, resentful that justice was delayed, they nevertheless stood still and listened. It was not a reprieve, merely a stay of execution, and he must know it.

He paused just long enough to be sure he had their attention, and then he went on, 'My friends, I was deep in the mire, a lost and wretched soul. There never was a soul so lost as I, who did not know how lost I was!

'I had freedom, brothers and sisters. There was none to check me, none to rebuke, none to care what became of me. I had my heart's desire.

'Freedom! What a word that is! Men have died with it on their lips, suffered torments to win it for themselves. And now, at last, it was mine!

'I went where I pleased, spent all I had, and no one questioned what I did, no one cared. Money does not go far when you spend it freely. The fortune my father had worked for all his life was little enough. Soon, there was nowt left. I was

62

free, but I was alone, unloved, destitute. I had no skills, for I was too young to have learned any, and too heedless. I had no home, for my proud heart kept me from it. The prodigal son was forgiven, because he threw himself at his father's feet and begged for mercy. I did not want mercy, I did not desire forgiveness. Freedom was my only cry.

'How soon I found that freedom was a bitter thing! What is freedom, without friendship, without love, without bread to eat, without respect? It is darkness, my friends, it is without form and void, a place of desolation. Lost in that trackless wilderness, my heart failed me. Strong drink, so long my deadly solace, became the staff on which I leaned, my only help. I was alone; I drank to forget my loneliness. I had hurt those I loved; I drank to shut out their tears. I drank to forget what I had become; I drank to shield myself from what lay before me; I drank to forget the past. I drank to hide from myself.

'And to buy drink, and the little food I needed to live, what did I do, my friends? For you know I must have found bread somehow; I am here speaking to you today. This is what I did, my brothers and sisters – I went on as I had begun. I lived as a common thief. Perhaps you think little of that, some of you here. Have you not always lived on the game from the Bishop's moors? Is that not what rich men call theft? Why no, my brothers and sisters, that is not what I mean by theft. I took not from the rich, not from those who had enough and to spare; I had not even that excuse. No, in my desperation and my need I robbed the old, the weak, the poor as they wandered the streets. I picked pockets; I begged with lies; I crept into back doors and stole from houses. That is theft, that is sin, in any man's eyes. And when I had money, I drank until it was gone. Not only drank, but gambled, went after whores, sought out every vice. Worst of all, I closed my heart to all compassion, to every cry of the hungry and the oppressed – in them I heard my mother's tears, and it was more than I could bear. One day word reached me, by a long route, that my parents were dead. I was drunk when I heard it – when was I not drunk, in those days? In my hardness of heart I did not weep for them, only cursed them for my condition, for the evil I had brought

63

upon myself. That, my friends, is the measure of how lost I was.

'But the Lord's ways are deep, my friends, unfathomably deep. Hear me just a little more!'

There was no sound in the crowd, as there had been none ever since he resumed his story. But by now it was not simple curiosity that kept them silent, but something else: the power of his voice. It was an extraordinary voice, unexceptional enough at first hearing, a young man's voice, neither deep nor high, which would have gone unnoticed in everyday talk. Yet it held them all spellbound. It rose and fell, one moment harsh and bitter, the next sharp with anguish, tender with grief, warm and cajoling, yearning, caressing, then cold as the rain carried on the wind. It was like music, all lilting vowels and rhythms, swinging their emotions in a second from anger to compassion, from grief to hate and back again. No longer did anyone want him to reach the end, so that justice could be exacted. The lure of his voice was too beguiling, had them too much in thrall, for any to want to break free.

'At last one day my stony heart was touched. How, I do not know, for I thought myself proof against all weakness. And she was little enough, this creature who touched my heart, a woman you would have despised, a woman whom even I, vile as I was, thought beneath my contempt. Aye, my friends, she was a lost woman, a woman of the streets, a whore.

'We were two of a kind, you will say; two sinners wandering far from home, drawn together in their sin. Who knows – God only knows. Whatever the reason, I loved her, brothers and sisters. And the greater wonder is that she loved me. You have all heard of the greatness of God's love, its power to work miracles. Why, I tell you that even our weak human love has the power to melt the heart. I know, because it melted mine.

'I thought I was a new man. I gave up my drunkenness, I gave up thieving, I studied, read books, strove to improve myself. I even found work, hard, real work, in a cotton mill – I hated that work, but the woman had need of bread too, and we had a bairn.

'Brothers and sisters, I thought I was a happy man. I had a

roof over my head, a woman who was a wife in all but name, an infant daughter. I no longer sought freedom, for I found there were things more precious even than that, a bondage more sweet. I worked long hours in the mill, only so I could keep my small family.

'And then a fever came to the great town where we lived, and few were spared. I fell sick, and then my wife who had nursed me so tenderly, and then the child ...

'I lived, my friends. To learn at last how helpless is man, how unable of himself to help himself. For they died, those two that I loved, all in one bitter winter night, and there was nowt I could do to save them.'

His voice broke, and fell away into silence. His hands – expressive hands, which had constantly moved to underline and emphasize his words – reached out in one last gesture of hopelessness and then dropped to his sides. He stood there, a broken man, reliving before them the grief of that night. Near Eve, a woman was sobbing, clear into the silence.

The voice resumed the tale, very low, full of desolation. 'My friends, I stood in that bare and silent room, and I was alone as I had never been alone before ... And then –' Suddenly, harsh, clipped, bitter, the voice cried out, 'And then, my friends, I did a terrible thing: I cried aloud and I cursed the name of the Lord! I saw His hand in my grief and I could not forgive Him for it. I cursed God, my brothers and sisters, aloud and for a long time.

'And then I lost myself in drunkenness for many days.

'I woke at last to despair so deep that no words can tell you of its bitterness. Darkness closed me in. Now at last no drink, no hardness of heart, no loving wife, hid from me the truth of what I was. It was night again, and all were asleep but me. In my desolation I seemed to see laid before me all my life and all I had done. That night the cries of my mother rang in my ears, and the terrible words I had spoken to her echoed mockingly about me. I saw one by one before me the men and women and children I had wronged, I saw myself as I truly was, in all my dirt and sinfulness. I saw all that, my friends, and I judged that man, as you judge me today. I saw that he was utterly beyond redemption, worthy only to be thrown into outermost darkness. Indeed, I saw that the darkness was already about me and within me, that there could be no worse to come than this. All that was left to me then in the bitterness of that night was death. I took a knife, my brothers and sisters, and sharpened it well and raised it to my throat ...

'And it was just at that very moment, just when the blade touched my flesh, just then – just then, brothers and sisters, that a Hand stayed me.'

Silence, a long silence; Eve shivered. Then the voice softly resumed, almost in a whisper, though everyone heard it. 'I did not see the Hand. I knew I was alone. Yet the Hand was there, and the Presence. I felt it all about me, towering over me, a terrifying Presence, a mighty Presence, the great Judge of all come to call me to account. I trembled before it, most dreadful sinner that I was. I trembled; and then I knew that now, in the depths to which I had fallen, in this moment when I was so low I did not even think to cry for help, when I felt myself too lost even to beg for mercy, *then* I knew in my heart that God is not only just, but He is merciful. I knew it, not because I was told it was so, not because I had read His word, not because I had faith. I knew it because it was His mercy that took hold of me that night; His mercy that came like a fire to warm me, to pierce my heart, to fill me, brimful and overflowing. In that night of despair I suddenly, wonderfully, found joy. I was nothing, and He, brothers and sisters, He was everything. Without Him I could not help myself, I could not bear to live, I was lost and alone. With Him, I had all the heart could need or desire. In my poverty and loneliness and grief, I was yet loved. In my sin, I was yet saved. With His loving arms about me, I need no longer fear, I could turn from my sin. In His service, I could find true freedom at last.'

Even from where she was, some distance away, Eve knew there were tears in his eyes; she could hear them too in the roughness of his voice. Yet it was warm, soft, full of tenderness, a voice that almost seemed to sing in its lilting joy, a lovely caressing voice that reached right into her heart.

'I came home, my most dear friends, to bring you the only thing I have to give, in reparation for the evil I have done – the assurance, the certainty, that if so great a sinner as I can be snatched from the burning, then how much more is there hope, is there salvation for each one of you!'

What followed then was the message Eve had been expecting, the message she had heard expounded with varying degrees of fervour all her life, from ministers and preachers and in her own home, a message always devalued for her by her father's example. Yet this was quite different. It was as if she were hearing it for the very first time.

Rowland's words seemed formed of fire, searing her to the very heart, scouring and warming her at the same time. This was not the harsh correctness of her father's religion, which however tenderly put by Sunday preachers or class leaders always seemed touched with his unyielding and intolerant spirit.

Not that there was toleration in this, or ease, or softness. Love, yes; God's love, that fiery searching out of the spirit, forcing its way into her heart – yes, that was there, demanding her attention, her response, her whole self. She felt ashamed of her littleness, her dirtiness, her appalling sinfulness; against this blaze she was a pale and useless worm. Yet let it burn within her, and anything was possible. She stood there, yielding to its heat, and knew that her whole life, her whole self was transformed, transmuted, changed for ever, irrevocably.

Rowland's voice fell silent at last, and then, a little after, he began to sing in a clear melodious tenor.

> *'Come, O Thou Traveller unknown,*
> *Whom still I hold, but cannot see ...'*

One by one the people joined in, hesitantly at first, and then gathering in strength, until the words swelled out, filling the market place, washing against the walls of the church and the inns and the little houses. Eve laughed aloud, softly, though tears ran unchecked, unnoticed down her face. She sank slowly to her knees in the mud, her arms outstretched above her head; and then she began to sing too, rocked by the music that was all part of her joy in the new life that filled her.

> *''Tis Love! 'tis Love! Thou diedst for me!*
> *I hear Thy whisper in my heart;*

67

The morning breaks, the shadows flee,
Pure, universal Love Thou art;
To me, to all, Thy mercies move:
Thy nature and Thy name is Love ...'

It was like the other night with Joe in the byre, but not like that, for there was no shame in this, and no fear, only hope and wonder and ecstasy. She wanted to embrace everyone here, all these other people, so many of whose faces were alight with the same joy, whose hands reached out to clasp hers, whose eyes shone with the same fire. She was weeping and laughing and singing all at once.

Saved – saved! There was no word like it, nothing else that could so express her sense of release, of coming home to a safe haven where she was sure of happiness at last.

4

Edward placed another log on the fire (it was cold tonight; hard to believe it was nearly May) and pulled his chair closer to its warmth, trying to ignore the constant eddies of smoke that drifted into the room, though he found a hand cupped over mouth and nose helped a little. He tried to read, but the words seemed to make no sense, and he found he was reading the first paragraph again and again without taking any of it in. The ticking of the clock, slow and sombre, seemed to echo in the shabby room, and in his head too, emphasizing the silence that surrounded it. Outside, the wind was rushing in the trees, men were singing drunkenly beyond the parsonage wall; staggering, as he supposed from his already considerable experience, from one inn or alehouse to another, or perhaps going 'prossing' (that, he had learned, meant gathering to talk – and drink – late into the night) in the cramped and malodorous closeness of a friend's house. Friday night was always noisy, with the lead miners released from work for the weekend.

In here there was no dirt, no nauseating odour, no strong drink (Peggy's tea could certainly not be so described), not even a great deal of warmth; and no company except his own. Nothing but solitude ... loneliness ... no, that was the wrong word. He was not lonely, of course he was not. He had his books, his meditations, a letter to his sister (begun and quickly abandoned), which was supposed to bring her closer but had somehow failed to do so. Loneliness was the sign of an impoverished spirit, and a faithless one. He had always enjoyed his own company, when none more congenial was offered to him, and even sometimes when it was. And it was not as if he had not been warned what life would

69

be like in Weardale for a young man of his class. Furthermore, he had found he was not quite so thoroughly isolated as he had feared. Mr George Crawhall, agent for the Beaumont mines in Weardale, had been present in church last Sunday with his wife and had proved to be respectable and even gentlemanly – 'benevolent and hospitable', so Edward had described him to his sister after dining with the family at Newhouse. But agreeable though the man might be in his way, even he did not provide quite the society Edward was used to.

It was not yet fully dark, but all the same he got up and pulled the curtains. Then he wandered to the piano and played a little, but its untuned condition jangled on his nerves and he soon gave up. Deciding to make a beginning on Sunday morning's sermon, he returned to his chair by the fire and picked up pen and paper, and a Bible that lay nearby, and considered his text. Last Sunday it had been 'Thou shalt not go after other gods', with particular reference to the lures of Methodism, as well as of sundry itinerant preachers. But its effect had been limited, since there had been only a handful of people in church, the enthusiastic but unmelodious band up in the gallery outnumbering the rest of the congregation by one. He was, he had realized, preaching to the converted, and they were few enough. Perhaps a softer approach was called for. Looking at Sunday's lesson he thought it unexpectedly apt: 'For the Lord thy God bringeth thee into a good land ... a land whose stones are iron, and out of whose hills thou mayest dig brass.' Not that brass was the same as lead, but it was close enough – or would the simple folk who heard him merely assume he knew no better? Depression settled further over him than ever. Could he hope to achieve anything in this place?

The clock whirred and clunked and then began to chime out the hour. Nine o'clock; the day was almost over ... *This is foolish*, he thought. *I have been here scarcely two weeks, I cannot be expected to have done very much as yet. There is ample time.*

What was more, he realized, startled at the discovery, he had not thought of Mademoiselle de Mortain for some considerable time, not for several days. In fact, she seemed

70

now like something from a dream, or a figment of his imagination. Strange that she had ever meant so much to him; even stranger to think he had once been convinced that she had broken his heart beyond repair.

He returned more resolutely to his sermon, but soon found himself, for some reason, wondering how Miss Emerson was occupying herself this evening, up there at White Lea. Perhaps he would go and see her again tomorrow – no, not tomorrow, Monday, while her brothers were at work. And he would of course be going to see, not her, but her father, as any good parson would have done in his place.

As every day this week, Rowland had been out preaching somewhere – over towards Rookhope this time, his aunt thought – and came home late, just as darkness fell, thankful to change out of his wet clothes and sit down to the supper she had kept hot for him. Lancelot had already eaten and gone out again, or Tabitha Hall might have felt less free to speak her mind. As it was, she waited until her nephew had finished eating and then sat down to face him across the table.

'How many souls have you won today then?' There was a slightly acid note in her voice, but Rowland did not appear to notice it.

'Two were awakened to the Lord,' he said, and smiled; he had always had a very sweet smile.

'That's two more than yesterday, I suppose,' said Tabitha, refusing to be impressed. 'How long do you mean to roam around with your message? I doubt there'll soon be none left who haven't heard it.' She paused, and then came to the point. 'You'll be staying here till the dale's converted, I take it?' When he hesitated, she continued, 'I'm not one to turn my own kin from the door – but I didn't ask you to come back.'

'And you've no wish to keep me, now I'm here.' He flushed slightly, and so did she, even fumbling for words a little, which was not like her. Rowland went on quickly, 'I had it in mind, aunt. I have since I came back. I shall find work.' He stood up suddenly and went to the window, though what he was looking at out there in the night his aunt

71

could not imagine. 'As it happens, I heard of something today that might do. I was waiting only to know if it is the Lord's will.' His voice had an oddly reluctant note, though she could not see his face to judge its expression. 'John Peart's partnership wants a new man.'

'Is that your father's cousin John Peart?'

'Why no, Cuthbert's John from Close End – no kin of mine that I know of. But one of his partners is too sick now for owt but light work. He knows I've not much experience, and that long ago, but he'd take me on trial for a bit.'

'Then what's holding you back?' Her tone was sharp. 'The Lord I suppose.'

'No,' he said, and then swung round, saying with sudden firmness, 'I'll go and see him in the morning.' He had the calm look of a man whose mind has been made up for him.

'Where's he working?'

'Guinea Grove.'

'That's where you were before you went away, isn't it?' It was in the westernmost part of the dale, almost in Northumberland. She seemed to remember that, while working there, he and his father had lodged through the week with a fellow miner at Lanehead, so as to have only about a mile to walk to the mine each day.

'Aye.' He was silent for a little while, then he said, 'They've built a lodging shop now, so I'll be a wallet man.' Miners lodging away from home were so called because of the large bolster shaped bag, or wallet, in which they carried their weekly supplies of food.

'Can you not find better?' It was not, she thought, what she would have wanted for any son of hers, if he had a choice in the matter. She began to understand what had made him hesitate, for he must know at least as well as she did what conditions were like in the lodging shops provided at the more remote mines.

Rowland shook his head. 'It'll do for me.' He smiled a little. 'So I'll only trouble you at weekends, if you'll have me. I'll pay for my keep, of course. Or find other lodgings, if you'd sooner I left altogether.'

Regretting her sharpness, Tabitha said, 'Why, of course I'll have you. Mary would have wanted it. Maybe I'll learn to think more kindly of you, in time.' She was surprised to realize even as she was speaking that she had already begun to do so. 'But what of your preaching then? There'll be the less time for that.'

'I've done what I was meant to do. It may be that I shall be required to preach again, from time to time. But for the most part it's my life that must speak for me now.'

'It'll have to speak loud, to drown out the past,' his aunt said drily. 'Folk don't forget that easily.'

'I know.' He was silent again, his thoughts wandering off on some course whose progress she could not follow, but which led him at last to say suddenly, in quite a different tone, 'I never knew why my father didn't set the law on me.' He came and sat down again at the table, his eyes on her face, his expression unexpectedly sombre.

'Why, he wanted to, never doubt it. Only Mary wouldn't hear of it. To tell the truth, I was surprised he heeded her. I know what that money meant to him. You couldn't have found a surer way to hurt him if you'd sought one out.'

'I know,' he said.

Surprised at some harshness in his voice, matching her own, she said sharply, 'Did you know that when you did it?'

His eyes were guarded. 'Maybe,' was all he would say.

She sat looking at him, thinking of the past, wondering about all that had happened. It had seemed simple enough at the time, but now that Rowland was back she was not so sure. 'Tell me, what there was between you and your father – was it more than just your wildness?' Then she added, as an afterthought, 'I never cared for him much, to tell the truth.'

Slowly he shook his head. 'It's over now. He's dead. I did wrong. Leave it there.'

So she did, and a little later he went to the small room, cleared of lumber, where he slept, and soon afterwards she heard the soft murmur of his voice at prayer. She sat on by the fireside until Lancelot came home, thinking about all the changes that the past fortnight had brought into her life; and realized that she was no longer angry at the way Rowland's return had opened old wounds. She even found herself beginning to warm to him.

*

73

William Emerson had failed faster than anyone had expected, and it was clear that he was nearing the end now, scarcely conscious most of the time, a thin, gaunt, gasping wreck of a man, with little left of the person he once had been. His old friends had gathered at White Lea tonight, as they had always done, at least once a week, for as long as any of them could remember – Ralph Emerson and George Lowes, and the younger members of what had once been William's partnership.

Tommy, who always loved to stay up and listen to the talk, had fallen asleep, weary as he was, and lay curled up in a corner of the settle, covered with a coat. Jenny had shifted his head so that it rested on her lap, heavy and warm against her thigh. Now and then she would pause in her knitting and stroke his tangled hair. Awake, he would never have permitted such softness.

Her heart ached for his weariness, for the youth lost in endless grinding toil ... What was it he had said at supper tonight? *Mr Bowman's always picking on me, for nowt I've done. It's not fair.* Nor was it, and she knew, as Tommy did not, what lay behind the inspector's unfairness. She felt both hurt and angered, more so than Tommy, perhaps, for he seemed to regard it as little more than a minor inconvenience, like the rain that left him so chilled at the end of the day. He would not have welcomed her sympathy, had he known of it. Offer him the chance to return to his carefree childhood days, and he would have scorned it; Mr Selby had been quite right about that.

She looked down at the boy's flushed face, ringed with soft gold-brown curls of hair. He looked so young, so innocent and untouched, though she had already noticed how the rough world of the washing floor was beginning to affect his speech and his manners, coarsening them. He was proud of his manliness; she felt only saddened that he had no other example to follow. Yet at the same time she envied him, because he believed he was happy, above all because he was able to fall asleep so easily, and sleep so soundly, hour after hour, until in the morning she would have to drag him into wakefulness to go to work. If only she could sleep like that! But then she would not even be able to lie down until all the men had gone. She spent the nights in this room, on a straw mattress laid on the mat by the fire, ready in case her father needed her; which he had done several times each night for she did not know how many weeks. She could not remember when she had last slept soundly, all night long. Even before her father's sharp decline she had been kept wakeful, often, by thoughts of Billy. Now it would have seemed a luxury to have had only thoughts to keep her awake.

In her weariness she did not follow the talk, not clearly. It came and went in her consciousness, mingling with stray memories, coming unbidden, disappearing as unpredictably.

... Mr Selby, calling last week to ask after her father ... He seemed somehow to breathe a different air from the common stuff of other mortals, so that the aura of it hung about him. Now, the mere thought of him warmed and cheered her ...

She could not hold on to the memory. Mr Bowman, pawing at her, came back into her mind, and she felt angry for Tommy's sake ... But then the curate had rescued her, so tall and handsome on his fine horse, with that look of strength and health and assurance, as if for him nothing could ever prove difficult or dangerous or embarrassing ...

'It took all that time to drive a way through to her, and then she was bad enough to get, what with the foul air,' Ralph Emerson was saying. In the interval between sentences he sucked at his pipe, empty because the smoke troubled his brother. 'And now there's this.' He glanced at William. 'It's what you always said, that she'd be a bitch, that one.' The man in the bed stared back at him from hollow, anguished eyes, the terrible sound of his breathing filling the room; but Ralph went on as easily as if William had grinned and answered him, as once he would have done. 'Right enough, she's every bit as bad as you said. I told you – didn't I? – the latest is we've met up with a twitch, and we don't know if it's worth going on with her, next quarter.'

For Jenny this talk of twitches and bad air and the difficulties of working the lead had been a part of her life for as long as she could remember. She knew that the awkward female they discussed was the portion of lead vein for the working of which the partnership had made a bargain with the mine owners, she knew a twitch was a place where the length of vein thinned to nothing, before swelling out again, she knew about hades and throws and strings and flats and the different strata under the ground, she even knew the distinctive smell of the mines, compounded of wet rock and pipesmoke and tallow candles and gunpowder and other stranger, less explicable odours, for it hung about the clothes she dried each night by the fire; yet she knew all these things only in her imagination, not in reality, from her own experience. That world underground, which they talked of with such familiarity, as of a close neighbour, was unknown to her, and probably always would be.

'I still think we should carry on next quarter, even if we've not got beyond the twitch by then,' George Lowes put in. 'I mind how my father's last grove looked. They all swore she wasn't worth the working. But what happened? He would keep at it, and he was proved right in the end. She was the richest they ever had, that last quarter. He reckoned they cleared a hundred pound that year between them.'

It was the lead miner's dream, the thing that kept them working through foul air and damp and dust, sickness and danger, the hope that one day they would find the ground that would make their fortune. Then they would buy acres of fertile land, move down the dale and breed horses, even develop a mine themselves perhaps. But a hundred pounds was not so very much between four men, and Cuthbert Lowes had died a year after he won his share; it had kept his widow and children from want for a time, but that was all. There was only one man Jenny could think of now who was said to have realized the dream. He supplied the mines with galloways from his prosperous farm east of Stanhope. But it was only a rumour, she thought, that his wealth had come from mining, and in any case it had been long ago, long before she was born ...

'Aye, I've got it,' Joe was saying now. (What had he got?) 'I had a read of it yesterday.'

... Mr Hall's pamphlet, of course; Uncle Ralph had just asked him about it, only she had scarcely heard him ...

'What do you think of it?'

'Why, there's parts are all right.' He got up and took the

pamphlet from the shelf. 'When he goes on about all the hardships of lead mining, how we're near starving, that's fine – fair moves you to tears.'

... What would it be like to sleep on a feather bed, sinking down into it, wrapped in warmth ...? With Mr Selby bending over her, perhaps, smiling, all golden and gentle, keeping her from harm ... Such a feeling of safety she had with him, as if in his presence she had no need to fear anything ever again, no need to strive, or struggle, or grieve ... She had never really had anyone to take care of her, in all her life ...

'While I advocate the cause of the miner, I by no means intend to induce him to be idle. I have always said, I thought he could work an hour or two longer in the day, in the mine.'

Jenny looked up, startled, and saw that Joe was reading from the pamphlet; she remembered now that he had read her the very same passage last night. He was standing with his back to the fire declaiming the words with full dramatic emphasis. Jenny woke up a little and watched the faces of the other men, interested to see how they would react.

'Labour is bountifully offered to the majority of the population, as salt is to the sea, to keep it from putrefaction and filth. And the labourer when he contemplates those whom he regards as rolling in wealth, would stifle his envy, if he could know the real situation of many, who abound in luxuries, attacked with gout and flatulence, and plethora, worn down by disease and vexation, arising from pride and fatal ambition, sitting down to tables spread with Eastern luxuries, without appetite to taste a morsel with satisfaction, and envying the poor man, the gratification of enjoying his humble fare with delight; the labourer I say would bless his situation, and sit down with gratitude at his humble fire side.'

Joe sat down himself, all apparent gravity. George Lowes raised a handkerchief to his eyes in a show of grief. 'Why, the poor gentlemen – to think we never guessed how they suffered!' And then they all laughed, slapping their knees in derisive enjoyment. Joe joined in with as much enthusiasm as

77

any of them, but he broke off long before the others, suddenly grave.

'Aye, it's good for a laugh, but just think about it, what he's wanting from us. It's no wonder Mr Crawhall was so sharp to let him speak. You were there, uncle; you know how he moved them all with his talk of the sufferings in the lead dales. Well, that's only one side of it.' He banged the pamphlet down on the table. 'If he would see us better fed, it's for his own ends. Hungry men can't work as long. And if we work longer and bring more lead up to the day, you can be damn sure we'll see little enough of the profits.'

'Rowland Peart had to work sixteen hours a day in the cotton mills,' said Ralph.

Joe brushed that aside. 'Why, cotton spinning's not man's work. Same as the washer lads – they work longer hours, for it's not so hard. But that's the only thing we have, the right to knock off when we please, more or less. What else have we got – what else do they want? Our very blood ...? How do we tend our land if we work longer hours? Our women folk already have more than enough to see to as it is.' He glanced at Jenny, who nodded her agreement.

'Maybe he thinks if you're paid more you'd have no need to make owt from the land,' she suggested. 'But that's the one good part of our lives, to have our bit land.'

Ralph Emerson nodded. 'Quite right, lass, quite right. Let's hope no one listens to him. There's too much change as it is, even since I was a lad. Then, what you did in your own time, that was your affair. Now they even try to have a say in that. Take poor Charlie Siddle – oh, I know I don't hold with poaching, but that's our business, not the masters'.' He caught Joe's eye, and smiled faintly. 'Mind, they'll have to watch out, sacking men for poaching, or I doubt they'll have none left to get the lead.

'But it's not just that. Take the washing; once every partnership looked to its own. It was up to them how it was done, and who by. Many of them had their wives there, and their daughters. I grant you, that's not what we'd all want – I wouldn't myself – but it was up to us. It was handy enough in busy times. Now the agent wants a say who he'll have, or who he won't have, and there's the inspector sticking his neb

78

in every minute. Why, maybe there was some cheating in the past, but there is now too, for we all know the inspectors aren't angels. And now they're bringing in machines for crushing, then you mark my words, there'll be something else for them to lay down rules about – that's already happened up at Breckonsike. Just one more bit thing maybe, but when you look at it, you see a pattern. Always, every time, it ends up with that bit more in the masters' hands. The Old Man was free to work as he pleased. The way things are going, there'll sharp come a time when we'll none of us have any say at all in what we do or how we do it.'

... Jenny had always liked to hear talk of the 'Old Man', that legendary figure who had worked long abandoned mines, by methods now disused. It had been some years before she had realized that there had never been one single individual 'Old Man', that the phrase was only the miners' way of referring to the workings of past miners. Even now, she still had in her mind the childhood image the words had conjured up for her, of a great tall, long-legged, shadowy figure striding forward through the centuries from some mysterious dark ages before time began, all flowing robes and long white beard. Not that she would ever have risked their laughter by telling Joe or the others what she thought ...

'They'd have us working like cotton spinners, if they could,' said George Lowes, 'starting and finishing when they please, working to the bell.' He turned to Ralph. 'Did you hear Rowland Peart the other day then?'

Ralph nodded and then leaned forward to give greater emphasis to his words. 'I tell you, George, I heard John Wesley preach when he came the last time in 1790, up at Ireshopeburn, and it was like that all over again. Not that they were the same, mind, but there's no denying the power that lad has to hold a crowd in his hand. None too keen on him they were either, not at first. There's a good many went only to jeer. But come the end they wasn't a dry eye from one side of the market place to the other, I'd say.'

'Then you'd say he won a good few over?'

'Why, now, that's another matter. There weren't more than a handful went up to him afterwards, that I could see.

Though there were more than usual came to High House chapel next day –'

'He was there himself too,' said Ralph's Joe. 'Mind, Jacob Todd was preaching, and he didn't look too pleased about it.'

'Aye, well, Jacob Todd's easily huffed,' said Ralph. 'But I don't doubt most of those who heard the lad on Saturday will have gone home feeling more kindly towards him. Maybe rightly, I don't know.' He shook his head again, wonderingly this time. 'Strange thing to see that, knowing how he went away ... Did you hear him, Joe? I didn't see you in the market place.'

'I've better things to do with my time than stand gawping at a wandering preacher,' said Joe, with a harshness that clearly surprised the others.

'I thought, though –? He was your friend once.'

'*Was*,' said Joe emphatically. 'That was long since.'

Jenny, watching him, saw how strained he looked suddenly, and restless too; he had been like that most of the week, on and off. It was something to do with Eve, she thought. On Monday night, he had gone out cheerfully enough, only to return much later soaked to the skin and in one of his most difficult moods. She had drawn her own conclusions, but knew better than to question him about it. Besides, she had troubles enough without seeking more to carry on shoulders that already felt too burdened ... Oh, she was tired, tired of everything: the constant anxiety, the constant struggle to keep going, the constant knowledge of what lay just round the corner – or if not this corner, the next one, or the one after; tired of watching her father die.

She looked from one to another of the familiar faces here tonight, and noted how each one showed marks of ill health or age, increased since last time she looked at them; even Joe's was paler than it used to be. Yet at the moment they seemed carefree enough, as if unconcerned by what life had in store for them. The light of the fire and the single candle glowed on faces creased with laughter, on eyes warm with friendship, on work-worn hands cupped around tankards. She found herself wishing she could get drunk, but Billy had always disapproved of drunken women, and besides she found no pleasure in it. Perhaps women were different from men in that ... Was that why all leadminers drank so much, because it helped them for a while to forget their fate? There were those few, of course, who abjured strong drink, but she supposed that for them religion was consolation and escape enough, offering heavenly joys in compensation for earthly suffering ...

'We've one thing we can use,' Joe was saying now (the talk seemed to have moved on from Rowland). 'They can't get the lead without us. If we refused to take our bargains, then they'd be in trouble. We're not like cotton spinners, two a penny, easily trained. A lead miner has to know what he's about. We know a damn sight more of what's underground than the masters, I'd say.'

'They'd sharp find someone else to do it,' Ralph said gloomily. 'One thing Weardale's not short of is men, even skilled ones, and many without work.'

'But would any Weardale man take the bread from his brother's mouth?' retorted Joe. 'I don't think so, uncle.'

'You're in earnest!' said Ralph's Joe, lowering his tankard and staring at his cousin. 'You'd have us lay off work?'

'If need be, if the Pay's delayed much longer – beyond the next bargains at the furthest. What right have they to keep from us what's our due? The way I see it, we risk our lives to get the lead – the masters only risk their money.'

'Oh, and their peace of mind!' George Lowes reminded him. 'What was it, all those Eastern luxuries that make life so hard for them?'

They laughed again, and the talk turned to lighter things. Not long afterwards, it being well after midnight, the men left, making their way in the moonlight (aided by a lantern) down the road to their homes. Joe saw them go and barred the door, and came to carry his young brother to his bed.

'Did you mean all that tonight?' Jenny asked, as she spread her mattress before the fire and laid a blanket over it.

'All what?'

'About giving up work if they don't make the Pay soon?'

'Why not? We're still free men, whatever uncle may say.'

There was a new sound from across the room, and Jenny looked round. 'Father's slipped down. Give me a hand.'

They went to the bed and Jenny rearranged the pillows

while Joe held his father upright in his arms. Through the coarse nightshirt, soaked with sweat, the sick man's body felt appallingly thin, little more than bones without flesh, a skeleton whose only sign of life was the endless shuddering struggle for air. Joe shut his eyes. *This is my father*, he thought. *This is the man who gave me life.* There was something so wrong about it, so horrible, that this wasted remnant of a man should have anything to do with the living being he had loved so much; that he, the son, should be holding his father as if he were a helpless infant. He wanted to weep, yet his feelings were somehow too complicated, too painful for tears. He felt as if he were choking too.

'Now,' said Jenny, startling him. She had the pillows ready and together they eased their father back into a sitting position against them. Joe studied Jenny's face. What did she feel, tending the sick man day after day? Had she felt the anguish of it, as he had done, the near-revulsion at something so unnatural? She looked only tired, dreadfully tired. She was gently brushing their father's hair back from his face, tucking the blankets more securely about him. Then she looked up and smiled faintly.

'It's been a long day,' she said. They moved away, but at that moment another sound stopped them in their tracks.

'Joe ...' This time it was clear enough, a word thrust harshly out in a sudden longer interval between the rasping breaths. Joe went back to the bed. Nothing had changed, yet somehow the eyes glittering at him from the dark sockets had a different look, as if William Emerson's spirit had temporarily returned from whatever dark and airless place it had been haunting, already half departed. He saw that the claw-like hand moved, just a little. He crouched beside the bed and took the hand in his.

His father seemed to gather together all the last tattered shreds of his remaining strength, though it astonished Joe that he had any left to call on. 'Joe ... have ... a care.' The voice came in a whisper, gasped out into the room. The sick man closed his eyes for a moment, before forcing out, 'Think first ... before ... you take on ... masters ...'

There was no more, though Joe was silent for a time, waiting. But even without further explanation he thought he

82

understood. He smiled, though his father's eyes were closed again. Then he said softly, 'I'll do nowt without thinking first. I'm not that kind. You know that.'

He thought perhaps he glimpsed a ghost of his father's old smile on the gaunt face, but he could not be sure.

It was Chapel market next day, and Joe had been waiting for it all week – or since Monday, at least.

He had gone as usual on Monday night to wait outside Hannah Milburn's cottage for Eve to come to him. But when she had emerged, later than usual, she had been in the company of two other girls. He had watched, helpless, from behind the tree across the lane, expecting her to make an excuse, to fall behind, to do anything to come to him; but she had gone steadily on her way, walking between her companions, and disappeared at last from view. He had hurried after her, as softly as he could, and seen her part from the others at the back gate of the shop and run quickly inside, not even looking round.

Frustrated and angry, Joe had gone home. There was, of course, some perfectly simple explanation – her father had become suspicious, for instance, and made sure she was accompanied; had perhaps even warned Hannah Milburn to see to it. But Joe would not be quite at ease until he had spoken to her and heard her explanation for himself. Besides, not to see her for so long was torment. He wanted to hold her in his arms again, to talk with her and make love to her, as that first time, to feel that she was as nearly his as she could be, given her father's obstinacy.

By Saturday, his longing for her was intensified by what had happened the night before. He wanted the comfort of her warm and living body, her youth and sweetness, the assurance she somehow seemed to offer that there was a future to look forward to, however hard the present might be. They would not be able to talk much in the crowded market place, but he would be sure to find her there and they could arrange a later meeting.

He walked quickly down to the village and wandered among the stalls until he saw her emerge from the shop, looking solemn and abstracted. He waited until she had

83

paused before a rather meagre assortment of vegetables laid out beneath the arches of the market cross, and then went and stood beside her, not looking at her, as if he was simply another casual shopper. At present there were too many other people nearby for him to risk speaking, even in an undertone, and he was still waiting, watchful for the right moment, when she startled him by saying, softly enough, but in what was by no means a whisper, 'I must speak with you, Joe.' He felt his heart beat faster, and only with difficulty prevented himself from looking round. 'In the back lane – wait there for me.' He paused only until she had wandered on to the next stall before going as quickly as he could without actually running towards the lane that skirted the back of her father's shop. It was there, very soon, that she came to him.

There was no one in the lane, so he drew her into a gateway and held her close. He was about to bring his mouth down to kiss her when he became aware of resistance, and he drew back again, surprised.

She placed her hands, palms outwards, on his chest, her eyes very intent on his face. There was a strange look about her, unlike anything he had ever seen before; at once exalted and very grave, as if she felt both joy and pain at once. 'Joe, you know I love you –' She paused, drawing a deep breath. 'More than ever now, I think.' He tried to answer her with a kiss, but still she resisted, her hands holding him away from her. 'No, listen – listen! . . . I must not see you any more.'

Of all the things she might have said he had not expected this. He caught his breath and found he did not know what to say in reply. All he could croak out was, 'Why?' though it fell far short of what he felt.

'I am changed,' she said, and the note of exaltation gave a lift to her voice. 'I have heard – seen . . . Oh, Joe, if only you could see too, if only your dear eyes were opened, then –'

He had no idea at all what she was talking about; it made no kind of sense to him. 'I don't understand.'

'No,' she said softly. 'No, that is the trouble. But I think you will, one day. Please God!'

He began, uneasily, to wonder if that last little phrase, which had rather the sound of a fervent prayer than a casual

84

interjection, might hold the key to what had happened to her. 'If you love me, and I you, then what cause have we not to meet?'

'Because my father has forbidden it, and it is my duty to obey him in all things. Because what we did together was a sin, and now I have been forgiven. I am made whole, redeemed and saved.' When he was silent, digesting this statement, considering its implications, she added, 'I heard Rowland Peart last week.'

So he had reached out into Joe's life again after all, the stranger who could hold a hostile crowd at bay with the simple power of his voice, and who had invited comparison with the great John Wesley himself. He might have changed from the Rowland Joe had known, but it seemed as if he was still as impossible to ignore as ever.

'When you hear the Word too, Joe, then perhaps we may see each other again, if my father comes round.'

When, if: the two impossible demands, which he could never meet, because it was not in him to meet them. Did she know that? Did she care? She said she loved him, there was that hint of pain in her voice and her eyes, but they were outweighed by the brightness, the joy, that lingered still from whatever it was that had happened to her last Saturday, the thing that seemed to mean more to her than all the sweet happiness of their times together.

Joe thought that in all his life he had never felt so much like committing murder as he did now. He argued with her, pleaded, urged her to change her mind, tried desperately to make her see that she was being foolish, emotional, hysterical; but he could not move her. She did not weep, she showed neither anger nor softness, only stood there with that look of solemn happiness on her face and let him speak, and repeated, now and then, in that quiet, grave voice, that they must not see each other, that it was over unless, until ...

When he left her, he marched unhesitatingly to Lancelot Hall's house, threw the door wide and strode in, interrupting with his fury and pain the little group of new converts at prayer in the room inside.

'Rowland Peart, you've stolen my girl from me!'

The young man swung round to look at him; and Joe

found himself suddenly and without warning engulfed by the past – a past in which he and Rowland and Billy were always together, and Rowland had been at the centre of their lives. He had thought he had remembered, but he had not; not until now, when that slight figure – older, graver, calmer, yet somehow the same – turned his eyes upon him. How could he have forgotten those eyes? Dark and glowing in the angular face, they had in them something that was at once gentle and fiery, and they seemed to look right into his soul ... Joe remembered their power, and shook himself as if to break free. It had all been a long time ago, and Rowland was a stranger now. He gave his attention firmly to the young man's waistcoat buttons (one was hanging by a thread and would be lost if no one repaired it) and said, 'Why can you not leave them alone, all those fools who come to hear you? We were better off without you. You've stolen her away.'

'Who? Who do you accuse me of stealing away?'

'Eve Todd. My girl –'

'She's not yours. We belong only to God, each one of us. If He's called her, then thank Him, and turn to Him yourself. You'll find her again there, for in His love we are all brothers and sisters.'

Joe flung himself forward, enraged by the man's calmness, his warm persuasive voice, the arguments that were the mirror of Eve's arguments, a smooth barrier in which there was no fingerhold, nothing to give a purchase, no aid to scale it. It shut him out, completely, and he was helpless against it. He wanted to pummel that calm face – with something, surely, of Eve's exaltation on it too – drive out the tranquil expression, silence the smug words. His fist shot out, he felt it strike soft flesh; saw Rowland stagger back, put a hand to his mouth, bring it away bloodied.

There was a sudden commotion, a rush of people about him. Hands grabbed his arms, several pairs of hands, or they would not have been able to restrain him as they did. He was dragged back, struggling, and flung out into the lane. He fell to the ground and heard the door barred against him. He scrambled to his feet and ran to it and kicked at it in helpless rage. 'Coward! Come out and fight like a man!'

But there was no response of any kind, only the sound of

86

voices singing a hymn, and the door was strong and securely fastened. After a time, conscious of the futility of it all, he gave up. He made his way to the King's Head and sat in a corner and got very drunk.

In that black mood he stumbled home some hours later, almost falling into the kitchen. There he was pulled up short by something in the atmosphere that reached even through his drunken and bitter consciousness. Something had gone from the room, something had changed irrevocably.

'Joe.' Jenny's voice was very soft, but had in it a new note of sadness. She was standing near the box bed, watching him; very still. Joe realized Aunt Ann was there too. Suddenly hardly drunk at all, he righted himself and went to them.

'Father died this afternoon,' said Jenny. 'About an hour since. Did you not see Uncle Ralph on the road? He's gone for Mr Selby; and Betty Shields, to do the laying out.'

Joe went and stood looking down at the motionless shrouded shape on the bed, stretched flat at last, the painful breathing stilled. It seemed very quiet in the room – yes, that was it, no coughing, no harsh breathing. The long struggle was over at last. He reached out and drew back the sheet from the still face. It was peaceful enough in death, with no sign on it now of pain or anguish, but somehow nothing either of the man whose spirit had finally, completely gone. Without that spirit, this was an empty husk, no more. So he had thought when Billy died, though then in his anger and grief and guilt he had felt none of this quiet sense of relief. He would miss his father, miss him terribly, he was sorry that he had not been here, and more that he had been behaving in a way of which his father would not have approved; but he could not regret his passing.

Jenny put her arm about him. 'He never really woke up, after last night.'

So William Emerson had not known who was with him at the end; no need then even for that small measure of guilt. Yet for some reason he began to weep, painfully and slowly. Jenny put her arms about him and wept too, but he felt ashamed, because he knew it was not his father he was mourning at all.

5

At sunrise, a long string of ponies threaded its way into Weardale by Killhope Cross, on over the bleak upland road. To either side the land stretched treeless and desolate, broken only by the scarred hush gullies and barren waste heaps of the lead workings. With the ponies rode, not a single carrier and his dog, but an escort of armed men, alert and watchful for the slightest threat.

For these were no ordinary ponies, carrying ore to the smelt mills or rye to the miners. In the bulging panniers on their backs were stowed thousands of pounds in cash, being carried from Coalcleugh in Northumberland, where the Pay had at last been made yesterday, over to Newhouse, where today the long-delayed Weardale Pay would take place.

Last week the cash had been laboriously raised at various Newcastle banks, against the output of lead ore from the Beaumont mines, much of which was not yet sold. It was the more bulky to carry, the harder to raise, because it must be supplied in the smallest denominations possible, bearing in mind the relatively small amounts due to each miner.

George Crawhall, riding with the escort, felt relief growing in him as the cavalcade wound its way down into the dale. Not long now, and the weeks of preparation and hard work would be at an end; and the growing murmuring of the miners against the long delay in making the Pay. He thought of cool drinks and the tranquil shade of his garden – the June sun was unbearably hot, even so early in the morning – but there could be no rest yet, not for some time, not for any of them.

From little houses scattering the hillsides, from villages strung out along the river, men and women and children

88

came to run and dance beside the escort, singing and cheering the coming of the Pay. By the time they were within sight of Newhouse the road was crammed from side to side with a noisy happy throng, slowing the passage of the caval-cade almost to a standstill. Here, on the fields around George Crawhall's fine seventeenth-century house, across the road and all the way down to the river, innumerable tents and booths had sprung up since the agent left it a week ago, bright with banners and bunting, crammed with goods to tempt the miners to spend their long-awaited cash. From dawn, men and boys had been gathering here, their families with them, to be first in line for the Pay.

The cavalcade came to a halt behind the house and the panniers were lifted from the ponies and carried inside. In the long, narrow entrance hall, the clerks took their places at a table almost as long as the room, account books opened, plates set out to be filled and refilled with cash as the Pay progressed. For weeks before Crawhall left for Newcastle, he and his clerks had toiled over the books, working out what (if anything) was due to each miner – how many bings of dressed ore each partnership had raised during the period under consideration, multiplied by the figure per bing agreed with them at bargain time; set against the cost of transporting and dressing the ore, charges for tools, candles, rope, gunpowder and other essential items used in the year's work, and the amount paid out month by month in subsistence money. Whatever was left over at the end of these elaborate calculations was divided between the members of the part-nership, and each man given a ticket with what was due to him written upon it, a process that had to be repeated for every partnership in the thirty five or so mines in Weardale.

George Crawhall directed the final details – banknotes here, sovereigns in one plate, silver in another, copper in another, their exact placing for greatest convenience, who would be responsible for which function – and all the time he thought with longing of the far-off evening of this day, when, having entertained all the officials to dinner, he would at last be able to settle back in his most comfortable chair, a brandy in his hand, and heave a heartfelt sigh of relief that it was all over for another year.

Jenny woke that morning in the box bed downstairs, feeling both refreshed and hopeful. The sun was already slanting in long lines past the windows and once again she had slept deeply and without waking all night through, from the moment she had laid her head on the pillow. She had still not lost her sense of relief and thankfulness at being able to sleep again. Harrowing memories of Billy's death no longer haunted her, as if her father's passing had somehow taken that other agony with it. She missed her father terribly, she mourned Billy still, but she felt as if she were in some way beginning to live again, to wake slowly from a long and terrible nightmare.

And now today there was the greatest holiday of the Weardale year to look forward to. Last year she had stayed at home. Held earlier in the year, the Pay had come too soon after Billy's death, and, besides, her father, who had lately given up work for good, had suddenly taken a turn for the worse. So Joe had gone alone and seen to the payment of bills and made the necessary purchases. This year she would enjoy herself, for she was still young and the sun was shining and it was just possible that Mr Selby, who had been so kind at the time of her father's funeral, but had only called at White Lea once since then, might be there to crown the day with excitement.

It was also possible that the holiday distractions – not to mention the unusual experience of having money in his pocket again, for however short a time – would jolt Joe out of the black and bitter mood that had hung about him since Eve rejected him. He had not told Jenny a great deal about it, but she could piece most of it together for herself, and her heart ached for him. To lose everything in one day was very hard. But he too was young, and there were other girls, as pretty as Eve and far more accessible.

Jenny put on her best print gown and set out with Joe and Tommy along the westward road, calling for her aunt and uncle and cousins on the way, gathering a crowd of other friends and neighbours as they went. Like Jenny, everyone wore their best holiday clothes, cheerful with ribbons and scarlet neckerchiefs and brightly coloured shawls and waistcoats. Clogs, freshly blackened, clattered on the dusty road. There was much laughter and gossip and singing.

As they descended the hill towards Newhouse, rounding the corner by the little square candle house that supplied the miners with lighting, Ralph said, 'Well, we've cleared the books this time. That's something.'

Joe reached into his pocket and took out two tickets, received yesterday, that recorded the pay that was due up to last September, for the ore dug since October two years ago. One of them was Billy's, and listed the small amount the young man had earned in the six months before his death – Joe had arranged to collect it and take it to his friend's mother. He returned that to his pocket and examined the other.

'Seven pounds, five shillings and sixpence – it's better than last year, I'll say that. But it'll not go far, not with what we've got owing.'

'We're going to have to look for more than thirty shillings a bing next time,' said Ralph. 'That is, if we keep on where we are.' The last two months had proved as unproductive as they had feared, with no sign yet that the twitch was nearing its end.

'I've given thought to that. What do you say to trying for a bargain that lets us free if we find nothing more after, say, a month from the start?'

Ralph considered the matter. 'That wouldn't suit Mr Crawhall. He likes it all neat and tidy, a quarter each bargain, no more, no less. And if we do come to an end after a month? He'll have let all the bargains by then. We don't want to find ourselves out of work.'

'Aye, that's true enough. It had better be a full quarter then, and the highest price per bing.'

'What we want,' said George Lowes, who had joined them on the way, 'is a war. The price of lead was never so high as when we were fighting the French.'

'Why, so it was,' agreed Ralph. 'But never so low as in '16, after Waterloo. War upsets things too much. Better to have a steady demand and fair prices. And more lent money, come to that.'

While the men attached themselves to the end of the long

91

patient line of miners stretching out from the entrance hall into the sunshine, and Tommy went with his friends to look for fish in the river, Jenny and her aunt stood in the shade of a tree to wait for their menfolk.

'We'll not have much left once the rent's paid,' Ann Emerson said; she looked worried, Jenny thought, as well she might. Unlike White Lea, Uncle Ralph's smallholding at Side Head was not his own, but rented from Mrs Beaumont, who leased much of the Weardale land from the Bishopric, along with the mines. Her land agent was here today, ready to take the rent due, before the men could spend it. 'Men don't seem to think of these things,' Ann added. 'To hear them, we'll all be rich tomorrow. We women know we never shall, but there's no telling them. All we can do is make the best of a bad job.'

When Joe had his pay at last, he handed most of it to Jenny for safekeeping, and she went to settle what was owed to the joiner who had made William Emerson's coffin, and to the miller and the other tradesmen who had come to Newhouse, and to buy one or two essentials for the house and land. And then, once that was done, she wandered along with the other women, pausing to examine cloth at one stall, shoes at another, to gaze lingeringly at the red coats, once worn by soldiers, that one enterprising tradesman was selling. There was already quite a fashion for them among the washer lads, and Tommy had badgered her for one, but she found to her regret that they were too costly; she had no wish to start running up credit so soon.

Fortunately, there were free entertainments to compensate for such disappointments, not least for those miners who were out of work or had not cleared the books this time. There were the travelling players, performing their noisy drama to a noisier audience of all ages, and a group of miners solemnly step-dancing, their footwork neat and nimble on the bruised grass; there were quoits to throw, pitch and toss, and the ale was cheap, with so many sellers competing for the miners' custom. Jenny watched and listened and laughed and talked, and told herself that this was fun, that she was enjoying herself. But memories niggled at her. Last year she and Billy had made plans for the Pay.

He would buy the wedding ring, and they would choose goods for their house, and then at last they would be married. Only they had neither of them come to Newhouse that day...

She must not look back, she must not think of how different everything might have been. She forced herself to talk cheerfully to her companions, to give all her attention to what she saw, and her eyes swept the crowd for any sign of Mr Selby's tall and handsome figure, offering excitement and escape. But everything seemed to lack its customary shine, as if the coating of dust thrown up by all the clogged feet had cast a cloud over their very souls. She could not see Mr Selby anywhere.

A sudden rush of people, pushing past her, separated her from the others. Looking round for them, she suddenly found she was standing beside the wrestling ring, and the winner of the latest bout – the champion from Cumberland, as usual – was raising his arms to the not wholly enthusiastic cheers of the crowd.

She was swept back two years to the moment when she had stood on this very spot and it had been Billy in there, and the cheers had echoed and re-echoed in her ears, for he was Weardale's champion and he had won. And she had gazed and gazed at him: Billy Hall, Joe's shoulder fellow, suddenly new and strange to her eyes, clad only in breeches and stockings, all gleaming muscle and bright hair. He had swung himself over the rope and come to join them and Joe had congratulated him warmly, but his eyes had stayed with Jenny, and hers with him, and later they had danced together, and planned to meet again, in secret, and after that it had all followed the only natural course ... until last year.

She should have expected it, but somehow she had not, and so it found her defenceless against it, that sharp sense of loss and grief, rising in her as if it had all happened only this very day. She had looked forward to a carefree holiday. Now she knew she could not bear to stay here for a moment longer. She found Joe – drinking hard in one of the tents with Ralph's Joe and the Siddle brothers and Jock Currah from Burnhope and one or two others – and told him she was going home, and then she turned and walked quickly up

93

the hill, away from the noise and the dust and the crowd, and the memories that would not let her rest.

Joe had no more heart for the holiday than his sister. The chief benefit of the Pay for him, apart from the obvious one of at last having a little spare cash, was the distraction it offered, in the shape of an apparently infinite number of ways and means of getting speedily drunk. It also offered a good company of friends with little else to do but join him in the undertaking.

First, for a time, they wandered over the hillside, looking to see what was on offer, assessing the qualities of the various drinking booths. Anthony Siddle, seeing Joseph Dawson engrossed in conversation in one of them, wanted to go in after him, but Joe caught his arm. 'Not in there, not today. Frank Johnson's around somewhere.' Frank Johnson was the constable, sole upholder of the law for miles around, and thus not much liked. But Joe knew Anthony's enthusiasm for tackling Joseph Dawson – there had been three major fights since Charlie was fined – and did not want to have his drinking disrupted by trouble of that kind. Fortunately Anthony, having drunk very little as yet, was still amenable to argument, and they moved on somewhere else and settled down to some serious tippling. By the time they reached the third booth they had got beyond appreciating the finer points of what they drank, or even, as far as Joe at least was concerned, noticing what it was. His companions, less drunk than he – they had after all less reason to give it such concentrated attention – dumped him on a stool by the entrance to the booth and the next round of drinking began.

Joe, dazed by alcohol fumes and the noise and the heat, sat staring morosely out over the busy scene, watching the bright moving mass of people. Some way off across the road, below a sky so blue it hurt the eyes, the grey walls of Short Thorns public house marked the western limit of the festivities. On a hummock a little higher up the hill, a circle of men, cheering and shouting, crowded round the cockpit; and on the low wall that surrounded it, his back to the bloody fray below, a man stood, haranguing the passers-by with vigorous gestures of the arms, though from here his voice was inaudible. That he was providing some kind of entertainment was clear enough, however, for quite a little crowd had stopped to hear him, with apparent attention. Joe narrowed his eyes to see more clearly, and then, realizing who it was, glowered with a sudden concentration of hatred. After a moment or two he rose swaying to his feet, one arm clinging to the side post of the booth for support, the other grasping Anthony Siddle's shoulder.

'Let's hoy stones at Rowland Peart,' he suggested, taking a step or two forward. James Craggs followed his line of vision to the small figure of the preacher, and then cheered his approval; so did one or two others. Anthony shook his head. 'What's up?' Joe demanded. 'Give us a bit sport.'

'Why, let him be,' said Anthony. 'He's doing us no harm.'

'No harm? No harm, you say?' He lurched round on his friend, clasping him by the lapels. 'D'you know what he's done?' He swayed again, and then sat down rather abruptly on the stool. 'Hypocrite! That's what he is. Slimy, whining hypocrite. He took Eve. That's what he did. Stone him out of Weardale, I say.'

Suddenly finding a precarious equilibrium, he got up again and lurched off up the hill, pushing through the crowd, towards the preacher. The others followed him, most laughing, enjoying the prospect, Anthony protesting and anxious.

'Since when were you so soft?' demanded Joe. 'Why, you'd have fought Joseph Dawson sharp enough.'

'That's not the same,' said Anthony. 'Joseph Dawson deserves it. Rowland Peart doesn't.'

'That's what you say.'

'Aye, and what I think too.'

'Then get your neb out of my affairs and let me be!' Angrily he shook Anthony's hand from his arm and pushed his way on. Anthony, suddenly glimpsing a familiar face in the crowd ahead, ran after him and held him more firmly.

'Watch out!' he warned. 'There's Frank Johnson.'

'What's up wi' you? What's he to do with it?'

'Why, he can have you up for being drunk and disorderly, that's what. Or worse, if you pick a fight. Isn't that what you said to me? Howay now, man. Let's get you home.'

Joe turned round and looked solemnly at his friend. 'I've to take Billy's pay to his mother.'

'Then,' said Anthony emphatically, 'we'd best get you sobered up. You're in no state to go calling on Tabitha Hall.' And with the help of the others he steered Joe down the hill towards the river.

Edward Selby had felt that duty obliged him to attend the pay at Newhouse, in his capacity as shepherd of this unruly and unwilling flock. He did not much want to go, having by now only too great an experience of his own unpopularity, but he had heard what fighting and drunkenness and other disagreeable behaviour could be expected on this occasion, and felt the more impelled to go and try and make his mark upon it. That he might fail was only too likely, but for that he could be forgiven, in the circumstances. For him not to have tried to make any impression would be unpardonable.

It was worse than he had expected. The noise and dust and drunkenness appalled him, even after two months' experience of the drinking capacity of the Weardale men. So did the brutality, the openly wanton behaviour of many of the girls, some as near drunk as their young men, and – as usual – the rudeness and incivility of the children (his desire to do a little teaching had already foundered on the native indiscipline of the boys entrusted to his care). Slithering in spilled ale and vomit, he made his way from one booth to another, trying to exchange a friendly word with this one or that, but though he was sometimes replied to with some degree of politeness, those around him always rapidly melted away, as if by magic, the moment he came to a halt among them. That he should make any impression on them either for good or ill was clearly impossible. He did not even come across Jane Emerson, as he had rather hoped he might, expecting her to be here. But, not seeing her, he told himself that she clearly found this place as offensive to her refined spirit as he did.

Feeling depressed, he decided he had done all that duty required of him, and set out on foot up the hill from Newhouse, drawn by some sort of half conscious impulse in the rough direction of White Lea. Once at the top, hot and breathless, he paused and turned to look back over the dale.

96

Somehow it seemed as inhospitable and alien today, shimmering in the midday heat, as it had in the snow on the day of his coming. He wondered if, when his time came to leave, anyone would notice he had ever been here. Even Miss Emerson, who was so often in his thoughts, who he had to acknowledge meant a great deal to him – would she notice any difference, when he went away? She was always kind, but no more ...

Odd, he thought, that he should expect any more. For her to be kind and polite was exceptional enough. What did he want? He knew he had not been hoping for her conversion; what he wished for was something quite different, which had previously lurked somewhere in the distant recesses of his mind, and now, intruding itself, startled and discomforted him.

Then he told himself that his frequent wish to seek her out did not imply any desire on his part for a change in their relationship, which was of course simply that of a man of God to one of his flock. What drew him to her was that rare quality she had, of offering him a glimpse of a world that ought to be, a world of simplicity and unforced kindliness, such as he had found nowhere else, certainly not in this dale – nor for that matter in the company of Mademoiselle de Mortain. In Miss Emerson's house, sitting by the hearth of which she was the presiding spirit, he could feel himself transported into a magical world of lost innocence, paradise before the intrusion of the serpent, in which she was Eve, not yet tempted to sin. When they talked together, there was about her views (when she was not, as now and then, parroting her brother's words) a certain untaught wisdom, which he found very touching. Oh, that he could be sure she would remain as she was, unspoiled by too much civilization, or, more likely indeed, by the barbarity that surrounded her! Perhaps the death of her young man had been a matter for relief after all: Edward thought it unlikely he had been worthy of such a prize, and marriage to him would surely have coarsened her.

There was no breeze today, even here on the hilltop, for the branches of the Scots pines above his head were motionless; that in itself was unusual, in this place where the hottest day was usually refreshed by a breath of wind. Yet, in spite of the heat, the landscape had a soft green look, as if spring was reluctant to fade into summer. On the bank beside the road, cow parsley blossomed in creamy luminosity and the flowers of the cranesbill were richly purple blue. Just over the wall, in the adjoining field, a few mountain pansies were still in bloom, bright points of purple and yellow and violet, and everywhere tiny white stars of spring sandwort patterned the cropped grass. Below him, he could see the line of the river, marked by its bordering trees, and beyond it the hills, dotted with the little houses in their surrounding green patches of cultivation, reaching gently up to the browner line of the fells. Even in his present sour mood, he had to admit that the scene had a certain charm.

Until, that is, he looked immediately below, past the hummocks of the Newhouse spoil heaps, through the trees, to the steep fields on this side of the river, from whence came the sounds of coarse shouting, shrieks and laughter, raucous singing. Narrowing his eyes against the glare, he could make out more than one group of men rolling over the ruined grass in ferocious drunken combat. *The usual entertainment of the dale*, he thought sourly. So much for the views so often expressed in fashionably intellectual circles (though not the circles he moved in if he could help it, even away from here) that men raised far from the corrupting influences of the city were somehow nobler and finer; or even that all men were capable of being perfected, given the right nurture. Just let those deluded philanthropists try and tame these men, he thought.

He was so absorbed in his gloomy reflections that he did not hear someone coming until she was almost upon him; then he looked round, startled, at the sound of clogged feet on the stony ground, and saw Jane Emerson about to pass him on the road. Confused, he felt himself colouring. He fumbled for his hat, pulled it off, made some sort of sketchy bow. 'Good afternoon, Miss Emerson.'

Then, his composure a little restored, he saw that in his self-absorption he had not noticed that she was clearly in some distress. He thought she might even have been weeping. 'My dear Miss Emerson, what is it?' His voice all

98

warm concern, he stepped nearer to her.

She shook her head, and he sensed that the tears were even closer than he had thought. The calm dignity that had so impressed him had crumbled at last; with reason enough, as he knew well.

'You have not stayed with your friends below,' he said gently, implying a question, should she feel it would be helpful to talk to him.

She shook her head again. 'I ... I could not –' She paused for a moment, clearly trying to bring herself under control, and then she resumed in the same rough, dry voice, 'We were ... Billy –' She broke off, with an odd choking sound, as if her words had stumbled against some impossible obstacle; and then her face dissolved into an ugly mask of misery and she began to sob wildly.

Edward could not bear it. In a moment, somehow, he found his arms were round her and he was holding her close, murmuring soft tender sounds that had no precise meaning, while his hand stroked her hair. She fell against him as if it was the most natural thing in the world, her face on his shoulder, her tears soon dampening the cloth of his coat.

He did not know what had made him do it. He had scarcely ever in his life before had his arms about a woman. Restraint, consideration, courtesy, had guided his manner towards the opposite sex in everything he did until now. Even his sister had never received more than the most decorous of kisses from him; and if his approaches to his mother had ever been warmer, if as a small boy he had been held and caressed by her, he did not remember it now. Yet he had not hesitated to put his arms about this woman who a few weeks before had been a stranger to him. Compassion, of course, had guided him, and the wish to give comfort, yet now that he was holding her a sense of awkwardness began to intrude itself upon him, and something more, something inside himself, a growing consciousness of the woman's body in his arms, its firmness, and yet its softness, in places where no man's was soft or rounded; and an awareness of his own response to that sensation. He knew these feelings well enough, for they had too often been stirred by some dubious woman seen in the street, by an actress dreamed of at night, even by Mademoiselle de Mortain (at least until he knew how she had been playing with him, how she had deceived him); but he knew too that they were evil, sinful, to be cast aside with horror. It appalled him that they should have any part in his dutiful care for a troubled parishioner.

Suddenly afraid of what had woken in him, he pushed her gently from him and steered her to a convenient fallen tree trunk, where she sank down and her tears subsided a little. She did not look at him. He wondered if she felt rejected. But what else could he do? Allow himself to be led further into sinful thoughts? How could he ever explain to her his present shame, or apologize for it?

'I am sorry.' It was she who spoke first, pulling a handkerchief from her pocket and blowing her nose with determined vigour.

What was she sorry for? he wondered. He might almost have suspected her of feeling as he had; but he rejected the idea at once. He knew that women did not have carnal feelings, or only depraved and corrupted women who had been lost long ago, and Jane Emerson was not like that. If she had clung to him, it had been because she needed consolation, and – for a time at least – found it there; nothing more. He hoped she would never know what he had felt, never even suspect it.

It was at that moment that Jenny caught him looking at her. Their eyes met, and for a long time they stayed where they were, just looking. Until then, Edward had been right about Jenny's feelings. In her sudden overflowing of grief and misery, she had not been thinking of him at all. Her only thoughts had been for her own losses, for her father and for Billy, and all the memories of them that this day had woken in her. Edward had simply been there, offering comfort when she needed it most, and an effective comfort too, for he was a rock to cling to in her weakness, such as life had rarely offered her. Bound up with that consolation had been the feel of his arms about her, of the fine cloth coat beneath her cheek, the heat of his body through it, the good clean smell of him, small things that only augmented her sense of being protected and cherished, of being able, for a brief interval, to cast her misery on to someone else's shoulders. It was only now, looking at him, that she saw from his expression that for him at least it had been more than just a simple matter of offering comfort. Her heart began to beat very fast, and she felt her colour rise.

She stood up, smoothing skirts that were not in any way disarrayed, but she had to have something to do. Then she glanced at him, and saw how he was watching her still, and breathing rather fast, his colour as high as her own. She had forgotten what it was like to desire a man, but she remembered well enough now, remembered the way her limbs had seemed to melt in response to Billy's least glance, and the ache in her body that he had always been able to satisfy, so sweetly. But this was another matter, for all that it felt the same. She might have little experience of gentlemen, but she had heard stories enough of their dastardly behaviour towards young girls of her kind, stories of betrayal and cruelty. There were of course a few romantic tales of rich men who married poor girls, but they were fantasies, as she knew quite well. In real life that did not happen. Wise girls took the greatest possible care when in the company of agreeable young men of gentry families, especially when the young men took more than an ordinary interest in them. It might seem flattering, but it was not, because young men of Mr Selby's class wanted girls of hers for one thing only. She would have thought a clergyman would be different from other young men, but then even the Bishop himself was scarcely a model of Christian charity and humility, from what she had heard. A lascivious curate should not be in the least surprising.

She looked him straight in the eye (it was hard, for he was handsome, very handsome, and she could not wholly subdue the response of her body) and said as coolly as she could, 'Good day, Mr Selby,' and then she turned and walked away from him. She told herself she was relieved that he did not follow her, though in reality she was more than a little disappointed.

After a ducking in the river and a brisk walk to John Kidd's house at East Blackdene, where that young man's wife plied him with tea, Joe was at last sober enough to make his way to

101

Chapel to take Billy's pay to Tabitha Hall. His clothes were not improved by the drenching, but at least they were drying quickly in the hot sun. On the whole he was grateful to his friends. He ought to have taken the money as soon as he got it, for fear of having it lost or stolen, and it was only his gloomy mood that had made him put it off, because it was one more reminder of the losses he had suffered over the past year and a half.

He knew quite well that, having done their duty by him, his friends had returned to their drinking. When he had seen Billy's mother he would go back and join them, and finish the job properly this time, and perhaps have another, and better, chance to get back at Rowland. It still rankled that Anthony, usually the first to pick a fight in a good (or not so good) cause, had got in his way. The man must be going soft, unless Rowland had cast his spell over him too.

Today, Chapel was pretty well deserted, for everyone was at Newhouse, apart from those few who had a conscience about clearing debts at the earliest opportunity, and were doing the rounds of the shops paying what they owed. He or Jenny would see to their village debts tomorrow, when the festivities would move into the market place, to continue for several days (and a weekend or two) more. Now, he was glad enough of the interval of quiet.

Until, that is, he came within sight of the market cross and saw Eve there, talking to another girl. He stood quite still, looking at her, all the bitterness at his nerve ends. He saw the other girl part from her, and then she turned to leave as well, and saw him in her turn. For a moment she coloured deeply, and then she smiled, a rather forced and uncomfortable smile. It won no response from Joe, who looked at her with deliberate coldness, as if to ask her who she thought she was smiling at. She coloured still more, and came a little nearer, close enough for him to hear what she said, even though she did not raise her voice.

'Joe, I would not have us enemies.'

'No? You've a strange way of showing it. What else can we be?'

The blissful serenity of her expression, which he found so infuriating, was ruffled a little; for a moment he even thought

102

she looked hurt. But then she lifted her head and said staunchly, 'I shall love you always, the more now I know that I am loved by my Saviour.'

'Once you were content to be loved by me.'

'Now I know to be content with that is sin.'

'So my love means nowt to you? Why then, that's as well, I'd say, for I love you no more. Remember that, Eve Todd – I hate the very thought of you and your cold religion.'

'I am sorry,' she said gravely, and he knew it was pity for him and not regret for what she had done that lay behind the words.

He was about to make some further cutting remark, expressive of his scorn for her and the new faith that had come between them, when he saw that she was no longer looking at him, but at some point beyond his shoulder. He glanced round and saw a group of men hurrying towards the market place from the Newhouse direction, pausing now and then to call out to someone as they passed.

'I must go,' said Eve quickly. 'I shall pray for you, Joe Emerson.'

'Don't trouble yourself,' he retorted; but before he could say more Jock Currah, the first of the hurrying men, reached him and gasped out, 'Joe, they've got Charlie Siddle.'

'Who has?'

'Frank Johnson. I reckon he had it all planned. Set Joseph Dawson to pick a fight with Anthony, then off and arrested Charlie before any of us knew what had happened. Took him back to his house in handcuffs, to seek a cart, Anthony says. We're to get together, meet by the bridge – sharp as can be.'

Men came from all directions, many drunk, some armed with staves or cudgels or even fowling pieces. They threw coats and waistcoats in a heap by the bridge and then crowded on to it, filling it from side to side, two abreast, swelling out at either end.

The cart came lumbering into sight along the road from the constable's house in East Blackdene, with Charlie handcuffed uncomfortably between a bruised Joseph Dawson and a triumphant Frank Johnson; triumphant, that is, until he saw the men barring his path, the prisoner's brother in front of them all.

Johnson urged the horse forward; Anthony stood his ground and the animal refused to budge.

'Get out of my way, Siddle,' said Johnson. 'You're obstructing a constable in the execution of his duty.'

'I'll obstruct you no more, when my brother's free,' said Anthony. Behind him, Joe and the others growled their support, and then they all stepped forward, closing round the cart. Charlie Siddle grinned; his brother reached up and grasped Johnson's coat, dragging him half off the seat. 'Let my brother go, or you'll rue the day!'

'Get your hands off me, or there'll be two charges of assault!'

'Dawson asked for it – and so do you!'

Johnson, held painfully half out of the cart, glanced round at Joseph Dawson, whose battered face seemed to bear eloquent witness to the imprudence of resistance; as too did the hopelessness of his expression, and the way he shrugged. Johnson was a courageous man, but he was not stupid. He looked at the crowd gathered before him, noting the determination on every face, and he knew he was defeated. He said, 'Why, let go of me then, or I can't get at my keys.' Anthony hesitated just a moment, and then let him go.

Without a word, Johnson took a key from his pocket and unlocked the handcuffs. Charlie, grinning cheerfully, jumped down, to be greeted by slaps on the shoulder and shouts of jubilation from his rescuers. Anthony flung his parting shot at the constable – 'You can tell the Bishop, if he wants his fine, let him come and get it himself. Then he'll see what a warm welcome we'll give him!'

Humiliated and miserable, Johnson turned the cart and made his way – unhindered, though to a chorus of jeering – back the way he had come. Joseph Dawson, judging it unwise to return home just yet, went with him.

The rescuers repaired to the King's Head to toast their success, and Joe, promising to join them soon, hurried to complete his errand with Tabitha Hall.

As he reached the house he saw Rowland, back from his preaching, just coming out. He came to a halt and stood scowling at the young man, and wished he was still drunk enough not to care about causing a disturbance outside

Tabitha's house. Rowland smiled, very sweetly. 'I'll not fight, Joe Emerson,' he warned. Then, before Joe could reply to that, he went on, 'What happened out there? I heard they arrested Charlie Siddle.'

'He's set free,' said Joe curtly.

To his surprise, Rowland nodded as if with approval, and then said, 'He's been badly used, to be fined so much. It wasn't just.'

'Why no,' said Joe, reluctantly; he would rather have been given cause to disagree. Then, as Rowland did not seem to be making any move to go, he said pointedly, 'I've got Billy's pay for his mother.'

Rowland nodded again and took a step past Joe, and then turned back and said gravely, 'It was not my doing that Eve turned to the Lord. I'm only His instrument.'

'Then if you'd not come back, He would have had no instrument and she would be mine still.'

Apparently Rowland had no answer to that, or none that he thought appropriate. He laid a hand on Joe's arm, as if pleading for some sort of return to their boyhood friendship, or so it seemed to Joe, who had no intention of allowing himself to be won over. He shook off the arm and strode into the house, where Billy's mother sat waiting for him by the window.

'May I help, father?'

Jacob Todd was busy entering in his account books a record of payments he had made today to suppliers from Newcastle and elsewhere. Though he had no time for the system of credit operated by most Weardale tradesmen, he nevertheless only settled his own bills annually, at the Pay. Now he looked round with astonishment into the gently smiling face of his younger daughter. It was by no means the first time in the past weeks that she had surprised him with her willingness to serve him, as a dutiful daughter should; in fact, it had become commonplace for her to do so, and the thought daily gratified his spirit and offered opportunities for him to speak to her with gravity and at some length, drawing all the morals to which she had never listened in the past and which she now heard with exemplary humility.

But that she should offer to assist him with the accounts, Eve who was so incompetent at figures that he would never allow her to serve alone in the shop, lest she offend some valued customer by giving short change – that left him temporarily speechless, the more so when she added the next moment, 'I should like to be taught how to do figures. You always said I could learn, if I applied myself.'

Jacob nodded, pleased that his words had at last been taken to heart by this daughter who had always declared that she hated arithmetic. 'I am glad to see you have given heed to my words. As I have always said, no one is beyond teaching. It is never too late to apply yourself. But ...' He paused, looking her up and down, as if calculating her usefulness to him, then added, 'I have not the time tonight, to take you in hand. Next week perhaps. Or it may be that your mother will teach you, when time allows.' He glanced at his wife, who bowed her head in agreement. 'Meanwhile, daughter, I am sure there is some sewing you can usefully do.'

'Yes, father.'

She had always hated sewing, almost as much as she hated working with figures, but she went meekly to a chair by the empty hearth and took up a worn stocking and set to work to darn the heel, watched with critical eyes by her sister. She knew her father too was still watching her, with that mixture of disbelief and satisfaction that had been so apparent since he realized what had happened to her.

'"By their fruit ye shall know them,"' he said at last. And then added, with ponderous emphasis, '"The fruit of the spirit is love, joy, peace, long suffering, gentleness, goodness, faith." I begin to see signs of such fruit in you, Eve. My prayers have been answered at last. The Lord has touched your heart.'

'Amen,' said Eve happily. She had long ago had to accept that her father would never be able to bring himself to acknowledge that someone so despised as Rowland Peart had brought about the change in his daughter that a lifetime of his stern discipline had wholly failed to effect. From the beginning (once he had overcome his suspicion that her changed manner was simply a new way of trying to deceive

him into ignoring her misbehaviour) he had attributed it to
years of strenuous prayer and the effect of his words and
beatings upon her. Like the dropping of water on a stone,
they had to make an impression at last, and he was the more
pleased with himself because it had taken so long. One
Sunday he had even preached on the virtues of perseverance
against all the odds, using his daughter's conversion as an
example. Eve had not much relished the use he made of her,
particularly as it was quite untrue, but somehow her new
faith lit everything around her with such an overwhelming
joyfulness and brightness that she could not resent anything,
still less feel hate or anger. Besides, she knew now where her
duty as a daughter lay, so she obeyed her father without
question and without resentment, even with gratitude that
she had some way of demonstrating how complete was the
change in her. She had, as St Paul said, put on the armour of
God (she had become an attentive reader of the Bible since
that momentous Saturday, finding all kinds of things she had
never noticed before, all kinds of delights, whole phrases she
tried urgently to commit to memory), and the shield of faith
protected her from all the fiery darts that might once have
had power to harm her soul.

That was not to say that there had not, now and then, been
some small anxiety or trouble. Her meeting with Joe today,
for instance – that had ruffled the smooth flowing river of her
joy just a little; but not seriously, and not for long. The main
sensation she had carried away from the meeting was one of
regret, because, loving him as she did, she wanted Joe too to
know the happiness she had found. Every day, morning and
evening, she prayed earnestly for his conversion.

There had been one other little trouble, too; a realization
that something that had become a part of her life, month by
month, had ceased. But an instant of alarm had soon been
dispelled. She knew she had been so transformed by her
conversion that it was hardly surprising if it affected her body
as strongly as it had her moods, her thoughts and feelings,
and everything else in her life. And it did affect her body, she
knew that, full as she was of enormous energy, and yet a
wonderful, tranquil happiness, all carnal lusts left behind
with the old impure life she had sloughed off at the moment

107

of conversion. She had never felt so well as she did now. She knew she looked different too, all her joy shining out of her eyes, driving away the look of harassment and fear that once had been there. For what now was there to fear, ever again?

She caught her sister's eye, and realized sadly that her prayers had not yet been answered as far as Judith was concerned, for the malice in them showed only too clearly how she resented Eve's change of heart, more perhaps than she had disliked the old unregenerate Eve with whom she had quarrelled frequently, but always with the satisfaction of being able to feel herself superior. Eve smiled faintly, but her sister's expression only hardened, so she looked down at her sewing and forced herself to think of the words of the hymn she had sung with such abandonment as she knelt in the market place.

Tis Love! 'tis Love! Thou diedst for me!
I hear Thy whisper in my heart;

'Joe Emerson's got his eye on Phoebe Dent. He was in the back lane with her when I came by just now. A good bit of land the Dents have, and no lads. He'd do well there.'

The morning breaks, the shadows flee,
Pure, universal Love Thou art;
To me, to all, Thy mercies move ...

She forced the words through her mind, pushing away her sister's spitefulness.

'She's bonny, too ...'

'Judith, it is not seemly to gossip!'

Eve had never before been thankful for an intervention of her father's. Her sister's sharply spoken words might not cause any real or lasting disturbance to her feelings, but she could not deny that they hurt a little, even more than a little. It was the one thing she had not been able to leave behind, the hope that one day, in spite of everything, her father might relent and accept Joe as a son-in-law. She did not want to think that by then it might be too late. But then, Joe had shown her today that he regarded everything that had been between them as over and done with, for ever. It was right that she should learn to accept that fact, with joyous resignation.

108

Thy nature and Thy name is love.

What was Joe's little human love, against that? What was her own trivial disappointment, against what her Lord had suffered for her? The very thought that she should be allowed to share in that suffering, in however small a way, added to the exaltation of her spirit.

6

'**W**here's our Joe?' Tommy exploded into the room and there came to a halt, poised just inside the door, breathing fast, face glowing, eyes shining.

Jenny looked at him in astonishment. He had been out all day – she had no idea where, but was simply thankful he had tired of playing the man in smoke filled alehouses, and taken instead to spending the long hot days of the holiday splashing in the river or roaming the hills, a boy again, the cares of the working world left behind. 'He went over to Rowantree Foot with Ralph's Joe to look at Tom Low's galloway.'

Tommy looked as if he was close to bursting. 'Will he be long?'

'Why, I can't say. You know how it is when men get together over horseflesh. But he's been gone a canny while now.'

Tommy stood in the doorway, looking out over the fields and the road, his eyes on its westernmost point. He hopped from one foot to the other, so impatient that he could not be still. Jenny, trying to concentrate on her spinning (she had been working outside at first, but the heat of the sun had driven her indoors, where it was always cool), soon grew irritated at his restlessness. 'Tommy, give over fidgeting so! What's up with you?'

'I've got to see Joe. Now. It's important.'

'Can you not tell me?'

He shook his head fiercely, but did not elaborate. She tried to find tasks to occupy him, but he did them so quickly that she would have only a moment's peace before he was back in the doorway, restlessly watching the road. She knew at once when Joe did come in sight at last, for Tommy let out

110

a great cry and flew off down the hill to meet his brother. Curious as to what should so have excited the child, Jenny put her spinning aside and went to the door.

She saw them meet, just where the track reached the road, saw Tommy gesticulating energetically, saw Joe come to a halt, listening with concentrated attention to what his brother was saying. Then she saw the two of them come slowly on up the hill to the house. When they were near enough, she saw that Joe too had something of Tommy's bright excited look.

'Why now,' she said, hands on hips, 'perhaps you'll let me in on this great secret.'

Joe grinned and glanced at his brother. 'Shall we tell her, our Tommy?' Tommy nodded, and Joe held out his hand towards Jenny.

She took the stones he held in it, three fragments, roughly globular, heavy and coated with white, though the greyness inside gleamed through. 'Shoad ore,' she said.

Joe nodded. 'Tommy found it.'

'Over there – just by the head of Middlehope burn,' put in Tommy.

'Whose land is it?' Jenny asked.

'The Bishop's, of course.' Joe made a wry face. 'Pity it's not ours. Or even the Quaker Company's. Still, that was never likely. Tommy says there's a canny bit of shoad ore lying about up there.'

His brother nodded vigorously. 'All over. So I had a scrat around. There's a vein there, I'll swear there is. A new one.'

Jenny looked questioningly at Joe, who said with a caution belied by the tremor in his voice, 'From what Tommy says it's beyond where the levels in Middlehope old mine cut through, and in any case that vein runs south-east to north-west. But it might be a shoot from it. If it was, it would have a canny length to it. Then, there are veins cut across from Rookhope, into the Middlehope vein. Where they meet, that's where some of the richest ore's been found.'

Jenny could see the hope in his eyes, that this might be such a vein as every miner dreamed of, its upper edge worked on by time and weather, until the fragments of ore that Tommy had found had crumbled away; it could be such a thing, or it might simply be scattered fragments from a thin

111

and negligible offshoot of a greater vein already being worked. Joe looked up at the sky. 'How long before dark? Have we time to get up there?'

'Why aye, of course we have!' Tommy tugged at his arm.

They went in the growing dusk up the hill behind the house and on over the fell; Tommy, eager and excited, leading the way. When they reached the spot, it looked quiet and innocent enough, a little shallow dip in the hills, grass grown and featureless. Tommy showed them where the shoad ore lay scattered at the foot of a shallow slope.

Joe walked slowly over the whole ground, his eyes intent upon every inch of it, sometimes pausing to dig with his heel or make a scraping with his hunting knife. It was on the western slope of the dip that he stayed longest, watched in a tense silence by Jenny and Tommy. At last he put the knife away and straightened, and even in the growing darkness they could see how his eyes shone. 'Well, our Tommy, you're a born grover, I see.' He flung an arm about the boy's shoulder. 'I reckon this is worth a trial. And just in time – the masters have all but finished riding the groves. A few days more, and we'd have taken our bargain.' He ran his eyes over the ground. 'There's not slope enough for hushing. We'd have to cut a trench, to see if it's worth going on with.' His voice suggested that he was already quite sure it would be. 'We'll all come up tomorrow and take a better look.' Then he added, 'Don't let on to anyone now, will you?'

Tommy shook his head, all happy pride. 'Why of course not, our Joe. Would I do that?'

Joe went down to see his uncle that evening, and did not come back until late, though Jenny heard him singing long before he reached the house.

The partnership spent most of that hot Sunday, once Ralph Emerson and his family were back from morning worship at High House Chapel, investigating the possibilities of Tommy's find; and returned convinced that it was well worth approaching Mr Crawhall, in the near certainty that he would agree that they should make a trial of the vein. 'We'll have the right to work it for a year, just the way we want,' Uncle Ralph said gleefully. 'It'll be like having our own mine.'

112

On Monday, Joe left the house earlier than usual, so as to call with the other members of the partnership at Newhouse to report their discovery, before there was any danger that anyone else might find it. Tommy, full of their praise for his powers of observation, went with them; usually the washing continued at bargain time, even though the miners ceased work, but Ralph Emerson's partnership no longer had any ore left to wash. His uncle's promise – 'We'll call it Tommy's vein' – rang in his ears all the way to Newhouse.

Jenny, touched by some of their excitement, found it hard to concentrate on the morning's tasks. Yet she told herself that she at least must keep her head. Tommy's find might prove to be of no significance at all, and even if it turned out to be the rich vein they hoped for, that did not mean that the partnership would inevitably find itself with undreamed-of wealth at its disposal. There was a long way to go yet, even if everything went as they hoped.

Little more than an hour later, returning to the house from driving the cows to graze on the fell, Jenny was surprised to see Joe coming up the track towards the house. She went to meet him.

'I thought you'd be gone longer.' She saw, with a tremor of anxiety, that he had lost the look of joyful excitement with which he had left the house, and even seemed preoccupied and grave. 'What's up? Have you seen Mr Crawhall?'

She was a little relieved that some of the weekend's excitement returned to his face, if only temporarily. 'Aye, and he's riding that way today. We've to call at the office tomorrow, to hear what he says.'

'Then, what –?'

'I've to go to Auckland.'

She stared at him. 'To Auckland?' They had neither of them been as far as Bishop Auckland in their lives. 'But what for?'

'Frank Johnson called at the Siddles' house this morning, first thing. Had a warrant for their arrest, he said, for assault.'

'The both of them?'

'Aye. And other eight, I think it was. John Kidd, James Craggs, Jock Currah, all those who stood foremost on the bridge that day. Not me, though.'

113

'What happened?' She was sure there must have been a fight.

'Why, Anthony said he'd come quietly.' He smiled at her obvious astonishment. 'Mind, most of the others aren't in work; he maybe fears he'll be turned off if he's awkward over this. But he did say if Johnson laid a hand on any of the rest, Charlie included, he'd call out all his friends. There's another thing too – he reckons what happened on the bridge was no assault, and he means to tell the magistrate so. He reckons Johnson made more of it than there was, just to put himself in a good light.'

'That would be like him,' agreed Jenny. 'But why's he going to Auckland? Mr Wilson's at Wolsingham.'

Joe's sombre look returned. 'He's taking him before Mr Faber.'

'The Bishop's lawyer?'

Joe nodded. 'He's the justice who issued the warrants. That's why we're going too. Not the ones who have warrants against them, of course. It's best they lie low for a bit. But Anthony may have to pay Charlie's fine to keep Mr Faber quiet, and if they fine him too, as I suppose they will – well, he'll need his friends to help out.'

'That'll be friends with money.'

'I know. But I'll take what I can. Maybe it'll be enough, put together with what everyone else has.' He studied her face. 'You don't mind?'

She thought of the tiny sum still remaining to them from the Pay, put aside to buy the oatmeal and other stores they must get in before next winter. She had even hoped they might just be able to afford a headstone for their father's grave. And then she thought how she would feel if Joe were in Anthony Siddle's place (a far from impossible situation), and relented. 'Why no, it's right you should go. You'll be wanting food too.' They went to the house, and she put bread and cheese together for him, and a flask of ale, and saw him ride away on the galloway.

'I'll not be home till late,' he said as he went.

When he had gone it seemed suddenly very quiet. She stood in the doorway long after he had disappeared from view, her eyes scanning the dusty road beyond their hayfield, which was almost ready for mowing, so richly scattered with clover, buttercups, forget-me-nots, yellow rattle, orchids, vetch and daisies, and a multitude of other flowers and seeds, that it looked bronze rather than green. Raising her eyes a little, she looked across to the slopes of Chapel Fell and the lesser heather-clad rise of Black Hill, and at their feet the little houses and fields that spread along the valley floor and up to the edges of the moors. There were at this moment no human sounds, only the cry of the curlew, larks singing, the soft sigh of the wind in the trees that sheltered the house, the bleating of sheep, the hum of bees on the meadow flowers; and the sound of water, so constant a sound that if she were asked what she heard that would be the last sound she would think of, since it was somehow as inevitable as her breathing – more so, for it would go on when her breathing had long ceased.

Joe had told her Tommy had gone off somewhere with Luke, and she knew she would not see him again much before supper time. She would very likely be alone here until dark, and that would not be until nearly eleven in these long days of early summer.

She wondered whether to go down to the village, or perhaps call on her aunt, and then thought better of it. She had work to do here, tasks she had put off for some time now. What better opportunity than this for tackling the worst of them? She went into the house and dragged all the furniture out of the kitchen, shook the mats and draped them on the garden wall to air, swept up the sand with which the flagstones were strewn each week, and set to work to scrub the floor.

It was hot work, and she had stripped to her heavy linen shift and bound up her hair away from her neck with a ribbon. The sun flooded in through the open door, quickly drying the flagstones, bringing dazzling light and warmth and the sweet fragrance of the moorland grasses into the room. The noise of the scrubbing brush filled the air, shutting out other sounds, so it was not until there was a sudden lessening of the heat and a shadow bent over her own that she realized someone stood in the doorway. She looked sharply round, and then sat back on her heels staring in astonishment (and

115

some considerable embarrassment) at the figure standing there, so immaculate in contrast with her own dishevelled state.

'Miss Emerson, I have come at an inconvenient moment, I can see –'

She smiled, trying to look nonchalant through her blushes. 'Why no, I'm glad to stop,' she said. She put the brush aside and scrambled to her feet, wishing that her shift was not so stained with dirty water. 'The floor's so wet, we'd best talk outside. Shall I bring a drink out?'

'That would be most welcome,' Edward said courteously. He smiled. 'They warned me that I would find the climate here uncommonly harsh, yet what do we have but weeks of tropical heat?'

'Why, this isn't Weardale weather! I can't bring to mind a year like it before. It's all ahead of itself.'

She left him outside and went to bring ale for them both, a little doubtful if it was a suitable drink for so refined a young man, but then it was much too hot for tea, and milk did not seem appropriate either. She set the tankards on the stone bench by the door and sat down beside them, expecting him to do the same, but he did not do so, simply stood where he was, looking uncomfortable and making no move to talk or drink. He appeared to be absorbed in gazing out over the dale; but after a moment he turned abruptly to her and said, 'Miss Emerson, I must ... I beg you to give me a moment of your time ... it is imperative ...'

She looked with astonishment into the blushing and troubled countenance of the young man. She waited for him to go on, though it was some while before he seemed to realize from her silence and her stillness that she was giving him the moment of time that he requested. She wondered if he knew that his hands were crushing his hat unmercifully. She doubted it would be wearable ever again, and smiled a little at the thought, and then raised her eyes and saw that the smile had not escaped him, and that he thought she was laughing at him. She controlled her features, assuming a suitably grave expression (it was clear that whatever he had to say was of a serious nature).

'Miss Emerson, I ... the other day ...'

116

'I haven't given it another thought,' she said quickly, sure that he must be trying to make some adequate explanation of that embarrassing lapse; but her words had the opposite effect to what she intended. He looked openly dismayed.

'Oh, no – I mean, Miss Emerson, I did not behave well, but ... there is an excuse. I ...' He bit his lip, and then appeared to get himself under control at least, for he said next, his voice low, quivering but fluent, 'Miss Emerson, I have never truly loved, until now – and I love you. I love you with all the passion, all the devotion, that a gentleman can feel for the lady he loves. I know you may think it strange. I know that if *you* do not, then others will do so. I told myself it was a delusion, that it must be overcome. I was – I am – convinced that my feelings are not returned. But I cannot go on as I am, without pouring out my heart to you, in the hope – the vain and futile hope – that I am mistaken as to the nature of your feelings.'

She could not move, or even take in fully what he was saying, except with a sense that she must be dreaming, that he could not be saying what she thought she heard. When he went on, she was even more convinced that her senses were deceiving her.

'Miss Emerson, you have my heart, whether you will or no. I offer you now all that remains to me – my hand, if you will have it.'

What was he saying? It could not be what she imagined, surely?

'In short, Miss Emerson, will you do me the great and inexpressible honour of becoming my wife?'

Joe came home well after dark that night. Tommy, exhausted but happy, had returned half an hour before, and had scarcely touched his broth before crawling into bed and falling asleep. He had said almost nothing to Jenny, but then in a way that was a relief, because if he had been talkative she might have found it harder to keep from him what had been devouring her all day; and Tommy must not know, not yet.

Joe, however, was full of his own concerns. 'Mr Faber's sent Anthony to the Quarter Sessions.'

117

'That's bad,' she said.

'Maybe. Anyway, he's out on bail now. We stood surety for him. It's only till October, and he'll not let us down. We couldn't let them shut him up in Durham gaol.' He smiled, a little grimly. 'The worst is, he has to keep his hands off Joseph Dawson till then. He'll take that hard, the way things are.' He went to the fire and peered into the pot keeping hot over the glowing peats. 'That smells good.'

Jenny went to spoon some of the broth into a bowl and set it before him on the table. She sat down facing him, but it was not until he had taken a few mouthfuls that he realized there was something odd about her silence and her expression. He laid down his spoon. 'What's up, Jenny?'

Now that the moment had come she found it very difficult to tell him; yet it was simple enough. She sat gazing at Joe, watching the increasing puzzlement on his face, wondering how to begin, and in the end simply blurted out, 'Mr Selby wants to wed me.'

She had not been sure how Joe would react to her news, though she had supposed that as her brother, who loved her, he could be expected to desire her happiness. What she had not anticipated at all was what happened, for he threw back his head and began to laugh, and did not stop for a very long time, so overcome was he by the humour of the situation. She watched him, angry and dismayed, and when it seemed as if he would go on for ever she sprang to her feet and began to shout, 'Joe, no! Give over!'

He stopped laughing, as far as he was able, though his shoulders quivered still, and he was rubbing eyes full of tears. He shook his head. 'Why, I'm sorry, Jenny, but it's comical, you must agree – that fine finicky gentleman, falling for you! I've heard nowt like it in all my life! Why, Jenny, is he very lovesick?'

She was hurt, all her happiness lost in the tight knot of angry apprehension inside her. 'You haven't asked what I answered him,' she said quietly; and now she was afraid, not of laughter, but of something much more threatening to her happiness.

And indeed the laughter left his face, warned away by her gravity. 'What could you answer?' he demanded, but he too

118

was clearly fearful now. He got to his feet and came and stood close to her, where he could look easily into her face.

She told him, her voice very quiet and matter of fact. 'I said yes. We're to be wed, just as soon as he has a place of his own.' And she knew that she had been right to fear for her happiness, for if Joe would not share it with her then it could not be complete; and he was staring at her with a look of appalled disbelief. Worse, she could see with unmistakable clarity the rejection in his eyes, not just of what she said, but of the person who could admit to such a thing.

'Billy's scarce been dead a year.'

It was an accusation, of the very worst kind, for it pointed the finger not at the ridiculous nature of her admission, but at her faithlessness, her betrayal, of her love and his friendship.

'Do you think he'd have wanted me to grieve for him all my life?'

'Fourteen months is little enough to ask. And at the end of it, to give yourself to him – to yon –!' He made a fierce angry gesture with his hand and swung round and walked away, as if to stay any longer with his sister was more than he could bear. He went outside, banging the door behind him. Jenny, listening to the sound of his feet clattering away down the track, began to shiver. He will come round, she told herself. He will get to know Edward, and care for him too. He will accept it, soon enough, given time. But she had an ominous sense that she was deluding herself, that this betrayal was something so fundamental that he would never bring himself to forgive her.

Joe called for Ralph and Ralph's Joe on his way along the road the next morning. The other two men were in a cheerful frame of mind, but it was clear to both of them that Joe did not share their good humour. Ralph glanced at him once or twice, but made no comment, guessing he would give nothing away while his cousin was there; otherwise he would already have spoken.

He cheered up once they reached the office at Newhouse and stood before Mr Crawhall's desk, all four of them (this was too important to be left in Ralph's hands alone, as it usually was), and heard the agent agree that Tommy's find looked promising and that they should make a trial of it.

'It looks as though there may be a fair quantity of ore near the surface. But I think it worth sinking a shaft to see if there's any great depth to it. It may even be possible to cut across from Middlehope old level, if it proves rich enough. But even if you find it amounts to nothing much, you should be able to raise sufficient ore to make it worth your while. I think we can see our way to offering twenty eight shillings per bing of dressed ore.'

'That's for a year, taking a tack on it?' Ralph returned, in the tone of one checking something of which he was already certain.

They saw the agent glance at the other two officials present. 'Indeed no; a quarterly bargain on the usual terms. A year's agreement is only desirable where extensive dead work is at issue, and likely to take as long to complete.'

'But it's our find. We've a right to a tack on it – a year at least, to work as we please. At thirty shillings a bing, we thought.'

'I acknowledge that so it has often been done in the past –'

'Always!' Ralph put in with impatient emphasis.

George Crawhall smiled faintly, indicating that (in the circumstances) he would overlook his employee's vehemence. 'I think you would find that it is some years since any partnership took a tack to work any ground in Weardale. I must also point out that the vein in question is not far from existing workings and almost certainly connected to them.'

'You can't be sure!'

'No, and for that reason, and taking into account all the circumstances, we are prepared to offer you terms that differ in some degree from what is customary. For this quarter, you shall have sole right to work the ground in question, and I undertake further that you shall have first refusal on any subsequent bargains there, for a year at least. But in other respects we must insist upon the usual quarterly agreement.'

There was a long silence. Ralph chewed at his lip, frowning a little. His partners watched him, hoping perhaps for some inspired intervention that would, after all, ensure them the terms they had hoped for. But before he could say

120

anything further, the agent added, 'My object lately has been to give employment in the mines to as many men as possible – you know what numbers there are without work in this district. If your find proves to be good, then I would wish to set on developing it with all speed, not have it tied up for a year or so with only yourselves working it, and that without the resources to develop it to its fullest extent. I am sure you see the force of my argument.'

It was, perhaps, the only argument that could have swayed them. After another pause, Ralph said, 'We'd want something for dead work.' His voice sounded dry and a little expressionless, inadequately concealing disappointment.

'I think not,' said George Crawhall. 'There should be no difficulty in sinking the shaft, and you will not be cutting levels or the like at this stage, nor should there be any difficulties of drainage so near the surface. Come now, if the vein proves good, then you will raise the ore with no trouble – and we agree that seems likely. But we all risk losing something if we are wrong. After all, you will still have your subsistence money, even if you make nothing. That seems fair to me. We take an equal share of the risk.'

Joe would have pointed out, sharply, that the risks were not at all equal, for if their trial proved worthless George Crawhall would still have his job and his salary; Colonel and Mrs Beaumont the income from their other mines to maintain them in luxury; the Bishop of Durham his ninth part of every bing of ore raised in all the dale's mines, and the rector of Stanhope his tithe; but Ralph Emerson's partnership would have nothing at the year's end, nothing but the monthly thirty shillings lent money, which was quite inadequate to keep a man and his family. But it was Ralph and not Joe who was speaking for them, and Ralph, knowing what was at stake (as Joe did too, under all his anger), said only, 'If you offered thirty five shillings a bing, that might answer.'

They waited in silence, holding their breaths, while the agent thought about it. He must know, as Ralph's partners did too, that by assuring them of their right to the ground he had denied himself the usual bargaining tool – to threaten to offer it elsewhere if they would not take it on his terms. They

121

might have been disappointed in their expectations, but they were still in a very strong position. 'Very well,' said Crawhall at last. 'You shall have the top price – thirty five shillings. But with no payment for dead work; except that, should you subsequently find difficulties of a kind we have none of us anticipated, then I may reconsider the matter.'

They looked at one another. Ralph saw agreement, a little grudging but clear enough all the same, in their expressions. He turned back to the agent. 'We accept.'

Mr Crawhall pulled the large leather bound bargain book towards him and opened it and entered their names in the left hand column, and the details of their bargain alongside.

Ralph Emerson and 3 partners agree to sink a shaft two fathoms north eastward of the head of Middlehope burn, and to raise ore at thirty five shillings per bing, till 30 Sept next.

Then all four men in the partnership signed the agreement, George Lowes with a cross, since he had never learned to write, and the clerk made a copy of it for them to keep, and then they left the office. Once outside the door, George said brightly, 'It's better than I thought we'd get, to start with – and if it turns out as we think, we'll still do well out of it.'

They agreed, cheered by the thought, and went across the road to Short Thorns to drink to the future. But at the door Joe suddenly halted and said, 'I'm in no mood for drinking. I'm away home.'

He was well up the hill when Ralph caught up with him.

'What's eating you, lad?'

'Nowt,' said Joe, without looking at him, and they walked on in silence for a little while. Ralph had begun to think he had been unwise to come after his nephew, when Joe turned round and asked abruptly, 'Have I any say who Jenny weds? By law, I mean.'

Ralph stood still, and Joe halted too, facing him. 'So that's it,' said Ralph. 'I saw you had something on your mind. Who is he then?'

'I can't let on. They want it kept quiet.'

'But you're not best pleased with him?'

'I –' he broke off, clearly unable to express what he felt;

122

not, at least, without giving everything away. 'Have I a right to stop it then? Seeing as father's dead.'

Ralph sighed. 'Why, I don't know, lad. I'm not skilled in law. It may be you've a right. But – think it over well first. You don't want to make an enemy of your own sister.'

'So I stand back and do nowt? Let her throw herself away on yon – yon . . .!'

Ralph shook his head. 'If he's that bad, of course not. But if it's just that he's not to your taste, why, that's another thing.' He hesitated, then said quietly, 'Did it make Eve Todd think the less of you that her father opposed you? At least, before . . .'

The memory of it struck Joe like a blow; he even flinched, visibly. Then he swung round and began to walk on, fast and in anger. 'Damn her and him, damn them all!' Ralph was not sure who precisely he was cursing, but he did not attempt to catch up with his nephew. He knew his limitations, and Joe with anger in him had the strength of giants. Ralph walked on slowly, wondering who could possibly have asked for his niece in marriage. It was usually well enough known who was following whom, but he had heard no coupling of Jenny's name with anyone, not since Billy died.

Jenny walked along the road, seeing nothing of the sunlit landscape about her. What was it Joe had said to her when he sat at breakfast this morning, just before Tommy came down? 'Jenny, tell me it's not true! Tell me it was just a bad dream!'

He had been wholly in earnest, she had realized. And for a moment, facing him, she had almost believed he was right, and that it had all been a dream. It seemed so extraordinary, so unreal, so very unlikely. It seemed to bear no relation to anything else in her life, now or at any other time. She did not at that moment believe that anything could change, that life would ever be any different. Perhaps she had dreamed it, perhaps she had wished for it so much that she had convinced herself it had really happened – except that it had never occurred to her even to wish for such an amazing thing to happen to her.

Now, descending the hill, she thought back to yesterday,

to Mr Selby (must she learn to call him Edward?) facing her in the heat outside the house, and the overwhelming sense of wonder and happiness that had filled her as she had realized he meant every word he said; that this beautiful, godlike young man did indeed wish for nothing less than that she should be his wife. She had faltered, said, 'What of Joe, and Tommy? They need me ...'

And he had said, 'They shall have you a little longer, for we cannot be married until I have been ordained priest. But as soon as I am presented to a living, by this time next year, I hope, then ...' He had broken off, leaving her to fill in the amazing conclusion, before going on, 'By then is it not possible that your brother will have found himself a wife? If so, then I am sure he will be glad to have the house to himself.' She had thought that very likely, for Joe was already past the age when most lead miners married. Now that Eve was lost to him, he showed every sign of looking elsewhere, though so far with little enthusiasm.

'Jane, I need you more than your brothers ever could,' Edward had continued, his voice very soft, his eyes imploring (*he* needed *her*!). 'I do not think I can endure life without you.' And then he had reached out and taken her hands in his, and she had been lost.

'Yes,' she had said. 'Yes, I'll marry you.'

After that he had drawn her into his arms, as he had on the day of the Pay, but it had been nothing like that, nothing at all, for he had kissed her, uncertainly at first and then with real passion, and she had responded with her whole self, and felt the life so long subdued by her grief return to her body, flowing through it, demanding to be satisfied. Her only disappointment had been that he had brought it all to an end far too soon, almost it seemed before it had begun, and that he had then been very correct, rather cool, as if trying hard to control his feelings. But she knew now what lay beneath that cool exterior, and looked forward to discovering more of it as time went by.

'It must be our secret for the time being,' he had said, to her great disappointment, and only considerable persuasion – and her firm assurance that Joe could be trusted with their secret – had made him concede that she should tell her brother.

124

And then Joe had thrown her happiness back in her face. She felt a surge of anger, sending her feet moving faster. What did Joe want, to tie her to Billy's grave for ever? To force her to go on suffering endlessly, to mourn Billy to the end of her days, while she watched her brothers sicken and die as her father had done? To go on carrying all the burdens on her shoulders, more and more of them, until she was left alone at last, a widow in all but name, in a land of widows; widows and children and young men who would never grow old? Why should she not live? Why should she not have someone to care for her and cherish her? Why should she not love again, and hope, and look forward to a future of living and loving and hoping? Why should she not escape from this place if she chose, and go with the man she loved to wherever he bade her go, and bear his children and watch them grow, with him at her side, her strength and support, into an old age of comfort and security? If Joe wanted to go on living here, to shut his eyes to what lay ahead, that was his choice. But she could not do it, because the future haunted her at every step. She could feel its grip tightening daily about her and knew that if she did not break free now she would never escape, for there would never be another chance like this.

This morning, as she hurried down the steep path to the village, she had no very clear thought as to where she was going, except that she wanted to get away from White Lea, to think over what had happened, to try and rediscover a happiness jarred and splintered by Joe's anger. She would go and see Tabitha Hall perhaps. She wanted the old woman's consolation, and she knew Tabitha would understand, for she always understood ... But no, because to talk to her in her present troubled state of mind, without being able to tell her of that trouble, would be hard indeed.

Instead, she found herself turning aside into the churchyard and making her way to the grave, already grass grown, where Billy's body had been laid to rest on a cold wet March day last year. She stood looking down at the simple grey headstone.

What would Billy have said? It was impossible to imagine, because if Billy had lived she would not be where she was now, thinking of Edward's strange proposal. Billy had never

125

proposed marriage, not in any formal sense. From the first moment they met they had both assumed, without need for words or decision, that they would marry one day. It had been in the autumn that Billy had said, 'I've got a bit land up at East Blackdene. Enough for a house and a cow or two. I'll start building this weekend.' Then, a few weeks later, he had said, 'I should have enough for the ring, at the Pay.' She had not questioned his decisiveness, or resented it, for she had taken him for granted as much as he had her. Their love had seemed a safe and solid thing, something that was meant to last for ever. So she had thought.

It had been a delusion, that sense of permanence in her love for Billy. But with Edward it was different. As far as anything in life was certain – and she knew nothing could be – he would keep her from harm, protect her from hurt. She would have his love with her through all her days, and the comforts (unknown, scarcely imagined) that he could offer her, in that world beyond the dale which she had never seen.

She became aware of someone coming towards her across the grass, and looked round to see that it was Edward himself. She glanced quickly about to see if anyone was watching, and then thought how foolish that was, for what was more natural, more seemly, than that the curate should offer comfort to a bereaved girl standing at her lover's grave?

And he did bring comfort, just by his coming. All at once she realized how lovely a day it was, how green was the grass under their feet, how delicate the flowers that scattered it, how bright the sky; and all their loveliness seemed somehow to radiate from his tall, golden presence, from the tender smile with which he greeted her, from the hands, warm and fine, that clasped hers. 'You look sad, my dearest Jane. What is it? I hoped I had charmed away all your sorrowful memories.'

So she had imagined nothing, dreamed nothing; it was all real. *My dearest Jane.* How soft his voice was, how warm and tender! She smiled. How could she be sad, when he looked at her like that?

'Did you tell your brother?'

He guessed then, with that sensitivity of his to her most anguished thoughts. 'Aye. He didn't much like it.' The

126

inadequacy of the explanation troubled her, but she could not find words to describe Joe's reaction, not words fit for Edward's ears.

She did not need to find them. He held her hands more firmly, looked into her eyes, all loving compassion. 'I think I understand. They were friends.' He gestured towards the grave. 'Perhaps it seems to him to be in the nature of a betrayal. It is not, after all, so very long.'

'Do you think it's too soon?' she broke in anxiously.

'No, my darling, of course not, if you do not. Love cannot be bound by rules. But be kind to your brother, and understanding. And I will endeavour to do the same. As yet we scarcely know one another, he and I, and that must be rectified. We will win him round, in time. We have time, remember.'

She felt happiness taking up its place again in her heart, firm and strong; its rightful place, with Edward at her side. She smiled up at him, and he said, 'Love will find a way. That is an ancient truth, my dearest Jane.'

He could not stay with her, for he had a sick parishioner to visit, but he parted from her with great tenderness, leaving her feeling more loved and cared for than ever.

When he had gone she went to see Tabitha after all, for the shadow had been lifted from her spirits. She was still unable to tell Billy's mother what had happened to her, but something must have shown on her face, for as she sat by the window facing the old woman across the table, Tabitha said, 'You look bonnier every time I see you.' Jenny smiled, wishing she could explain. 'It does me good to see you so,' the old woman went on. 'You've had a hard time of it this past year. But now –'

'It must be the sun,' said Jenny.

Tabitha scrutinized her so closely that Jenny thought she must inevitably read the truth in her happy face; but all she said was, 'I wish the sun would do as much for our Rowland. He has a poor look these days, since he went up to Guinea Grove. But then it'll soon be haytime.'

'Very soon, maybe two weeks early, at least,' Jenny agreed. 'I've never known the hay so far on, though it'll be a light enough crop this year, for want of rain.' She loved

127

haytime, the high point of the short Weardale summer, for then the mines closed and the miners toiled in the fields with their families, gathering in the hay crop against the winter, and it was as good as a holiday.

She was smiling at the thought, when Tabitha said suddenly, 'You're young yet, Jenny. Don't mourn Billy too long. To my mind it's time you had thoughts of some other lad.'

Jenny had no answer to that, except to smile and shake her head, in wonder rather than disagreement, though Tabitha did not know that.

'I'd like to see you with bairns, lass. It would be a bit like having Billy's young ones about me. Mind,' she went on, 'I'm getting greedy. I doubt I've weddings on the brain. Did you know – our Lancelot's started courting at last? He has his eye on Rodger Emerson's widow from Daddry Shield. A good name for our family, Emerson. He'll not hurry, mind. He's not exactly lovesick, but she was left well off, and she's still young enough for bairns ...'

Jenny looked at the lined dark face of Billy's mother, and thought that leaving her would be one of the hardest things about marrying Edward, almost as hard as leaving Tommy and Joe. In a way, she thought, Tabitha had taken the place of the mother she had never really known. *I shall come back to see her*, she thought. *I shall bring our children to her, for she will be a grandmother to them, in all but name.* She imagined how it would be, the happy return to Weardale, coming back to the joyful welcome of her friends, with Edward at her side and his children hanging on her arms.

7

M iss Georgiana Selby, tall, blonde and self assured, travelled north with her maid two weeks after receiving her brother's letter. She would have liked to have come sooner, but various family commitments (the gentry in their neighbourhood habitually marked the summer season with a series of balls, picnics and visits, for which Miss Selby's presence was indispensable) had made that impossible. Now, however, having refused two not very tempting invitations, with a proper show of regret – in her letter telling her brother of her plans she mentioned only the regret and not the lack of temptation – she found herself free to set out.

In wet weather, her brother had told her, the roads beyond Stanhope were often impassable, but the recent hot spell allowed the chaise in which Miss Selby travelled to proceed all the way to St John's Chapel, though with much jolting in the ruts and at the cost of great veils of dust, which swiftly coated even those within the vehicle, in spite of Miss Selby's forethought in closing the windows and enduring the excessive heat inevitable upon her action. As a consequence, too, she saw little of the countryside as they passed, for the windows were too dirtied, and the dust thrown up as they passed shut out the view.

She was the more delighted, then, when the chaise came to a halt and the door was opened by Edward, who handed her out into the sunny market place of the village. She looked round at the picturesque cottages – all of stone, many heather-thatched, others roofed with fine stone slabs; the handsome market cross, erected in celebration of an election victory twenty-eight years before, by no less a person than

Lord Byron's father-in-law; the sturdy but simple church; the goats and pigs and geese wandering at will over the little green, beside which rushed a swift stream; and, surrounding all, the high green hills, as romantic as any she had seen in more fashionable resorts. True, at the merest glance she could see no less than five inns or alehouses, bearing out what Edward had said of the habits of the population, and there were considerable odours of an unpleasant kind, hinting at inadequate drainage and rather too close proximity between human and animal living quarters, but then her brother had warned her how primitive the place was. It was just that she had not expected it to be charming as well.

'This is delightful, Edward,' she said, having planted a faint peck upon his cheek by way of greeting. 'You did not tell me: an unspoiled paradise.'

He gave her a rueful sideways look. 'Where "only man is vile",' he said. 'I have lost several illusions since I came here.'

'Ah, but perhaps you have gained some too,' she returned archly, and saw him colour (then she was right in that anyway, she thought). But the things she really wanted to say must wait until they were alone. She gave one last look round, commented on the fineness of the hills, and followed him into the parsonage (a respectable enough house, if small), her maid coming behind with the lighter bags, the coachman bringing the rest of the luggage.

She did not find herself alone with Edward until, rested and changed into a fresh muslin gown, she joined him in the dining room for dinner. Peggy served them with a curious tasting soup and then left them alone.

As soon as the door closed behind her, Georgiana laid down her spoon. 'Now, Edward, I must know – what is all this about?'

'All what?' he asked, with a look of innocence, belied by his rising colour.

'Don't tease, Edward. Your letter was full of the virtues of a certain nameless young lady of this parish, about whom you managed to write a great deal without enlightening me at all. What is more, there was no word about her in your letter to mama and papa. And I don't believe it was entirely a coincidence that you were so pressing in your invitation for

130

me to come. You want me to meet her – that's it, isn't it?'

Edward paused to take a spoonful of soup. 'Yes, there is something in what you say,' he admitted carefully.

'Which means, I suggest, that your interest in her is of the warmest kind. Is that not so?'

He coloured still further, and then, as if abruptly bringing himself to a point of decision, he too laid down his spoon and then linked his hands round his plate, looking his sister straight in the eye. 'Georgiana, I have not been quite open with you, still less with our parents. I – Miss Emerson has done me the honour of accepting my hand in marriage.'

Georgiana was too well bred to whistle, but she came as near to doing so as refinement would allow. 'Edward! So your heart was indeed touched! But to do so –'

'I know. I know I should have spoken to our parents first, to appraise them of my intentions. I know that, failing that, I should have informed them the moment it was decided. But it is not yet made public, of course. It is just between ourselves, and Miss Emerson's elder brother.' He caught her eye and smiled ruefully. 'It all happened so suddenly, without forethought.'

His sister looked a little anxious, and reached across and laid her hand on his. 'Edward, are you sure that she is the right one?'

'Oh yes, entirely sure, as sure as I have ever been of anything in my life.' He coloured again. 'This is nothing like – well, that other unfortunate business. I am astonished now that I could have been so foolish, so green. I had only to see Miss Emerson to know how deluded I had been. From the first – almost from the first – I have known the nature of my feelings for her, and they have left no room for doubt. That is why I did not pause for thought, because there was no need. And – she is no conventional young lady. I could not approach her as I would have done had she – if she were ...'

Georgiana's eyes sparkled with interest. 'Tell me, what is she like? ... Emerson, you say her name is? Is she perhaps connected with the Lincolnshire Emersons?'

'Not so far as I know,' returned Edward carefully. He wondered whether to hint at a link with the only well-to-do Emersons he knew of in Weardale, but that would be less than ingenuous, and besides Georgiana would be sure to find him out. He did not, however, add that Emerson, like Peart, was one of the most common surnames in the dale.

'Of course, you told me that there were no families of our class in the parish; more than once you complained of it. I take it then that she is – well, what kind of young lady is she?'

'She is a – farmer's – daughter.'

'Ah, the bucolic paradise! Yes, I remember you referred to her as an unspoiled child of nature. Then there are some farmers of substance in this area? I imagined from what you said that they were all lead miners.' Her tone had a faint note of amusement.

'Many lead miners are farmers too, and in many cases one member of a family will do one thing, one another.'

Georgiana digested the information, and then said slowly, 'Edward, I do hope you have not been very foolish.'

He smiled happily. 'No man is ever wise in love. But for all that, I know this is right.'

'You had better tell me more about her.'

With the same reflective smile upon his face, Edward tried to convey to his sister something of his sweet inner vision. 'She is not tall; fair of skin, fresh complexioned, healthy yet not lumpish. I have seen many less graceful in a country ballroom, but she has none of the affectation you would see there. Her eyes – they are grey, very fine. She has suffered great grief. There was a young man who died, a short while before they were to have been married; her father passed away soon after I came. Yet she is young still, virtuous, unspoiled by all that has happened. Her name is Jane, Miss Jane Emerson.'

Georgiana gazed at him in silence for a little while, and her expression did not, he thought, suggest that she yet saw his future bride with his eyes.

'Jane ...' she said slowly at last, as if trying to remember what the name brought to mind. 'My maid is called Jane.'

'And we have a cousin Jane,' Edward reminded her with a trace of impatience. 'What of it?'

She looked at him. 'Nothing – merely a passing thought, that is all.'

132

'You will like her, I know you will. She has some education, you know. She can read and write –' Perhaps he realized what he was saying almost as he said it, for he broke off then, wincing at the look of disdain on his sister's face.

'Good heavens, Edward, what kind of young woman is she, that you can count it in her favour that she is not illiterate?' She shook her head with obvious alarm. 'Oh, Edward, what have you done?'

'I have followed the dictates of my heart,' he returned calmly, and then he closed his hands about hers. 'Georgiana, you will love her the moment you see her; I know you will.'

As they walked up the hill to White Lea next morning to call on Jenny (Georgiana insisted on going on foot), Miss Selby stopped often to look back the way they had come and exclaim with pleasure at what she saw.

Haytime was nearly at an end, accomplished in half the usual time because the weather had held so long. Everywhere, wherever they looked, the little fields were full of men, women and children at work in the sun, turning the hay, leading it to the byres, singing as they worked. The bright, hot, grass-scented air seemed to vibrate with songs and laughter. With so much to draw the eye away, it was easier to overlook the scarring of the landscape that, up here above the dale, was so marked a feature of every slope and hollow.

'It puts me in mind of Dr Johnson's Happy Valley,' said Georgiana. 'Oh, Edward, this is charming!'

He said nothing, hoping only that she would say the same when they reached White Lea. He told himself he was quite sure that she would.

They were turning the hay at White Lea, Jenny and Joe and Tommy, working their way steadily across the field. But they had seen the approaching visitors, that was clear. Edward saw Joe halt, and call to the others, and then they all looked along the road; and then Joe flung his fork aside and marched off the field, soon disappearing behind the house. A little later Edward saw him walking briskly up on to the fell.

He had mixed feelings on the subject. He had been a little apprehensive about how Joe would behave towards Georgiana, or (more problematic still) what Georgiana

133

would make of that uncouth young man. On the other hand, he regretted Joe's flight, for once again his determination to make friends with Jenny's difficult brother had foundered on Joe's greater determination not to be won over. Whenever Edward called at White Lea, Joe would refuse to speak to him and leave the place at the earliest opportunity. On the day they had begun mowing, Edward had walked up to White Lea and offered his services in the hayfield. On that occasion Joe had stayed long enough to say bluntly, 'We don't need help from the likes of you,' before going back to his work, his scythe swinging ferociously through the grass. Jenny had apologized for her brother, but she had not been able to move him, so Edward had missed the pleasure of working alongside her in the fields.

Now, as they turned up towards the house, Jenny came to meet them, Tommy following. The boy looked quite present-able, a healthy country lad, tall for his age and strong limbed, with loose curls clustered about his flushed face, and eyes that were enquiring without being unduly hostile. As for his Jane, she looked enchanting, Edward thought; all rosy and pretty, with her hair agreeably dishevelled beneath her wide brimmed hat and her fair skin lightly freckled.

Edward took Georgiana's hand and drew her forward. 'Georgiana, may I make Miss Emerson known to you? Jane, this is my sister, Miss Selby.' His manner and his voice expressed his hope – no, his certainty – that they would soon be friends.

Jenny stepped forward, smiling; and then came to a halt. Cold eyes – like Edward's, yet how unlike! – looked her up and down, glittering with critical appraisal. Jenny might not be familiar with the ways of fine ladies, but she knew dis-approval when she saw it, and there was no mistaking the nature of the cool greeting that followed. 'How do you do, Miss Emerson.' A languid hand was extended towards her, just touching the tips of her fingers as she reached out to clasp it, and then hastily drawn back again.

Jenny was only momentarily daunted by the coldness of the greeting. In an odd way, it made her feel somehow closer than ever to Edward. They might be separated by class and breeding and education and every experience almost that

134

they had ever known, but in this they were alike; they each had to contend with the disapproval of someone close to them. Jenny had Joe, Edward had Georgiana, a much loved brother and sister whose opposition had somehow to be overcome.

But it appeared that, whatever her feelings on the subject, Edward's sister was at least willing to try and break down the barriers. She looked about her and then turned to her brother and said eagerly, 'Oh Edward, may we help with the hay? I should so much enjoy it!'

'I am quite sure Miss Emerson and young Tommy will be only too happy for us to give them our assistance,' Edward said, trying not to notice the look of surprise and suspicion on the boy's face.

Before long, forks had been found for them and they were following Jenny and Tommy over the field, watching how to turn the hay so that the last of it should dry in the sun. 'We should be leading tomorrow,' Jenny said, and then had to explain that the expression meant that they would take the hay on a sledge to the hay loft at the western end of the farmhouse.

Jenny had to concede that Edward's sister worked hard and learned quickly. By midday the work was finished, and – at Georgiana's request – Jenny brought bread and cheese and ale out to them in the field, so that they could eat under the trees. Georgiana, tackling the sour rye bread with great self control, made a determined effort to engage her in conversation, though Jenny was not deceived by the careful politeness of her tone into thinking that her hostility had in any way diminished. She was quite kind too, in a lofty way, to Tommy, though to Jenny's dismay the boy became almost as sullen as Joe, as if he had unwittingly taken his cue from his older brother. He even, once, used one of the more colourful words learned on the washing floor, though to Jenny's relief (she looked sharply at the faces of her guests) neither Edward nor his sister seemed to have recognized it for what it was.

Later, when the curate and Miss Selby had gone, Jenny said to Tommy, 'You should have been more friendly, Tommy. They were kind to you.'

135

Tommy looked at her with some resentment. 'I don't know what they want with us. I liked it better without them.'

Over supper that night, Edward said to his sister, 'You see, she is charming, as I told you. I think you saw it yourself today, did you not?'

Georgiana nodded gravely, 'Oh yes, she is charming enough, in her quaint country way. As you say, a fresh little country girl, and as such I found her company agreeable. But as a sister-in-law . . . that is quite another matter.'

Edward was clearly disappointed, but he consoled himself with her limited approval. 'It's a beginning,' he said. 'I am sure you will come to think differently.'

'I think it more likely that you will,' his sister retorted.

On Saturday, Georgiana – who showed a lively curiosity about local life, even an enthusiasm for it, at least in so far as she was not expected to make it a part of her own – insisted on inspecting the market. She found great amusement in watching the buyers and sellers haggling with earthy vigour over the goods, and in listening to their gossip. Unlike Edward, she had a quick ear for dialect, and that evening planned to make her brother laugh with her accurate mimicry of certain members of his flock on market day.

She was not, however, so impressed with the market itself. Seeing Jenny standing lost in thought before a row of sacks containing various kinds of cereal, she went over to her. 'I must confess to some disappointment, Miss Emerson,' she said, the first greetings over. 'I have travelled a good deal and sampled many a market, but of them all this must be the most ill-supplied. Even our little market at home has more to offer, in variety of produce – and quality too. I have to admit, I should not like to have to depend upon what I see here today for my sustenance.'

Unlike Georgiana, Jenny had been impressed by the quality of the cereals displayed for sale this morning. Usually she went to the mill for oats and rye, but it was never so good as this. It was, however, much less expensive, and the miller always allowed credit, and Jenny was in no position, with prices rising so fast, to be particular about its quality. As she

136

turned regretfully away from this morning's tempting display, she was not inclined to respond kindly to her companion's criticism. 'You can afford not to,' she said, with a sharpness she would normally have avoided.

All the same, she was a little disappointed that it did not appear to trouble Georgiana. 'Really?' Edward's sister said. 'I understood from Mr Crawhall that many miners have quite a substantial income, worthy of comparison with any in the land – among the labouring classes, that is.' She and Edward had dined at Newhouse the previous day and, as was her custom, she had set out to inform herself as far as she could of local conditions. Then she said, before Jenny could reply, 'But do not let us dwell on such sordid matters. Pray tell me, have you ever seen inside a lead mine? You must have done, I suppose, though I understand them to differ from coal mines in having no women employed underground.'

'No,' said Jenny quietly, curbing her fury at the studied insolence of the tone. 'I've never been into a mine more than a little way.' Then she saw Tabitha coming into the market place from the lane. 'There's someone I must see,' she said, and smiled politely and went on her way. Georgiana might not openly have insulted her, but Jenny knew quite well that every remark had been barbed. Perhaps, after all, Joe's outright rudeness was to be preferred, though it was not easy to see how either of them could be overcome.

Tabitha smiled at her scowling countenance. 'Has she been trying to put you down, lass? Pay no heed.' Evidently she had seen who Jenny had been talking to.

Jenny's face lightened. 'She means to be kind,' she said, not believing it at all.

'I heard she was up at White Lea the other day,' Tabitha went on casually. Her expression was, Jenny thought, faintly disapproving.

'Aye,' said Jenny. 'She wanted to see how she liked haymaking.'

'And how did she?'

'She made a canny hand at it,' Jenny admitted. Then she added, 'I think Mr Selby felt she might want company of someone her own age, a lass, I mean.'

'Aye, well, she's a long way from home, I suppose,' said

137

Tabitha. She looked across at the tall figure observing the market from her vantage point in the shade of the market cross. 'A bonny enough lass, if she didn't look down her nose so,' she observed. Jenny giggled, feeling better at once and wondering how Miss Selby would like to be so described.

Since her engagement to Edward, Jenny had begun to attend Sunday morning service at the church, a little self-consciously, though she knew that it would merely be assumed in the village that she was responding gratefully to the curate's ministrations to her, following her father's death. Edward had said nothing to her on the subject, and she still had little idea what marriage to him would mean for her, but of one thing she was quite clear: she would certainly be expected to share his religious beliefs and attend church as regularly as he did. It seemed as well to get into practice at once, even if it meant braving Joe's sarcastic comments whenever she made ready to come out on Sunday morning.

She had been very nervous on the first occasion. She had rarely been inside the church, except for the occasional baptism and only too frequent funerals, and she felt very strange and out of place. She did know, however, that most of the pews in the nave belonged to the more well-to-do among the churchgoers in the district, even if few of them chose to occupy them with any regularity, so she crept up the stairs to the furthest corner of the gallery, hoping that the musicians would be too occupied with their playing to take much notice of her. Her position did at least have the advantage of a good view of what went on, without exposing her to the critical gaze of those who sat below.

In fact she had found, a little to her surprise, that she rather enjoyed the services. The ordered words had a certain pleasing charm, their sound and rhythm like an old song, and the stately yet vigorous playing of the band gave body to the thin singing of the sparse congregation. But of course it was Edward above all who filled her thoughts and brought a deeper significance to everything that happened within those solid walls. Here he was at home, in his own sphere, the focus, the master, of all that took place. She loved to watch

138

what he did, with such simple unhurried assurance, at each
stage of the service, loved to hear his fine deep voice intoning
the prayers, reading the lessons with such grave dignity,
admonishing the congregation from the pulpit. She did not
take in much of what he said, for she was too wrapped up in
watching with delight the gracefulness of his gestures, the
poise of his head, the perfection of his profile, and smaller
things too, like the spotless freshness of the linen at his wrists
and throat, the gleam of the signet ring against the long slim
fingers of his right hand. Sometimes, during the sermon, she
would catch his eye, and see him colour a little and stumble
over the words. He always controlled himself quickly afterwards, but it delighted her that he should love her so much.
She would feast her eyes upon him and think, *He has chosen
me; out of all the women he has ever met in all the world, he
has chosen me.* It was a thought that sometimes went to her
head like wine, making her feel that she could do anything,
overcome any difficulty.

At the end of the service she always lingered as long as she
could, trying to leave last of all, in the hope that they might
be able to talk unobserved for a little while. But of course on
the Sunday after Miss Selby's arrival, Edward was not alone
when she reached the porch. She felt disappointed, but only
for a moment, for Georgiana welcomed her with a greeting
that was warmer than usual and then said, 'We should so
much like you to come and take tea with us tomorrow.
About three perhaps.'

It was as well, Jenny thought the next afternoon, that work
had started again in the mines today, and that neither Joe nor
Tommy would be there, when she left the house, to ask
where she was going. She dressed with care, putting on her
very best flowered print cotton gown, draping a fresh white
shawl over it, slipping on the neat buckled shoes, hardly ever
worn, which felt so odd and light to feet used to clogs. Then,
her heart beating fast, she made her way down the hill
towards the village.

She had never been in the parsonage before, and it seemed
vast and rather frightening, the rooms inside so high
ceilinged, so polished and elegantly furnished that she was

139

daunted by them – with reason, for the hour that followed was, socially speaking, the most uncomfortable of her life.

She sat perched on the edge of one of the parlour chairs, fearful of relaxing in case she should look clumsy or disrespectful, pausing always before she spoke, so as not to disgrace Edward with some incomprehensible piece of dialect (she had discovered he did not always understand everything she said). She sipped at her tea, spilling a little in the saucer in her embarrassment and then afraid to drink any more in case the liquid under the cup should splash over her gown or (worse) the upholstery of the chair, which, though a little worn in places, had clearly once been very fine. She was too nervous to eat any of the sandwiches or cakes presented to her with supercilious condescension by Miss Selby. She remembered very little of what was said for the first half hour or so, either by herself or anyone else, though she knew the conversation (if it could be called that) somehow made progress, in a painful and halting manner.

After a time Edward broke into a rather longer silence than usual to say brightly, 'Jane, you told me once you had never been inside a lead mine.'

'No,' she said, a little warily, remembering Saturday's brief, spiteful conversation with his sister.

'Then we have a treat in store for you. Tomorrow Mr Crawhall has agreed to take us all three on a tour of one of the mines. What do you say to that?'

She stared at him, hoping she had misunderstood him, but knowing she had not, wondering what on earth she could say in reply. She thought of these two comfortable, refined, well-dressed people walking into one of the many levels, and she with them, while they looked about with happy enquiring eyes, all agog at the entertaining prospect of observing the miners, her neighbours and friends, for all the world as if they were a sideshow at a fair – the two headed man, the bearded lady – not men like themselves working deep underground in darkness and discomfort and danger, hacking and blasting a living from the rock. She was appalled. The very thought of it made her shudder and feel cold. Yet Edward looked so pleased, as if he was quite sure that she would be delighted at what he proposed. After a time, when still she

140

said nothing, he looked puzzled. 'What's the matter, Jane? Is it not an excellent plan?'

She shook her head and struggled for words. 'I ... I cannot. Not like ... Please, Edward ...!' He frowned, and she only faltered the more.

For once Edward's sensitivity had failed her. He seemed quite unable to understand her reluctance. True, she was not able to explain her feelings to him in any coherent manner, but she had grown so used to his capacity to know how she felt without being told that this seemed the more remarkable. Worse, she knew he was displeased with her. He said, 'Perhaps you would consider that it is my wish that you should come,' with such severity that she felt chilled right through.

Desperate for any means of escape, Jenny said next, 'Why, if I go with you, then everyone will know – about us, I mean ...' But Edward's mouth only tightened the more; she had never seen him look like that before. She felt as if all her support, all her strength, were falling away from her, leaving her alone, without help. She knew she must have done wrong, for why else would Edward be displeased with her? Struggling to see it with his eyes, she thought she understood where her fault lay – her repugnance at the very thought of accompanying him down a mine was a weak and foolish thing, unworthy of the woman who was to be his wife. He was not being insensitive, simply asking of her what any man in his position would have asked. Yet try as she might she could not bring herself to agree to what he wanted.

'They will only suppose you have befriended my sister and have come to keep her company. What could be more natural?' Since Jenny, talking to Tabitha yesterday, had already encouraged such a view, she could not argue with it. But what then was she to do?

To her surprise, it was Miss Selby who came to the rescue. 'Edward, my dear brother, I think I understand Miss Emerson's feelings. After all, we shall be – how shall I put it? – distanced by our connections from what we shall see. In Miss Emerson's case that cannot be so. The miners are her own people, perhaps even kinsmen of hers. Come now, spare her this ordeal!' Georgiana might be quite right in what she said, but Jenny knew perfectly well that she did not mean her intervention in any kindly sense. It was not made on Jenny's behalf, but as a way of reminding her brother how very much beneath him Jenny was. Perhaps, too, she wanted to enjoy the proposed visit unencumbered by Jenny's presence. But, whatever her motives, Jenny could only be grateful to her. It did not much matter why Miss Selby had intervened; it was enough that she had.

Fortunately, Edward saw the force of her argument and relented. 'Then so be it,' he said. She knew he was still disappointed in her, not only about this, but also because of her failure to shine in the awkward social situation to which he had introduced her this afternoon. She determined that, at the earliest opportunity, she would take steps to learn how to conduct herself in polite society. It was, she suspected, one of the accomplishments that would be required of her after her marriage. She could even begin her education at once, by listening to, and observing, the way her companions behaved.

As a consequence of that decision, the afternoon did not after all end as badly as she had feared. She was even quite pleased with what she already felt to be an improvement in her self-assurance. When Miss Selby began – as she had done more than once before – to talk of a book that Jenny, naturally, had not read, she no longer remained silent, crushed by a sense of her own inadequacy. Instead, she questioned Miss Selby about the book, expressed an interest in it, and found herself very soon with a copy of it to take home and read. She felt almost as though she had scored a triumph of some kind.

Watching carefully, taking her cue from the others, she judged when the time had come for her to leave, and thanked them both as gracefully as she knew how, and rose to her feet.

Edward came, alone, to see her to the door; and there, before opening it, he took her hand and said, 'Dearest, forgive me if I caused you distress. I would not hurt you for the world.' When she smiled at him he kissed her, lightly but with great tenderness. She felt as if his protective love, momentarily withdrawn, had wrapped her round again like a shawl.

Back at White Lea, Joe was already home from work. 'Why, I'd have thought you too fine to come back to this poor house,' he greeted her, with heavy sarcasm, when she told him where she had been.

She tried to argue with him, but as usual he left the room as soon as she began to speak. Much later, after a silent supper, she heard him outside, talking to Tommy, his voice warm and animated. 'She's so easy, Tommy. Comes away in our hands, rich pure ore, with hardly need for dressing. When we make our fortune it'll all be your doing.'

Jenny knew then how completely Joe's anger had shut her out, as if she were now no more than a housekeeper, reluctantly tolerated as a regrettable necessity. It was at moments like this that she found it hard to keep alive her confidence that one day Joe would relent and welcome Edward as his brother-in-law. But then once she had left the dale behind her and made a new life, with Edward's help, in new surroundings, with new friendships about her and a new family to call her own, it would not matter what Joe thought. He would no longer have the power to hurt her.

It was not until Georgiana had been in Weardale for a week that Edward broached with his sister the real reason for his invitation to her to visit him. 'You must agree, our parents should not be kept in ignorance much longer. It is not right that it should have been kept from them so long already.'

'Certainly not. What do you want of me then? That I should find some tactful way of breaking it to them?' Her tone suggested that she thought that an impossible task.

Edward shook his head. 'No, no – that is my responsibility, of course. But I wish them to meet her.'

'Do you really believe that will help your cause?'

'Yes, I do,' returned Edward coolly. 'But you must see that it would not be proper for her to travel to Nottinghamshire all alone with me. Naturally she has no maid, nor has she any suitable female relation. I had hoped ...'

'That I would agree to chaperon her on the journey. I see.' She paused, studying his face. 'You know my feelings about the whole business. I hope – indeed I am convinced – that

143

you will see sense before it is too late. But meanwhile I suppose it is better that you take her to Ashfield than that you should not. It may help to make up your mind for you.'

'My mind is made up,' he retorted, and then added, 'But you will stay and travel with us both?'

In the end, it was Jenny who presented the chief obstacle to the projected visit to his parents.

'Why, I can't leave my brothers, not just now,' she said, when he told her. 'Tommy needs me – and who will see to the animals if I'm not there?'

'One day, dearest Jane,' said Edward, with commendable patience, 'they are going to have to learn to do without you.' If he was displeased, he was hiding it well. 'We should be away only a very short time. I have my duties to attend to here, remember ... And I do feel that we owe it to my parents to tell them of our betrothal.'

'Can you not write?'

'I can, but it would not be the same.'

She tried again. 'If I come away with you, why then everyone will know about us. It will not be a secret any more.'

'Naturally, but then it was only to be kept to ourselves until my parents had been told. Once we have seen them, then the world may know. We shall give a small party, perhaps,' he concluded thoughtfully. But she would not commit herself to come away with him, her only concession being that she would consider the matter.

Meanwhile, Edward seemed determined to wear Jenny down by the force of his love for her, inviting her two or three times a week to join him and his sister on expeditions and outings during which he took every opportunity of demonstrating his tenderness and consideration towards her, as far as the restrictions of his sister's presence would allow. Whenever Georgiana was sharp with her, he would intervene, rebuking her, sometimes quite severely, for her ill manners. Jenny was astonished at how little Georgiana seemed to resent her brother's behaviour, on the surface at least. But then neither brother nor sister seemed very ready to show anger or dislike in the open way she was used to.

Jenny, appealed to, had many suggestions for places to

see, none of them with the painful associations of the visit to the mine, about which Miss Selby had talked, pointedly, for some days after she and Edward had made their tour. There were the fairy holes near Stanhope, caves that riddled the hills, enchanting places, which had weird and frightening legends associated with them. Jenny told her companions of children spirited away by fairies, of feasting companies seen in the caves at night, only to vanish with the dawn. Miss Selby, hearing her, said wonderingly, 'I do declare you believe in fairies yourself, Miss Emerson!'

Jenny coloured a little at the mocking tone, and then returned steadily, 'All I know is, there are three children I know of, went missing one day and were never seen again, nor any trace of them found.' Then she pointed out some quite harmless natural feature, by way of changing the subject.

There were strange ruins of who knew what ancient dwellings, and tales of love and murder and ghosts and border raids to go with them, and ballads to be sung. There were waterfalls hidden in almost every cleft and gully of the dale, and the greatest fall of all, several adventurous miles over the moors in Teesdale: High Force, a cascade so magnificent, so awe inspiring, that even Miss Selby, confronted by it, was temporarily lost for words.

One evening early in August, Jenny made her way home up the hill path, walking a little awkwardly because she was stiff from riding. Used, like most Weardale girls, to riding the shaggy galloways astride like a man, she had been alarmed to find that Edward's sense of decorum confronted her with a sidesaddle – a precarious and uncomfortable affair, she had thought from the first, and no amount of familiarity with the thing had convinced her otherwise.

But, that apart, it had been a lovely day. For her companions such outings as this, undertaken purely for pleasure, were a normal part of summertime. For Jenny they were extraordinary, wonderful, something she thought she could never learn to take for granted, as they did. It was such a joy to leave behind all her cares and responsibilities, all the unpleasantness with which she was now surrounded at home, all the watchful eyes of neighbours and friends, and to ride in the sunshine (even on a sidesaddle), to eat food of a delicacy that would have been astonishing on the Christmas table at White Lea, spread on a cloth on the grass in the shade of trees, sometimes even with wine to wash it down; to feel that the whole day lay before them, in freedom and pure enjoyment. And almost always there would be some moment, however brief, when Georgina would wander off alone to inspect something she had seen in the distance, and Edward would seize the opportunity to put his arms about Jenny and kiss her. Somehow, out in the open, her desire for him was intensified almost beyond bearing; his for her too, she suspected. But he was always very correct, as of course he had to be, for all too soon his sister would return, full of something she had found, and the moment would be over. Jenny wondered sometimes if there would ever be a time when they would be alone together for long enough, without fear of interruption ... it had always seemed so easy with Billy.

She found herself longing suddenly for all this to be at an end – not the picnics and outings, of course, but the secrecy, the waiting for their marriage, the tactful distance between them. She wanted to marry Edward, to go away with him to their new home, to share his bed and conceive his children and give birth, and to live again, to the full. And she wanted it now.

She reached home rather later than she had intended; Joe was particularly unpleasant if she was not there when he returned from work. But to her surprise it was not Joe but Tommy who was sitting on the steps to the hay loft, watching for her return. He scrambled to his feet and came to meet her, and she anxiously scanned his face.

'What's up, Tommy?'

'We're laid off. Burn's dried up.'

She could not remember that happening before, ever. Even in the finest summer the burns would continue to run. But the long hot weeks without rain had been exceptional, and now it had happened. 'Then you'll have holiday till it rains,' she said cheerfully, while her mind grasped the realization that Tommy's small but useful wage would be lost to them, at this time when they needed every penny they could lay their hands on.

146

And then she realized that Tommy would be at home, for some indefinite period, with nothing to do but care for the animals and see that the essential tasks were done. For a short time at least they could manage without her at White Lea.

8

Jenny felt strange, unlike herself. It was not just the fine clothes, bought for her on Georgiana's advice in York, where they halted at the end of the first day's journey; or not them at all, perhaps, though they were so much in the height of fashion – the gowns so light and fine and high waisted – that she felt very self-conscious when she first stepped out in them. But she had worn fine clothes before, or fine by Weardale standards.

No, what was strange was to find herself wholly and exclusively in the company of people like Edward and his sister, who talked in prim, careful, polite voices, who never expressed anger, who always seemed to think before they said anything at all, and then to speak as if trying rather to conceal what they really felt and thought than to reveal it; who behaved in so many ways as her family and friends never did, with a gracious courtesy that from Edward alone had flattered and pleased her, but when it was all around her, in the confined space of a chaise, became tiresome, the more as she knew it was expected – assumed – that she would behave like that too.

There was, of course, one other traveller in the chaise who was much more like herself: Jane, Miss Selby's maid. But Edward and his sister treated the girl almost as if she were invisible, scarcely speaking to her except with a command or a request. When Jenny, distressed by such behaviour, tried to talk to the maid as she would have done to any neighbour at home (they were, after all, much of an age), she received a look of such chilly disdain from the girl's eyes that she did not dare to try it again. Quite clearly, different rules applied in this, as in everything else. She must simply resign herself to learning them, as quickly as possible. But it was all very unreal, and in a short time she had an overpowering headache, and wished she was safely back at home – or at the end of her journey, where she might hope, perhaps, for a little time to herself, in which to consider all the implications of this new life she had chosen.

They had left Weardale behind with astonishing speed, covering in two hours a distance greater than any she had travelled in her life before. Outside the chaise the hills had diminished and then disappeared altogether, giving way to a strange landscape of unrelieved flatness, or so it had seemed to Jenny's daleswoman's eyes. On the third day, leaving York and bowling south on the Great North Road, she felt as if she had left her home for ever, as if it was now so far away that she might never see it again. For a time there was a harsh constriction in her throat and she was swept by a wave of homesickness. If only, she thought, she could have been alone with Edward on this journey, then she might have felt better about it, even found pleasure in it.

But then she began to take an interest in the countryside through which they were passing, the inns at which they halted to change horses or eat or spend the fourth night of their journey, the landmarks that Edward and Georgiana, nearing home at last, pointed out to her as they went, and she felt happier. The land rushing by outside the chaise was less green than Weardale, for the sun here had a greater heat – like stepping into an oven, she thought, when she emerged briefly into it at one of the halts – and the leaves were already beginning to look tired, hinting at autumn. But in other ways it all had an overpowering richness. She had never seen so many trees – not only such a number, but so tall, so heavy with foliage, so luxuriant in their growth, so straight, as if no rough wind had ever stirred their branches, or snow made them bend beneath its weight. And there were great herds of cattle, fat, smooth-coated, red-and-white cattle, their udders heavy with milk; and vast cereal fields, their crops gathered now, but the stubble still golden where the corn had been. It was a land of hedges, not walls, of fruit trees glowing with ripening fruit. In the villages through which they passed the gardens were full of brilliantly coloured flowers, and everywhere there were not only women and children, but old men and middle-aged men in greater numbers than she had ever seen them before, working in the fields, driving carts, busy in workshops and yards, as alert and active as their womenfolk.

Then, on the last day, they rattled along a narrow winding road between neat hedges, and even Edward and Georgiana became excited and clamorous, pointing out people and places as they went, sharing memories (Edward remembered now and then to tell Jenny about them too), commenting on small changes. And then the chaise turned between high brick gateposts into a long straight drive lined with yet more of those luxuriant trees, so tall and wide that they met in a great green arch overhead; and came to a halt at last on a gravelled space before the front door of a mansion four times the size of Mr Crawhall's great house at Newhouse.

Jenny had known Edward came from a prosperous home. After all, he lived better, in more refined circumstances, than anyone else in Chapel. But she had somehow not expected anything so grand as this, the wide façade, three storeys high, the long graceful windows, the small pillared portico. 'Just an ordinary house', he had told her; but in Weardale it would have been a palace. She wondered that he did not realize it.

They went inside, and Edward's parents came to meet them. They greeted Jenny with the same cool politeness as Georgiana had shown, and then a maid led her up a wide staircase to what seemed to her a vast bedroom.

'Your room, miss,' said the girl. Then: 'Would you like me to stay and help you?'

Bemused, Jenny gazed around her. Help her? To do what? 'No thank you,' she said instinctively, and when the girl had gone stood where she was for some time longer, just inside the door, staring at the room. *Your room*, the girl had said, as if she had some sole and exclusive right to it. She had never before had a room that could be called her own, never to be shared with others, or given over to them completely when need arose. There was one upstairs room at White Lea, and otherwise the hay loft and the kitchen had to serve as sleeping quarters.

This room, on the other hand, was almost a dwelling in itself. As well as the pretty curtained bed (huge for one person), there was a dressing room with washstand and dressing table and long mirror, a massive wardrobe, a desk by the window, comfortable chairs and an elegant little sofa, and a fireplace on whose marble mantelpiece a gilt clock stood, the hearth below filled with a vase of roses, their heady scent pervading the room. Going to the long windows, hung with brocade, she found she was looking over a beautifully laid out garden, enclosed by trees through which she glimpsed a lake.

Her two small bags had been brought up with her. What should she do now? Unpack them, find places for her new clothes and the hairbrushes and other items (essential, so Georgiana had said) bought in York? And what then? What was expected of her? *Dinner will be served as soon as you are ready*, they had said, kindly enough. She was expected to go downstairs again then. But when? And should she change first? Perhaps the maid could have told her, but she had been sent away. There was a bell pull in the room (she supposed that was what it was), but she dared not presume to ring it.

She wished she knew where Georgiana's room was. Edward's sister might look down her nose when asked for advice, but at least she always gave it honestly when applied to. But in this huge house it might take her hours to find Georgiana, with all kinds of possibilities for embarrassment on the way. In the end she undressed to her new silk petticoat, washed a little at the porcelain bowl in the dressing room (there was a deliciously scented soap), and put on a gown of primrose silk with a lightly frilled hem, and what she hoped were suitable gloves. About her neck, she fastened Edward's first gift to her, bought on the way here, a necklace of clear stones that sparkled like the quartz on the hearth at White Lea ... *Finer than any rich man's jewels*, Billy had said ... She pinned up her hair with a satin ribbon and slid her feet into tiny satin slippers (she loved the feel of them, so soft and light that she wanted to dance), and then she made her way downstairs to the drawing room, a lofty ornate room into which she thought the whole of White Lea could have been dropped with space still to spare.

The family were assembled there, engaged in light conversation, and she was relieved to see that Georgiana too had

151

changed, into something not very different from her own gown. Nor had she kept them waiting. 'As soon as Arthur comes down we shall go in to dinner,' Mrs Selby said.

Studying them as they talked (fortunately with so many people in the room she did not have to say much herself), Jenny saw where Edward got his looks; the fairness was his mother's, the height and the fine profile his father's. But even so his parents surprised her. To have a son older than Edward they must be at least as old as her father had been, for he had been married young; yet, had she not known that, she would have taken them for ten, even fifteen, years younger than William Emerson. True, Mr Selby had white hair, but beneath it his face was plump and rosy, his eyes clear and bright. He had a look of health and vigour such as she could not remember ever having seen before in so old a man. His wife, too, had something of the same clean, well-cared-for look, though her complexion was pale enough, like her daughter's. But there was nothing careworn about her, no sign that she had lived long or suffered or borne children. At her age, a Weardale woman would have been old; but Mrs Selby was in the prime of life.

Jenny had a sudden clear recollection of the passage Joe had read to them last spring, on the night before their father died. She had not believed then – they none of them had – that the sufferings induced by riches were truly something for which the rich must be pitied. Now she was quite sure of it. What did these people know of suffering? If they were ill, they could afford the best physicians, the most tempting food, warmth and comfort, and strong medicines to ease their pain. If they worked hard, it was by using their minds and their pens, seated on comfortable chairs, with clear air coming in on fine days through wide windows that looked on to a gentle and pleasant landscape, without any blight of industry or toil upon it. If they were bereaved, their grief would not be made worse by want. It was not the discomforts of wealth that gave these people their look of vigour, after years that would have brought the average lead miner to his grave and his wife to exhausted widowhood.

'Edward tells us you come of a farming family, Miss Emerson. Have you much land?' The voice broke in on her

152

reflections, startling her. She thought of the vast acres of farmland she had seen from the carriage windows (*My father's land begins here*, Edward had said), and then of White Lea's three acres, with rights to peat and grazing on the fell; and then she looked Edward's mother straight in the eye and answered her question, candidly and without self-consciousness.

Edward's brother came in at last, a large young man, darker and more thick-set than Edward, with none of his grace or elegance and no trace of his beautiful manners. He looked Jenny up and down, said in a bored voice, 'How do you do, Miss Emerson?' and then ignored her for the rest of the evening. His wife, who was, they told Jenny, in a delicate condition, came down only after dinner, looking pale and languid and heavily pregnant, that being, Jenny supposed, what they meant by a 'delicate condition'. She paid even less attention to their guest than did her husband, but then if she was unwell, as Jenny supposed, perhaps she had some excuse.

It was a bewildering and uncomfortable evening, and it seemed interminable. Jenny's headache had returned long before it ended, and she was greatly relieved when the time came for her to retire to the vast bedroom and sink into the softness of the bed (already warmed for her, she noticed, even on this warm night) and lie listening to the strange silence of this place so far from home. This then, was the world beyond the dale, or a small corner of it at least, the corner which was to be hers ... As she drifted into sleep, she realized that there was no sound of water to be heard, from anywhere.

Georgiana went into her mother's room to say goodnight, and found herself steered at once to the sofa by the window, on which Mrs Selby sat beside her, clasping her arm with great earnestness. 'Georgiana, what do you think of all this? You've seen rather more of the girl than we have.'

'I have done my best to become acquainted with her,' said Georgiana carefully. Her mother pressed a hand to her forehead, as if her anxieties were threatening her with one of her headaches.

153

'Do you think he has thought what it will be like, to have such a young woman at his side throughout his ministry? How will she ever be able to receive his guests, or accompany him on visits? Has he given thought to these things at all?'

'I am afraid thought and reason have had nothing to do with it,' said Georgiana. 'He is simply besotted, and that is all there is to it.'

'And I thought, after that other unfortunate affair, he was settling down at last!' Mrs Selby sighed. 'He has learned nothing, it would seem. But at least the French girl was a lady, and quite enchanting, in her sly way. This business I find very hard to understand. Miss Emerson is pretty enough, I suppose, if you like those fresh country looks, and she has a fetching manner, unusual in someone of our class. But I imagine she is nothing out of the ordinary in her own setting.'

'I have no reason to suppose so. But there we are. Edward has lost his heart, and his head into the bargain, I am afraid. Perhaps you should say to him what you have just said to me. It might make him see sense.'

Mrs Selby shook her head. 'Your father and I feel it would be wiser to say nothing at all. If we express disapproval, I fear that may only make him the more determined to go through with it. Leave things alone, and he may see sense without any help from us. But it is very hard to watch and do nothing.'

'I suggest, then, that you arrange for them to go into society as much and as often as possible. He has only to see her floundering her way through visits to our neighbours to realize that it just won't do. And first of all, I suggest you call on the Stranges. You always thought he and Lydia might make a match of it. Put a creature of such obvious loveliness and accomplishment against little Jane Emerson, and he cannot help but be struck by the contrast.'

Her mother kissed her. 'My dear, how wise you are! That is an excellent notion. She must have a day to recover from the journey and find her feet – that is only kind – and then I shall do exactly that!'

Jenny opened the door and stood looking across the dale to Chapel Fell. It was a beautiful morning. The air was like

154

crystal, fresh and sweet and dazzlingly bright, full of the sound of running water. The breeze bent the meadow grass, so that it shone like silver.

Joe came into sight on the road, his fowling piece under his arm, the dog panting at his heels. There would be a bird for the pot today. She started to walk down to meet him, and he waved cheerfully. The dog saw her coming too, and ran up to her, tail wagging; then he barked, the noise sharp in the quiet morning –

It was not the dog. The noise came again, and it was quite a different sound, strange to her ears. She realized her eyes were closed, so she opened them. The maid had pulled back the curtains (that was what she had heard) and the sun came hot and heavy into the room to lie on the floor some distance from the foot of the bed. It was very quiet, except for the soft footfalls of the maid and the singing of a bird somewhere across the garden. There was a smell of chocolate and roses. She was a very long way from Chapel Fell, and the sweet fresh morning, and the sound of water.

She sat up, pushing aside the sudden sense of loss that had come with waking. There was a cup of hot chocolate on the bedside table. The maid said, 'Good morning, miss,' and then she was left alone, propped on pillows, warm and rested but still half asleep. She sipped at the drink, new to her, but delicious, and realized with a half guilty pleasure that at home she would by now have been up for hours. All the last traces of her dream vanished, to be replaced by happy anticipation, only a little tinged with apprehension. She looked forward to the coming day with a sense of adventure. It might hold many things that would be unfamiliar to her, embarrassing, perhaps even frightening, but she would, she decided, take each moment as it came, learning as quickly as she could from those around her.

She knew now that Miss Jane Emerson was someone quite different and distinct from Jenny of White Lea, less sure of herself perhaps, but capable of all kinds of behaviour that Jenny would have thought affected and a little ridiculous. She must learn, when necessary, to put aside her common sense and do what was expected of her; because it was, after all, Miss Emerson who was one day to become Mrs Edward

Selby, and as much a part of this strange new world as Georgiana or Arthur's wife or Edward's mother. Mrs Edward Selby would live what would seem to Jenny a life of idleness and luxury, waited upon by servants, watched over and protected, with no need ever to be anxious or burdened by cares; but the price she must pay was to become, with Edward's help, the kind of wife he wanted her to be.

So she accepted the maid's assistance, when it was offered to her again, even though that meant help with dressing, a somewhat disconcerting experience. Why, she wondered, was it assumed that *ladies* were incapable of doing for themselves what all the women she knew did every day as a matter of course? It was, she supposed, yet another of those unexplained oddities that she must learn to accept. The most uncomfortable part of it was to be waited on by a girl as much like herself as anyone at Ashfield, who was yet separated from her by a gulf that the unwritten rules of this place would not let her cross. It would be a long time, she thought, before she would grow used to that.

The first day went well, on the whole. Certainly she enjoyed it – as how could she not, when every aspect of life at Ashfield Hall seemed designed to shield its occupants from every difficulty and discomfort? She suspected that Edward's parents disapproved of her as much as Georgiana had done, but like everyone else they concealed their true feelings beneath a veneer of politeness.

Next day, at breakfast, she was faced with a new challenge. 'This morning,' said Mrs Selby, quite casually, 'we shall call on dear friends of ours. We should like you to make their acquaintance.'

Before they left, Jenny managed to seize a moment alone with Edward (not so easy to do, she had found, even in this great house with all its empty rooms). She confessed that she was terrified of the impending visit, and asked for his advice. 'Never fear, my dearest,' he reassured her. 'Just be yourself. What could be more charming?'

It was flattering, but not, she thought, particularly helpful; for who, after all, was 'herself'? Miss Emerson, who was so new to this world, or Jenny of White Lea, who could have no place in it at all?

156

*

Edward had mixed feelings as he sat among the chattering young ladies and watched how his beloved behaved. She looked enchanting, he thought, setting off the sprigged muslin and the pretty bonnet as delightfully as she did her simple country clothes at White Lea. But she was not quite his Jane. The fresh simplicity of her manner was not lost exactly, but she had suddenly acquired a store of little mannerisms he had not seen before, gestures and ways of speaking of a kind that any young lady learned at her mother's knee, ready for her first steps in society. Even her accent seemed to have diminished, though it was still suffi- ciently in evidence to give rise to an occasional raised eyebrow among the less well-mannered of her companions. In a way he was pleased that she did not appear coarse or ill- bred – but then could his Jane ever have appeared so, in any company? He was not sure. He only knew that he was relieved when the visit came to an end.

Once back at Ashfield, he found an opportunity to walk alone with her in the shrubbery, away from the eyes of his family. He drew her arm through his, and she moved closer to him, gazing up into his face with all the sweet ingenuous- ness that had so delighted him from the beginning. He felt happier at once, and came to a halt, looking down at her. 'It was not so bad then, was it, my dearest?'

'Why no,' she agreed. 'I thought they would all be very clever, but they weren't, not at all. In fact,' she added, her tone edged with surprise, as if she had made a startling discovery, 'they said some very silly things.'

He laughed, delighted by her artless frankness. His dear Jane, so wise in her simple way! 'Ah, but then you see, my darling, being clever is a dangerous tactic for a young lady. She fears it will only frighten away the young gentlemen, and what she wants above all is a husband. And no young man of only ordinary cleverness wants to be made to feel stupid by his wife.'

Jenny stared at him, wide eyed. 'How very silly!' Her voice was rich with scorn. Then: 'Is that what you think – that your wife must not be clever?' Implied was: *Is that why you chose me?*

157

Once he would have denied the accusation with indignation, but now he found himself hesitating. Could it be true? But no, he thought, brushing the imputation aside. He had been attracted to Jane not for her lack of education, but for her simplicity and innocence, that untouched, unspoiled quality she had, which was quite a different thing. She was, after all, a young woman of considerable intelligence, in her way.

And that, of course, was why this morning he had been a little frightened by the new Jane he saw in that refined but foolish company (she was quite right about them). What if she were to change, beyond all recognition? It was inevitable that she should change in some ways, once she was transplanted permanently from her native dale into his more complicated world. In fact, as he had seen this morning, she had already begun to change, quite markedly. But then she would have changed if he had never found her, become corrupted and coarsened in ways he could not bear to think about. Here at least, in his care, she could be guided and directed, so that she would develop her mind and her soul without losing her simplicity and native wisdom. He felt privileged to have so precious a charge laid before him.

'Well, my dear,' said Mrs Selby to her daughter that evening, 'she rose to the occasion much better than I had anticipated.'

'Yes,' said Georgiana slowly. 'She is clearly a good deal cleverer than I gave her credit for.'

'Perhaps, after all, Edward knows what he is doing. Perhaps it will turn out for the best.' Mrs Selby sounded as if she was trying very hard to convince herself of it.

Georgiana shook her head. 'I think it more likely she has calculated the advantage to herself of appearing to be as we would wish.'

Edward's mother was alarmed. 'You think her calculating then? Sly, perhaps, seeking advantage for herself? But Edward is not a rich man.'

'By her standards he has untold wealth. To marry a young man of our class must be beyond her wildest dreams. You cannot imagine, mama, how very far beneath him she is, in reality. I have seen where she lives, remember.' Then, suddenly contrite, she bent to kiss her mother. 'Perhaps I misjudge her, mama. Perhaps you are right, and Edward has chosen well, against all the odds. We shall see.'

Jenny floated through the days that followed in a curious state, bordering on intoxication. She had never dreamed there could be such luxury, such comfort. She felt pampered, even though no one did anything for her that they would not have done for anyone else in the house.

There was so much to enjoy, so many riches. There was the food, wonderful food of a variety and delicacy beyond her wildest imaginings, which was placed before her at meal times as if by magic, without the need for her to do anything to prepare it. There were the picnics and visits and even a few modest dances, though these had their less agreeable side. She did not know most of the steps, though she did her best to learn them; she had no musical skills, such as seemed expected of all young ladies; often she would find herself patronized unpleasantly by one of Edward's neighbours. But she learned to return veiled insults with a sweetness tinged with acid, and to acquit herself tolerably well on most social occasions. She did not think she ever brought disgrace on Edward.

And there was the garden, of course. Gardens in Weardale, with the exception of that at Newhouse and a few others, none of which she had seen, were small and grew only useful things. The garden at Ashfield was larger than all the White Lea land, and designed, apparently, simply for pleasure, laid out in such a way that there seemed endless things to explore, a series of quite different gardens: formal areas full of roses or clipped evergreens, wilder spaces shaded with trees, grassy paths that led to a statue, a fountain, the lake or the shrubbery. She supposed that it must take hours of work each week simply to keep all of it tidy, yet not once during her stay did she glimpse a gardener or see anyone at work out of doors; just as, in the house, floors were swept, flowers arranged, furniture dusted, silver polished, linen changed, all without the least sign of anyone lifting a finger. The household routines seemed designed to create an illusion that hard work simply did not exist, that it was no more than a figment of someone's fevered imagination.

Not, Jenny gathered, that the family saw themselves as idle. They occupied themselves with reading aloud and talking and sewing and playing musical instruments and calling on one another, and even, sometimes, carried nourishing gifts of food to the sick and poor in the neighbourhood. In their eyes, their lives were busy and purposeful. To Jenny, for whom work of the kind they scarcely saw had been the centre of her existence until now, as inevitable as sunset and sunrise, their lives were idle in the extreme. Yet before long she was as content as they were to fill her days with trivial things, finding new pleasures and new interests, and only occasionally troubled by a sense of guilt that she should be doing so little.

One of the pleasures she discovered was the library. Here she found, not a few precious books like those they had at home, worn from being passed round among so many eager readers, and almost all on some subject having a direct bearing on the work of the dale, but a whole room set aside for nothing but books, shelf after shelf of them, filling every wall from floor to ceiling, and covering every subject she could think of, and many she had not known existed – poetry and plays, novels, theological works, books on hunting (Joe would have liked that, she thought, and then remembered with a pang that if she were to tell Joe about it he would simply turn round and walk away), books of speeches and sermons, books in many strange languages, history books and political works, books on natural history and mathematics and geography. There were far too many for anyone to read – even in a lifetime she thought. And no one here seemed to read them much at all, so far as she could see. She took to coming into the library almost every day, when the others were occupied somewhere else, and taking down a book at random, and curling up in a chair to read until she was summoned to join in some other activity. Edward laughed at her. 'My country girl, becoming quite a little bookworm', he said. But she sensed that he did not quite approve, though she could not think why. It was a pleasure she relished the more because she had come to it so late.

Sometimes, when especially delighted by some new experience, she would draw a deep breath and close her eyes and tell herself, 'This is how I shall live, as Edward's wife. I shall belong here, as he does.' It was a thought that filled her with amazement, a thought too massive in its implications to grasp as yet. She had dreamed of leaving Weardale behind, with all its heartache, but without any very clear idea of what she would escape to. Now she knew, and it was more wonderful, more astonishing, than anything she had ever imagined. She began to feel as if she had been at Ashfield all her life. If at any moment she found herself longing suddenly for the hills, for the wind from the fells, for Joe or Tommy or Tabitha or any of those others she had once loved so much, then the feeling was only fleeting and soon ended. They all seemed so remote, as if they no longer had anything to do with her. Edward was her life now, and his world was hers, or soon would be. In a week or two, for a short time, she would return to the dale, but then, after only a few months more, at the very most, she would leave it again for ever. And then, settled in leisured comfort with Edward at her side, she would learn to feel as much at ease as he was, as if she too had been born to this privileged existence. Before long, this world would be reality for her, and the one she had left behind simply a troubled dream.

9

In the month of Jenny's absence, the sun had baked the roadside grass to brown and taken all the freshness from the meadows along the river bank. The water ran sluggishly, low on its stony bed, and many of the burns had dried up, or dwindled to a faint trickle. Fat rosehips glowed in the woodlands, and the blackberries were massive and luscious and black, ripened far sooner than usual. In contrast, the cattle, grazing in fields nearly bare of grass, were lean and listless, their ribs showing through their coats, as they tried to lick the last remnants of moisture from the drying beds of streams and ponds. Men and boys, many laid off work because there was no water to wash the lead or drive the pumps that drained the lower levels, lingered on street corners or leaned on walls, gazing into emptiness, or spent their last pennies on drink, to roll home forgetful of their troubles until dawn should bring them crashing back again.

'I've never seen it like this, never!' said Jenny again and again, as she stared out of the chaise window at the parched landscape.

'I expect it will rain soon,' said Edward soothingly. 'It is nearly autumn.' From what he had heard of Weardale weather it was unusual enough that there should have been no rain for so long; that the drought would continue for many more days seemed unlikely in the extreme.

The chaise came to a halt in St John's Chapel. Edward warmly pressed Jenny to come into the parsonage to take tea before going home, but she refused, agreeing only that he should have her luggage sent up after her. Now that she was back, she wanted to return to White Lea as quickly as possible, to see how they all were. Only now did she realize how much she had missed them. Miss Selby, who had travelled north as chaperon, but was going home again tomorrow, was clearly glad to be taking her leave of Jenny, though she managed parting words of conventional politeness.

The market place was quiet, but there were a few people about. None of them spoke to Jenny, though they watched her from a distance, in silence. Some, smiled at, looked away, or returned the smile with a cold stare. Jenny was puzzled. What was wrong? Surely she had not changed so much that they did not know her? She was wearing one of the new gowns, spotted cambric, with a graceful shawl draped over it, and a straw bonnet, but a fine surface did not change the essentials.

Then she heard a shout. She turned, saw a small boy – one of the Walton lads, she thought – jeering at her from a back lane. She did not catch what he said, but its tone was clear enough. And she realized then, her heart beating fast, what was wrong with everyone. They knew where she had been, and why – as how indeed could they not, when she had been away so long? And, like Joe, they saw in her engagement a betrayal, not perhaps of Billy, but of all the long years of hatred for the Church and what it stood for. It would have been bad enough to have tied herself to an outsider, some upstart from Stanhope perhaps, or a mine official; that would have earned her many rebukes and a good deal of rough teasing. But this – for this there would not readily be forgiveness.

She called a greeting to a woman she knew well, standing watching her from Jacob Todd's doorway, and when the woman turned her back she went on her way, trying not to feel hurt. Once they had all shown their disapproval, then perhaps they would consider the point made and learn to accept what she had done. Somehow she must help them to understand why she had done it, for surely that would make a difference.

But first there was Joe, and Tommy. She crossed the river and walked on up the hill, glad to be alone for this little space, for this walk that led her from one life, the one she had chosen, to another, the one into which she had been born. She knew quite well that, just as she'd had to learn to adjust to life at Edward's house, so it would take a little time for her to become accustomed again to the more familiar world of home, grown unfamiliar during the past weeks.

She came within sight of White Lea, and felt a lump tighten in her throat. It was just as she remembered it, yet touched with strangeness, as if a part of her was seeing it for the first time. The Jenny who returned to it was a different person from the one who had gone away, and this Jenny was almost an outsider. She slowed her pace and approached the house with something close to fear, as if she did not quite know what to expect; nor did she, for how would Joe and Tommy receive her, after this absence?

The ponies trotted to the wall to lean over and whinny their greeting, and Spot barked from somewhere inside the house. She pushed open the door and went in to the cool interior.

Inevitably, perhaps, the order and cleanliness of her reign had receded before the less stringent regime of her brothers, but there was nothing too dreadful waiting for her. Spot leapt up at her, tongue licking, tail wagging, all impatient delight. She patted him, and wondered where the others were. It was about supper time (she was hungry herself), but there was no pot over the fire and no sign that a meal had just ended. She looked upstairs, but, finding no one, went outside again, Spot at her heels.

Joe was behind the byre, concentratedly mending a wall. She stood watching him for a moment as he carefully chose precisely the right stone to build up each stage of the wall, settling it slowly into place before moving on to the next. She felt a warmth about her heart, a great welling up of love. Dear Joe – whatever she might feel for Edward, there was no denying that her brothers had a special place in her heart and her life and always would.

He turned suddenly and saw her. For a moment his face was lit with joy; he stepped forward, arms reaching towards her. And then, abruptly, he stopped, his expression cooling, his hands falling to his sides. It hurt more than Jenny would have thought possible. She stayed where she was, as her brother looked her up and down and said, 'Why, I hardly

164

knew you.' It was worse because it was clearly untrue, designed to hurt, to remind her that they were estranged, and why. At that moment Tommy came round the corner of the byre with two stones in his arms. He saw her, dropped them, and gave a great joyous shout. 'Our Jenny!' Then he ran into her arms. Jenny was so relieved and delighted at his spontaneous welcome that she began to cry.

'We'd best go in,' said Joe at last, and she realized it was a grudging gesture towards her, acknowledging that they had somehow to rub along together if life was to be bearable, that all their communication could not be hostile, much as Joe might feel it ought to be.

'Have you had supper?' she asked as they went into the house, her arm about Tommy.

'No,' said Tommy. 'Now you're back we'll do better.'

Jenny caught Joe's eye, and saw there not (as she had expected) a sheepish acknowledgement that his cooking was not all it might be, but something graver, which made her uneasy. 'What'll we have then?'

'There's only oatmeal,' said Joe. 'We've finished the day's milk.' She looked at him in surprise. 'The cows have all but dried up; the grass is eaten right down.' She went to the meal chest and saw to her dismay how little of that there was left. 'The potatoes'll be ready soon,' Joe consoled her, adding, 'Though I doubt they'll be poor enough. There's been no rain to swell them.'

She did the best she could with oatmeal and water and salt, and her brothers were glad enough of it, but her appetite, cherished and flattered during the past weeks at Ashfield, felt repelled by the comfortless mess. She ate little, passing most of her portion untouched to her brothers. 'Too fine for Weardale food, I see,' said Joe, which did not make her feel any better about it. 'I bet the curate's folk don't go hungry.'

Jenny said nothing for a moment – what after all could she say? She felt shame enough that she should have been living so well, while her brothers had so little. Studying them now she could see that they were both thinner than she remembered, and Joe looked weary as well. She turned to him and said gravely, 'Joe, I know you don't like what I've done.

165

You've made it plain enough. I'd hoped you'd have had time to think better of it, but it seems I was wrong. But that doesn't mean we can't put it aside, just for now. We're brother and sister, and we live in this house together, and I've no wish to fight with you over everything.'

'Maybe you should've thought of that before,' Joe retorted. Jenny glanced sideways at Tommy, who was watching them both with unease in his blue eyes. She saw that Joe had noticed it too, and he shrugged. 'All right then, I'll let it be for now. But I'll not come round, you know that. And if I can do owt to make you think better of it, then I shall.'

Jenny began to clear the bowls from the table. 'Is there any tea?'

'No, nor ale neither.'

She looked at the shelf near the fire. 'The rum's gone too, I see.' She saw from Joe's expression what had become of it, but she let it pass. He had reason enough to want to drown his sorrows. 'What'll we do, Joe? We have to eat.'

'I'll be out on the fell again tonight,' he promised. 'But there are too many after the game, and Joseph Dawson's got eyes in the back of his head.'

'And Frank Johnson,' put in Tommy.

'Aye, and him. He still has a mind to present the Bishop's warrants.'

'He won't,' said Tommy. Joe ruffled his hair.

'Why no, our Tommy, of course he won't.' He stood up. 'Anyway, it's coming up to Michaelmas bargains. If we can get the lent money up, we'll do better. We mean to try for forty shillings a month.'

'Do you think you'll get it?'

'The Quaker Company pays as much. I can't see Mrs Beaumont holding out against us, not when she's told how things are, with prices so high.'

Later, when Joe had gone out, Tommy came to Jenny and said in a low voice, 'Are you really going to wed Mr Selby?'

She could hear the faint note of disbelief in his voice. 'Yes, Tommy, I am.'

'Oh,' he said, and turned and went upstairs, very slowly.

*

166

The next day, shopping in the village in her old clothes, put on with just a trace of regret, Jenny was forced to recognize how greatly she had offended in the eyes of her neighbours. Women turned their backs on her, men stood staring at her, their eyes hostile, saying nothing, children jeered and shouted. When she ventured a smile or a greeting, the best response was silence; more than once someone spat deliberately on the ground near her feet. As bad, prices everywhere had risen greatly since she went away, yet many shopkeepers coldly refused her the credit on which everyone depended until the next Pay.

Desperate to find that something at least had not changed, she went to call on Tabitha Hall, taking with her a small gift – a brooch, simple but pretty – which she had bought while she was away, encouraged by Edward.

She pushed open the door of the house, smiling. Tabitha, scrubbing the table, looked up; and then straightened, her dark eyes suddenly very cold and hard. 'I don't know what brings you here, Jenny Emerson, for I've nowt to say to you.'

Even Joe's anger had not hurt her like this. She caught her breath, stood for a moment quite unable to move or speak; and then she turned and walked out of the house and back along the lane, trembling so much that every step was an effort. Not knowing what else to do, she went to the parsonage and asked for Edward. Peggy (surely she could not be disapproving too?) admitted her to the study, where he was working on tomorrow's sermon. Jenny stood in the doorway, looking at him, shaking, unable to speak; and then she burst into tears.

Edward took her to the parlour, sent for tea, put his arms about her and tried to comfort her, but since it was some time before she could tell him what was wrong he was at a loss to know what to say. When she did tell him at last, haltingly and between bursts of sobbing, he was enraged. 'What stupid, narrow minded people! Pay no heed, my darling – there's not one of them fit to lick the ground beneath your feet!'

Quite illogically, that brought Jenny's anger down on him. After all, she thought, her neighbours had reason enough to hate what she had done, when they had been trodden beneath the heel of the Church for so long. But somehow she could not begin to explain that to Edward. In the end, almost as troubled by his consolation as by her own unhappiness, she left him and went back home.

There Joe inadvertently gave her one crumb of comfort. 'I should have warned you, there's no credit for miners now, not with things so bad. It's all used up, for most of us anyway. That's another cause for a rise. We've months to go before next Pay, even if they're sooner with it this time.' So that at least had not been a rebuke for her behaviour, but simply something in which, like all miners' families, she shared.

That night, it rained at last, heavily and for several hours. The long drought was at an end. On Monday, the washer lads returned to work, and those miners who had been laid off because the machinery had failed.

In the King's Head, Tom Walton posted someone at the door to keep watch, in case of unwelcome intruders, and joined the miners crammed into his only sizable room, filling the smoky air with angry talk. Then he shouted for quiet. 'You all know why you're here, lads, so we'll waste no more time. John Peart, Close End's going to speak first.' They all looked towards the man who had stepped forward into the only remaining space in the centre of the room.

'Tommy Thompson there and me, we've got up this together,' John Peart began. He held up a large piece of paper. 'It's an address to every miner in Weardale, asking for support. I'll put it up outside afterwards, and I'll thank you to see that all those who aren't here get a look at it. Read it out for any who can't read. I'll read it to you myself in a moment, but first, I'll tell you in plain words what we have in mind.

'Like all of you, we've gone hungry a few times this year. And things don't look to be getting any better. Now, we were promised, when lead prices went up, we'd get a rise too. True, we got five shillings on the top price at Ladyday, but that'll still leave a vast of us not clearing the books this year, and the lent money's starvation money, as I see it. If you've had your eye on the price of lead, like I have, you'll know it's gone up a canny bit these past months. But it's no use us

168

going in dribs and drabs to the masters begging for more. That way, they'll just pick us off one by one.' There was an increasing muttering from the men, already guessing what John Peart was about to put before them.

'So, lads, here's what I say: we stand side by side. Tonight, we pick our representatives, men we can trust, to speak up for us. They'll be the ones to go and put our case loud and clear to Mr Crawhall, first thing tomorrow. And what do we demand? Nowt less than forty shillings a month subsistence and ten shillings more per bing for raising ore. And if we're not promised it, then the very next day every partnership in Weardale stops off work, and not one partnership, not one man, not one washer lad, goes back to work till the masters give in.'

The last words were almost drowned in a chorus of cheers. But Joe noticed that not everyone was joining in. Not far away from him Jock Wilson from Level Gate shouted, 'We tried it before, just two year ago. It didn't get us far then.'

'Why no,' John Peart retorted swiftly, 'for then lead prices were on the bottom. The masters could ride out a strike. It saved them money – what more did they want? Things are different now.'

'Aye, that's right, they are.' That, Joe saw, was Anthony Coulthard. 'And I'm for a strike. I don't see we've any choice. But there's no denying it'll be hard. When my father was alive he used to talk about the '95 strike, often enough. I'm old enough to remember it a bit myself. All those weeks of bitterness, nowt coming in, and for what? A few bushels of rye brought in, and my father and Jack Kidd and a good many more thrown out of work. And in '95 we were at war. There was a call for lead.'

Suddenly eaten up with impatience at all the misgivings, Joe cried, 'Demand's up now, and prices. If the Quaker Company can pay more, then so can Mrs Beaumont. They know that as well as we do.' He jumped to his feet. 'It's only justice. How else do we eat? Scrat around for crumbs from the masters' table? No, lads! We're not animals, we're men – no more nor less than Mr Crawhall and Colonel Beaumont and his lady. Are they better than us? Of course not! We have as good a right to eat as they have, and to live.'

This time the cheers roared to the rafters, and at the end, John Peart said, 'Right now, that's agreed. We send our delegates to Mr Crawhall to put our demands –'

'We'll send you!' someone shouted, to general agreement. 'And Tommy Thompson.'

John Peart silenced them again. 'Thanks for your confidence, lads. But let's take care about this. What we need is one man picked from each part of Weardale; that way we all get a voice, as far as we can. That would be maybe six, eight men. Then we'll have enough to choose from, so it's not always the same men speaking for us. We don't want the masters blaming a few of us for what we all do together.' He looked round to check that he had their support. 'Right then, I'll stand for Guinea Grove and the west, if you'll have me, and Thompson for Burtree Pasture.'

'Joe Emerson's our man!' called Anthony Siddle.

There was an immediate growl of agreement; and then one dissenting voice broke in, saying something Joe could not catch. An odd silence settled momentarily over the room, and everyone looked at Joe. 'What was that?' he demanded, crossing to where the man sat.

'I said, how can we be sure you're to be trusted?'

Joe frowned. 'You know you can trust me. I'll thump any man who says otherwise.'

'Aye well, maybe. But what of your sister?'

'What of her?'

'She's thick with that curate fellow. What say if she goes gossiping to him about what we're at?'

'I'd stake my life Jenny's loyal.'

'Would you? You have no more liking for this match than any of us.'

'No more I do, but that's not to say she'd play false to her own.'

'Let him be, man,' John Peart urged. 'We know she'd not stoop that low. More to the point, we make sure she's told nowt that can hurt us.'

'Right, then I say we pick Joe Emerson.'

This time there was no dissent.

Eve put down the pail and slowly straightened. Judith,

170

standing in the doorway, eyed her critically. 'You're getting fat, Eve,' she said. Eve looked round and caught her eye, and at that moment saw the dislike, casually expressed, a mere passing observation, change quickly to something speculative, questioning; and knew then precisely what it was that her sister was thinking.

For what seemed a long time she stood there, staring at Judith, while the full implication of the words spread steadily into every corner of her consciousness, and all the warmth of the day seemed to recede from her, leaving her utterly chilled, like an exposed rock in an empty wilderness.

She knew Judith was about to say something more, so she pushed past her sister and hurried into the house, going at once to her room. There, she sat on the bed and tried to face the horrible thing that now possessed her mind.

It could not be true; it could not be! It was a nightmare, from which at any moment she would wake. She was saved now, redeemed, free of the filthiness of the past. A new life had begun. A new life ... no, not that, not that ...!

She began to shiver, uncontrollably. She must be wrong. It was a mistake. She was sick, perhaps ... yes, that was it, she was unwell; perhaps she would grow worse and die. Suddenly that seemed an infinitely desirable end.

But she knew she deluded herself. The moment Judith spoke, she had known the truth, for it had only put into words, dragged up to the surface of her mind, the thing that had been lurking half hidden there for weeks now, the thing she had not wanted to admit, that she had explained away as best she could and smothered with the excitements of her new life, in the hope that it would prove illusory. Only you cannot smother the truth, not for ever.

It must have happened that very same month. Her thoughts went back to that time, to the two April days, the two moments of ecstasy, so alike and yet so different in their significance: in the hay byre in Joe's arms; in the market place, where through wind and rain had come those burning words of hope and love. Set apart from one another by – how long? A week perhaps? Scarcely that, though in the intensity of all she had experienced it had seemed like a lifetime. No, rather it had been like a death and a rebirth, in

171

which all that was the old Eve Todd had been sloughed off and left behind for ever. Except that it had not, for this remained, as if to tell her that there could be no renewal, no leaving the past behind.

Oh God! Oh God! The cry was not spoken aloud, but it came from the heart and there was no blasphemy in it. It was a desperate cry for help to the loving Father whose power she had felt so overwhelmingly. For if this were true, if her fears were justified, what then did that tell her of the love so newly known? What kind of love was it that could exact this punishment from her, after all her repentance, all her joyful acceptance? It was a love as harsh and cruel and merciless as that of her father, the only kind of love – save Joe's – which she had ever known, until now. It was no love at all, nothing that could console or support her, for it left her at the mercy of the supreme tyrant who had ruled her life from infancy.

Two days of torment, two days of utter darkness, convinced her that there was no escape, that this dreadful thing had indeed happened to her, that her punishment was complete. She could go nowhere for help. She had turned Joe away, and now he hated her; he was said to have found another girl. She thought of Rowland, but knew there was no way out there either. What could he tell her, but that she was indeed utterly cast away? There would only be punishment piled upon punishment, and it was already more than she could bear.

Very early next morning she crept from the house and made her way along the river bank to a place where the trees grew densely, shielding from view a deep fast flowing stretch of water (she was glad it had rained at last), and there she filled her pockets with the heaviest stones she could find and slowly, with determination, waded into the river. It was cold, tugging at her feet and then at her skirts, so that she slithered on stones slimed by the summer heat. Just a few steps more and she had lost her footing altogether and was torn from the shore and swept into the rushing stream.

'You'd best sleep in the hay loft tonight,' Joe said, when Tommy had gone upstairs, 'else you'll be up very late.'

Jenny, gazing into the fire while her hands were busy with

172

her knitting, looked sharply round. She presumed, from what Joe said, that he had friends coming prossing tonight. 'I'm not that tired,' she said. 'I can wait up.' She studied her brother's face, and saw that all its usual resentment was overlaid by a hint of anxiety. 'Who's coming then?'

He shrugged. 'One or two. We have things to talk over. Private things.'

'Since when were your affairs too private for my ears?'

He said nothing, but she knew the answer all the same: since she took up with Edward Selby. His mistrust chilled her. This was, almost, worse than his disapproval of her choice of husband, for this implied that her very loyalty was suspect.

'How could you ever think I'd do you harm, or any of your friends? They are my friends too, even if you'll not believe it any more.' Still he said nothing. 'Joe, what's going on?' All this week, she had sensed something uneasy in the atmosphere, but Joe had evaded her questions. He had simply gone out early every morning, as usual, and returned from work rather later than he generally did. If Tommy knew any more, he was not telling either.

'That's my business,' Joe said now. 'If you're not tired, then maybe you could go out. Didn't you say you'd take one of the moor hens to Aunt Ann?'

'I told you – I took it this afternoon.' A combination of Uncle Ralph's declining health, the dizzying rise in the price of food, and the ending of credit for miners, had worn down Ann Emerson's resistance to receiving the proceeds of poaching. She had been pathetically glad of Jenny's gift.

'You could go somewhere else then.'

This time it was she who was silent. She wondered only that Joe should suggest such a thing, for he must know there was nowhere she was welcome now, nowhere except the parsonage, and Edward's strict view of propriety would not allow her to call there after dark, unchaperoned. But to say all that to her brother would only be to invite further unpleasantness. She knitted to the middle of the row and folded her work and stood up. 'I think I'll go to bed,' she said, as if the thought had just occurred to her. She made her way out to the hay loft.

173

The men came close on midnight, the seven chosen, with Joe, to represent the different areas of the Weardale lead mines. They took their places about the table, their faces all deep shadows and hard angles in the candlelight: John Peart, Thomas Thompson and Anthony Coulthard, old by lead-mining standards, with fifteen years or more of experience behind them, and four younger men.

'I must say,' Coulthard began, 'I'd hoped we'd have no need of this meeting.'

'Why, we all hoped that,' John Peart agreed. 'But you can't say we weren't prepared for it.'

'But he did make some kind of offer, at least?'

Thompson smiled bitterly. 'If you call five shillings more per bing an offer, and that not till the New Year. He wouldn't budge on the lent money. What's more, he didn't sound to me like a man who was ready to change his mind, either.'

'He says he cannot,' John Peart reminded him, though there was derision in his tone. 'Says it's not in his hands to give us more.'

'Why then,' said Joe, 'we've no choice but to go on as we promised – no work till they give us what we ask.'

Around the table the men nodded in agreement. Coulthard said, 'There's one thing, though. Last time we were off work, there was some talk of the masters taking us to court.'

'Aye,' said Thompson, 'for breaking our contracts. They wanted to make out our bargains were binding in law.'

'And if we stop off work now, before the bargains are out, then we're putting ourselves the wrong side of the law.'

John Peart shook his head. 'I thought of that. But the bargains only have days to run. There are none that go on beyond September 30, and that's only next Wednesday. The masters aren't going to trouble themselves to take us all to court for those few days.'

'In any case,' said Thompson. 'We've got to stop off now, before the new bargains are let. Mr Crawhall will be going to Newcastle in a week or two to fix next year's prices, and we don't want him in any doubt how strong we feel about it. We've got to do it this way.'

'I agree,' said Joe.

'Mind, it could be a long fight.' That was George Robinson, one of the younger men. 'And there's any amount of men already going hungry, even before we've started. If we're going to keep everyone together, we need to be sure no one starves.'

'I thought of that,' said Coulthard. 'We should get up a collection. There are some have cash still, and the tradesmen might give us something. If we can make sure no one starves it gives us that bit longer.'

'There's always the Bishop's game,' Joe put in with a grin. John Peart frowned.

'No, man, not that – not till this is settled. I don't care who else goes out on the fell, but the eight of us have got to keep the right side of the law. Owt else does our cause no good.'

'Aye, you're right,' Joe agreed soberly. Then he said, 'But we've got to do more than sit back and wait for Mr Crawhall to come round, because it's my belief he won't. He'll think he has only to hang on till letting day and we'll sharp come crawling back. We've got to force his hand.'

'Seems to me,' said John Peart, 'if he says he's no power to give us more, then we go to them who have.'

'To Mrs Beaumont?' exclaimed Thompson. 'All the way to Wakefield?'

John Peart shook his head. 'Young Mr Beaumont's only at Hexham, and he's a Member of Parliament too. He might put in a word for us. And there's Mr Morrison in Newcastle.'

'One thing more,' said Robinson. 'We've got to make sure every partnership stands firm. What say we take a paper round to all of them, get them to sign their agreement to strike? Then we know we've got them behind us.'

That was agreed and Joe brought pen and paper and ink, and an extra candle, and they set to work on the wording of the agreement. After that, they turned their attention to composing petitions for the delegates to take to Newcastle and Hexham. It was harder than they had expected to frame the words that mingled precisely the right degree of respect and firmness, and many false starts had been screwed up and confined to the fire before they had it right. By then it was almost day and their faces were grey with weariness. It was at

175

that moment, crashing into the quietness, that the hammering came on the door.

No one said anything. Eight pairs of eyes met across the table. John Peart shuffled the papers into a heap and pushed them under the settle. Joe knew they were all thinking as he was, though quite who they thought it might be out there, and what kind of threat he offered, none of them quite knew. At last Joe rose to his feet. 'We've just met for a bit crack, that's all,' he said.

He opened the door, letting in the first of the dawn light, and John Kidd fell into the room, red with exertion and too breathless to speak. Joe led him to the settle, where he sank thankfully down, gasping noisily. The relief among the other men was almost tangible. John Kidd, whose father had been thrown out of work in '96, was no threat at all to men who had chosen to risk the same fate.

When the newcomer had recovered enough to look about him, he seemed troubled by the other men in the room, as fearful of them as they had been of him. 'They're friends,' said Joe. 'They can keep quiet if need be.'

Kidd nodded, and then said in a low voice. 'It's Eve Todd.'

It was the last thing Joe had expected. He sat down beside Kidd, feeling suddenly cold and afraid, more afraid than before. All at once the strike seemed supremely unimportant, even unreal. He knew that all he had ever felt for Eve was as fresh as it had always been. He knew that if she was dead he could not bear it. He braced himself, and then whispered, 'What of her?'

'Found her in the river this morning.' He caught a glimpse of Joe's face, and went on hurriedly, 'She's alive. I got her out. She's at my house. My lass is watching her. But she doesn't want her father told. Nor anyone, she says. She cries all the time. I thought it best to tell you, all the same. When she said why she'd done it, that is.'

'Done it?'

'Threw herself in the river. On purpose.'

Around the table, the other men were talking softly, tactfully conscious that Kidd's message was not for them. In any case, he had spoken so quietly that it was unlikely any of

176

them would have heard what he said. Now, Joe stood up. 'I'll come for her. We'll have her here.' He called to the others, 'Get a drink for John. I'm going to wake Jenny.'

Joe and Jenny took the galloway down to John Kidd's house and there Joe went in alone to where Eve was, and emerged a long time afterwards with his arm about her, and lifted her on to the pony's back. Her face was stained with tears, but she seemed calm enough as the three of them made their way slowly back to White Lea.

'This is your home now,' Jenny said, as they reached the house. 'We'll take care of you.'

In spite of John Kidd's caution, Lancelot Hall heard the news in the smithy that afternoon, and carried it back to Rowland when he went in to supper.

Rowland listened to him in an odd silence, his face grave enough, but showing no sign of emotion. Not for the first time, Lancelot wondered what he was thinking. Up in front of a crowd, giving his message to them, he seemed to tear out his very heart for them to see, exposing himself to hatred, ridicule, all the things the very thought of which made Lancelot shudder. Yet in private, except when speaking directly of his faith, he kept his feelings very much to himself; or perhaps, thought Lancelot, he had no feelings, apart from religious ones. Even then, he would have expected something more from his cousin, when told the sad, sordid little tale – especially in view of the ironic fact that the fallen girl was one of his own converts, supposedly saved. But Rowland said only, 'I see,' and soon afterwards went out, though it was almost dark and he had little taste for inns or alehouses, except sometimes for the company found there.

It was not human company that Rowland sought this evening, but the wind-blown austerity of Chapel Fell. He climbed without pausing, and fast, until he reached the fell top; and there he stood still, struggling to get his breath, the noise of the wind all about him, its coldness chilling him.

He scarcely noticed. His thoughts were too full of what he had heard. It was a small enough thing, and hardly uncommon. He was surprised himself at the effect it had on him. He should have been able to explain it, to find an answer to it in his faith. He had grown used to doing that, with ease, in every situation that presented itself, but this time it seemed almost as if – for the moment at least – his faith had failed him.

He thought back to his first meeting with Eve, when she had come forward to speak to him in the market place the first time he preached. He had hardly spoken to her since then, though he had been able to see for himself how changed she was from the wayward, rebellious girl who had been the despair of her father. He had a certain fellow feeling for her, as the wild offspring of upright parents. He had wondered too how nearly her experience had matched his own, before that moment of conversion, how like his own father Jacob Todd had been – not much, he thought, on the surface, but there were many different kinds of tyranny. Perhaps he was being unfair to Jacob Todd. He did not like the man much, but then he was not asked to like his fellows, only to love them, which was rather a different thing.

Back to Eve, that dark pretty girl whose face had shone among so many others at that first meeting, whose joy in her new faith had been palpable. He knew that feeling of joy, though for him now it only occasionally came with the intensity of the first days. But it had never quite left him, even in his more difficult moments. It gave him peace of mind and a consuming sense of purpose, and a stubborn ability to persist in the face of the most impossible odds, without doubting the rightness of what he did. Had Eve experienced her new faith with the same intensity? He thought so, he had no reason to doubt it; he had seen the happiness shining from her whenever he saw her at worship or passed her in the street. And if that were so, then the implications were deeply disturbing to him. How was it possible to go in one short space of time from joy so complete to the darkest despair? He had known despair too, but only in the days before his conversion, and as a prelude to that conversion. He had been sure it was something he need never fear again. But then he, as a man, could never find himself facing what Eve had to face.

It brought him up short. He had not previously considered what it must be like to be a woman. He had experience

178

enough of women, in relation to himself, the closest experience. And yet somehow he had never thought what it was that marked their condition out from his; they were simply people, like himself. After all, it was what they had in common that had first drawn him to the only woman he had ever loved, the woman he believed he had known as intimately as he knew himself. Now he had to recognize that there was something she shared with Eve of which he had no experience and no knowledge, and he knew that it was of the greatest importance that he should understand what it was, if only to enable him to help Eve, if help were possible – as surely it must be.

He thought back to the first moments when he had felt assured of God's love and salvation, and tried to imagine what dreadful thing might have happened to him, comparable to this, something that would have brought on him consequences that were both very public and deeply shameful. All the sin that had mired and snared him in his life until then had been cancelled without trace at the moment of conversion, leaving nothing behind. That, after all, was what salvation meant. But what, for instance, if he had afterwards been arrested for some crime committed before then? If, perhaps, his father had still been alive, and had tracked him down at last, demanding retribution for the theft? It would have been painful for him, dragging back to his memory all kinds of experiences he had hoped were buried for ever, but he thought he would have been able to face the consequences, remembering that God's love was with him through it all, that he was never alone.

But he knew too, realized it even as he imagined it happening to him, that it would have been a very different thing. What had happened to Eve was nothing like that, could not be. He had heard what people said when a woman fell pregnant, seen what became of her. That, after all, was how his wife (he called her that, though they had been through no formal ceremony) had first found herself in the streets, used and then abandoned by a man, a plight made the more dreadful because that man was her own stepfather. Eve, of course, had not been abandoned, had genuinely wished to marry Joe Emerson; but while her father forbade

179

it, and she was under age, there was nothing she could do. Besides, she had turned Joe away. She could not expect him to stand by her.

Rowland sat on the grass and for a little time tried to imagine he was Eve, to enter into her shame and her fear, the horror that had wiped out in one instant all the happiness she had found, all her faith. Yes, it must seem to her as if God had held out salvation to her, only, mockingly, to snatch it back again, marking her out for ever as lost and cast away. For that was how everyone would see her. The theft he had committed, the dark sins of his youth, had not branded him as this single sin branded Eve, as it would brand her always. There was something in a woman's condition that made the sin of impurity more unforgiveable than any other, at least when there was no man for her to wed in haste; something that often allowed her partner in sin to evade any public guilt, as she could not. It was, he thought, her dependency, like that of a child. Few women had a separate, independent existence, as men did; poor women in particular could not live without husband or father to maintain them, to govern their lives and offer them protection. Protection: it was an ironic word, in the circumstances. The protection of a father, a stepfather, of a man like Jacob Todd . . . perhaps possession would fit the case more nearly.

He considered Eve's sin, that gravest of all sins that a woman could commit. Every sin was a serious matter, of course, but he could not feel that this one was so very grave, born as it was of love and a moment of forgetful passion; less evil by far, so it seemed to Rowland, than the filthiness, the cruelties and deceptions of much of his own life. If he was pardoned, then so much the more was Eve. But without her conviction of pardon, it was ineffectual.

Full of a searing pity, he prayed that he might be given the words that would help her, and then he made his way at once down the hill and across the river and up again, towards White Lea.

Joe stood, arms crossed, in the doorway, leaning against the post at one side, his foot lodged firmly against the other. He glowered at the young man facing him.

180

'What do you want, Rowland Peart?'

The dark eyes met Joe's gaze without flinching. 'I'm told Eve Todd's here.'

'What if she is? She's nowt to do with you any more.'

'She's always my concern, as are all my sisters and brothers.'

'Then go away and leave her in peace. You've done her harm enough already.'

Rowland ignored him and went on, 'You'll wed her then?'

'You know I cannot. Her father will not give his consent.'

'Then I'll see him and get it.'

Joe's eyes widened. 'You're very sure of yourself!'

'Why no,' said Rowland. 'I'm sure of my Lord.'

It was not a good day for Rowland. The message he took back to White Lea some time later was not, after all, what he had hoped for, even expected. 'I neither give nor withhold my consent to any marriage,' Jacob Todd had said, as little inclined to welcome Rowland as Joe had been. 'I cannot do so, for I have no daughter but one, and she is here, obedient and dutiful, under my roof. You can tell that to whom you please. It's my last word on the matter.'

Joe, standing outside the door this time, having shut it firmly behind him so that no one should see who was there, heard the words (or a slightly softened version of them) in silence and then said, with a certain grim satisfaction, 'It seems your Lord has let you down. As well I've never put any trust in Him. Now get off my land, and keep off it.'

Jenny opened her eyes. The room was still in darkness, lit only by the glow of the dampened peats in the hearth. Tommy still lay sleeping soundly on the mattress by the fire. Whatever the sound was, it had not wakened him.

Then it came again, unmistakable this time, the creak of a foot on the stair. She slid from the bed and pulled a shawl about her and crept into the passage.

'Joe!'

She could just make him out in the darkness, sitting on the stairs, quite still. She reached out and laid her hand over his;

181

it felt very cold. 'You'll catch your death sitting out here. What's up?'

She was relieved that he did not reject her. It was the old Joe, her friend and companion, who got to his feet and came down to her and allowed her to rub his hands to bring the warmth back to them. 'I couldn't sleep, that's all; or lie quiet. So I came out here, not to wake Eve.' It had been the obvious arrangement, that Eve should share Joe's bed, for she needed all the comfort he could give her.

'Come in by the fire. Tommy'd not wake for the Day of Judgement.' They went into the kitchen and Joe stretched his hands towards the fire. Jenny said softly, 'What kept you awake?'

'My thoughts.'

She smiled. 'Aye, that I could've told you. Now perhaps you'll say what thoughts.'

He sat down abruptly on the settle, with Jenny beside him. He was frowning now, the dark reflections that had dragged him from his bed reclaiming possession of him. 'Some of us went to see Mr Crawhall yesterday. He wouldn't listen.'

It was not what she had thought he would say, for the catastrophe that had happened to Eve had driven everything else from her head. 'Did you expect owt else?'

'It seemed clear enough, in justice, that we had a case.'

'When have they ever cared about justice, if they can get away with paying less?'

He looked as if he had never expected so disparaging a view to come from her; not now, at least. 'Would you not've thought he'd have given in?'

She shook her head. 'Not if he sees no cause to, no. Why should he?'

'So,' he said slowly. 'You see the need to give him cause.'

She was silent then. It was the obvious conclusion, but for all that she had not thought of it. 'So that's why they all came, last night. There's to be a strike.'

'Aye. We agreed it the other day, all of us. We stop off work till we get what we ask.' He gave a brief rueful grin. 'And no poaching meanwhile.'

'It won't be easy.'

182

'No. That's why I can't sleep. If they give in quickly, that's one thing, but ...'

Jenny thought of the little they had, even with the poaching, of the struggle week by week to keep them fed, on that and the lent money. Without money, without credit, they would have nothing at all but what the land gave them, and in this high country that was little enough even in good times. If all else failed, there was the parish, and what meagre charity it might pay out; already there were many who depended on it, too many. And winter was coming, the cold and the snow. To face all that on empty bellies would be misery indeed.

'Have you thought what you're doing, Joe? Truly thought?'

He nodded. 'Aye. But it came home to me tonight. There's Eve to think of now.'

'She'll need food and care, with the bairn coming.' Jenny studied his face, seeing something more.

'I know it shouldn't be in my mind at such a time,' he went on reluctantly, 'but there's Tommy's find too, our trial.'

She understood, for she knew how much his hopes were bound up with the find on Middlehope Moor, how much it had already begun to fulfil those hopes. And she recognized that a strike would put them all in jeopardy.

'What does Uncle Ralph say?'

'He sees the need for what we're doing. He says we must do what's right, whatever the cost.'

His expression was so bleak that she asked, 'Would you step back now, if you could?'

He shook his head. 'I promised father I'd do nowt without thinking first, nor have I. If there was any other way, then I'd have taken it. But there isn't. They'll not listen to reason, so – we must put reason aside, and try other means. What else is there?'

'And if that fails?'

'It mustn't fail. We mustn't fail. Not this time.'

10

Joe was woken by Eve's thrashing in the bed beside him, and the little cries that broke from her, frightened whimpers and moans that cut him to the heart. It had happened three nights running now, and with it went days of silent unhappiness about which she would not speak.

He rolled over and took her in his arms, murmuring lovingly to her until she woke. She clung to him, relieved to be awake, but, he knew, not really comforted.

'Come now, Eve, what's up? I've a right to know if anything's wrong. Have you a pain?'

'No,' she murmured against his shoulder. Then she said, 'It was a bad dream, that's all.'

'Tell me about it.'

For a little while she said nothing and he thought she would refuse what he asked, but at last, suddenly, she murmured in a low reluctant voice, 'I dreamed I was in Hell.'

He kissed her and stroked her hair. 'You know that can't be, my hinny. There's no Hell, truly there's not. And if there was, there are far worse people who'll go there, not you.'

'But I did wrong. I'm doing wrong yet.'

'To lie here with me, without a ring on your finger? You know in your heart it's not wrong. The only thing that's wrong is that your father won't let us wed. Besides, what's a wedding service but words? We know we belong together. We don't need any priest or minister to tell us that.'

She seemed to be pondering what he said, for it was some time before she spoke again. 'Joe, I was so happy before. I'm happy now, in a way, but not like that. If only ...'

'If only what?'

'Do you think Rowland Peart would come? I want to talk

184

to him. Maybe he knows the rights of it.'

At that he said nothing, but simply moved a little away from her, though he kissed her lightly on the top of the head. 'Whisht now, my hinny. He's all in the past. He shall have no more to do with you. Go to sleep now.' Then he kissed her a little more and caressed her and she forgot her troubles for long enough to respond to him, and then they drifted back to sleep.

'Has Joe gone?'

Jenny looked round as Eve came into the kitchen, noting with some anxiety the dark circles round her eyes and the haunted look that still hung about her. That Eve was physically unwell, constantly tired and afflicted by frequent blinding headaches, was clear enough; but it was more than simple physical weakness that troubled her. 'Aye. They're all going to Newhouse again today.' As Eve sat down, Jenny put a bowl of crowdy before her, though Eve merely picked at the food. 'You slept better then, not to know Joe was gone.'

'I was awake through the night.' As if suddenly resolved to confide in Jenny, she laid her spoon down and said, 'Jenny, I want to see Rowland Peart.'

Jenny sat down facing her. 'Won't that make it all worse?' She knew from Joe something of what preyed on Eve's mind and, like him, very largely blamed Rowland for it. On the other hand, Eve was already her friend – her sister – and she felt a deep sympathy for her.

Eve shook her head. 'I want to ask him what he thinks. He will understand, I know he will. Joe doesn't believe, so he can't help. But he doesn't see that. He seems to hate Rowland.'

'He blames him for what happened to you. And I think maybe he's a bit jealous too.'

'Why should he be jealous? It's Joe I love.'

'Maybe. But Rowland means a lot to you, doesn't he?'

'He ... why yes, I suppose ... he's like no one else, you see, Jenny. The way he speaks, the words seem – why, to shine somehow. And when he looks at you, his eyes see right into your soul, and see the very worst, but the best too, and they look with such love.' She coloured hotly. 'I know it

185

sounds as though Joe's right to be jealous, but that's not what
I mean, not really. Loving Joe – well, he's Joe, and I know
him like I know myself, and I know he does wrong sometimes and I feel easy and comfortable with him, as well as –
well, other things. But Rowland – it's not him, it's what's in
him, that's the difference.'

'I see,' said Jenny, who did not. She thought the distinction
Eve drew was rather a dubious one, but she had to accept it.
Besides, it was clear enough that the girl was troubled.
'Loving is a strange thing,' she added thoughtfully.

'Aye.' Eve came and put an arm about her. 'I think you're
right to take your happiness while you can. Don't let Joe or
anyone come between you.' Then she said with sudden
determination, 'I've a mind to go and see Rowland myself.'

'No, you mustn't do that,' said Jenny. 'You're not strong
enough for so long a walk. Besides, Joe would be angry. I'll
see if there's owt I can say will move him. We'll find a way
somehow.'

Mr Martin Morrison, chief agent of all the Beaumont mining
interests, making a tour of his area (routine, so he wanted it
to be thought), rode from Alston over the bleak wastes of
Upper Weardale eastward to Newhouse. Warned in advance
by George Crawhall that an angry and menacing crowd had
gathered outside the Weardale headquarters, he took a long
way round, up on to the fell by the Breckonsike mine and
then down again, approaching Newhouse from the north.
Even so, as he came within sight of the gabled roofs of the
old stone buildings, set so close into the hillside that they
almost seemed a part of it, he could hear quite distinctly the
low ominous sound of men muttering angrily together, and
glimpse the growing mob (for what else were they?) gathering outside the Short Thorns public house and spilling on to
the green slopes where in June the booths and sideshows had
marked the holiday. One or two men passed him, but they
were deep in grave talk and apparently (rather to his relief)
did not know who he was, so that he was able to reach the
house without incident, to be welcomed with great warmth
by a clearly distressed George Crawhall.

'Thank God you are here,' the Weardale agent said, as he

186

led his superior into the office. 'I tell you quite without exaggeration that if this is not cleared up soon there will be violence. I've hardly dared put my nose out of doors these past days, at least not without a fair escort.' He poured brandy into two glasses, and handed one to Morrison. 'One of my washing inspectors had a stone thrown at him yesterday. There is a most regrettable spirit abroad. They seem lost to all feelings of respect and duty.' He got up suddenly and went to the window, throwing it wide. 'Listen to that!'

The air was full suddenly of noisy anger. Morrison nodded. 'I saw them,' he said.

'The trouble is,' Crawhall went on, 'I can't see that matters will be calmed unless we promise something more. Yet to yield to men in this wicked and turbulent frame of mind is to threaten an end to all subordination.'

'I cannot but share your sentiments on that score. And we are not in any case in a position to offer any further increase.'

'Indeed no. But how to put that over, how to convince the men that it's in their own interests to accept what's offered?'

'What is in their own interests is that they return to work. There can be no question even of considering their demands while they are in breach of their agreements. However, it seems to me imperative that I should fully explain the position to them. They must be told in the plainest possible language that it is in the power of none of us – even of Mrs Beaumont herself – to raise prices or subsistence money, certainly not for the immediate future. So what we must do now is to inform them that I am here and will make myself available to hear any of them, and answer their complaints.'

'Then I will send to let them know,' said Crawhall, leaving the room.

It was Joshua Bowman who went out to face the increasingly impatient men now waiting on the road outside. He took up a position well above them, on a corner of the wall that edged the field behind the house, concealing his anxiety behind a scowl. He conveyed Mr Morrison's message (with some difficulty, for much of what he said was drowned in shouting, and he had to repeat himself several times) and then jumped down into the field.

'Wait, Bowman!' He turned back, to see a man step forward at the front of the crowd (it was Joe, he noted, brother of that stuck up Jenny Emerson, who thought herself too good for a mere Weardale man). 'We've an answer for you!' He stood still, listening. 'You can tell yon Morrison, if he wants to speak with us, then he must come out here. We'll not come crawling to him. We've had our say, and we stay out till he gives us what we want.'

An increased roar from the men behind him backed him up.

Flustered and unhappy, Bowman turned and went to report to the two men inside.

Morrison scowled. 'How dare they! Such insolence is insupportable!' He thought for a moment, then said, 'Go out and inform them that, since no one appears to wish to speak with me, I am leaving for Newcastle within the hour. That may encourage a greater sense of urgency.'

It took some time, but the strategy worked at last. After about two hours (when Morrison was on the point of putting his threat into effect, since it seemed he had no other choice), six delegates from the miners appeared at the house, asking to speak with him. Relieved, he resumed his seat behind the desk, Crawhall seated a little behind him.

As the men entered, Morrison did not rise, nor did he ask the men to sit down. 'Ah, I believe some of us met in Newcastle the other day ... so, you've decided to come after all. Now perhaps we can talk sensibly about this matter.'

'That's all we want,' said Anthony Coulthard. 'We're reasonable men. And our demands are reasonable ones, the very least we require to live.'

The agent made no comment on that, only said, 'You must know that the rise you have been offered is as much as the mines can afford – no, to be frank with you, it is more than they can afford.'

'We were promised a rise as soon as lead prices were up, and they've been up a canny while now.'

'Indeed, so they have, to a small degree. And Mrs Beaumont has kept her promise, to offer a rise as soon as it was practicable. Unfortunately, there are other factors affecting the decision. I know she would greatly wish to offer more.

She is fully aware of the difficulties so many of you are labouring under. But she has to remain cognizant of what the mines are able to bear, in the matter of increased costs. It is in no one's interests – yours or hers – that the whole enterprise be rendered bankrupt.'

Coulthard looked him up and down, as if estimating the cost of the man's well-cut clothes. 'I've seen no sign of that, nor any hint of it. It's we who are hard up. We can scarce afford to feed our families, still less live without anxiety. There's a vast of us on the poor rate already. It'll get worse if there's no rise in our lent money.'

'That is precisely the problem,' said Morrison. 'Do you know why there are so many burdening the poor rate – one of the highest in the country, may I point out? I will tell you why. Because Weardale is trying to support a population far in excess of what the land can happily maintain. There are, to put it bluntly, simply too many of you. But that, may I point out, is hardly our responsibility. We have done all we can, and shall continue to do so. We employ many more men than the needs of the mines require. Further, we have more trials under way than any other enterprise, in the hope of findings new veins to provide work for this excessive population. But that is an expensive process, as you very well know, and rarely repays the outlay on exploration. Further, by increasing the price per bing, we have offered more than the mines can legitimately afford. We cannot in honesty do more.'

'Then how does the Quaker Company do more?'

'I would suggest their expenditure on exploration has been rather less ...'

'Or they don't have to pay out to keep the Bishop in comfort,' muttered Joe, unheard by the agent.

'... or they are taking a risk we are not able or prepared to take. If they make severe losses that will help no one, least of all the miners contracted to them.'

George Robinson took a step forward. 'We're wasting time with all this talk. We didn't come to haggle. What we want is simple: forty shillings a month subsistence and ten shillings more per bing. No more and no less. And you'll get no ore raised till that's what you offer.'

189

'And how many men do you speak for, pray? I would hazard that no more than a few hotheads are behind you – or will be once they know how reasonable we have been.'

'There you're wrong. We speak with one voice on this. Every man in Weardale has signed to say he'll not work till we have our rights.' It was, the other delegates knew, a slight overstatement, but they were not going to contradict it.

Morrison shook his head. 'I wonder if you know what you are doing. This is a most irregular proceeding in every way, and most regrettable. Nor is it in the interests of any of you. I trust very much that you will be brought to your senses before you go any further down your present road.' He sighed, as if his regret was very real. Then he said suddenly, 'I'll tell you what I will do – to demonstrate that my concern for your plight is as real as I claim, I will make an alteration to what Mr Crawhall has already put before you. He has offered five shillings more per bing from January the first; I will undertake that the increase shall be paid at once, from the onset of this quarter's bargains. I may find it hard to justify such an offer to my superiors, but I take the responsibility on myself, in the interests of bringing peace once more into Weardale. Return to work, all of you, let the placing of bargains go ahead unhindered, and I will keep my side of the agreement. I can't be more generous than that. I am sure you will agree that we have been more than fair.'

There was no flicker of interest or acquiescence in the faces opposite him. Coulthard said, 'We will carry your offer to the men,' and then the six of them turned and left the room.

Outside again, Joe, whose voice was loudest, conveyed the offer to the increasingly impatient men, in words which Morrison himself might have used; but the chief agent, standing at the open window of the house behind them, caught the ironic sneering tone in which they were put, and frowned angrily. The next moment the surging thunder of the men's jeers and shouts reached him in a great wave of rejection and fury, and he knew that however the message had been carried the answer would have been the same.

'They've been well worked on already,' murmured

Crawhall behind him. 'I fear there never was much hope they'd accept.'

Morrison shot him a keen glance. 'Then you think the men as a whole are not fully behind the strike – that they've been talked into it? By whom then? The six who were here just now?'

Crawhall shook his head. 'I don't know. They may simply have been delegates, chosen to speak for the rest. Or they may be directing the action. I have heard that there is some sort of committee behind it, but who they are I do not know.'

'That is something we must find out. Look into it, Crawhall. It is of the greatest importance. If we are unable to break the strike by appealing to the mass of the miners, then we may need to find another way. Meanwhile, it is essential that we act as if wholly indifferent to the outcome of their proceedings. Calmness is everything. Once you are ready to let the bargains, then I should like to predict that the majority of the men will see sense. We only need to sit it out until then.'

When the deputation returned with the men's response, Morrison heard them in silence, and then said, 'I am very sorry, more sorry than I can say. I fear they will come to regret this step. But there we are.' Then he added, 'I suppose you realize that your men are in breach of the law?'

'In wanting a fair price for the fruits of our labour? I don't see how that can be,' said Robinson.

'You are combining together to conspire for a rise in wages. That is illegal. Every man who signed your paper is similarly in breach of the law. I warn you only in friendship. I have no wish to use the law against any of you. I suspect you rather of being misguided than wicked. But for that reason I urge you to return to work with all speed.'

'You've had our answer to that,' Coulthard said.

On his way out of the house to where his horse was waiting to carry him back to Newcastle, Morrison went to speak directly to the men. 'All of you, I urge you, as I have urged your delegates – return to work at once. I am convinced that is what many of you wish. If you are afraid of the threats of your workmates, then be reassured: every protection will be offered to you. That is my promise, and that of Mr Crawhall.'

191

The derisive roar that greeted the promise was hardly encouraging.

On his way to meet his beloved Jane the next afternoon, Edward found himself accosted by two men with a bowl. 'We're collecting for the miners' fund, sir. Like to give us something?'

'If the miners wish for money, then they should return to work,' he said primly. 'They have no one but themselves to blame if they go hungry.'

One of the men muttered something he didn't quite catch, but did not want to hear. He wondered if they would have been any more pleasant towards him had he made a contribution. If so, it would have been something of a landmark, to be remembered. The strike was not going to help him feel comfortable in this place, he reflected. There was an atmosphere of angry excitement hanging over the village which to him seemed ominous in the extreme. Men stood in groups on the corners, talking in low urgent voices and watching every passer-by, as if suspicious of strike breakers. Not that he thought there was any danger (if that was the right word) of anyone breaking the strike. He had never felt so isolated and shut out by the people around him as he did now. It was as if this new, self-inflicted tribulation bound them all together against the world in an indissoluble bond, which was inevitably characterized by hostility to all who were not held by it too.

He began to think he had been unwise to ask Jane to meet him by the ford, down river from the village. It had seemed a good place, far enough from her home and sufficiently out of the way not to draw attention to their meeting, but he wondered now if it was not after all dangerously close to the village and all its resentment of those who were not a part of it; and Jane was no longer a part of it, for she had been rejected by her churlish neighbours even before the strike began. Knowing something of the unpleasantness she still suffered, he would have preferred to call for her at White Lea and escort her all the way to the parsonage, but that would have been to risk a confrontation with her brother, more hostile than any of them. Edward had no wish to find himself drawn into a quarrel with that hot headed young man.

Jane was there, standing on the nearer bank of the river with her shawl pulled about her. She came to meet him, smiling warmly, all her sweetness in her eyes, and he forgot his qualms. What did all those other trivial problems matter, so long as he and his Jane could be together?

He took her in his arms and kissed her, rather more effusively than propriety allowed, but then it would not, he hoped, be very long before they were married; and for a girl unused to the constraints of a chaperon, dependent always on her own self restraint and natural modesty, the rules to which his sister was accustomed did not quite apply.

He felt a surge of excitement at the thought of their impending marriage, of the wedding night, when all he desired would at last be permitted. He had often imagined it, though a little shamefully. She would be shy perhaps, but not coy, modestly content to surrender to him, eager to bear him children and serve him as the perfect wife that she was so clearly born to be.

'Peggy has prepared something for our refreshment,' he told her, drawing her arm through his. He looked forward to the little feast he knew awaited her, by way of a surprise. But first there was that other, more delicate matter, about which he must speak in spite of his very clear reluctance. It was not an easy thing to bring to the attention of an innocent maiden like his Jane. Better to get it over with quickly, before they reached the parsonage, before they came (as they very soon would) to the first cottages of the village. He cleared his throat and began, 'My dearest, something has come to my ears which I find greatly distressing. I trust you will be able to set my mind at rest.' He looked down at her and saw that she was troubled by his tone. 'Is it right that Jacob Todd's daughter has been given refuge under your roof – the one who has so sadly gone astray?'

'Aye, that's right,' said Jenny. 'She tried to kill herself – but you'll know that. Joe always wanted to wed her.'

'I am aware of that, and I have a degree of sympathy with them both – indeed, great sympathy for her in her plight. It is entirely proper that someone should take pity on her and

193

give her shelter until the birth of her child. But to invite her to share the roof of an unmarried girl ...! My darling, I know you do not like me to speak ill of your brother, but I think very ill of him for taking such a step.'

'Do you think I had no say in it then? Where else was she to go? It's Joe's bairn she's carrying. They'd have been wed long since if it hadn't been for her father. Joe will take her to Gretna once the bairn's born.'

'That's as may be, but it remains that they are not yet married. Her position is most irregular. Your charitable spirit does you credit, my love, but I think even so you must see the impropriety of it, for someone in your position.'

She stared at him, and then shook her head. 'Why no, I can't say I do. She's done no more than most lasses. It's not her fault it's turned out as it has.'

Edward pressed his lips together with disapproval. 'That, my love, is why there is so much immorality in Weardale, because even young ladies so naturally innocent as yourself have not been taught to call wrongdoing by its proper name. Have you any idea how many brides go to the altar in – well, a less than pure condition?'

'Why yes, but then till lately they had to go all the way to Stanhope to wed. They're used to putting it off till the last minute – or till the Pay, at least.'

'That is not the point. I am not talking about delays in the wedding ceremony, but an undue haste in – well, I believe you understand me.' He was, Jenny saw, beginning to grow very red, but he persevered nevertheless. 'I am sure you do not believe that such minor inconveniences are any justification for unchastity.'

Jenny sensed that to admit that she did not share Edward's views on the matter might lead her into serious difficulties, and so she said, 'No, of course not.'

'Then,' he said, 'you see the rightness of what I have been saying about that young woman's presence beneath your roof?'

She knew she could not go that far. 'Why no,' she said, 'I don't. Eve's got to stay somewhere, and Joe's the best one to look after her. And I don't see how it has any effect on me.' She smiled ruefully. 'If she isn't a warning against what can

194

happen if you're not careful I don't know what is!'

She saw at once that she had shocked Edward. 'I am not talking about being careful, I am talking about doing right. And I do not think it a matter for levity.'

'No,' she said meekly. 'No, it is not. But I am not going to turn Eve out, even if I thought Joe would agree to it, which he won't. So I'm sorry, but there it is.' Her instinct told her he would accept that, however reluctantly, and she was right.

He said nothing more until they reached the parsonage, and if he had been Joe she would have suspected him of sulking. Even the highly uncomplimentary shouts of a group of miners watching them from outside the King's Head did not seem to penetrate his mood; certainly he gave no sign that he had heard them. But once at the house he seemed suddenly to shake off his gloom. He ushered her into the dining room with a conspiratorial air, as if anticipating her pleasure.

In the doorway she stood still, gazing at all the food spread upon the table, her mouth watering, her heart beating fast, her eyes wide. Edward watched her with tender amusement.

'Come, dearest, are you not going to eat?'

She looked round as if the words had startled her. 'Oh – what? Why yes ... No, I can't eat all this!'

'I'm not asking you to eat all of it.' He laughed and came to kiss her tenderly. 'You dear little goose! Just eat your fill. I have been afraid sometimes you might not have enough to eat.'

'No.' She took her seat, all gravity. 'But I don't want to eat like this when so many have nothing at all ... We never have enough at home.'

He leaned over the table and earnestly took her hands in his. 'Then, my darling, you shall take home with you as much as you wish of what I have, to feed all those hungry mouths. I have little sympathy with the strike, but I cannot let you suffer.'

Jenny already knew that he condemned the strike, for he had preached against it very firmly in church on Sunday, doubtless to the satisfaction of Mr Crawhall, who had been sitting in his pew just below her. It had brought home to her, in a way that made her feel deeply uneasy, how much more

Edward had in common with the mine owners and agents than with the miners who formed the vast bulk of his flock. It was only to be expected of the Church's representative, of course, but Mr Whitelock would have been less ready to take sides openly on such a matter. In looking forward to escaping from Weardale, Jenny had not thought before that in doing so she would be moving into a world that was not only very different from her own, but also in many ways utterly opposed to it. 'Don't you think the miners have a right to a share, when prices go up?' she said at last, desperate for some reassurance that Edward was not, after all, so alien as he had suddenly begun to seem.

'Of course, my love,' he said, and she was surprised at the depth of her relief. Then he went on, 'But I do not think this the way to achieve such an end. If all working men were to take the law into their own hands, think what would happen – nothing less than the overthrow of all order and authority! The revolution in France should have taught us the dangers of such a course. But at a human level – yes, of course I wish to help my hungry brothers and sisters.'

She had to be content with that; on the whole she thought it was enough.

Not having any money for drink (or anything else), Joe slipped into the King's Head as unobtrusively as possible and joined his friends in the corner by the window. Not that Tom Walton, being sympathetic to the strike, minded his customers using his inn merely as a meeting place, but Joe felt awkward about it all the same. 'No, I don't want a pint bought for me,' he said quickly, as he sat down.

'Wasn't going to offer you one,' said Anthony Siddle. 'What I've got I need for the court.' It was only two weeks now to the Quarter Sessions. 'We don't see much of you these days,' he added.

'Aye, well, you know –' A hand settled itself with some force on Joe's shoulder. He looked round sharply and saw the landlord standing beside him.

'You're wanted,' said Walton. Joe shrugged, said, 'I'll be back,' and followed the man across the room.

Once they were away from the others, Walton said in a

196

low voice, 'Upstairs! Thompson and Peart are back.'

Joe slipped up the stairs to Walton's bedroom, where the other members of the strike committee had already gathered. John Peart and Tommy Thompson had just returned from Hexham. Their deputation to young Mr Thomas Beaumont had been delayed because of an unfortunate fire at his Northumberland mansion, just a week ago; it had not seemed quite tactful to trouble him with their own difficulties at such a time, and tact was supremely important in putting over their case. But when every other possible move had proved fruitless, they had agreed that they should not wait any longer. In less than two weeks the bargain prices and lent money for the coming year would be fixed, and by then it would be too late.

But this evening Joe sensed the optimism in the air, even before he took his seat on a chest near the bed, on which most of the others were seated. 'It went well then?'

Thompson nodded. 'I'll say one thing for young Mr Beaumont; he listens to what's said to him.'

'Come on then, man!' said Joe impatiently; lately, what with hunger and anxiety, he was more short tempered than usual. 'He'll put in a word for us? Is that it?'

'So he says,' Thompson returned. 'Mind, it's on condition we go back to work. Once we're back, then he promises he'll speak for us to his mother.'

'Can we trust him?' asked Coulthard.

'We thought so,' said John Peart. 'He heard all we had to say, and told us he thought we'd good reason to be aggrieved. Then he said he would most certainly promote our cause with his mother.'

'But will she listen, that's what I want to know?' Joe asked. 'It's not much of a promise otherwise. Not to end the strike for.'

'Mrs Beaumont thinks the sun shines out of his ears,' said Thompson. 'The Colonel too.'

John Peart nodded. 'Remember the Great Drink?' That event five years before, paid for by the Beaumont family to celebrate the coming of age of their eldest son, was already legendary among the Beaumont miners. Nothing quite like it had ever been seen before or since. It had made the average

197

Annual Pay look like a festival of moderation and abstinence.

For a little while it seemed as if the proceedings would be washed away in a torrent of reminiscence, until Coulthard said, 'Come now, lads, we need a decision. What are we to do? Are we sure enough of Mr Beaumont to advise going back to work? Because if we're not, then we should stay out. Once men have gone back, then it'll be hard to get them to come out again, if owt goes wrong.'

'But how much longer can we go on, if we do stay out?' said Thompson. 'The strike fund isn't doing so well.'

'Why, now there you're wrong,' Robinson put in. 'I took it into my head to go down to Stanhope this morning, to call on Mr Rippon at the Castle. A canny fellow, just a bit lad really. He must have liked what I said, for he made a very generous donation, and what's more he promised he'd send corn and rye as well.'

'Mind, we shall need that even if we go back to work next week,' said John Peart. 'Things were bad before the strike began.'

'The way I see it,' said Joe suddenly, 'we didn't go through all this just to throw it away because a soft-spoken young gentleman makes a promise that costs him nowt. How are we to know he wasn't just saying it so you'd leave him in peace? Or so you'd do just what you are doing, and advise us to go back to work?'

'We only have to wait a week or two to know if he meant what he said,' John Peart pointed out. 'The masters will be fixing the price any day now. We'll know then if we've got what we want.'

'And if we haven't? If Mr Beaumont fails in his promise?'

'Then we stop work again.'

Joe shook his head vehemently. 'Oh no, not once we've all gone back. Coulthard's right there. You'll never get everyone out again. We're solid now. We've got to stay that way.'

'Then Mr Beaumont won't speak for us. He made that plain.'

They talked on for some time, revolving the same arguments and coming to no agreement, increasingly ill-tempered about it all. In the end John Peart said, 'There's only one thing for it. We put it to the others and let them vote on it. That's all we can do.'

'Then I say we call a meeting here Monday and tell them what's happened,' said Joe, to general agreement. 'But until then, not a word. We've got to keep together, whether we stay out or go back.'

Nearing home later that afternoon, Joe caught up with Jenny, who was returning from the village with a basket on her arm. They walked the last few yards together, talking without saying a great deal, but once inside the house, Jenny laid the basket on the table and, with a flourish, removed the cloth that covered it, waiting for the exclamations of wonder and pleasure. Joe said nothing, simply stared at what she had revealed. Eve took a step nearer. 'That's real wheaten bread!' She sounded awed.

Joe reached out to restrain her, his eyes on his sister, severe and accusing. 'Where did this come from?'

'Does it matter?' Jenny asked. 'It's good food, and honestly got.'

'Not honestly, if it came from him,' said Joe.

'If you're too proud to eat it yourself, then at least let Eve have what she needs. She has the bairn to think of.' Joe looked from Jenny to Eve and back again and said nothing, merely turned away and took a book from the shelf and then went to sit down with it by the window. It was, the two women supposed, the nearest he was likely to come to giving in. Jenny grinned at Eve, and they sat down at the table and began to eat.

Afterwards, Eve went and put her arm about Joe and kissed him, ruffling his hair. 'You're a good man, Joe Emerson, in spite of yourself.' Then she said in a pleading tone, 'Joe, please let Rowland Peart come. I want to talk to him.'

Joe's face assumed the mutinous look that Jenny knew very well. She wondered if Eve had yet learned its significance.

'You wouldn't see the minister, or Hannah Milburn – and it was a hard walk for her, to come up here. The both of them know more of religion than Rowland Peart ever will.'

199

Eve shook her head. 'But not the same way.'

'Besides which,' said Joe, hardly listening to her, 'I can't see how talking to him will make you feel happy again. It was all his fault in the first place.'

'No it wasn't ... Joe, please!'

When he continued with his reading, ostentatiously turning the pages (though far too quickly for him to take anything in), she went on pleading and pleading, until in the end he flung down his book and said fiercely, 'He took you from me once. I've only just got you back again. I don't intend to let him take you from me again.'

'Eve is not your property,' said Jenny sharply. 'She's not anyone's property. If she wants to speak to Rowland Peart, or the devil himself come to that, that's her right.'

'You would think that, of course,' said Joe, but Eve continued to plead.

'Joe, you will not lose anything. I just want to talk to him. I'll give you no peace till I have.' After a pause, she brought up the ultimate threat. 'If you'll not ask him to come, I'll go and seek him myself.'

There was a silence, and then Joe said grudgingly, 'I'll think about it.' Eve, sure of success, kissed him warmly, but he only added, 'I make no promises. I'll see, that's all. Now let me be.'

11

Walking down the hill to St John's Chapel on Monday morning, Jenny wished she had not been so ready to offer to go in search of Rowland, when at last Joe had given in, late last night.

True, she had been afraid that, feeling as he did, Joe would be more likely to quarrel with the preacher than invite him to White Lea. But somehow, momentarily at least, she had forgotten what kind of reception she herself was likely to receive. Worst of all, to find him she must go first to Tabitha Hall's house, and risk the hurt that would inevitably bring.

But she had promised Eve, and so she walked as quickly as she could through the taunts of the market place and on along the lane (fortunately deserted) to the smithy, where she knocked on the house door.

It was no sooner opened than it slammed shut again, before a word could be spoken. Jenny had time only to catch the briefest glimpse of Tabitha's small figure at its further side. With a sense of desperation, she pressed her face to its unyielding surface and called, 'I want Rowland Peart! Is he there?' But there was no reply.

Lancelot was working in the smithy, shoeing a horse for a man who sat waiting nearby, shouting to him over the noise of hammer on metal. Jenny hovered in the doorway, wondering whether to shout herself, or to go in, or if Lancelot too would ignore her. Then he looked up and saw her, and studied her for a moment in silence, before taking the shoe to the horse and beginning to fit it to the hoof. At least it was quiet enough now for her to make herself heard.

'Do you know where Rowland is?'

He jerked his head in a vaguely westerly direction. 'Blackdene way, preaching.' Then he bent again to his task.

'The Methodists won't like that,' said the waiting man. 'They've threatened to throw him out if he keeps on preaching.'

'They can't do much,' Lancelot returned. 'He's not a full member, just goes along to worship with them. To tell the truth, I can't see him fitting easily into any church.' He did not seem to notice that Jenny had already thanked him and gone on her way.

She found Rowland at East Blackdene, speaking to a small crowd from the top of a flight of steps leading to a hay loft. He was in full flow, so she attached herself to the fringe of his audience, glad that they were too intent upon his message to take much notice of her, though those nearest to her, glancing round, edged away from her, as if fearful of contamination.

In front of her, two men hovered, occasionally speaking in low voices to one of the people there, and holding out a bowl. 'For the miners' fund,' she heard them say. She supposed they were taking the opportunity of touching hearts already softened by a spiritual message. If so, they had judged badly, because few put any money in the bowl, and one or two seemed rather to resent the interruption. After a time, the men slipped through a momentary gap, into the heart of the gathering, out of her sight.

Rowland's message this morning seemed to be that all God's children were united by their common parenthood, brothers and sisters one of another, and as such each was responsible for the other, a responsibility that had no limitations, no boundaries, and for which each would one day be called to account. It might not be a principle that she had often heard emphasized, but it was unexceptionable enough. What startled her were the conclusions he began to draw from it.

'"I was an hungred, and ye gave me meat: I was thirsty and ye gave me drink: I was a stranger and ye took me in" ... Why, how easy that sounds, how consoling for our consciences! How sweet the path to salvation! But wait, my brothers and sisters, for there are other words, the words the

202

Lord speaks to the damned who are cast into Hell. "I was a stranger and ye took me not in: naked and ye clothed me not: sick and in prison and ye visited me not." There it is, my friends! It is not the evil we do that will send us to the eternal fires, but the good we have failed to do.

'Remember rich Dives, who sat feasting while the poor man begged at his gate?' His voice changed, as it did so often, but now it became prim and educated – uncomfortably like Edward's, Jenny thought. His appearance seemed to change too, as if the slight shabby figure was suddenly transformed into a man of the world, elegant and assured, his manner full of self-justification. 'A fine hospitable man, Dives, wouldn't harm a fly. Worked hard all his life. Not one to sit back and let his money go to waste – oh no! No idler he! He put nearly all he had into those mines of his, worked every hour that God gave, suffered many a sleepless night over it all. What could be more just and right than that he should enjoy his wealth in his old age, when he's worked so hard all his life? He always has a warm welcome at his table for his own kind, his friends and family; a most benevolent gentleman, and such good company.

'As for that unsavoury beggar Lazarus at his gate, he really does intrude upon the fine view from the house. Not that Dives, good hearted man that he is, would ever have him turned away. He's even content for Lazarus to pick up the crumbs from his table, any scraps that are going. I can tell you, many a poor man would wish to be in his shoes (I speak metaphorically, of course, for Lazarus has no shoes – and as for his feet, well!).' Here, Rowland pinched his nose, with an air of fine disdain that set his hearers rocking with laughter. 'Besides, just look at him – he could have found work if he'd really wanted to. There's always work for those who want it. And all those children he had – such improvidence! No wonder he's poor! It's nothing more than he deserves. Why, the scraps from the table are a feast for him. Let him have any more and who knows where it will end? Before we know where we are he'll be clamouring to sit at the table with the rest of us and share the feast, for all the world as if he were our equal! The Lord preserve us from such a prospect!'

There was more laughter, richly appreciative, but at that

203

very moment the gentleman somehow slipped away and Rowland himself stood there once more, all burning indignation.

'Brothers and sisters, they died, those two men. You know the tale. One went to Heaven, the other to Hell; each rewarded as he had lived. And God's judgement does not give place before the rich and the powerful, it does not respect the rulers of this earth. No, my brothers and sisters, it was the poor man who found himself in Abraham's bosom, the poor man, who had died unheeded and unmourned at the rich man's gate. As for Dives, what use were his feasting and luxury and his magnificent funeral, when the Lord called him to account? All his wealth would not buy him a place at the Lamb's feast in Heaven, it would not even buy him the least bit crumb from that feast. For him there was only everlasting torment in the burning fires of Hell. For this Dives, who did no harm to anyone – did *nothing*, my brothers and sisters, nothing for any but himself. And for that he is being punished yet ...'

He did not need to underline the point any more. It was clear enough to everyone precisely what lesson he drew from his texts. Around her, Jenny saw, people were smiling, nodding, as delighted and astonished as she was. They were not used to preachers who attacked authority, who cast doubt on the wisdom of their masters. As for one who did so right in the middle of a strike, that was unheard of. But then, just as they had all been lulled into a comfortable sense of unity against the common enemy, Rowland turned the whole argument on them.

'To do nowt, my brothers and sisters, to sit at home and close our eyes and ears, that is the way to Hell. That is sin. The man or woman who says "I've done no wrong, I've never harmed anyone," that person condemns himself as surely as if he stood before the Lord on the Day of Judgement.' His eyes swept the throng, and Jenny felt as if they touched her too, seeing into some uneasy part of herself, though just at the moment she could think of nothing she had failed to do about which she ought to feel uneasy. Then Rowland's arm swung out, pointing into the crowd, moving on to this person and that with dramatic emphasis, and his

voice was sibilant with accusation. 'Be quite sure, my
brothers and sisters, this is not a sin of the rich alone. Search
your hearts, ask yourselves now, as you will be asked before
the throne of God when He comes to judge the world, "Have I
not turned my back on my neighbour when he was in need?
Have I not seen grief and suffering and passed it by? Have I
not made use of another's trouble for my own ends, shutting
my ears to the voice of conscience?"

'I see one here today who wallowed in drunkenness while
his children went in rags. I see one who kept every penny
meanly to himself while his wife died for want of a few pence
for a doctor. I see one who shut her ears to the cries of a
tormented child. Worse, I see those who claim to serve God's
cause, who claim to work for their hungry brothers and
sisters, who go among you as benefactors, but underneath
they are as ravening wolves.' His eyes had settled somewhere
in the depths of the crowd, and a hush fell over it. 'Aye, let
your conscience hear my words! Make amends before it is
too late! Give back the money you drank away last night,
money that was given in generosity for the needs of the
hungry! Repent, for tonight it may be that your souls will be
required of you, and the Lord you have cheated will accuse
you – "I was an hungred, and ye gave me no meat!" What
then will you say?'

There was a sudden commotion, in the exact spot where
his eyes had rested. Someone began to push his way out to
the edge, angrily gesticulating; two people, the men who had
been collecting for the strike fund. The next moment there
was a roar from the others, the men took to their heels, and
there was a wild pursuit down the hill, on towards the river.
Rowland, with a look of some concern, ran after them,
calling out that there must be no violence, but his voice was
drowned in angry shouting.

Right on the river bank the pursuers caught up with the
men, stripped them in search of any money they had and
then swiftly and unceremoniously flung them in the water.
Rowland stood helpless on the bank, watching in dismay, but
held back by the jeering crowd from doing anything to intervene. Jenny supposed he felt responsible for what had
happened, as he most certainly was. Not that she blamed

him. If the men had indeed been collecting for the miners' fund under false pretences, then at the very least they deserved their fate; which was not so very bad, after all, since the river was too wide and shallow to be dangerous for two grown men in full daylight. They were already climbing out on the far bank, swearing profusely and followed by the jeers and catcalls of their neighbours. Someone said, 'Take the money to Anthony Coulthard. He'll see it gets to those who need it.'

Rowland began to walk briskly along towards the bridge, as if he intended to follow the men and speak to them, though Jenny thought that a most unwise action, in the circumstances. Besides, she wanted to speak to him herself. She hurried after him and caught his arm. 'Rowland Peart!'

He turned sharply, his eyes scarcely focusing on her, clearly too deeply preoccupied with what had just happened to waste time on anything else.

'I must speak with you.'

He hesitated for a moment (was he too going to reject her?) and then, after one swift regretful glance towards the departing men, gave her his full attention. She knew she had it, by the intensity of his gaze on her face, the sense she had that all the force of his mind, his soul even, was concentrated on her alone. It was a somewhat disconcerting sensation, but at least he was not hostile. 'What's your trouble?'

'Oh, it's not mine,' she said hastily, not wanting to be mistaken for one of his converts. 'It's Eve Todd.'

'Why yes – the stranger you took in.'

'She's no stranger,' Jenny pointed out sensibly. 'But she's troubled, very troubled.'

He considered the matter in silence. His eyes were, she noticed, more or less on a level with her own; perhaps that was why they seemed to see right into her. Before today she had felt no awkwardness or unease, on the few occasions when they had met – irritation perhaps, but nothing worse. He was, after all, a man who had been Billy's friend, a Weardale man, more like her than Edward or his family. But now, suddenly, for no reason that she could think of, she felt herself colouring under his gaze.

'Then why come to me? Your brother showed me the

door, last time I was at White Lea.'

'I know. But since then Eve has – well, it's preyed on her mind. Joe loves her, you know. He wants what's best for her.'

'What would be best would be for them to marry, but I told him what her father said.'

'Aye.' Then she burst out, 'How can a father be so cruel to his own child? I don't understand it, not at all.'

'You've done well to know so little of evil,' said Rowland sombrely. 'But we're straying from the point. What do you want of me?'

'To come and talk to Eve. She asks to talk with you. But –'

'Well?'

'She is convinced that she is bound for Hell. That's what troubles her. She has bad dreams, and can find rest neither day nor night. But if she talks to you, and all you can offer her is the assurance that Hell is the punishment for sin, and she is more of a sinner than ever, then –'

'Why then her case will be the worse. Do you truly think that's what God would want of me, to offer her such cold consolation?'

'I don't know. I hadn't heard you've ever urged tolerance for sin.'

'No, nor shall I. But this is a different matter. Eve knows she sinned, and she repented long ago. That is forgiven. What she has before her now is the consequence of her sin. As for living with Joe, as she is now ... She will be none the worse for anything I say to her. And of course I will come. Trust me, Jenny Emerson.' There was something so intimate in the way he spoke those last words that for a moment she forgot all about Eve and Joe, about anything at all. She was instead aware with an extraordinary intensity of conscious-ness of Rowland's face, its taut angularity, the long lines that marked it, the wide supple mouth, the eyes very dark under the heavy brows, eyes that seemed to hold her spellbound, so that she came to a complete halt and simply stood there, unable to move or think or lower her gaze.

Then, abruptly, he looked away and said, 'I've someone else to see, and this afternoon a meeting for prayer, but I'll come after that. Will that content you?' and the spell was broken.

'Yes,' said Jenny, feeling quite shaken. Then, her mind clearing, she remembered. 'No, for Joe won't be there. He says he must be at home when you come.'

'Of course, we meet in the King's Head tonight – I'd forgotten. I should be there too. And tomorrow I'm promised to go to Bollihope.' He frowned. 'She shouldn't be left waiting. Will tomorrow night be too long?'

As she walked back up the hill, Jenny thought, *Eve is right; there is something about him, about the way he looks at everyone.* But even knowing that others felt it too did not make it any less disturbing.

Rowland was a long time with Eve that next evening, but when he came outside to where Joe and Jenny and Tommy were tactfully sitting on the bench by the door, he said quietly, 'I think you'll find her calmer now.'

'She'd better be,' said Joe. 'If she's any the worse, you'll not get home in one piece.'

Rowland ignored that. 'There's one thing.'

'What?' Joe's tone was wary.

'So long as she lives with you unwed she can never be quite easy.'

'And you've made damn sure she's not easy about it! I might have known. I've promised I'll take her to Gretna as soon as the bairn's born and she's fit again. I can't do more than that.'

Rowland put up a hand. 'One moment, Joe! She doesn't need me to tell her of her sin. She has a conscience, and that will not be at peace, truly at peace, until she is your wife in more than your eyes. But there is one way, if it seems right to you.' It was clear that Joe was not in the most receptive of moods, but though he folded his arms and stood stony faced while doing so, he did listen. 'To go to Gretna is the only way you can be wed without her father's consent, but that cannot be done for many months yet. Otherwise, there can be no legal marriage, nor I think would any minister of religion wed you. I'm no ordained minister, but ...' He cleared his throat. 'I would call for a blessing on you, and I do believe in God's eyes that would be sufficient, in the spirit if not in the law.'

Joe gave it some thought. 'Did you say that to Eve?'

Rowland nodded. 'I think she liked the notion.'

'Why then, if it's what she wants, I'm content,' said Joe. 'As for me, since I don't hold with Hell, or Heaven either, it makes no odds. But I'd swear owt to make her happy.'

'That will have to be enough for the time being,' said Rowland quietly.

'You need not think you'll get your claws in me for your God, Rowland Peart,' Joe warned him.

Rowland merely smiled.

It was an odd occasion, the ceremony that was not a ceremony, yet had all the solemnity of one. Eve, her face shining with a happiness as great as that of any lawful bride, stood at Joe's side, facing Rowland across the hearth. Jenny and Tommy, their witnesses, watched quietly from a little distance away as Rowland, using what he remembered of the words of the marriage service, made the young couple promise to love and be faithful to one another, and then held their clasped hands and prayed for God's blessing. He looked exalted, Jenny thought, his eyes closed, as if he had been carried away from the homely room to some far place. Afterwards, it was a moment or two before he appeared to realize quite where he was.

Eve kissed Joe first, eagerly, and then, with a hesitant shyness, Rowland too; and then everyone relaxed and laughed and Jenny went to bring what food and drink they had to the table. At that point Rowland said he must be going. Joe, already delighted by signs that the Eve he knew and loved was fully restored to him, with all her sweet teasing ways, protested almost as warmly as if there had never been any cloud on their friendship. 'Why, but you must stay and drink with us! This is a wedding after all.'

Rowland shook his head. 'I've to leave for Guinea Grove early tomorrow, and it's already late. Besides, I don't touch strong drink.'

'You were not so lily livered once,' said Joe, with obvious regret. They went together to the door, and Joe laid a hand on the other man's shoulder and said simply, 'Thank you.'

'Not me,' said Rowland.

'I know no one else to thank, in this case,' said Joe, and

patted his shoulder. He watched Rowland walk off into the dusk.

Rowland made his way down the track and on to the road, coming soon to where the sheltering belt of trees marked the western border of White Lea. Here, where the fringe of the plantation crossed the road, it was already deeply shadowed, with a cold wind setting the leaves rattling overhead. In the darkest point under the trees he did not see the two men waiting for him. He knew nothing until they were on him, thumping and kicking him with joyful savagery. 'That's for preaching against us – and that! And that!'

He did not know how long it lasted. It all had an air of unreality, as if it was happening to someone else, though the pain was real enough, the savage blows, of fists and some sort of weapon, a club maybe. At first, from instincts long buried, he fought back, ferociously, with all his strength, but he was slight, unarmed, outnumbered, his eyes as yet unused to the dark. How it ended he was not sure. There was a sudden agonizing pain in his head, worse than any before, and then a merciful moment of blackness; and then a little later again he opened dazed eyes on a blur of light – from a lantern, he realized, whose light flickered on a face bent over him. It was hazily familiar, but his brain was too fogged with nausea and pain to consider whose it might be. He felt an arm slide under his shoulder, raising him a little; then the pain came again, and he was sick, and the blackness returned.

Joe, coming into the kitchen early the next morning, went at once to look anxiously into the shadowed depths of the box bed. 'Good thing you sent for me,' the surgeon had said last night. 'Though I don't think there's any permanent damage. Time will tell.' Rowland had looked bad, though, when Joe, alerted by some unusual sound, had discovered him on the road; for a moment or two he had even thought he was looking at a corpse. He would need to be in bed for some days yet, at the very least, Mr Scott had said, before refusing payment and going home.

'It crossed my mind, maybe Eve had taken a turn for the worse, after all.'

Joe jumped, and then realized it was Rowland who had spoken. He was not smiling, but his eyes were bright with amusement. The bruises on his face were already turning red and purple, and he looked more battered than he had last night, but at least he was conscious and apparently no worse; except that Joe wondered briefly if the blows had addled his brain, since what he said seemed to make little sense.

'You threatened me yesterday,' Rowland reminded him.

'Why, so I did.' He pulled a stool to the edge of the bed, remembering with sharp suddenness when he had last done this; only then the man in the bed had been dying. 'Who were they, do you know?'

Rowland managed a sketchy shake of his bandaged head. 'There were two I spoke against yesterday. But I can't be sure.'

'That would be the two who were cheating the miners' fund?' Jenny had told him about it, and he had heard of it too at the meeting last night, from Anthony Coulthard, who had been full of praise for Rowland.

'There's one thing I wondered,' said Jenny, looking up from attending to the fire. 'How did you know those men were keeping the money for themselves? Were you sure of it?'

'I wouldn't have said owt otherwise. I saw them collecting at Wolsingham one day, and other places where they weren't known. And I knew they weren't any of the men Anthony Coulthard had picked. They were in the Black Bull one night, so I spoke to them. Their answer was to tell me to mind my own business.'

Joe frowned. 'Then they can't be let get away with this.' He went to put on his coat.

'Where are you going?' Rowland asked, suddenly finding considerable force from somewhere.

'To get a few together to see to it,' said Joe.

'No – no, I don't want that!'

Joe stood still, looking at him with clear astonishment. 'Why, what else is there to be done?'

'Nowt,' said Rowland. '"Whosoever shall smite thee on the right cheek, turn to him the other also."'

'It was a damn sight more than your cheek they smote,'

211

said Joe humorously; and then added, suddenly serious, 'You don't mean it? That they should get away with this?'

'What good would it do to use violence against them?'

'Teach them to leave you alone. And that there's more than just you think little of their cheating.'

'And that all I say against fighting and violence, all the Gospel I live for, that is worth nothing?'

'It was your preaching got them a ducking.'

Under the bruises, Rowland coloured a little. 'That was not what I intended. I didn't think they would give themselves away as they did.'

Joe came to the bedside. 'Do you not feel angry? What are you made of, man?'

Rowland smiled faintly. 'Aye, I feel angry. But that is Rowland Peart's way, and the Devil's. God's way is different.'

Joe shook his head. 'I don't understand you, that I don't. You've changed, that's certain.'

'But you'll let things be?'

'If I must. If that's truly what you want.'

'Tommy, it's time for bed, if you're to be up for work tomorrow.'

Tommy, sitting drowsily on the rug before the fire, looked up at his brother. 'Why have we gone back, Joe? Will they be paying more, when the new bargains are made?'

'That's what we all hope.'

Jenny caught the note of doubt in his voice, and when Tommy had gone out, on his way to the hay loft, she said, 'You'll feel better about it, once you've been back a few days.'

'I'll feel better about it when we have what we asked for. Not till then.'

'It was what the meeting decided,' Jenny reminded him gently. The events of yesterday seemed to have broken down part of the barrier between them, and Joe had now told her all about the long and angry meeting on Monday night. It explained the sullen mood in which he had returned to work this morning. 'You have to abide by it.'

'I'd not mind so much if the vote hadn't been so close.

There was next to nowt in it. To go back for so little – why, it seems such a waste of all we've been through.' He glanced round at the box bed. 'John Peart said you voted against.' Then he saw that Rowland was asleep, as far as he could tell in the dim light. 'I envy him, not being able to go back yet,' he added to Jenny.

They talked on for a little while, with something of their old affectionate ease, and then at last Jenny made her way out to join Tommy in the hay loft, cheered by Joe's softening towards her.

She had reached the top of the steps by the byre, and her hand was on the latch of the door, when some sound behind her in the night made her turn. There, coming up the track towards the house, a lantern bobbed and swayed, lighting first one, then another of the men who came with it – two of them, Jenny thought, her breath caught in alarm. She ran back to the house and told Joe, who came to the door to look.

'It's Robinson and Stephenson,' he said at last, his voice lightening with relief. 'What the hell can they want at this time of night?' They were not close enough friends, even after their days of working together on the strike, simply to have come prossing. He went down to meet them.

Jenny continued on her way to bed. She knew quite well that Joe's apparent partial forgiveness of her would not be shared by anyone else in the neighbourhood.

'We were right to vote for stopping out,' Robinson said, as he stepped into the house. 'I just wish to God the others had heeded us.'

Without waiting for Joe to question them further, Stephenson enlarged, 'It was Jock Wilson's partnership, from Level Gate. They found their grove so fouled up with bad air, what with standing so long, they couldn't work. So Wilson went down to Newhouse, to report it to Mr Crawhall. And while he was there he was left alone in the office, just for a minute or two, and he just happened to see this letter on the table –'

'I wish to God we'd known of it before we voted,' Robinson broke in vehemently. 'I know damn sure there'd have been none voting to go back, if we'd only known.'

213

'We didn't know, did we? Jock had a read of it, you see – it was lying there, not quite covered over. It was from Mr Morrison in Newcastle, written on Saturday – *Saturday*, two whole days before we met! Mr Morrison had spoken to young Mr Beaumont, he said, put him right on what was offered to us. And Mr Beaumont swore he'd promised us nothing, only said we should go back to work, for our own good.'

'He does not interfere – that's what he said,' put in Robinson. 'He has nowt to do with the mines and the running of them, nor does he want it. So much for his promises!'

There was silence, while they all three stood there, staring at one another. Then Joe turned and crashed his fist down on the table and swore savagely and at length. 'I knew we shouldn't go back – I knew it! We should never have trusted them. What the hell do we do now?'

'That's why we've come,' said Robinson. 'We've got to decide.' He broke off and glanced uneasily at Rowland, who was awake now and watching them.

'He's all right,' said Joe. 'He voted to stay out.' They sat down at the table. 'What does John Peart say? And Thompson?'

'We haven't seen John Peart. Thompson says he still doesn't believe they were deceived. He thinks Mr Beaumont will speak for us yet. He says he'll not believe otherwise till the bargain prices are set, and the lent money. He says he'll come out again then, if there's no rise.'

'And how long will it take till then? Two weeks? No one will come out again after all that time. He was a fool to believe Mr Beaumont in the first place – I always said it.' Joe frowned, bending his head on his hands and running his fingers through his hair, dragging at the roots. 'How many know about this?'

'All that were in the King's Head tonight, and we've told as many more as we can. There'd be a strong vote for laying off work again, if we took one now, I'm sure of it.'

'Then that's what we go for – not a vote, there's no time for that, and no point. No, we just send word round the strike's on again, and tell them why.'

214

Robinson shook his head. 'That's easier said than done. Now they're back, there'll be some who won't come out again. Thompson, for instance – and he won't be alone.'

'If they won't join us, then we'll have to make them,' said Stephenson. He lowered his voice. 'Smash the waggon ways, and the pumps, make sure they can't work even if they want to.'

Joe shook his head doubtfully. 'That puts us outside the law. I think it would be best not, not yet anyway.'

'From what Mr Morrison said, we're already outside the law,' said Stephenson. 'Though I can't see why.'

'Nor can I,' said Joe.

'It's simple enough.' It was Rowland's voice that broke in on the discussion, faintly but with determination. All three men turned to look at him. 'The law says men may not combine together for an increase in wages. The penalty can be transportation, if the courts have a mind.'

There was a long silence. Joe felt as if an icy finger had traced a path down the length of his spine.

'You didn't know?' asked Rowland.

Joe shook his head. 'Mr Morrison said something of the sort, but we're not learned in the law. And who would think ...?'

'Who would think so reasonable an action could be against the law? Who indeed. The masters can combine all they like to keep prices up and wages low. But that's another matter, of course. The masters make the law. Remember your place, Joe Emerson.' He spoke slowly and carefully, but his voice was edged with bitterness.

'But we're not employed men, like cotton spinners. We're free men. We make bargains, to work as we please.'

Joe looked at Stephenson with some scepticism. 'I doubt that's how the masters see us.'

'Why then, can you see the masters taking every miner in Weardale to court? There's over a thousand men. They'd be fools to try.'

'They only have to make an example of the leaders,' said Rowland. There was another silence.

'What would you do, in our place?' Joe asked at last. The thought of court action, of risking transportation to some

215

unknown land on the other side of the world, had temporarily quelled his vehemence.

A faint painful smile twisted Rowland's mouth. 'I'd not give in till I had justice. But then I've no one dependent on me. If they shipped me to Australia there's only myself would suffer.'

Joe looked puzzled. 'You're not like other preachers. Jacob Todd's been preaching obedience and duty ever since this all began, so my uncle says. And he's not the only one. To hear them speak, the only justice we'll ever get is in Heaven. That's meant to make up for all we suffer on earth. Well, it's not enough for me.'

'Nor for me,' said Rowland, with such conviction that the words came fluently, forcing their way through weariness and discomfort. 'Nor for the Lord, I do believe. He will call the wrongdoers to account and bring about the day of justice.'

'On the Day of Judgement!'

'On this earth, in our time – I am convinced of it. Read the gospels, Joe. You'll see the promise in every line. "He hath filled the hungry with good things; and the rich he hath sent empty away." That's not a promise for heaven, but for the earth, for us now.'

'When you've done with all your talk,' Stephenson broke in, 'can we get back to what we're here for? If we're outside the law anyway, I don't see that it matters what else we do. What have we to lose? Unless you want to go meekly back to work after all?' he added to Joe.

Joe shook his head. 'No, I don't want that. But we damage no property till we know what the others are going to do. If they all come out again, then we don't need any means to make them.'

'And if they won't, then we use every means we can think of. Not just smashing machines, but more – why, *personal* means.' The menace in Robinson's tone made it quite plain what he had in mind, though he added, as if to leave no possible doubt, 'Nothing like a night visit from his friends to put a man in mind of his duty.'

As he turned back to the table, Joe caught the look of dismay and disapproval in Rowland's eyes, but he ignored it. Even his kind of piety had its limitations.

*

Much later that night, when the others had gone, Joe went to
see if Rowland needed anything before he himself went up to
bed. The young man appeared to be asleep, but his face was
deeply flushed beneath the bruises and his breathing was
rapid and uneven. Joe laid a hand on his forehead and was
alarmed to feel how hot it was. In the end, he went to wake
Jenny.

By dawn next day Rowland was delirious. Joe, setting out
for Guinea Grove to see John Peart, called on the way at Mr
Scott's house and asked the surgeon to go quickly to White
Lea.

That day, too, George Crawhall, warned that the strike
was threatening to break out again, promised that every man
who now stayed at work would be paid lent money for the
entire time he had been on strike. The worst of it was, Joe
knew that was a promise that would be kept.

12

E dward, concerned that it was so very long since he had seen Jane, waited one more Sunday and then, when she was once again absent from morning service, resolved to go and call at White Lea, braving whatever unpleasantness might await him.

He rode up the hill with apprehension growing in him every inch of the way. What could have happened? For a few days it had seemed as if the strike was over, but she had not made any attempt to come and see him during that time, and then the whole thing had flared up again with a new bitterness, all the old unanimity gone. Jane's brother was clearly up to his neck in it, even, it was said, one of its leaders, though on the whole the miners were evasive about who precisely was leading them and what planning had gone into running the whole unhappy business. Not that any planning was much in evidence now, only a furtive and desperate policy of intimidation towards those who resolutely remained at work. Yet it must, Edward thought, be quite clear to any but the most hopelessly blind and fanatical that nothing was going to be achieved by such tactics, that no further rise was going to be offered.

There had been a considerable increase in violence, not out in the open like the usual drunken village brawls, but in back lanes, on the fell near some lonely mine shaft, behind alehouses. At several of the mines, men had come in to work in the morning to find vital machinery or waggonways smashed beyond use. Some working miners had their windows broken, or their wives and children jostled and shouted at in the street; more seriously, others received menacing visits at dead of night, from men with faces blackened to prevent recognition. Edward would have been glad to think Jane was avoiding all this by staying at home, had he not begun uneasily to fear that, as Joe Emerson's sister, she would be more likely to be among the attackers than their victims. Except that he could not bear to think she might support such behaviour ... No, he did not really believe that she would, not for one moment. And as his affianced bride she was naturally distanced even from her brother. Only why, then, had she not come to see him? Could it be – dreadful thought! – that the obnoxious Joe was keeping her a prisoner at White Lea?

He hoped that her brother would be safely away from the house this morning, on some subversive errand of his own. But even if he were not, then the curate was prepared to face him. It must be done, for he could not bear this uncertainty any longer.

The house looked, he thought, alarmingly deserted, approached in the cold rain of the late October morning. Outside, the cows fed, as did so many in the dale at present, on ash branches cut from the trees. In normal years the cattle grazed throughout the autumn on the aftergrass that followed the hay harvest, but this year the drought had meant there was no aftergrass worth mentioning, and no one yet wanted to begin on the meagre quantity of hay stored against the winter proper, which could be no more than a few weeks away. There was one pony in the field, bedraggled and miserable looking, but that at least suggested Joe Emerson was out somewhere, riding the second pony; or Edward hoped it did.

He went to the door and knocked, and when there was no immediate reply, pushed it open.

He stood in the doorway, astonished at what he saw. Jane sat on the rug before the hearth, one hand resting on the pretty stones that stood there, her eyes on someone seated, beyond his vision, on the settle. As he drew nearer, Edward saw that the object of her attention (which was disagreeably concentrated, he thought) was the preacher he so disliked. What, he wondered, was that young man doing here, looking thinner than ever, and pale and drawn, but ensconced in a corner of the settle as if he belonged there, with Tommy close

219

beside him and a book (it had the look of a Bible) open on his lap, as if he had been reading to the two of them; except that, precisely at the moment of Edward's arrival, he was looking at Jane as intently as she looked at him, with all the close familiarity of long acquaintance. It was bad enough that she should be in her brother's power. That she should be – intimate, was the word that sprang to mind, though he quickly rejected it – with this deplorable young man only increased his dismay and alarm.

She looked up, and then scrambled to her feet, colouring in a way he found disquieting. 'Edward!' She came and put her hands in his and kissed him, and then led him to the fire. 'Come and warm yourself.' She looked from his thunderous face to Rowland and then back again. 'You know Rowland perhaps?'

'We have not met,' said Edward frigidly, and not quite accurately. 'I was not aware,' he added, 'that he was an *habitué* of this house.'

Jane looked faintly puzzled at the unfamiliar word, and then said, 'He's been very sick, for three weeks now.'

Which, Edward realized, exactly explained why she had not called on him. His first sensation was not one of relief at the straightforwardness of the explanation, but of overwhelming anger, fury that a young lady promised to him should give nearly a month of her life to nursing a shabby, disreputable hedge preacher friend of her brother's (that, Edward presumed, was why he was here in the first place, for he was just the kind of man Joe Emerson would have as a friend), when she ought to have been thinking only of the gentleman with whom she intended to spend the rest of her life. It was, Edward realized, high time he took matters in hand, before they became any worse.

But he could not, of course, simply burst out baldly with what he wanted to say. He must work up to it in a tactful manner. So he enquired after the young man's health, and heard something of how he had come by his injuries in the first place (only what one would expect from someone who played on people's worst emotions as a means to win them for his dubious beliefs, Edward thought, unsympathetically), and asked how Jane and her family were managing in these

220

difficult times, and made one or two kindly remarks to Tommy, who hung down his head and mumbled an inaudible reply, until prodded into greater politeness by Rowland (which exasperated Edward even more); and then he talked of the weather and other trivial matters, until he felt that he had met all the requirements of courtesy and could safely come to the point.

He rose to his feet. 'My dear, I must take my leave.' He was pleased that Jane looked distressed that he should be intending to go so soon. 'Perhaps you will walk a little way with me?'

Outside, with the door safely closed, and sufficiently far from the house to be sure that they would not be overheard, even by scruffy preachers with no scruples, he took her hands in his. Conscious of his gravity, Jenny looked up into his face, gratifyingly unconcerned by the rain.

'My darling Jane,' he said, 'there is something we must most seriously consider.' He paused then, not quite knowing how to go on. He knew what he wanted to say, and why, but he was not certain that his reasons would convince her, in the circumstances. How would she react if he were to say, *Not only is Eve Todd under your roof, but from what I hear of your brother's doings, White Lea is becoming daily a more unsuitable place for the young woman I have chosen as my wife. And now I find that a man of doubtful if not un-balanced character has also taken up residence there, and has been daily in your company?* In the past he had been quite sure that he would always be able to convince her of the rightness of his opinion on any matter, but that conviction had lately been shaken, more than once. Further, might she not be offended if she were to think that was the only reason for his wish to speed matters up? Which it was not, of course. The main reason must be – well, the one he would put before her now.

'My darling, we have lived apart too long. I think it is time we fixed the day when we shall at last be made one.'

He wondered for a moment if she had failed to understand what he was saying, for she looked rather blank. He even wondered if he did not see just a hint of dismay; but surely that could not be so?

221

'Then you've been found a parish?' Jane asked; she was a little vague as to the precise mechanism of these things.

'Not yet. But there is no reason why we should not live together at the parsonage, until I am ordained. That cannot be long delayed now.' A wife of his own class could not have been expected to live on such limited means, but Jane was different, of course.

Jenny was surprised at her own reaction to what he suggested. Surely this was exactly what she had been longing for, the imminent arrival of their wedding day? This, at last, would mean the end of all the unpleasantness, the final break with everything that had made her so unhappy. She would have Edward to protect and care for her at all times, the comforts of the life he offered her, the prospect very soon that they would move away from Weardale altogether and make a new life in some prosperous parish where no one would know her origins and she could finally and for ever put all the unhappiness behind her. Yet her first reaction was one of alarm and dismay, as if what he suggested was the very last thing she in fact wanted. She could not understand it. After a moment she decided it was only because what confronted her was such a big step, that she would inevitably be saddened at the prospect of leaving family and friends (those few who remained) behind. Perhaps too she was fearful of moving into the village as Edward's wife, in daily contact with the neighbours who hated her for what she had done; though that could be very little harder than the way she lived at present. On the other hand, she need no longer fear for the well-being of her brothers. Eve would be there to care for them when she had gone; or at least she would once the baby was born. That, of course, was the only obstacle.

'I think,' she said slowly, 'that we should wait until Eve's bairn is born. She's not well enough yet to look after the house. When the bairn comes it will be different.'

He was shocked that after all he had said she should use such an argument against him. On the other hand, looked at from a purely practical point of view, what she said was incontrovertible. It was only from a moral point of view that it was indefensible.

'I am sorry you do not see the urgency of the matter,' he said, very gravely. 'I do beg you to reconsider. You are in a most irregular position here, the more so with that young man – a single young man, may I remind you – also under your roof. I know it is not of your choosing, but ...'

For the second time since their first meeting, Jenny felt sure that in an important matter she was right and he was wrong. She said with equal seriousness, 'Edward, I've looked after my brothers since my mother died. I can't just turn my back on them. It's only for a little while. Eve's more than six months gone now.' She smiled, but not very confidently. 'We can be wed in the New Year.'

Still he looked displeased. 'I am sure there is some suitable woman who can be called on to care for your brothers and – anyone else. What of your aunt, for example?'

'Uncle Ralph's sick. He needs all her care.'

'There must be someone. Some respectable middle-aged widow perhaps. In fact, if she had been a mother herself, she would be far better fitted than you are to take charge of the – er – impending event.'

Jenny could not deny that there was sense in what he said. Except that she could not easily think of a suitable woman; and, more to the point perhaps, she felt a curious reluctance to do anything so irrevocable as to agree to that course. When she said nothing, Edward went on, 'I shall expect you to discuss the matter with your brother. I really do think something must be done. In fact,' he added, as a new thought occurred to him, 'best of all would be for you to go and spend the weeks until we can be married at my parents' house. You have said yourself you have much to learn, and who better to teach you than my mother?'

That sounded even less appealing to Jenny. In Edward's company, life at Ashfield had been a blissful dream; without him to shield her from the hostility of his family, she suspected it would be both alien and intimidating. 'I'll talk to Joe,' she promised at last, knowing full well that such a step would be unlikely to bring her any nearer to agreeing to what Edward wanted. He bent and kissed her then, tenderly enough, but without his usual passion. She knew as she stood and watched him go that he was still displeased with her. For her part, she had never felt so out of humour with him as she did now.

Just outside the parsonage, Edward was accosted by Frank Johnson. The constable had a harassed and anxious look, as well he might, for he was helpless to prevent or control the disorders that so gravely afflicted the district. He asked for a word and then looked about him so nervously that Edward took him inside and rang for Peggy to bring tea, while the man told him what he wanted.

'You maybe know, sir, that I had business at the Quarter Sessions this past week.'

'I had heard the poacher Siddle was to go before the Sessions, yes.'

'Oh, it's not that. Or that's not the whole of it. In any case, he was bound over to the next Sessions. But there was more than him had a hand in the assault at the Pay.'

'A disgraceful affair,' Edward murmured. He had heard several conflicting versions of the event and was not convinced that Johnson's colourful account was the most accurate, but he felt that at present the man needed all the support and sympathy he could muster. In any case even the most peaceable pressure exerted on a constable in the course of his duty was at the very least undesirable.

'Well, you know I've tried to bring the men concerned to justice. But I've had no help in it, none at all, save from Joseph Dawson and one or two others, but that's not near enough. They just give me the slip, every time. So Mr Faber said he'd apply for Quarter Sessions' warrants, being more forceful, so he thinks. And now we've got them. But ...'

Edward could already see what was coming, and braced himself, his mind working quickly, searching for the most diplomatic reply.

'You've got standing in this place, sir. Men look up to you.' At the most generous estimate, Edward thought, that overstated the case. 'There's another thing, too – it's the Bishop's game we're protecting. They'll see the warrants as coming from him; and you, sir, you're under the Bishop. I know that's not quite how it is, but folk round here see things simply. So, you being who you are, I thought maybe you'd

224

come with me to serve the warrants. We'll choose our time well, there'll be others to help, but with you there – well, it could be just what we need.'

Edward looked at Johnson, a large man, who knew every inch of the dale and most of the men in it as he himself never would; and he thought of Joseph Dawson, as cunning as any poacher (naturally, since he had been one of the most skilled of that fraternity), and the other burly men who would certainly be called on to help. And he thought how few they were, set against the great mass of Weardale men who had no time for game laws and who lived by the assumption that the fruit of the fells, of whatever kind, was put there for their use and benefit, especially in these hard times.

In these hard times – that was just it. In the present ugly mood of the miners only a fool would risk trying to serve arrest warrants on any of them. It would look to the men like a deliberate act of provocation. Edward thought of the things half heard, half witnessed during the past weeks, and imagined what such an act as Johnson invited him to perform might bring down upon him, upon all of them. He did not think he was a coward (he hoped not), but he was not utterly foolhardy.

'I think,' he said slowly, choosing his words with great care, 'that my presence alone would make little difference. It might even inflame the situation. I suggest that the wisest course would be to bring in additional constables, from outside the district, to your assistance.'

'I've tried that. No one will risk it.'

'If there were enough of them, well armed, well paid too ... in truth, it seems to me the only course likely to meet with any degree of success.'

He knew that Johnson was disappointed in him, and when the man had gone felt suddenly ashamed and was almost tempted to run after him and say he had changed his mind. Almost, but not quite. Miserably, he sat down by the fire with a book and wondered what had become of all his ideals, all the hopes he had carried with him on the day he rode into the dale. He knew that he no longer even tried to work for the reformation of this ungrateful and barbarous population, that in his heart he had already dismissed them as beyond hope of reform – all but Jane, of course, and he was afraid that the corruption was beginning to reach her too. Somehow he must find a way to free her from it, to bring her finally and completely under his benign influence, before she was irrevocably tainted.

Joe looked round at the faces of the other men in the upstairs room at the King's Head, and saw his own bitterness reflected in them all.

There was another face fresh in his memory, too; Aunt Ann's. Pleading last night with tears in her eyes for him to call an end to the strike, before they all died of hunger, while his uncle still had strength left to work ... The pittance the poor rate allowed them was not enough, and never could be, not compared with the lent money three working men brought in.

And there was Eve, who needed so many things he could not afford to buy, clothes for the baby, delicacies to tempt her to eat and make herself strong and well for the birth.

And Tommy, with a young boy's healthy appetite, who was growing thinner and more listless every day.

'Did you get anywhere at Allenheads?' he asked George Robinson, trying abruptly to push those other pleading faces out of his mind.

Robinson shook his head. 'Nor at Coalcleugh, neither. They're ready enough to say they want more, but not to do owt about it. Besides, they've taken their bargains now.'

John Peart seemed about to speak, and then clearly thought better of it. He and Thompson had remained in work until the new bargain prices were announced, and then, faced with proof that Joe and the others had been right and Mr Beaumont's promise had been an entirely empty one, they had rejoined the strike. But their old ascendancy over the committee had gone. They knew their action was resented still, and they were wary ever of expressing their views again.

In fact, for a long time no one said anything. From below came the noise of talk, fairly subdued tonight, for the men gathered there were waiting for Joe and the others to come down and tell them what they had planned, what they

226

thought the next step should be.

Joe knew the others had all reached the same gloomy conclusion as himself. The strike had been going on now for a month, and there had been nothing coming in during that time and the plight of their dependants was growing daily more desperate. That haunted them, and the realization that the masters were not going to offer anything more, that it was too late now; that they had lost the fight the moment the first men went back to work after that fatal vote.

Someone had to say it, and since the others remained silent it was Joe who spoke at last, putting into words what they were all thinking.

'We've lost, lads. There's no more we can do, not without everyone behind us.' His voice suddenly sounded very harsh in the stillness. 'I say we go back to work.'

Jenny went out to hang the lantern by the door for Joe's return, and then to check that the byre was securely barred. As she came back towards the house she saw that the door was open and Rowland stood there, outlined in the candle-light.

'You'll catch cold,' she warned, but he came out to meet her.

'I'd a mind to look at the stars. It's a grand night.'

'Aye.' She turned to look across the dale, and he came and stood beside her. It was clear, but not cold for the time of year, the sky soft and dark as velvet, brilliant with stars. They said nothing, standing there side by side, he clearly wrapped in wonder, she more conscious, for some reason she could not explain, of his presence at her side. Perhaps it was Edward's warning that had made her aware of him as someone, if not threatening, at least in some way unsettling.

Then an extraordinary thing happened. She heard him catch his breath. 'Look!'

Struck by the awe in his voice, she looked where he pointed, and saw, hovering above the black outline of the fell behind them, a weird light shimmering and dancing, red and green, zigzagging, leaping in the sky. It could have no human origin, for it did not touch the ground, nor did it have the noisy, fleeting brilliance of fireworks, which she had seen

227

once, years ago. This was utterly silent, more strange than fireworks, more magical, more unearthly. She stared and stared, almost afraid, and then she whispered, 'What is it?'

'The northern lights,' he said, softly. 'The merry dancers, some folk call them.'

Then she felt his hand reach out and brush her arm, whether by accident or design she did not know, but at once a fierce tingle ran its whole length, and then on through her body. It was somehow of a piece with the weird light flickering and dancing over the dale, bound up with its strangeness. It was as if suddenly everything came together in this moment, earth and sky, all the hidden powers of the universe, all the vast unknown forces, drawn down and through the two people standing side by side on the dark hillside.

His fingers closed about hers, thin, nervy, warm, workroughened. With a sense of inevitability, even of rightness, she closed her own about them. For a little longer they stood quite still, though Jenny was no longer conscious of the lights, but only of the man beside her, his nearness, his quickened breathing – or did she imagine that?

Then he turned towards her, and he was very near, just a breath away; and then she knew he was going to kiss her and that no power on earth could stop her raising her face to meet his.

His mouth was soft and warm, just touching hers, and then gently exploring. She held her breath and gave herself up to him, and her whole body, her whole self was suddenly alight and alive with a consuming torrent of feeling.

Yet it was just one kiss, soon ended. He drew back, and once more they stood there, side by side, without moving. The sky was dark again, lit only by the tiny insignificant stars. He was no longer even holding her hand. It was as if nothing had happened. Yet what had happened was everything.

She heard his voice come suddenly out of the darkness and the long silence. It was low, and husky with emotion. 'I thought I'd been given grace to resist temptation. I can do without strong drink, without all else. But this –' He broke off, and after a tiny pause went on in something approaching his normal voice, 'We'd best go in.'

228

'Aye,' she said. She thought that would be the end of it, and turned to the door, but his whisper caught her.

'Jenny, you were tempted too? It was not all me?'

'Why no,' she said. 'It was not all you.'

As she lay wrapped in her blanket in the hay loft that night, on the edge of sleep, Rowland's face seemed to float in her mind, his presence as close as it had been out there on the hillside. She turned over, trying to push him from her thoughts, trying to drag Edward back there where he belonged. But it was no use. Rowland's image was too powerful, too strong for her. Edward, pale, insubstantial, glimmered briefly at the fringes of her mind and then fled. When she dragged him back again, she could not hold him for more than an instant before Rowland returned, haunting her.

It had all happened so quickly. She thought back over the past weeks, and could see no clue, nothing that might have warned her that this was waiting for her. Even that odd moment when they spoke together by the river, and she had felt disturbed by the way his eyes held hers, had seemed to be a single isolated incident, of no particular significance.

He had been very ill. With skills born of long and bitter practice, she had nursed him, doing all the doctor said, moved to pity by the desperate, unhappy ravings of his delirium, so much at odds with the certainties of his everyday waking self. For a time, they had feared for his life.

But he had recovered, and in convalescence all his serenity had returned. With the days, a gentle friendship had developed, or so it had seemed to Jenny, until tonight. He had talked to her, often, of Billy, remembering things from the past; though, knowing what kind of life he and his cousin had led together, she suspected that he left out a good deal. But there were stories she had never heard before, and memories that showed Billy's kindliness, his steadiness in spite of everything, his strength of character. And Rowland had listened as well, with great attention, to all she had to tell him; which was a great deal, for she was surprised to find what a relief it had been to talk, in a way she had never done to anyone since Billy's death. Sometimes Joe had been there too, and shared in their memories. She knew that for him the old friendship had been renewed, changed but strengthened.

Rowland had quickly won Tommy over, too, talking to him without superiority, in a friendly manner, as to an equal, but without any of the coarseness of the washing floor masculinity the boy so admired. Rowland had even taken to reading him stories from the Bible, carefully selected for their appeal to the child. She had been grateful, on wet cold days, to have Tommy so happily occupied.

But what was there in all this to explain what had happened tonight? Nothing at all, as far as she could see. He had become a friend, though they none of them knew much more about him now than they had before, since he never talked about himself, deftly evading any questions that came too near the personal. Besides, she knew that the man she had kissed tonight was no mere friend. Even Billy had not so seared his image on her heart. As for Edward ...

She could not understand it. Edward was beautiful; she had felt that from the first moment they met. She never tired of watching him, awed that someone so perfect, so flawless, so completely the ideal, should love her, out of all women. There was nothing beautiful about Rowland. Where Edward was tall and perfectly proportioned, golden haired, with features of exquisite regularity and fine blue eyes, and always elegantly dressed, Rowland was small and thin and untidy, the only quality that made anyone look at him twice the burning conviction that fired him. Why then in heaven's name did he haunt her so, why did her pulses race and her breathing quicken at the very thought of him? Why did she return again and again to that moment under the stars, reliving it in her thoughts, longing for him to kiss her again? She could not understand it. And while she longed for it to happen again, she wished most desperately that it had not happened at all.

Dawn next day was grey and wet and cheerless. It was, Jenny thought, coming in, yawning, to grope her way about the kitchen, very difficult to believe that last night something so strange and magical had happened that even Joe's home-coming had not been able to destroy its power. Now, she

230

wondered if she had imagined it all.

She glanced towards the box bed. Rowland was still asleep, his back to the room, only his tousled hair visible. She looked away quickly, afraid he might wake and she would see some consciousness in his eyes of what had happened last night; if it had. She hoped it had not happened, wished it had not, and yet she knew that to find it had been only a dream would bring an inexcusable sense of loss.

Once the fire was stirred to life and the crowdy prepared, she went to wake Tommy, and returned to the kitchen just as Joe came downstairs. Jenny gave them breakfast, troubled to see how little her older brother ate. 'You'll not work on that,' she chided him gently, but he simply pushed the bowl from him, saying nothing. Then he rose and put on his coat and went to say goodbye to Rowland, awake but not yet out of bed.

'Well, you'll be off work a bit yet.'

'Not much longer,' said Rowland. 'The worst thing is to know I did nowt to help, when it was wanted.'

Joe patted his shoulder. 'You were best out of it. Look where it's got us.' He turned away, and Jenny reached up to kiss him.

'You've no choice,' she said. 'You did all you could. Don't take it so hard.'

'How else can I take it? We led them into it. And all we've got for it is a few weeks of hunger when we might as well have eaten, for the good it's done us.'

Jenny stood in the doorway to watch them go, and then closed the door and turned back into the room, with a sense of apprehension churning inside her. Rowland was sitting on the edge of the bed, rather clumsily putting on his clogs. On previous mornings, she had helped him put them on, unconscious of any awkwardness about it. Now she simply stood and watched him. He looked up at her, and she knew she had not imagined last night.

What was it Eve had said? *It's not him, it's what's in him?* It might be true for Eve, but Jenny knew now, as she had known instinctively last night, that for her it was not the fire that burned in Rowland's soul that reached out to her, but the man, the small, fiery, untidy young man who was looking at her now, his colour rather higher than usual on his still pale face, his breathing – like hers – ragged and uneven.

'Jenny,' he said quietly. 'I'm going back to Chapel today, to Aunt Tabitha's. After breakfast.'

'Oh,' she said. She felt as if a bell had begun to toll inside her, ringing the slow deadly end of all joy. Yet that was foolish, even ridiculous. She was promised to the man she loved, and he was not here with her; more to the point, he had objected very plainly to Rowland's presence in this house. For their guest to leave now, today, could only make things easier for all of them. And he was, she thought, well enough to ride down the hill on the pony. His aunt, with fewer calls on her time, would be better able to care for him until he was fit enough to go back to work. 'I suppose that's best,' she said.

'It is,' he assured her, but like her he sounded as if he meant the opposite.

Joe realized as he walked to Newhouse that there had been more miners loyal to the strike than he had thought, for the road was busy with men: but it was not a noisy and cheerful busyness. There was none of the usual talk or singing or laughter. They knew it was a defeat. Joe, trying to hold his head high, wondered how many of them blamed him for what had happened, for all the unnecessary hardship.

He could not walk at his normal pace, because Uncle Ralph had insisted he was well enough to come with them today, which meant that they had to stop often to wait while their partner got his breath or rested a little after a bout of coughing. No one made any comment on his condition, or argued with his decision to come with them. They knew he would go on working as long as it was humanly possible, as any of them would when his own time came.

Outside the office at Newhouse there was already a huddle of men waiting to take what bargains were left, conscious that the pick of them would have gone to the partnerships that had stayed at work. For Ralph Emerson's partnership, there was one small consolation for the humilitation of defeat: so far at least, George Crawhall had kept his word to give them first refusal for their ground on Middlehope moor.

It had been offered to no one else.

It was still early, and Mr Crawhall had not yet opened the office, so they stood hunched against the rain, cold and miserable. Ralph's Joe put his own coat about his father, as additional protection.

'Here he is,' said George Lowes at last, as the door opened. But instead of standing back to admit the first partnership, the agent stepped out into the rain and began to walk among the waiting men, glancing round as if looking for someone.

'Joseph Emerson!' Joe jumped, and saw to his astonishment that Mr Crawhall had halted beside him. 'What brings you here this morning?'

It was such an odd question that Joe simply stared at him. At last, when the man continued to stand there, clearly waiting for an answer, he said, 'We're here to take our bargain, of course.'

'There you are in error. Your partners must look for another man, if they wish to continue in the same ground, that is. There is no work for you here. I wonder you thought there would be, after what has happened.'

For just a moment longer Joe was genuinely puzzled as to what the agent could mean; and then he understood, with a sudden clarity that was like a blow to the stomach and for a moment quite took his breath away. This time Mr Crawhall did not wait for him to say anything further.

'There will not be work for you at any mine owned by Colonel Beaumont, now or ever again; those are his instructions. Good day to you.'

And that was that. Joe was about to exclaim, to protest at the injustice of it, perhaps even plead for the man to think again. But only for an instant; then he recognized that he would be wasting his breath. There was no fight left in him, still less in his friends, and in any case to fight any longer would only be to invite further humiliation. Better, then, to salvage what dignity he could from the situation, by accepting it, here and now. He looked the agent in the eye, said as firmly as he could, 'Good day,' and turned to go. He felt Uncle Ralph's hand on his arm, detaining him, but he shook his head. 'Take Luke on, uncle,' he said softly. 'It's better this way.' And then he walked away, looking neither to right nor left, his head high. From the corner of his eye he saw that the agent had halted again, beside George Robinson this time.

His chief feeling as he walked back up the hill was a strange one, with something in it very like relief. He need no longer fear blame from the men who had followed him, or walk among them with a sense of shame. He had paid a price higher than any he had ever asked of them; and this morning, walking away from them, he was proud of it.

Jenny, coming in with the milk (the soothing mechanical action of milking had not after all calmed her nerves), saw Joe come striding up the track, and stood still. She knew at once what brought him home so soon. Somehow she had expected it all along. She knew that even if the bulk of the striking miners were forgiven for the anxiety they had caused the masters, those who had led them could expect no leniency. She put down the pail and went to meet him, slipping her arm through his. 'I know,' she said gently. Then: 'We'll manage somehow, never fear.'

Fleetingly, she thought that she might ask Edward to speak for him, but she rejected the idea almost before it took shape. It was doubtful if the curate would agree to interfere, as a matter of principle, but more to the point Joe would never forgive her were she to do such a thing.

Together they walked to the house. Eve, looking tired and awkward, came to the door to meet them, roused from her bed by the sound of Joe's voice. They told her what had happened.

And then, suddenly, Joe grinned, and all the strain of the past month seemed to fall from him. 'Time I got my fowling piece cleaned, I'd say. There's nowt to keep me from the moors now.' And he took the gun from its corner behind the settle, whistling as he did so.

13

They came at night over the fells, four men from Bishop Auckland and five from Darlington, with a Weardale man as their guide. They were all big men, in the prime of life and fully armed, handpicked for their resolve.

At first the moon favoured them, lighting their way over desolate land that to unfamiliar eyes had no track or landmark to show the way. Later, the moon disappeared behind a cloud, and even their guide faltered. It took longer than they had expected to reach Chapel, and by then the chilly December dawn was already breaking.

Rowland, starting on the long walk to Guinea Grove for his week's work, his wallet slung over his shoulder, saw Joseph Dawson open the door of the Black Bull to them. Something odd and furtive about the action, performed with such unlikely quietness, and the number of the men (none of whom he recognized), penetrated the now habitual gloom of his thoughts and set him wondering what they were about. He waited where he was, just out of sight, watching them. And then he slipped quietly back the way he had come to the Siddles' cottage.

It took some time to rouse the sleeping inhabitants, particularly as he did not want his knocking to be heard too clearly, but Anthony came at last, shivering in nightshirt and nightcap, peering suspiciously round the door. 'There's a band of strangers just come to the Black Bull,' Rowland whispered, 'I'd guess they're the Bishop's men.'

Anthony thanked him. 'Get word to Jack Kidd, if you can,' he returned in a low voice, before closing the door again. 'And the others.' Rowland heard him slide the bolts firmly home on the inside.

235

He hurried to take the warning to John Kidd at East Blackdene and from there went on to Side Head, where James Craggs lived.

'He's out,' said the man's mother, answering his knock. 'Went up to White Lea just a bit since, to call for Joe Emerson.'

There was nothing for it then but to go on to White Lea, though it was not fear for James Craggs or his friends that filled his thoughts and set his heart beating faster and more painfully even than did the brisk energetic walk. Ever since he had left the house on that bleak morning after they had seen the northern lights, there had been no room in his head for anything but Jenny and his desperate longing for her; and in all that time, a whole month now, he had not been back to White Lea. Now he was both glad and full of agony to be going there again.

James Craggs was not there, and nor was Joe. Rather confusedly he stammered out an explanation to Tommy, who had answered the door to him.

'They're up on the fell,' said Tommy, which meant, Rowland supposed, that they had gone poaching. The family at White Lea would have no other means of support, apart from the indignity of the poor rate, now that Tommy was laid off for the winter. He stood staring rather stupidly at the boy for a moment or two, while Tommy looked at him in some puzzlement. In the end, Jenny came to see what was the matter.

'Tommy, who – ? Oh!' She came to a halt, her eyes on Rowland, her face filling with colour.

'I – I'm looking for James Craggs, to warn him. The constables have come with the warrants.' It was as much as he could manage, so overwhelming were his feelings, face to face with her again.

It was a moment or two before she had herself sufficiently under control to stand aside and say, 'You'd best come in.'

He took a step forward, without thinking, and then came to a halt, shaking his head, as if to rouse himself from sleep. 'No ... Do you know which way they went?'

'Harthope or Burnhope,' she said. 'Somewhere over there.'

236

'Then I'll go that way and keep a look out for them.'

There was an awkward, painful little pause, before Jenny said, 'Take care then.'

'Aye.' He pulled his plaid more closely about him and walked away.

The constables quickly surrounded the Siddles' cottage, hammering on the door and calling for the brothers to surrender themselves. When there was no immediate reply, they banged louder, with pistol butts this time, and booted feet, splintering the wood. The noise was appalling, and Mrs Siddle whimpered with fear. Very soon, it was clear, they would have the door down. 'We'll get out through the roof,' said Anthony. 'They'll maybe not be watching the yard out back. We can get up on to the fell that way.'

He and Charlie together pushed away sufficient slates at the back of the house for the two of them to clamber through on to the roof, shivering in their nightshirts, for there had been no time to dress. Up there, bent double so that the watchers from below should not see them, they eased themselves down to the roof's edge. They were almost there when Charlie suddenly lost his footing and fell with great speed straight into the yard – and the waiting arms of the constables. Anthony, having no alternative open to him, descended with more dignity and submitted, like his brother, to being handcuffed and taken with an escort of armed men to the Black Bull, where his arch enemy Joseph Dawson sat drinking at the bar and gloating volubly over the downfall of his detested neighbours.

The men on Harthope Fell, alerted by Rowland and others, slipped down by way of Harthope burn to the cottage at Rowantree Foot, where Tom Low lived. There, in the yard, they heard from John Kidd – who had made his escape from his house seconds before the constables reached it – all that had happened.

'I had one of them in range of my gun,' he said. 'I could have had him there and then. But I spared him. Mind, when I heard they'd got both the Siddles, I wished I'd let him have it.'

'Anthony too?' said Joe. 'But they know he'll be at the next Sessions. What's more, if they wanted him, why didn't they take him in October, when he was right under their noses? That sounds like malice to me.'

'Joseph Dawson will have made sure of it,' said Jock Currah. 'He'll be after the reward.'

'Why then he can't be let get away with it. I say we go to Chapel now and free them both.'

The others agreed with enthusiasm. There was much cleaning and priming of fowling pieces, and one or two men sharpened knives on the stone sills of the cottage windows. Then, with the quietness of skilled poachers, they made their way down the line of the burn, along the lane and into the market place.

They were too late. Out in the street, Mrs Siddle stared up at the shuttered windows of the Black Bull, hurling furious curses at the men who had taken her sons. But there was no sign of them, or of the constables, and the old woman was beside herself with anguish and rage. It took some time to learn that the brothers had been put into a cart, securely handcuffed to two constables, and that the party had then set out down the dale. 'They broke up the house,' Mrs Siddle wept. 'You should see the state of it. They had great pistols, pointed at me. They shoved me around.' She demonstrated a bruised arm. 'They took every gun in the house, and food too, all I had.'

Joe patted her shoulder. 'We'll get everything back for you, never fear.'

She shook her head. 'I pled with them, but they wouldn't hear me – just laughed and cursed. They said they'd take all Weardale for a black pudding.'

Jock Currah grinned, not pleasantly. 'We'll see about that. They can't go that fast, with most of them on foot.'

It soon became clear however that the constables were moving quickly, for at every stage of the way they had reports that the party had passed through about three quarters of an hour before. 'We'll never catch up with them,' James Craggs said despairingly.

But, approaching Stanhope, their luck changed. There they learned that the party had stopped at an inn, where the constables were sitting down to a large breakfast. The members of the rescue party whooped joyfully and slapped one another on the back. 'The fools!' cried Joe. 'The great fools! What men in their right minds with prisoners to get to safety would stop on the way?' Subsiding a little, they conferred together as to what to do next.

'We've got surprise on our side,' Jock Currah said. 'I say most stay here, in reserve, and maybe six of us go ahead and see how we get on.'

'Will that be enough?' asked James Craggs.

Joe's eyes shone. 'If six Weardale men aren't a match and more for a dozen Bishop's men, then I'm not Joe Emerson. Besides, any more wouldn't be sport.'

They agreed, excited and full of laughter, all wanting to be of the advance party. Joe was among those who slipped quietly into the town, taking back roads until they reached the market place and the squat, thatched building where the constables had stopped. Joe had not felt so happy for a long time, free of any care, untroubled by the implications of what he did, full of excitement and a sense of adventure, uplifted by the comradeship of those around him. This was pure enjoyment, a release after the long painful weeks of the strike, with all its bitterness and humiliation.

'If they've any sense, they'll have guards posted,' Jock Currah whispered. 'Keep your eyes open. And no firing unless one of us is hit.'

As quietly as if stalking game on the fell, pausing to listen after each soft step, the men edged their way into the inn. The parlour was deserted, but the door into the kitchen was closed, and from there they heard voices. They gathered just outside it, looking at one another; and then at a nod from Jock they pushed it wide.

One moment, to take in that the landlady was stooping over the fire, that the Siddles were seated near her – in the vast chimney corner, handcuffed either side of a constable – that other men sat or stood about the room, pistols laid aside, on the table, in corners; and to mark each one a man for himself. Then they sprang forward.

The room dissolved into a mass of kicking, thumping, shouting, brawling men, hitting with gun butts and fists,

239

sending stools and chairs flying. A pistol went off, the bullet veering off into the chimney and sending down a cloud of soot and smoke, adding to the confusion and setting everyone coughing. The landlady ran shrieking into the parlour, where she watched through the half open door, wincing every time a blow struck her table or the wall, or a plate or tankard crashed to the floor.

Then as suddenly it was over. First one constable, then another fled from the inn; then all with any power left to run. One, his feet caught in the tongs, clattered his way to the market place and did not stop to free himself until he had found refuge in a joiner's yard.

In the kitchen two men lay senseless on the bloody mess that was the floor, among spilled and broken furniture and smashed plates, while the victors gathered up weapons and discarded clothes. The landlady pushed wide the door and marched in, fury submerging all her fear.

'Just look at the state of this place! Just look at it!'

Jock Currah laughed and gestured towards the bloodied floor. 'Why then, bring us a bushel of oatmeal to mix with this lot, and you'll have a fine black pudding!'

Enraged, she shrieked, 'Get out! Get out!'

They got out, cheerfully enough, with the two prisoners, still handcuffed to their now frightened captor, walking between them. They hobbled, leaned on one another for support, but they were singing and cheering as they went.

Outside, their friends were waiting. They enlisted the aid of a passing tinker to free the prisoners and then hoisted them shoulder high and bore them in triumph back up the dale.

There had never been such rejoicing in Chapel as there was that day. The news had gone ahead of them, and by the time they reached the market cross a crowd had gathered to cheer their return. Mrs Siddle came running to hug her sons, and then the victors crowded into the King's Head with their friends, leaving the less fortunate to fill some other inn or alehouse, or stand drinking out in the street. Only the Black Bull stayed empty, barred and shuttered, its owner sourly listening to the sound of revelry and fearful of more broken windows before the day was out.

Word went to all the outlying cottages and farms. Jenny longed to go down and join the celebrations, and see how Joe was (though she had been told he was unhurt), but she did not dare. On the day the Bishop's men had been so soundly routed, the girl who had outraged the neighbourhood by allying herself to the Church's representative was hardly going to be welcomed in the village.

The drinking went on all day and the whole of the next night. So too did the singing and the talking, the endless retelling of the day's events, the 'Did you see how – ?' and 'What about when – ?' and the uproarious laughter that followed each retold incident, each shared anecdote. By midnight, someone had composed the beginnings of a ballad, added to every minute by another would-be minstrel, put to an existing tune someone dragged up for the occasion. It was long and heroic and its joyful notes rang endlessly in the night air, reaching even Joseph Dawson's ears.

At dawn on Tuesday most of the revellers spilled out into the streets. Some – the least drunken – made their way bleary eyed to work. The others staggered back to their homes and to bed. A few, once revived by a breath of cold air, returned to the King's Head and resumed their drinking, though by now the singing had a subdued and ragged sound, and snores formed a frequent rhythmic accompaniment.

Anthony Siddle – who, though convivial enough, had drunk little, compared to most of them – rose from his seat of honour by the fire and went to where his coat lay discarded on the window sill and pulled it on. His face had an odd expression, which was perhaps what alarmed his mother.

'Where're you going, lad?' she asked. She was comfortable enough there in the chimney corner, the centre of attention, with her sons safely restored to her.

'Durham,' said Anthony, putting on his hat as well.

There was a stunned silence. The others stared at him, open mouthed.

'But – but they'll lock you up!' Joe protested.

Anthony nodded. 'Aye.' Then, before anyone could say any more, he continued, 'It seems to me we've had our fight,

241

and we've won. We've given the Bishop's men a proper drubbing.'

There was a faint cheer, soon extinguished. Anthony went on, 'More to the point, there's two men stood surety for me. for my appearance in court next month. It's a bit soon maybe, but the way things are I think it best to get there in good time. If I'm not there, then it's not me that loses my money, it's my mates.' He looked at Joe, who seemed suddenly to have become completely sober. 'Seems to me,' he went on, 'that's no way to use a friend.'

Around him, his hearers digested his words as best they could through drink-fuddled brains. There was much nodding and murmuring. His brother pushed back his stool and stood up, a little unsteadily, 'I'd best come too then.'

Anthony pressed him down again. 'No, lad, there's no sense in that. No one stood surety for you, or anyone else. There's no call for any but me to get himself locked up.' His mother, shaken already by the events of the past day, began to sob. He put an arm round her. 'Now then, mother, you see I've no choice but to go. Like as not they'll be lenient. I had cause enough for what I did.'

'But there's yesterday,' said Charlie.

'Why yes, there is, and they'd no call to arrest me. I was bailed to come before the court anyway, and they'd no reason to think I wouldn't; if they had, then they should have locked me up when I was there, back in October. As I see it, they'd no right to come after me as they did, and so I shall tell them.' Then he grinned. 'There's one other thing. If I go to Durham by myself, that does Joseph Dawson out of his reward, and Frank Johnson too. It's worth it just to think of that.'

They went with Anthony to the door, and a group of them accompanied him for a mile or so, to see him on his way. After that, he walked on alone, an oddly dignified figure, in spite of his homespun clothes and rough appearance.

14

Rowland was woken by the coughing. Not that there was anything unusual in it, for it was a constant noise in the lodging shop, but this time for some reason it broke into his sleep. He wished it had not. Sleep, however fitful, had given him, for a little while, release from the fetid atmosphere of the windowless room, which on waking seemed to flow in again to his mouth and his nose, down his throat, nauseating and choking him. His head ached, as it had last night, and probably would for the rest of the day.

There was no glimmer of daylight through the hole that led down to the floor below, so no one would be up for some time yet. He lay quite still, concerned not to disturb the man stretched on the bed beside him, or the boy at their feet. Not that lying still was easy. Awake, he was only too aware of the constant irritating attention of the bed bugs that crept up each night from the straw mattress, seeking the warmth of the men who slept there; and of the ache set up in every joint of his body by the damp that seemed to pervade the whole atmosphere, from the drenched walls and the sodden thatch, and the wet working clothes hung on strings across the corners of the room in the vain hope that they might somehow have dried themselves by the time morning came. But it was the stench Rowland hated most. Without it, he could have borne the damp and the bugs and the dirt and the rats. They would not have set him wondering, as the smell did, if endless burning fires had not less of Hell in them than a Weardale lodging shop. He could not imagine any torment worse than this.

All at once, he could bear it no longer. Moving as slowly and gently as he could, he slid from the bunk, pulled his plaid about him, and felt his way between the tiered ranks of beds to the descending ladder. Downstairs, he crossed the earth floor, trying as best he could to avoid the stinking puddles, slippery with rotting potato peelings and worse, and reached the door and pulled it open. Once outside, he closed the door again on the smell that had flowed out with him. Then he stood quite still, eyes closed, and took deep long breaths of the cold morning air.

The relief was so great that it brought a lump to his throat. He wondered now if he would ever be able to force himself back in there again. But then, he thought that each morning, when day released him from it, and each night he went back. At least in winter it was just within his capacity to do so. During the summer, when the atmosphere inside had been thickened and intensified by the heat, it had required what seemed to him a superhuman effort of will to drive him into the place at the end of the day, a will that was not his own at all. It was no wonder that in summer most of the men lingered outside until well after midnight, talking, dancing, drinking, throwing quoits, ignoring the too-close attention of the hungry midges. But, however vile this place, not once had Rowland considered seeking work, or even lodging, elsewhere; for, unlike most of his fellows, he had chosen to come here, deliberately and knowingly, because he was sure that God meant him to witness them, not by setting himself apart, but by sharing with them all the harshness of their daily life. The trouble was that when he had made that choice he had still been sustained by the joy and certainty of his faith.

Now it was almost as if it had never been. He was hanging on grimly to the outward show of what had once been a living reality, trying to demonstrate daily a joy and hope he did not feel, while inside he wandered restless and lost in the dark, seeing no way out. In the past he had despised the hypocrites who professed a faith that had long gone cold, reduced to no more than empty ritual. It did not seem to him now that he was so very different from them.

He had failed. He had preached God's endless love, but at the first real test he had let it go, turned aside somehow, without knowing quite how or when. Faced with Eve's despair, he had tried to understand it; and succeeded, he had thought, enough to bring her a lasting comfort. But now that same comfort eluded him.

The ultimate degradation, by God's grace, was still spared him. Last night he had been very close to it, so close that he had thought he was lost. He had been sitting on a bench in the downstairs room, where the men, their supper of crowdy or potatoes at an end, gathered to drink and smoke and play cards before bed, and he had tried with desperate concentration to form his thoughts into a prayer, any prayer, so long as it came from the heart and was not just empty words; but without success. Then one of his partners (the man who had replaced John Peart, sacked after the strike), seeing perhaps how sombre he looked, had stretched out a hand towards him. 'Here, Rowland man – have some of this. You look as though you could do with it.'

'This' had been a leather flask of rum, and the next moment Rowland had found himself clasping it, instinctively, without knowing what he was doing. An instant later, he had drawn his hand back sharply, but then he had sat there for what seemed a long time, without moving, staring at the bottle, its stained leather caught in the dim flickering light of a candle stuck on the wall above their heads. Around him there were the normal evening sounds, the scuttling of rats in the shadows, the voices of the other men, laughter and a snatch of singing, all somehow very distant and unreal. At the heart of the room there seemed only him, and the liquid in that flask, and his longing for it.

Years ago, a washer lad just starting work, he had first learned what it could do for him, discovered its power to close the door on the darkness he carried with him, to blunt the edge of guilt and pain and turn the frightened, tormented child that lurked inside him to a young devil of inventiveness, wit and bravado, unafraid of anything or anyone. For years it had been his consolation and his strength; until the day when he had learned that there was a better defence against the darkness, one that closed no doors, but instead burst them open with a light so dazzling and so fearsome in its power that it laid bare the most secret corners of his heart and shrivelled up every last shred of the darkness until there

245

was nothing left of it but a harmless dust.

Perhaps something of that fire lingered in him still, without his knowledge, for yesterday in the face of overwhelming temptation he had been able at last to mutter, 'No, thank you,' and then to get to his feet and walk out into the night, not returning until he knew the danger was past; for the time being, at least. He did not know how long it would be before that hidden strength would fail him altogether.

Now, outside in the breaking dawn, he tried again to pray, but what had once been so easy, so natural, had gone. In the end he simply stood there, staring at the gradually lightening sky, heedless of the cold, his mind empty of anything but a dreary longing for Jenny, and a wish that he need never spend another night in this place.

At least today, thank God! was Friday, and this afternoon he would be going home, leaving the lodging shop behind him again until Monday. The thought made it possible for him to go back inside as soon as he heard the other men stirring. One of them came up to him and asked him to lead a small group of them in prayer, as he often did at the beginning and end of each day. So he went with them to a corner of the downstairs room and did as he was asked (hypocrite that he was!), clutching at the only words he could find. 'Lord, send Thy Spirit into the dark places of our hearts ...'

By the time he and his partners were making their way along the level into the mine, it had begun to snow; the long-delayed winter had come at last. 'Better not stop us getting home,' someone said, and he could only agree, fervently.

St John's Chapel was still buzzing with the events of last Monday. Rowland heard of them first from Lancelot and his aunt, and then from almost everyone he passed as he made his way across the market place. It was as if all those who had played a part, or had heard about it afterwards, wanted to be able to repeat the tale to someone who, by some miracle, did not already know it. They sang it to him as well, and the raucously lilting strains of the newly composed ballad floated to him from every alehouse and inn and many ordinary houses too, heroic, boastful, and very long. There was only

one line in it with which Rowland was inclined to agree –
And I hope such a battle will ne'er be fought more.

He listened patiently to the tales and the songs, acknowledging the sense of triumph the men felt, sympathizing with their delight at scoring a victory over the 'fat man of Oakland', the detested Bishop of Durham, but unable to share their unrepentant delight in the violence that had taken place. Once, he said quietly, 'The constables are men too,' but received an odd startled look in return, and realized it was not the moment to pursue the matter.

He thought then that he would go and hear Joe's version of events, since his friend was said to have played so large a part. But he knew that what he really wanted was to see Jenny again.

Joe was out, Jenny was not sure where. Eve was in bed – as she was for much of the time these days, since her ankles had begun to swell alarmingly – and Tommy too was asleep in the hay loft, after a day spent joyfully at play in the snow; he would normally have been at school during the winter months, but there was no money to spare at White Lea for schooling. Jenny led Rowland in silence to the settle, and made him some tea from her precious store, and for a long time they said nothing to one another. After a while, having sipped at the tea without once looking at Jenny, Rowland stood up and went to lean on the mantelpiece, gazing down into the fire.

Jenny watched him. He looked tired, she thought, his face hollower than ever beneath the strong cheekbones, his eyes more deeply shadowed, as if he was not sleeping well. It might be the strains of the work already making their mark, but some instinct told her it was more than that. When he swung suddenly round and faced her she knew she was right.

'Jenny, I cannot go on like this. It is torment. I'm ashamed of my weakness, more ashamed than I can say, yet –'

'I don't think it very kind of you to call it a weakness to love me,' she said quietly, through her hurt. Yet with the hurt went a painful understanding, even sympathy for what he felt.

His eyes burned in his gaunt face, consuming her, searing away every conscious thought but of him. His capacity to do

247

that was a terrifying thing, so complete was it, and so inevitable. 'It is a weakness, because I should have nothing left to give to any woman, nothing but God's love, offered in equal measure to all His children. To love you so much – sometimes I think it takes all I have from me, that I have nothing left for anyone else, no passion but for you. How can I give myself to God, if I have let you steal a part of me – all of me – from Him?'

'Do you think so badly of human love?'

'It's not that. Of course not. But for me ... it was what I knew I must renounce from the very first. I did not know it would be so hard, but it was a choice that was made for me, a choice I must stay with, else I betray all I hold dearest to me, all that's good. How can I give myself heart and mind to the Gospel if I'm distracted by the needs of a wife and family, by love for them, or fear for them? It would be a stumbling block.'

'Other preachers have married. John Wesley was married.'

'That's not the same. I'm not John Wesley. For some, I know, a wife is a help and a support. But then she must be chosen for what she has to offer in God's service, not just because to live without her is torment.'

Was she glad or sorry that he should be so troubled by his love for her? Both she thought, in different ways.

'I knew,' he went on, 'when everything was taken from me, and God came to me then, that it was His will for me that I should go empty handed into the world, that I should have only what He provided –'

She gave a little cry. 'You're not saying it was His will your wife should die, and the bairn?'

'No, no!' He denied it vehemently. 'He does not will suffering. But He can use it. There is a difference.' Then he added, with a quiet gravity that was like a rebuke, 'And have you forgotten, Jenny? You're promised to another. That alone should make me able to put you from my thoughts.'

'It has not helped me,' she said. 'I've thought perhaps – why, that it was not right to stay promised to Edward. That we are not right for one another.'

He was silent then for some time, his eyes still on her face. Her longing for him was so intense that it was all she could do not to cry out; or, worse, to stand up and cling to him, at which she knew he would be beyond any control, or any wish to control himself, and so would she.

'If you're not right together, then you should not wed him. that's clear enough. Marriage is a sacred thing, not lightly to be entered into. But –' He bent his head then. 'It could make no difference to me, whether you were promised to him or not, whether you were his wife or not. I know that what I feel for you must be put aside; that it is a distraction and a snare. I know that somehow, with God's grace, I shall be able to do it at last. Somehow.' The repetition of the word seemed only to emphasize his desperate need to convince himself of the possibility of what he said. But it was the pain in it that struck at Jenny's heart. She understood it, because it was like her own. Yet it angered her too, because she felt that it should not have been necessary or desirable.

'Then I'd best marry him soon and go away where I can't see you any more, and then perhaps I can have some hope of being happy,' she said. 'Or at least of peace.'

She knew from the way he looked at her that the very thought of her doing that was almost beyond bearing. She was aware too precisely why she had said it, not because she really believed it was any useful kind of solution, but because she wanted him to face the prospect of living without her, and to realize that he could not do it.

Unfortunately, she was faced instead with yet further proof of the strength of his resolve and his will.

He turned away, saying with dull low-voiced misery, 'That's no reason to wed. But it's for you to decide. I can offer you nothing. What I feel is something I must face and conquer alone, with God's help.' Then he said, 'It's time I was gone,' and began to walk towards the door.

She stood staring at him for a moment, and then on impulse reached out and caught his arm, not wanting them to part so painfully. 'Rowland!'

He looked round, and halted; and then, without knowing who moved first, they came together, and he held her fiercely to him and kissed her, and she clung to him as if she could not bear ever again to let him go. It was bliss and agony at once, and they did not know how long it lasted; only that

249

Eve, hearing voices, came downstairs, and seeing them gave a small strangled cry, which broke sharply into their embrace.

They sprang apart, frozen for a moment in guilty dismay. Then Rowland began to go to Eve, but Jenny caught his arm. 'No!' she murmured. He looked at her, then again at Eve, and then he turned and left the house. Jenny went quickly to Eve, who was staring at her as if at some terrifying stranger, struck dumb with horror.

'I know how it looks,' said Jenny slowly. Then she realized that how it looked was precisely how it was; there was no evading that. Conscious that she was shaking – as much from unsatisfied desire as from reaction to Eve's discovery – she went and tried to put an arm about Eve, but the girl shrank from her. 'You should be in bed,' she went on. Eve sat down on the bench by the table, looking dazed. Jenny sat down beside her. 'It was not of our choosing it happened,' she said quietly. 'And we know nothing can come of it. It was – it was just that we couldn't help ourselves, this once.'

'So that's why he went away so suddenly, the day the strike ended,' Eve said. Jenny nodded. 'He loves you too.' Jenny nodded again, feeling the tears rise at the thought of that momentous and painful fact. 'I did not think', said Eve slowly, 'that he would ever feel like that, for one woman, not like other men do.'

'I'm not perfect enough for him, I suppose,' said Jenny, a little harshly. She could not bear Eve's idolatry, for if Rowland was more than a man, then he had the less to offer her, as a mere woman.

Eve considered the matter for a moment, then said, 'No, that's not it.' She smiled very faintly. 'If he had to love someone, he could do worse. But ...'

'You thought him more than human, above such things.'

'Aye.'

'I'm sorry I should be the one to show you it's not so.' Then she thought, with sudden humility, that Eve probably understood better than she did why Rowland was so tormented by his love for her. It was not that he thought himself more than human; it was rather that he believed that God's grace working through him was enough to endow him with superhuman strength to resist temptation. And she, by threatening that belief, was threatening the whole justification for his existence.

'Maybe it's better that way. I don't know.' There was compassion in Eve's dark eyes. 'What will you do?'

'Nowt,' said Jenny. 'What can I do? Except – except that as soon as can be, I shall be married and go away, for ever.' She said that, not as if it would be the fulfilment of a girlish dream, but as if it were a punishment, inflicted on her for some terrible crime. 'When the baby's born and you're well again,' she added. She had been thankful that Edward had after all accepted that condition for delaying their marriage a little longer, but now she wondered if it might have been better had he not done so. Better to have got it over with soon, perhaps.

She was startled when Eve suddenly reached out and hugged her, pressing her cheek against her own. 'Oh, Jenny, and I thought it was all right for you, that you at least were truly happy, even when I was not.' Jenny realized then that she was crying.

'Eve, love, what is it? You're not crying for me?'

'Aye ... No ... I don't know.' Then it came out. 'Jenny, I'm so frightened.'

'Frightened? Of what?' But she knew; it was obvious enough when she thought about it, for Eve had not been well since she came to White Lea, and she knew that Mr Scott, who had seen her when he called during Rowland's illness, had been concerned about her, urging constant rest. 'Why, all will go well,' she said soothingly. 'I promise you it will. Just you see, come next month you'll be fit and sprightly again and rocking your little one in your arms, and Joe will be that proud and happy he'll be near bursting.'

Eve laughed, a little tremulously, and allowed herself to be comforted. But Jenny could only think that when that time came she would have no excuse any more to put off what she wished (yet did not wish) she had never put off at all.

She slept little that night, and woke in the morning with a nebulous resolve taking shape within her. She would go to Edward. She would do something decisive, something irrevocable, that would secure his place in the centre of her life once and for all.

It was unfortunate that when she reached the parsonage she was told that he had gone out and would not be back until late, or perhaps not even until tomorrow morning.

Edward had been invited to dinner by the Reverend William Wilson, rector of Wolsingham. It was a great relief to be welcomed into the comfortable rectory, to sit down in congenial and refined company to a tolerable meal, to put all the burdens of his duties behind him for a while.

Once the meal was over, the two men retired to the study to enjoy a quiet pipe together, and an uninterrupted talk. It was then that Edward realized that the purpose of the dinner was not, after all, purely social.

'You have a difficult task, young man,' the rector told Edward. 'I am not insensitive to the problems you face, and to the need you must feel for solace from time to time. However, there is one matter that has come to my attention.' Edward did not know what was coming, but he braced himself to face it, whatever it might be. 'Are you determined to go through with this marriage? I have to say that it does not sound very suitable to me.'

Edward stared at him. 'Has my family written to you?' He realized that the words sounded discourteously bald, but it was too late to retract them.

The rector smiled. 'As you surmise – yes, I had a letter from your father. He is very concerned about the matter, though I am not sure what precisely he thinks I shall be able to do about it. Would you like to tell me something more about her? I am aware that your father's view may not wholly accord with your own.'

'I do not think that would serve any useful purpose, sir,' said Edward carefully. 'I intend to marry Miss Emerson, whatever my father's view. I believe it is a marriage made in heaven.'

To his relief the rector seemed content to accept defeat. 'Then I suspect the wisest course is for me to hold my tongue. I suppose we must all be allowed one piece of foolishness in a lifetime, and for many of us that is our choice of

252

wife. I can only wish you may not live to regret it. But there we are.' Briskly, he put the matter behind him and changed the subject; though it was clear that his intentions were still not wholly sociable. 'I have a good deal of first hand acquaintance with the problems of Stanhope parish, from my duties as a magistrate. The poaching fraternity are a constant thorn in the flesh; I am forever having them up before me. You would have thought a five pound fine would be enough to deter any lead miner, but no, they come back again and again – that's when anyone can catch them, of course. A slippery lot.'

'Yes. It is so easy for them to escape arrest with all those miles of open moorland to hide in.'

'Indeed.' The rector sighed. 'In fact, the problems of law enforcement are really very serious. You heard about the incident last Monday, I suppose?'

'When the constables were so savagely attacked? Yes, I did indeed. One of the men was near death for a time, I understand, and is still not fit to be moved from Stanhope. A shocking business. The more so as the whole population is crowing over their "victory".'

'It has my fellow magistrates worried, I can tell you. This is strictly between ourselves, but they've called a special meeting of the Quarter Sessions in Durham next week, to discuss the matter. Something must be done, before this lawlessness gets completely out of hand. However, you have closer experience than I of the state of things in the parish. For example, you may perhaps know the identities of the chief instigators of this crime?'

Edward wished very sincerely that he did, but honesty obliged him to shake his head. 'I could make an informed guess as to one or two of them, sir, but even then not with complete certainty. I am the last person who would be trusted with such information.'

'A pity,' commented the rector. 'But keep your ears and eyes open and let me know if any information comes your way. Meanwhile, with such knowledge as you have of the district, have you any thoughts as to how the civil power may best enforce its rule on this occasion?'

Edward felt flattered that his opinion should be sought on

253

so important a matter. 'It's very difficult, sir. I have found that Weardale men stand by one another in almost every circumstance. In general, loyalty to their own kind means far more than abiding by the law. Further, as you have indicated, there are more than enough hiding places in which men familiar with the landscape may seek refuge, in the event of any attempt to enforce arrests.'

'Some of the magistrates, I know, are for sending in troops.'

Edward whistled silently. 'That would be a Draconian move, if I may say so. They would have to send a massive force to have any hope of enforcing the law effectively. A mounted one too, I imagine.'

'But you think it might work?'

'If it did, it would hardly endear the population to the authorities.'

'There are those who would say that would not matter, so long as they could be brought to fear them. But what alternative would you suggest, were you on the bench of magistrates?'

Edward, by instinct inclined to think that the most violent suppression that armed and mounted troops could inflict was the only possible solution, knew better than to say so. He did not want the other man to learn the extent of his disillusionment. 'I fear, sir, that the only hope lies in a much longer and slower process, that of education. I was glad to hear you say that the Bishop has it in mind to establish schools in the dale. It has long been my view that the provision of good schools, well endowed, would do more for civilization in the parish than any increase in the number of constables. Though it does not help, of course, that so many families have means too small to provide themselves with an adequate living.'

The rector nodded. 'Yes; because there are quite simply too many of them, on land that cannot support them.'

'Emigration might be an answer to that,' Edward put in brightly. 'Subsidized, perhaps.'

He was disappointed to see that the rector looked doubtful. 'In my experience, it is quite difficult enough to get dalesmen to move away even as far as the Durham collieries, where they are crying out for men ... Too large a population, and too many of them young and energetic and under employed ... If there were a higher proportion of older men able to set an example and offer guidance, things might be different. You have, I suppose, given frequent emphasis in your sermons to the duty of every subject of the King to obey the laws?'

'Certainly, with great frequency. But –' Edward smiled ruefully, 'since my average congregation consists of, at most, half a dozen men and women, nearly all of them entirely respectable, I cannot expect to make any great inroads on the lawlessness of the parishioners.'

The rector shook his head. 'It is a sorry state of affairs. In many ways the miners are an admirable race of men, intelligent and courageous. But they must be brought to respect the law, and true religion and virtue ... The matter of the late strike was another regrettable business – though I am convinced that it would all have been over far sooner, had it not been for the intervention of a few fanatics.'

'Mr Crawhall handled the whole business admirably. Without his cool head it might have gone badly. But there, that is over and done with now.' Anxious to make a favourable impression as a young man of ideas, Edward searched his mind for any further suggestion he might make. The rector of Wolsingham did not perhaps have the influence of the rector of Stanhope, but at least he was resident in the area, with occasional access to the ear of the Bishop.

He rejected the idea of suggesting that a more energetic and resolute curate was to be recommended, in place of the culpably inactive Mr Whitelock, and said instead, 'Another solution might be a Society for the Prosecution of Felons.' He knew that William Wilson had been instrumental in setting up just such a body in Wolsingham some years before.

The rector's eyes lit up. 'Indeed. We have found our own organization to have a most beneficial effect on this parish, at least so far as certain kinds of minor lawlessness and damage to property are concerned. There must be those in your district who would support such a scheme.'

'I did venture to speak of it to Mr Crawhall. He seemed to regard it favourably, as did others present at the time. But, of course, that again is neither a quick nor an easy solution.'

255

'I think we have to agree that there are none such, sad though it may be. But I cannot all the same think it right that the perpetrators of Monday's crime should be allowed to get off scot free. They must somehow be brought to justice.'

'Then I suppose troops are the only answer,' said Edward, with apparent regret.

Jenny was still up when Joe came in, rather drunk, just after midnight. There had seemed no point in going to bed when she knew she would not sleep, so she sat knitting by the fire and trying not to think of anything in particular; which was a pretty hopeless endeavour, and only meant that Rowland filled her whole mind.

Joe came and planted himself in front of her, and she realized he was angry about something. 'I asked Rowland to come back here with me tonight,' he said. 'He wouldn't come.'

She said nothing, simply looked at him questioningly, though she knew quite well what he meant to imply. He made it clear the next moment, in case the significance of it should have escaped her. 'Eve told me what happened.'

'Oh.'

'What do you think you're doing, Jenny? It's bad enough you should fly in the face of all decency to wed your curate, but then to mess about with Rowland Peart! He's a good man, Jenny. You've no right to hurt him – because, believe me, that's what you've done.'

'It's not like that,' she said quietly. But Joe was too drunk and too angry to be open to any explanation she might give.

'Come to tea,' Edward had said happily, when Jenny spoke to him after morning service, 'at three o'clock.'

As she walked down the hill that afternoon, she was not very sure what her feelings were. She was not particularly happy; but then she was not unhappy either. She had a strong instinct that today would settle things finally, put an end to her restlessness. By the time she went home again she would somehow, by some means, have resigned herself to marrying Edward, and taken some further irrevocable step towards securing that end, if any such could be found. She tried very hard not to think of Rowland at all. Fortunately, he would be at worship at High House chapel this afternoon, so there was little danger that they would meet.

At the parsonage, Edward welcomed her warmly and took her shawl and ushered her into the parlour, and then rang for Peggy to bring the tea tray. When they had talked about nothing in particular for a little time, while Jenny wondered how she was going to steer the talk into more productive channels, he suddenly said, with apparent casualness, 'Tell me, my love, do you know much of this disgraceful incident last Monday?'

All innocence, she looked at him. 'As much as you do, I suppose,' she said.

'Perhaps, though, you know the identity of the perpetrators – the men responsible?'

She had no more than the very slightest doubt that he was deliberately seeking information, presumably to pass it on to someone in authority. 'I'm not a tale bearer,' she said.

He looked impatient. 'My dearest, you really must rid yourself of these false notions of loyalty. It will not do. Law breaking is law breaking, whoever commits it, however close you are to those who are guilty.' He broke off, thinking for a moment that he saw some recognition on her face that he had touched a sensitive spot. 'Your brother – was he involved?' Part of him felt a certain unworthy and almost malicious pleasure at the prospect of that young man eventually getting his just deserts: another part was alarmed to think that so embarrassing an incident might touch him so nearly as this.

'Why should Joe be involved?' she retorted, and after all he decided to leave it at that. He had no doubt that the authorities would be able to gather the information themselves somehow. It was not discovering the culprits that would be a problem, it was bringing them to justice.

He was distressed, however; after all, if he could not convince Jane of the wrong of what had happened, then his fears for her were indeed well founded. He took her hands in his and said earnestly, 'My dearest, you must recognize that it was really a very serious matter, not something to be rejoiced in, as so many people here seem to do.'

257

'I know,' she said. 'People were hurt.'

He was greatly relieved at that sign of right judgement, though there was still something in her eyes that disturbed him, some kind of barrier he had not seen before and feared he might not be able to break down. 'It is a very grave matter indeed when those who are appointed to enforce the law are prevented from doing so; it is something that might well be destructive of all principles of order. No one with any respect for due authority could be otherwise but gravely disturbed. Indeed, I rather think we can expect very severe measures to be taken.'

The barrier fell then, and it was his Jane's eyes, full of alarm, that looked quickly up at him. 'What severe measures?'

There could be no harm in telling her. 'Possibly even troops.'

'Troops?'

'Soldiers. Sent into Weardale to arrest the wrongdoers. Armed and mounted, I don't doubt.'

She stared at him. It sounded so unlikely. Why should anyone care so much about the actions of a few poachers? 'Why are you saying that?'

'Because it's true. Such a step is being considered. I have it from one of the magistrates himself. Just think, my love, what that would mean.'

She did, and it was not a cheering thought. On the other hand, the fells were broad, the dales deep, there were even the mineshafts and levels, if it should come to that, many of them well known only to the lead miners themselves. So long as they had warning, and time to make their escape ... She would tell Joe tonight, and they would make sure there was always someone on the watch.

Edward, seeing from her expression how seriously she took his warning, and reassured by it that she would not any longer put loyalty to her brother first, smiled gently and passed her a plate of little cakes. Then he changed the subject altogether, recounting some small piece of news Georgiana had sent in her last letter.

Jenny watched him while he talked, studying him with great attention. He was indeed very beautiful to look at. Her

258

eyes, her senses, found real pleasure in simply gazing at him; that had not changed, not in the least. She could have done so for hours, without the slightest trace of boredom, especially if he was moving around, riding, walking, talking to someone, with that hint of restrained animation, that look of health and vitality, the more attractive because it was clothed in such controlled courtesy. Yet no longer did she feel any sense of excitement in watching him. It was a purely intellectual pleasure, without emotion. She wondered now if she had ever felt any more than this cool enjoyment. There was nothing in her, as she watched Edward, of the tumultuous sensations that tore her in pieces at one glance of Rowland's eyes. But then even with Billy it had not been like that.

As for Edward the man, the human being beneath the perfect profile, the exquisitely proportioned body, she wondered now if she had ever known him, or come anywhere near knowing him. She had begun to realize long ago that the perfection of his physical presence was not, after all, as she had at first supposed, wholly reflected in his character. She had even found sometimes, with increasing frequency, that she disliked some of the things he said or did. At the moment she saw only a handsome stranger, from whom she was further apart than she had ever been; or perhaps it was simply that it had taken Rowland to show her how far apart from him she had always been.

That did not, of course, alter the fact that Edward loved her (however blindly) and that she had given her word to marry him, and that he could be supposed to have feelings like any other man, which could be hurt by betrayal or deceit. She had two choices – to be honest with him and tell him what she felt; or to keep that to herself, let things take their course and do her best to be the kind of wife he wanted, in the hope that love and understanding would come with the years. If Rowland had not made it clear there was no future for them together, she would have taken the first course, unhesitatingly. As it was, she knew that she must take the second, because at the very least it offered her the only escape she could hope for from inevitable pain.

'Edward,' she said quietly, putting down her cup. 'Eve's

259

bairn will be born in less than a month now. I cannot leave her till then, but perhaps I could stay at White Lea for a bit after we are married, just till the birth. Or Eve could even come here till then. It would be closer to the midwife and the doctor. And you would not mind, would you, once we were married? It was because I was unwed you thought it wrong I should live in the same house with her.'

She saw his face light up. 'You are saying we should be married at once, as soon as possible?' She nodded, and he came and sat beside her and took hold of her hands. 'Oh my love, what can I say but that it would be the answer to my heart's desire?' Then he bent and kissed her, correctly, on the forehead.

She felt a sudden fierce impatience at his restraint. Somehow even his words, for all their apparent fervour, were spoken without impetuosity. She wanted to force her way behind the exterior of this courteous and distant stranger and seek out the man beneath, if he was there, a man she could love, a man who was capable of impulsive actions, of passion, even sometimes of anger. All at once, she reached out and pulled him to her and then, as soon as he was past the first moment of shock and hesitation, felt him yield to her.

Perhaps it was the unexpectedness of it, breaking without warning through his customary careful defences, perhaps what she had said before had already begun to soften him; but she knew at once that this was going to be different from all the other times. He was breathing fast, his mouth moving hungrily over her face. His hands caressed her, pushing her back against the cushions, while his body pressed closer and closer to her. It was what she had wanted, yet now it had come she felt herself recoil, momentarily repelled by what she knew to be passion without love, on her part at least ... But then he was on her, and all the long abstinence of the two years since Billy's death flooded her, reducing her to a great mass of longing, a longing that had nothing to do with Edward himself, for it was simply that of her body, demanding to be satisfied, somehow, and soon. She slid her fingers through the thick soft waves of his hair, eagerly arching her body against his. Why was he so slow, why did he

260

not go on, further and further?

His hand edged up to her throat, and then slid beneath the neck of her gown, finding its way at last to her breast. She heard him moan, and she was moaning too. His other hand groped beneath her skirts, pushing them up as it found its way to her knee, her thigh, and then to the bare flesh above her stocking. 'Oh Edward!' She knew it would happen now; all she wanted was for it to come soon.

Then suddenly, terribly, he stopped. She heard him give a little cry, not of longing but of dismay. He leapt up, right away from her. Her eyes flew open. She saw the horror on his face, even while he still breathed so fast. She saw how fiercely he struggled to bring himself under control. She sat up.

'Oh, Jane, how can you ever forgive me!'

'Forgive you?' She was utterly bewildered. 'Don't stop then. Come!' She held out her arms.

He took a further step back. 'What are you saying?'

'Why, what's wrong? We're going to be wed, and very soon. There's no harm in it.'

'No harm – !' He looked at her as if she were a stranger, and a repulsive one at that. 'Jane, I do not believe you know what you are saying, I do not believe it.' He took out a handker-chief and mopped his brow; she saw that his hand was trembling. All his customary calm had entirely deserted him. He looked flushed and deeply troubled. 'What I did was unforgiveable, utterly unforgiveable. How I could have ... I cannot understand it. I ask you most sincerely to forgive me. But if you cannot, then I understand, indeed I do.'

She began to laugh.

'I see nothing remotely amusing ...'

She went to him and put her arms about his neck, though he stood there very stiffly, as if determined at all costs to resist any temptation she might offer. 'Edward, we're going to be wed soon. What harm is there in it?'

'To threaten to take from you that most precious thing, your virtue –'

She looked puzzled. 'Isn't that what always happens when a girl weds a man?'

'After the marriage ceremony, of course. Not before!' He

261

sounded shocked that he should have to explain it to her.

'That's not the way in Weardale.'

'I am aware of that,' he said, his expression grim. 'As I have said before, that –' Then he broke off, an appalling thought suddenly occurred to him. 'Jane, you were not … You did not … The young man … ?'

'Billy?' she asked helpfully. 'Did I lie with him? Of course I did. I was his lass. He'd have thought it strange if I hadn't. So would I,' she added cheerfully.

She was not sure what had made her admit to everything. She knew well enough – he could have left her in no doubt – what he would think of such a disclosure. She had known since long before this afternoon, instinctively, that what had been between her and Billy was something she must keep from Edward, if she was not to shock him beyond words. Yet now she had told him, quite openly, and without the least hesitation or remorse. The next moment she made things worse by repeating the whole terrible truth. 'You know yourself it is the way of things in Weardale, when two people start going together. It's the way it's always been.'

'For others, yes. But you …'

'Why should I be different? I'm a Weardale lass like any other. It's only you put me on a pedestal and thought I was someone like your sister.'

'I knew you were not that; but that you should …' He broke away from her. 'You knew, just now – ? You meant …' He stumbled over the words, and looked as if at any moment he might be sick. Then he said with bitter accusation, 'I thought you pure and untouched, an innocent country girl!'

'There is no such thing, except in poetry and story books,' she retorted. 'That is the trouble with education. It does not teach you about life.'

'It teaches about morality, of that I have no doubt. I can only regret that you were never so taught. And I pray that this parish may one day receive the moral leadership it so deplorably lacks. God knows you all need it. I think you are more sunk in corruption than ever I dreamed … Yes, you are right, Miss Emerson. I have been utterly deceived, by myself as well as by you. You are not after all the young

262

woman I thought to marry; or, indeed, I regret to say, the one I wish any longer to marry. God forgive me that ever I thought you were – and for what I allowed you to lead me into this very afternoon.' He went out into the passage and came back with her shawl. 'Goodbye, Miss Emerson. We can have nothing more to say to one another. Ever.' And then he held the door open for her to pass through. He watched her coldly and in silence as she walked away, out through the gate and into the market place. Peggy, who had overheard the last part of the conversation with undisguised interest, hurried to bring fresh tea and exasperate him further with her sympathetic but probing questions.

Jenny walked up the hill, briskly, trying as she went to understand what she felt. She was perhaps a little sorry that it should have ended in quite this way, with Edward turning her from the house in such patent disgust. Yet that was the only regret she did feel, and it was alarmingly small. On the whole she felt light, free, as if she were, like the Siddle brothers, suddenly released from chains that had been taking her inexorably where she did not want to go. What a fool she had been to think she could ever find happiness with Edward! He might be a good man, but to be honest she really had no idea if he was. She knew she had not even come close to knowing him. If he had been blinded by self deceit, then so had she.

That evening, after dark, Joe appeared at the kitchen door of the parsonage with a large bundle, which he handed to Peggy.

'My sister sent these for Mr Selby,' he said, his voice full of undisguised satisfaction.

When Edward unwrapped the bundle, he found inside it every one of the clothes and jewels and other gifts that he had given to Jenny since their first meeting. He pushed them quickly away in a trunk in a spare bedroom, and wondered if he would ever be able to bring himself to look at them again. He had already written to his parents, briefly telling them that his engagement was at an end and begging his father to do all he could, with all speed, to find him a suitable living, as far from Weardale as possible.

Joe, meanwhile, had gone across to the King's Head to celebrate.

Rowland did not fall asleep until just before dawn, and minutes later his aunt came to wake him. He felt cheated, for the weekend was already over, and it had not after all offered him any refreshment to strengthen him for the week ahead.

It had, in fact, been a painful and difficult weekend. It was not just Jenny, and that agonizing meeting on Friday night; there was yesterday too. Not, of course, that he had expected it to be easy. With everyone so proud of the victory won at what they were all calling in grandiose terms the 'Battle of Stanhope', a preacher who spoke against violence was unlikely to meet with an enthusiastic response. But he had not expected to be received quite so badly. Until yesterday, he had never failed to move at least a considerable portion of those who heard him. Not that his hearers in the field at Burnfoot, where he had gone after afternoon service, had been unmoved; far from it. Most of them had been so enraged that they had begun to drown his words in angry shouting less than five minutes into his address. And then, all but a few had turned and walked briskly away, refusing to hear any more. Those who did stay continued to shout, and there were even a few stones thrown. He had gone on to the end, but it had been an experience he hoped he would never have to repeat.

On the other hand, he knew he had been right to speak out. He had only proclaimed the truth, and if none wanted to hear it that was not his fault. Christ himself had been vilified for proclaiming the truth; His servant Rowland Peart ought to rejoice that he had been allowed to share in that apparent failure. Perhaps he would have been able to rejoice if he had still been fired by his old certainty.

He crawled wearily out of bed and dressed, beside the open window where he could breathe the clear air, fresh off the fell. Ironic to think that he had lain sleepless in this sweet atmosphere, which he would remember and long for through each of the four nights that lay before him.

In the kitchen his aunt set breakfast before him and then packed his wallet with food for the week. A little later,

Lancelot came in and took his seat at the table.

'Heard a good piece of news in the King's Arms last night,' he said. 'They were all talking of it.' He was looking at his mother, as if he knew it would interest her. 'Jane Emerson's not to marry the curate after all.'

Some sort of explanation followed, though what it was Rowland did not hear. There was such a crashing in his ears, such a wild pounding of his heart that he could scarcely breathe. He lost all the little appetite he had, longing only for air. 'Excuse me –' he said, and got up and left the house.

'What's up with him?' his aunt asked, but her son's narrative caught her attention again and she began to question him. 'Why, I'm that glad,' she said at last. 'It hurt me that a canny lass like Jenny Emerson should do such a thing. I used to wonder what Billy would have said; I was glad he never knew. And now she's seen sense at last.'

Outside, Rowland walked rapidly up the hill a little way, along the wooded bank of the Harthope burn, until he was out of sight of the village. Here, where the burn cascaded noisily down, he lowered himself on to a rock beside one of the falls, closed his eyes and struggled to bring himself under control. After a time, his breathing steadied, the pounding in his ears lessened and he heard again the splashing of the burn, the faint sound of a cock crowing in the village, the distant bleating of sheep on the fell, sweet tranquil sounds, suddenly enhanced by a sense of wonder and hope.

But no, he must not hope. For what after all had changed? He had told Jenny that her engagement made no difference to him, that if she had been free it would have been just the same. He knew that was right. That her circumstances had changed was an incidental matter, of no importance, except that it would make it harder for him to resist temptation. With eyes still closed, he raised his face to the bitter dawn wind and clasped his hands.

'Oh Lord, give me strength to withstand –' he began. Then he stopped. The next moment he bent his head on his hands, pressing them to his face, 'Guide me, Lord, show me the way!'

15

As he rode out of Stanhope, Edward was conscious of an enormous sense of relief, of release even, as if he had suddenly been freed from prison. Had he not felt that it would be rather an indecorous thing to do, he would have sung aloud. As it was, he smiled happily, already beginning to imagine himself at home again, welcomed by his family, a welcome the warmer because of their delight at the ending of his engagement – their recent letters to him had been effusive on that score. He would still be in time for the end of the New Year round of social events, where he might well come across a number of attractive and eligible young ladies.

And, of course, there would be his ordination to the priesthood. His father, spurred on by relief at his son's sudden restoration to good sense, had already found the ideal living for him, not far from Ashfield, in an area he knew well, where the local gentry were plentiful and congenial. Once ordained, later this year, he would take up permanent residence in his new parish and, secure in the possession of an adequate stipend and a good parsonage house, look about him, at leisure, for a suitable wife.

He felt rather as if he were awakening rapidly from a nightmare. He thought he must have been a little mad during the past months, to have behaved as he did. He was ashamed of himself now, looking back, ashamed that he should have been so blind as to have thought Jane Emerson a suitable wife; and ashamed too of his complete failure as curate of that benighted place. Not that, in the circumstances, he could have hoped to achieve very much, but perhaps, if he had not been so besotted with the girl, he would have been able to achieve more, or at least have given more of his time and energy to trying to do so.

He decided that the days of allowing himself to be swept off his feet by the most unsuitable girls, simply because they inflamed his passions, were at an end. Reason now would govern his choice, and common sense, and the most practical calculations. Not that it would be difficult to find a lady who was both eligible and personable. He knew that he had a good deal to offer, and without any great effort he could think of several young ladies who might suit him very well. There was Miss Lydia Strange, for example, a charming girl, whom he had undervalued until now simply because she did not set his pulses racing. He would renew and broaden his acquaintance with her at the earliest opportunity.

At Wolsingham (already the day seemed warmer, the air softer) he saw the rector emerging from Church Lane, and dismounted to speak to him. William Wilson shook his hand and wished him well for the future.

'You are well out of it, my boy,' he said. 'I fear we are not at the end of our troubles yet.'

Edward had already travelled mentally so far from the concerns of the past months that he did not at first know what the other man was talking about. Then, with an effort, he recollected their last meeting and assumed an expression of grave attention. 'What happened about the troops?'

'The Secretary of State was not wholly sympathetic to our plea for military assistance. A single troop of hussars was put at our disposal, from the regiment stationed at Darlington, with a meagre reinforcement of infantry. Quite useless, as you can imagine. It was also made very plain that any use of them would be seen as an excessive reaction to a minor difficulty.'

'So they were not used?' A foolish question, since the arrival at St John's Chapel of even a single troop of hussars would hardly have gone unnoticed, but he could think of nothing else to say.

'We held a meeting of magistrates here two days ago, and decided we would be unwise to try. Undoubtedly, news of their coming would have preceded them, and by the time they reached the district every single rogue would have taken

267

to the heather. Some of our number still have hopes of moving the Secretary of State to reconsider his position, but London is a very long way from Weardale and I would surmise that our troubles must seem very insignificant at that distance.'

As already they did to him, Edward reflected. 'Will matters be left as they are after all?' he asked, though he was no longer remotely interested in the reply.

'That would be most undesirable. But to be honest with you, I should prefer a peaceful solution, could one be found. We shall see ... However, I must not keep you from your journey. I imagine you have a good way to go before the day is out.'

They parted in a friendly manner, though Edward reflected as he rode away that if he never heard of Weardale ever again in his life he would not be sorry. It had been a disastrous episode.

'See there,' said Jenny. 'Now all's ready.' She gave the cradle a little push and it swayed gently on its rockers. Inside it, small blankets lay neatly folded, ready for the birth, and a pile of tiny, carefully made garments, which she and Eve had knitted and sewed during the past weeks.

Eve gave a faint weary smile. She clasped her hands over the vast curve of her belly. 'I wish he'd come then,' she said. 'I'm sick of waiting.'

Joe, who sat beside her on the settle carefully cleaning his fowling piece, leaned over and kissed her. 'Not long now, hinny.'

'It'll be strange having a baby in the house again,' said Jenny reflectively. She grinned at Tommy. 'To think you were the last. I used to rock you in here, just like this.' She pushed the cradle again, and Tommy looked sheepish. 'Have you thought of a name?' she asked her brother.

If he had, he did not tell her about it then, for there was a knock on the door, and very soon half a dozen or so of his friends had made their noisy entrance, Anthony Siddle among them. Joe stowed his gun in the corner and went to fling an arm round the shoulder of the returned prisoner.

'Why man, you're back! Come, sit down, tell us what happened.'

They gathered about the fire, filling every available seat.

'Is it done with then? You're free?'

Anthony nodded. 'Fined sixpence and bound over for a year.'

'So that's it?'

'Aye. For me anyhow. But I heard there are new warrants out.'

'Oh aye? Who for, do you know?' Joe's tone was casual.

'I do know you're one of them. You can guess the rest. Seven, all told. I don't doubt Joseph Dawson gave them the names.'

Eve bit her lip and held tight to Joe's hand. He grinned at her reassuringly. 'Issuing warrants is one thing, enforcing them is another. They know that well enough.'

'But if they send soldiers, like Jenny said they might?'

'They'd have to send an army first.'

Eve, who clearly did not find that in the least reassuring, visibly shivered.

'I've been thinking,' said James Craggs. 'I heard what Rowland Peart said, when he preached against us.'

'So did I,' said Charlie Siddle. 'Hoyed a stone at him for it too. Nowt personal, mind.'

James shook his head. 'Why no, I wasn't meaning that. It's true, I didn't think much of what he said. But there was a grain of sense in it all the same. That about dignity, making them look bad by the way we behave – there's something in it.' There was a little pause, during which they all waited for his conclusion. 'I think we should go and give ourselves up, like Anthony there did.'

'That was different,' objected Joe.

'Aye, I know it was. But all the same, if we did that, then ... why, it seems to me, Frank Johnson would look a fool, and Joseph Dawson too, and they'd neither of them get owt for turning us in, and it would show the justices Weardale men aren't cowards.'

'Why yes,' agreed John Kidd, 'and maybe they'd be more lenient with us for it.'

The others considered the matter for some time, and then

269

several of them began to murmur in agreement. 'There's something in what you say,' Jock Currah agreed. 'A canny bit sense.'

'Then we'll do it, all of us, together?' James looked round at the faces of his companions. There was a general rumble of consent into which one word broke sharply.

'No!'

They all stared at Joe, who said vehemently, 'I'm not going anywhere, not with Eve's bairn due any day. I won't leave her now, not for any man. I'd sooner risk transportation.'

James looked disappointed, but he clearly understood. 'Aye, well, I can see that ... I tell you what, then. We keep watch for Frank Johnson, or anyone else they send, and lie low, just till your lass has her bairn. Then we all go to Durham together. How would that be?'

Joe nodded. 'Why aye, that would suit me.'

The men stayed a long time that night, so that it was well after midnight when Joe and Eve went up to bed, leaving Jenny to damp down the peats in the hearth and bar the door and put out the lights. Eve was very quiet, tired Joe supposed. He put his arm about her as they mounted the stairs, supporting her, and felt how heavily she leaned on him. Half way up she came to a complete halt and he thought she was about to fall. 'Soon be in bed,' he said softly, his mouth on her hair. He tightened his grip about her. 'Come now, hinny; three steps more.'

She did not move, or make any apparent attempt to do so. Within his supporting arm, her body seemed tensed, as if she braced herself against something. Then he heard her give a sudden sharp intake of breath, and she moaned softly. 'Joe!'

There was no mistaking the fear in her voice, nor – as it dawned on him what was wrong – his own alarmed response. Heart beating fast, he half carried her the last of the way and got her to bed. By now it was clear that she was in considerable pain, great waves of pain that came and went with terrifying frequency. He ran down to Jenny and she roused Tommy to go for the midwife and then came up to sit with Eve and hold her hand.

Joe sat with them too, for as long as he could. In the end it was too much for him. He could not bear to see Eve in such pain, to hear her crying for help, to him, to Jenny, to anyone at all, or reciting fast frightened little prayers, as if they might somehow act as a charm to ease her agony. He fled downstairs, and there paced the floor, straining his ears to catch all the sounds he had tried to escape.

Half way through the morning, the midwife advised sending for Mr Scott, and Jenny sent Joe, who was better, she felt, given something to do. Once the surgeon was there, Joe resumed his pacing. It was not until well into the afternoon that he heard Eve give a great agonizing shriek of pain; after which there was an odd and – to him – uncanny silence. And then a strange thin wailing cry seemed to fill the house. Joe stood quite still, frozen, a shiver running the length of his spine, though whether it was from awe or fear he was not sure; a little of each perhaps.

Jenny found him like that when she came down, moments later. She was smiling, though she looked tired. She slid her arm through his. 'You have a bonny little daughter. Come up now. Eve wants you.'

He went with her, and knelt by the bed, where his Eve lay propped on all the pillows in the house, looking appallingly grey and tired and frail, but smiling at him as if all her being, all her strength was concentrated in that smile; and in the crook of her arm lay a tiny red faced crumpled little creature who somehow took him quite by surprise, for in all the months of waiting and planning he had for some reason never really thought of the forthcoming birth as something that would produce a new and separate being. Yet here she was. He touched the infant's cheek, very gently, afraid that he might somehow hurt her. It felt soft and warm, and she stirred a little, blinking deep blue eyes, half opening a tiny triangular mouth, and then settling again into immobility. He looked up at Eve, who was still smiling.

'Can we call her Jane?' asked Eve.

'If we call her Eve too,' Joe said. Then he kissed them both.

For three days the snow had fallen without ceasing, blotting out hills and sky, tracks and road, all but the nearer buildings, a swirling mass of featureless whiteness. It howled and rattled about the lodging shop at night like a malevolent spirit, and by day stung the faces of the miners as they struggled between mine and lodging, snatched at their clothes, fought a battle with them for their very breath.

Like them all, Rowland feared that when Friday came they would find themselves marooned at Guinea Grove, unable to get home. Some, well prepared, had brought their skis with them, but the battered pair that had belonged to Billy were still lodged behind the door at his Aunt Tabitha's house, and in any case if it did not stop snowing soon it would be too dangerous to risk the journey, even on skis. No Weardale man ever took snow lightly, or underestimated its power.

But by Friday morning the snow had ceased and the wind dropped a little and by the time they had finished their breakfasts the sun had come out. They would make it home somehow, before nightfall.

It was a hard journey. Rowland and four others, keeping together because it was safer that way, struggled through drifts and bitter wind, trying to find the path in a landscape transformed and distorted by the snow. A journey that normally took scarcely two hours stretched out to an inter-minable five, and it was fully dark by the time they came within sight of the lights of St John's Chapel. Rowland did not think he had ever been so thankful to reach home as he was that night. He hoped in a vague sort of way that it would now snow ferociously all weekend, so as to make any return to Guinea Grove on Monday out of the question. But he suspected that the weather had done its worst for the time being.

He had looked forward to his aunt's warm welcome, the hot supper enlivened by gossip which now, again, often included news about Jenny, no longer an outcast. But he found that Tabitha was confined to bed with a feverish cold, and his cousin was on his way out to join his friends at the King's Arms (more to his taste than the miners' favourite, the King's Head). Rowland washed as best he could; usually he plunged into the burn below the mine to free himself of the worst of the week's dirt before resuming his weekend clothes and setting out for home, but today of course that

272

had been impossible. Tonight he had to make do with what water was left, ice rimmed, in the pail in the back kitchen. He put on fresh clothes, draped his working clothes around the kitchen to dry, and then got his own supper and settled down to its rather cheerless comfort beside a fire already banked down for the night.

As always, he had mixed feelings about coming home. It was, of course, an indescribable relief to be free of that horrible place for three blissful nights, and pleasant not to have to spend a large part of each day below ground. He would have time to preach (if the Spirit led him to do so and the weather allowed), and share in worship at High House chapel, and talk with friends not seen for a week. The hard part would be, as always, to avoid meeting Jenny.

He had been scrupulous about keeping away from her. It was, of course, not as easy as it might once have been, when she was still an outcast, rarely coming down to the village, and then furtively, when there were few people about. Now that she had seen sense (Rowland still did not know precisely why she had broken with Edward Selby, but he did not greatly care; the fact was enough), she was welcomed back among her old friends as if the breach had never happened. Saturday was the most dangerous day, when she often came to market. Lately, Rowland had taken to going for long walks on Saturdays, or preaching some distance away. Sundays were easier, for she no longer came down to church, even though Edward Selby had gone and Mr Whitelock, much restored in health, had returned unobtrusively to his duties.

It was not that he did not want to see her. But he knew that he needed a little time of calm, a little time to reflect on what he ought to do. He knew now that he had been quite wrong about one thing: it made all the difference in the world to him that she was not going to be married, that she was not promised to anyone else. He was not sure why. After all, if he was not to have her, did it really matter what she did or who she married? Yet somehow it did. It took much of the torment from his longing for her to know that she was free and could love him single heartedly, if that should prove to be permitted to them. He had not perhaps found again all the

273

single mindedness he had felt before he loved her, but a degree of serenity had returned, and he knew now that he had not after all lost his faith, or not completely.

What was more, the experience had taught him that things were not quite as simple as he had thought. Faced last year with Eve's despair, trying to understand it by imagining himself in her place, he had come to the conclusion that it was a consequence in part of the female condition. Now he knew, because he had suffered them too, that despair and doubt were on the contrary simply intrinsic to the condition of all humanity, as much a part of life as to believe and to hope. The joy of conversion was not, after all, a permanent and fixed state of mind and heart, even for him. Nothing was final, until earthly life ended, nothing certain, except that even in the deepest darkness God's love was still there, somehow, somewhere, and one had only to trust. That was the gift of conversion, not a constant state of unruffled bliss, but to know that in the worst despair no man or woman was alone and unloved.

He had learned to trust again. Now, as he went through the routines of each day, whenever he prayed, he waited alert, watchful, for some sign, some hint or impulse, some message of whatever kind that would show him with unequivocal clarity where his path lay, if only by assuring him that the one he had chosen at the moment of his conversion was the right one in every respect. He felt now that he would even find the strength, were it to be asked of him, to face the prospect of Jenny being married to someone else (as she surely would be, in time), if he could only receive that sign. It had not yet come, but he was borne up by the certainty that it would.

He finished his supper, washed the utensils and put them away, looked in on his aunt – who was asleep – wrapped himself again in his plaid and went out into the bitter night. Reaching its doors, firmly closed against the cold, Rowland could hear that the usual company had gathered in the King's Head. They welcomed him noisily, making the inevitable joking remarks about the tankard of water Tom Walton set before him with his customary mocking ceremoniousness. By now he was more or less forgiven for preaching against last year's most important event, or rather they had decided to overlook what they regarded as an unfortunate lapse, in view of other less reprehensible sides to his character, such as his support for the strike; and the fact that he remained stubbornly friendly, even to those whose actions he could not approve. What was more, he always took their teasing in good part.

His coming had briefly interrupted their singing, but they resumed it as soon as he was seated, taking up where they had left off, at the fifth verse.

'Now the times being hard and provisions being dear,
The miners were starving almost we do hear;
They had nought to depend on, so well you may ken,
But to make what they could of the bonny moor hen.'

By the time they began on the seventh verse the whole room was reverberating with it, tankards banging on the tables to beat out the rhythm, clogged feet clattering on the flagged floor.

'Oh, these words they were carried to Weardale with speed,
Which made the poor miners to hang down their heads;'

Charlie Siddle, his nose red from the cold, came over to the corner where Rowland was, and tapped the shoulder of Jock Wilson, who sat beside him.

'But sent them an answer, they would have them to ken,
They would fight till they died for their bonny moor hen.'

With obvious reluctance, Wilson gulped down the last of his ale and went outside. Charlie took the vacated seat.

'His turn!' he shouted to Rowland above the din. 'On watch for constables!'

'Joe's lass not had her bairn yet then?' Rowland shouted back.

He saw at once from the man's face, and from the little pool of quiet that suddenly surrounded them, that something was wrong.

'Why aye, she's had the bairn, a girl. Monday, I think it was. But she's bad – Eve Todd, that is; the bairn's thriving,

275

so far as I know. But the doctor's been up there a few times now.'

Rowland put down his tankard and said goodnight and left the inn, and set out at once through the snow for White Lea.

It was Tommy who opened the door to him; that in itself was a bad sign, at this time of night. The boy let him in, saying no more than, 'I'll tell them,' and a little later Jenny came down. She looked thoroughly weary, Rowland thought, feeling anxiety catch in his throat. She showed no self-consciousness, as if all that had ever been between them had no place in this house at this time, as if there was only room for one concern in her thoughts. If she realized that this was their first meeting since she parted from Edward, she showed no sign of it.

'Come up,' she said. 'Joe thinks that's what she'd want.' Then, as they went, she said quietly, 'Dr Scott says its only a matter of time.'

Eve lay still and scarcely conscious, looking somehow shrunken and fragile in the wide bed, beside which the baby lay asleep in her cradle. Joe sat on a stool at the other side, one hand holding Eve's, the other gently stroking her forehead, though she gave no sign that she knew he was there. He glanced round as Rowland came in; he too looked exhausted.

Rowland came and stood at the foot of the bed. He heard Joe say softly, 'Here's Rowland come to see you,' though there was no visible response on the grey face. Watching her, Rowland had a sudden piercing, anguished recollection of just such another scene, of another much loved wife being carried inexorably into death, beyond the reach of the man who looked on in helpless agony. Only then, two years ago in the dank, bare little room in Manchester, he had been the man, kneeling where Joe was now, and for him there had been two deaths, and no friend, no brother or sister, to share his grief; or so he had thought.

He went to Joe and laid a hand on his shoulder. 'Would you like me to pray?'

Joe nodded, though he did not look round. Rowland bent his head over his clasped hands and asked – his voice husky,

276

uneven, imploring – for healing and comfort and strength, whatever could rightly be given. After a little time, Eve's eyes flickered open and focused on him, and he fell silent. She seemed then to be struggling for words, trying desperately to say something. Joe leaned over, listening, watching her cracked lips, as again and again they silently formed one word. 'Sing,' Joe murmured at last. He sounded a little puzzled. 'She wants us to sing, I think.'

Then she said something more, and he leaned over her again. '*Traveller* – I think she said; *traveller* ... and *unknown*?'

'*Come, O thou Traveller unknown*,' said Rowland softly. He swallowed hard. 'It's one of Charles Wesley's hymns. We sang it the first time I spoke.' Watching Eve's face, Joe saw recognition there, and something that was not quite a smile.

'Aye, that's what she wants. Can you sing it?'

Rowland began to sing, though with difficulty, his voice unsteady, yet sounding to his ears very loud and harsh in the quiet room. Beside him, Jenny tried to join in, though she did not know the words and had to pick up the tune as she went along, and after a time, her voice breaking, could not continue at all.

> *'Tis love! 'tis Love! thou diedst for me!*
> *I hear Thy whisper in my heart;*
> *The morning breaks, the shadows flee,*
> *Pure, universal Love Thou art ...'*

Before the hymn reached its end, Eve had drifted completely into unconsciousness. She died little over an hour later.

Tommy was sent for the midwife, to lay out the body, for her skills encompassed both ends of life. Joe had taken Eve into his arms when she died, and he held her still, without moving, his face hidden against her breast, as immobile, as apparently without life, as Eve herself. Jenny touched his shoulder and spoke to him, very gently, but he did not stir.

'I think he's best left alone,' Rowland said quietly.

Jenny nodded. She looked about her, as if trying to find something to do, and seemed relieved when the baby began to cry. She got Rowland to help carry the cradle downstairs to the chimney corner, where she busied herself feeding the baby with watered cow's milk from a makeshift bottle. Rowland stood looking down at her, intolerably moved by that tender maternal image; and fearful too for the infant. The life of a child was such a fragile thing ... no, so was all human life, all human love. He wanted to kneel down beside Jenny and put his arms about her, to give comfort and to receive it. But she seemed somehow remote from him, absorbed in what she was doing, and besides he had no right to ask that of her. He could only be her friend, no more.

The baby was fed and returned to the cradle to sleep and Tommy came back with the midwife and Rowland took charge of Joe, loosening his clasp from the body, guiding him gently to the mattress in the corner (he would not leave the room), persuading him to drink a sleeping draught and then sitting with him until it took effect. Downstairs again, he found Jenny mechanically tidying away the accumulated clutter of the past week. She looked more weary than ever, now that it was all over.

'Is there owt else I can do?' he asked. His longing to hold her was almost overpowering, though he fought it with all his strength. If he had thought it would help her, he would have had no hesitation, but he could not be sure, and she had troubles enough without complicating things. Besides, so long as he did not touch her his self control was strong enough; once he had her in his arms he knew it would be gone. There was no hint in her grey eyes that she had any thought of him in her head, except as a friend who could be of use. He ought, he supposed, to be thankful for that.

'There's one thing, if you would, though it's hard. We sent word more than once to her family, but none of them came. Now –'

'They've to be told she's dead. Why yes, I'll do that for you.'

He turned and walked away from her, without another word.

It was clear that Jacob Todd had retired to bed for the night. The house was in darkness, and it took long and vigorous knocking to bring him to the door, holding a lantern and wearing only nightshirt and cap. He looked far from pleased.

'What time do you call this, Rowland Peart? Some of us keep Christian hours, I'll have you know.'

'I'm sorry,' said Rowland, 'but the news I bring will not wait. I've come from White Lea.'

There was a little silence. Rowland was not sure – the lantern light was weak – but he thought he saw a spasm of some kind pass over the other man's face. Then Jacob said, 'So what if you have?'

With difficulty, Rowland curbed a rush of anger. 'Your daughter –'

'I have no daughter but one.'

'She died tonight, just three hours since. I'm sorry.'

Again there was a pause, before the other man said, 'She's gone to judgement then.' He nodded. 'Good night, Rowland Peart. I have a bed to go to, if you have not.'

'The bairn's living yet. They call her Eve.'

There was no reply. The door was already closed. Rowland stood there staring at it for some time, trying to suppress the rage and hatred in his heart. Somewhere, surely, beneath that unmoved, relentless exterior, Jacob Todd must be suffering?

As he turned to go, he glanced up at the house. There was a light upstairs now, shadows moving against the curtain, voices. Outside, it was still and very cold. Chilled, weary, he began to walk away.

Half-way across the market place he was stopped in his tracks, transfixed by horror. A cry so appalling, so full of anguish that it seemed scarcely human, pierced the frozen silence of the night, echoing on and on as if it would never end. He stood quite still, eyes closed, unable to move, the sound filling his head. Then it broke off, resumed, wavered, and gave way at last to a woman's unrestrained sobbing, wild enough still, but earthbound, ordinary, the unmistakable sound of bitter grief. As he walked home, Rowland found he was weeping too.

Even without her family, there was a good company for Eve's funeral two days later, for all Joe's friends came, and Rowland, James Craggs, Charlie Siddle, George Lowes and

279

Ralph's Joe helped him to bear the coffin down the hill to the church.

Afterwards, as they left the graveside, walking quickly because of the cold, Jenny glimpsed a woman turning away, hurrying from the churchyard ahead of them, her shawl pulled close about her against the wind. She looked round at Rowland, who was walking near her, and saw that he had been watching the woman too. 'Mrs Todd,' he said softly. By the time they reached the gate, there was no sign of her. When Jenny turned to comment on it to Rowland, he had already moved away, to talk with Joe.

She hung back a little, to allow Uncle Ralph, just behind her, to catch up. He looked terrible, she thought. Several times already this winter he had been too ill to go to work, and now even their slow pace set him struggling for breath, but his talk, between coughs, was all of the wonderful grove they were working on Middlehope moor and how they would have more money at the year's end than they had ever dreamed of. Jenny was glad that Joe was too far ahead to hear what his uncle was saying.

They went back up the hill and the mourners crowded into the house at White Lea for the cake, cheese, wine, brandy and tea that Joe's slender resources had somehow been able to supply, helped, discreetly, by those of his friends who could afford it. Jenny, busy attending to them all, had little time to join the talk, full of the customary funeral reminiscences. Once, she thought Rowland was about to come and speak to her, but at that moment the baby woke and cried, and she had to take her upstairs and see to her, away from the noise and the bustle.

Jenny had scarcely wept at all since Eve's death, partly because there had been too much to do. Now she did weep, but she knew it was not only for Eve, not at all perhaps. She was suddenly overwhelmed again by all the sorrow and harshness of her life, by all the things that she had hoped, by marrying Edward, to escape. She did not now regret that he had gone. It was not, after all, so easy to escape from pain, or only by leaving behind all that she held most dear, and there had been no other reason for marrying him. Perhaps in a way that episode had helped her to come to terms with

280

Billy's death, to move beyond the bitterness of her sense of loss, to accept that he had gone, but that life would continue somehow. Yet at the moment it was not acceptance that filled her, only a desolate loneliness.

Since she had parted from Edward, she had daily hoped that Rowland would seek her out, so that she could somehow convince him that he was mistaken and that they were after all meant to love one another. But a month had gone by and he had not come. In fact, she thought sometimes that he was deliberately avoiding her, for he and Joe met often enough. Knowing that he saw their love as a snare, she did not try to make the first move. If he had learned to overcome his feelings, then it was not for her to disturb that hard won serenity, however much she longed to do so; that would only make him resent and blame her. But now that they had met again, she was bitterly hurt by his calmness, his apparent ability to look upon her simply as a friend. She did not want him to suffer, but still less did she want him to stop loving her.

He was as calm and controlled as ever when he came to meet her as she descended the stairs. 'I'm going now,' he said. 'But I must speak with you first.'

She did not know whether hope or fear was uppermost in her as she waited for what he would say next.

'Mr Wilson came to Chapel yesterday,' he said, and when she looked puzzled, enlarged, 'The rector from Wolsingham. He came with a constable from Durham, with the warrants.' She realized then that what he was saying had nothing at all to do with their feelings for one another. She hoped he did not see how disappointed she was. 'They found no one, of course, and we stopped them from coming up here, but myself and some others entertained them as kindly as we knew how – at the very least, that can't hurt the case against Joe and the rest. To be fair, they were courteous enough themselves, the two of them. The end of it was, we gave our word all the men would give themselves up, tomorrow, at Wolsingham. We said they would come with sureties, so they could be given bail. That's all arranged.' He paused, as if what he had to say next was not so easy. 'I know it will be hard for Joe, but they've waited a long time, and it's best to get it over with. I told him I'd come for him, but I don't think he heard me. Can you try and warn him?'

'I'll try,' she promised, though with little hope of success. They began to walk towards the door, two acquaintances talking casually together. 'But will you not be at work tomorrow? You've missed a day already.'

'They know I'll not be there for some days. I'm not greatly grieved at it.' He opened the door and stepped out into the snow, which had begun again, though gently this time, a lazy downward drift of flakes. 'I'll come early. It'll be bad travelling in this weather.'

'Thank you,' she said. Now, surely, he would say something, give some hint that his feelings had not changed, even if his resolve was still as strong.

He did hesitate for a moment, looking at her, as if about to say something more, but in the end he simply turned and walked away. She closed the door and went back to see to the few mourners who were left.

As he had promised, Rowland came early next morning, before it was fully light, though with the snow lying so deep it had never been completely dark. Jenny said nothing, simply held the door while he came in, and then closed it again.

Joe was standing by the fire, looking down into the cradle where his infant daughter lay sleeping, absorbed in thoughts so profound that he did not glance round or show any sign that he was aware of someone coming into the house. Rowland crouched down beside the cradle and began to stroke the infant's cheek with one finger, a little absent-mindedly, but with great tenderness. Then he raised his eyes to Joe. 'It's time, Joe,' he said quietly, after a moment. 'The others are waiting for you.'

Joe did look at him then, but blankly, as if he did not really see him.

'I'll come with you to Wolsingham,' said Rowland, standing up.

Joe stirred a little, and he must have taken something in after all, for he shook his head. 'I'm not going.'

'But you gave your word.'

'I did not know then –' He broke off, distress distorting his

282

features; he looked close to tears. Rowland laid a hand on his arm.

'I know. But this is something that has to be done. If you don't go they'll come for you, and then it will be worse.' After a pause, he added, 'All that will happen now is that Mr Wilson will bail all of you, till the next Sessions, at Easter. You'll be home again by nightfall.'

Joe swallowed hard. He bent his head, clearly pondering the matter. Then he said, 'But if he does not? It's not certain, is it?'

'No,' Rowland admitted. 'It's not wholly certain. But as sure as it can be.'

'And if he does not, if I'm sent to Durham gaol, what then? Jenny will be here all alone, to care for Tommy and the bairn, with no one to bring in any money, only the poor rate. I cannot do that to her.'

The baby began to whimper, and Jenny picked her up and sat on the settle with her, rocking her gently. 'We'll take no harm,' she said.

'I shall care for them,' said Rowland. 'We're going to be wed, me and Jenny.'

There was a sudden astonished silence. Brother and sister stared at Rowland. The odd thing was, Jenny thought, that he looked as surprised as any of them, as if he had no idea at all what had made him speak, had done so without knowing what he was doing. She saw him colour, and thought he was about to deny what he had said, or explain it away. But instead a look of joy came over his face, just such a joy as was putting out hesitant shoots inside her, woken by his declaration. It was as if he had heard rather than spoken the sudden and wholly unexpected announcement, and was as astonished by it as she was, and as delighted: as if he wanted to leap up and cry aloud for joy.

Joe looked from him to Jenny and back again. Their eyes seemed to be held together by an invisible thread, which he had no hope of breaking. Both were smiling, a tremulous, wondering smile, hovering on the brink of exaltation. Puzzled, he said, 'When – how ...? I didn't know.'

'Why, nor did I, but now I do!' Rowland went to Jenny and took the baby from her, passing her to Joe. 'Here, take

283

your bairn. I want to kiss my sweetheart.' And then he held out his arms.

Jenny looked at him and gave a great gurgle of laughter, which welled up suddenly from some long suppressed spring of delight. 'Now then, Rowland Peart, you've taken a canny bit on yourself! I don't remember being asked what I wanted.'

He grinned, looking boyish and full of mischief. 'So you'll not have me?' It was perfectly obvious that he had no doubt what her answer would be.

Just for a moment longer she held off from him, her head on one side, her eyes bright with teasing laughter; and then she said, 'What do you think?' and allowed him to gather her into his arms and kiss her with a fierce and hungry abandonment, to which she responded with laughter and tears together; and then with a passion as great as his own.

Then Jenny recollected with shame that Joe was there, that he had just lost the woman he loved; and at that same moment Rowland pushed her gently from him and looked with obvious distress at her brother. 'Joe, I'm sorry. I didn't think ...'

Joe shook his head, smiling a little; it was the first time Jenny had seen him smile since Eve died. 'It's the best thing that could have happened, for me too,' he said, his voice husky. 'If she wasn't to have Billy, there's no one I'd sooner see her wed than you.' And then he laid the baby in her cradle and came to clasp Rowland's hands.

It was all settled very quickly. Joe agreed to go to Wolsingham, and Rowland undertook to go with him and the others, returning with them this evening if all went well. If things went badly, he would come back to tell Jenny the news. And whatever happened they would be married as soon as possible.

Rowland was silent as he walked down the hill at Joe's side, though Joe tried to get him to talk. He was thoroughly intrigued by the whole business, astonished that it should all have been planned without his knowledge, without even, so far as he knew, any recent meetings between the two of them. All Rowland would say was that he had planned nothing, it was not his doing, which only made it more mystifying than ever as far as Joe was concerned.

To Rowland there was nothing mystifying about it at all. It had been, quite simply, the coming of the sign he had sought. The words had come into his mouth, just then, without warning, through no choice of his own, because that was how he was to be shown what to do. And so everything had fallen into place, and in the way he had scarcely dared to hope it might. He saw the path before him now, and it was, miraculously, the one he would have chosen if he had allowed his own impulses – wayward, unreliable as they were – to guide him. He knew now, with shame that he had ever doubted, that God's love was so great, so all embracing, that it did not exclude his love for Jenny, but rather encompassed and transformed it. That, for him, was the greatest wonder of all.

At White Lea, Jenny held the baby in her arms and danced round the room, singing as she went. Tommy, coming down for his breakfast, stood in the doorway, watching her in bewildered amazement, until she saw him and laid the child down and danced him round instead. Only then, laughing and breathless, did she tell him why she was behaving so strangely.

16

The curlews had been calling all day, their cry echoing over the fell, mingling with the mournful bleating of new lambs and the distant sound of the river. Towards evening, the wind had dropped, and it was very still, the shadows like velvet, the landscape all rich soft colours, the hills somehow brought closer by the gentle light. It was almost as warm as summer.

Jenny paused just outside the door, sighing with happiness, and expectation too. Her eyes scanned the track, followed the road until it dipped out of sight. Any moment now, surely –

Forcing herself not to watch for his coming, she went to dig a little more of the potato patch. It was time the potatoes were planted, but Joe did not like digging and now that washing had started up for the summer she no longer had Tommy's help. She wondered again if the change she already saw in her younger brother would continue now he was back at work. She hoped so. It pleased her that he no longer swore (except by accident), or got drunk with his friends, and that, even without formal schooling, he was learning to read widely and ask questions and improve his mind.

The dark earth was full of stones – like all the dale earth, it bred stones, so people said, for no matter how many were cleared from it each year, next year there would be as many again. Time after time she stooped to gather a stone and throw it aside, on to the pile in the corner of the garden, and each time she did so she glanced down the hill, just in case, before resuming her digging. She began to sing, softly, without words. It was the tune of some ballad or other, which Rowland had been singing last weekend, trying to fit it to more uplifting words, to Joe's derisive amusement.

The geese cackled in warning. She flung down the spade and ran; and there he was, coming up the track towards her. He waved and called and broke into a run.

They clung together, and he swung her round, laughing and kissing her again and again. It was some time before they drew apart and began very slowly to walk on to the house, their arms about one another.

'What news then? Is Joe home?'

'He's down in Chapel just now, about the sale of the galloway, the one he's just broken. But he's home. Fined and bound over, like the rest of them. That's why he wanted the pony sold. He's a bit short since Monday.'

Rowland halted and turned to face her, holding her very close. 'Tommy still at work?' She nodded, smiling in excited anticipation, knowing what was coming. He went on, his voice slow and caressing, 'Then we've just time ...'

She ran from him, laughing, into the house, and he followed, caught her just inside the door, and steered her quickly to the box bed; and there they came together, all laughter and tenderness, teasing and slow, then hungry for one another, coming through fierce desire to an exploding mutual joy. It was this, each Friday, that redeemed the misery of Mondays, when Rowland set off again for Guinea Grove, and Jenny had a whole five days to endure without him; this, and every wonderful moment of their Saturdays and Sundays together.

She had never dreamed there could be a happiness like it, so intense, so complete. When they were apart, every day dragged; together, it was like the northern lights they had seen at the moment of falling in love, a shimmering dance of fire and enchantment, transforming the most mundane of activities into something magical. It had surprised her at first, to discover what joyous sensuality there was in Rowland's love for her, apparently existing without any sense of incongruity side by side with the burning seriousness of his religious faith. But then each moment of their life together brought a new discovery, a new adventure.

She had no illusions about what lay ahead. It would never be easy, and they would certainly never be anything but poor, even if Rowland's partnership were to hit a rich vein, for if there was ever money left over when the bare necessities were paid for he gave it away, to Joe's frequent exasperation. But her experience with Edward had taught her that material things were not enough for happiness, and that to try and escape pain and hardship was a futile exercise, only made possible by ceasing to feel anything much at all. If she had chosen that path, she would have turned her back on the happiness she had now, and she knew, with certainty, that for this happiness she would endure any pain, any loss that might lie hidden in the future.

After a time they lay still in one another's arms, very close but no longer joined, each content to look into the other's eyes, smiling a little, at peace. Across the room, baby Eve woke and began to gurgle in her cradle. Rowland said softly, 'What you told me – is it still the same?'

Jenny nodded, smiling all the more. 'I'm sure now, quite sure.'

He reached down and patted her stomach. 'You'll have your hands full then, with two of them.' Then his hand moved on, downwards, and she pulled him to her again.

Later they went out into the dusk, to stand quietly together by the open door, watching for Tommy's return.

'Did you know,' Rowland said after a moment, 'I've been back in Weardale a full year now?'

'And now you're tied to it, chained and bound.' She laughed, teasing him.

He kissed her, slowly and thoroughly, and then stood looking into her face. 'God has been good.' After a little while he went on, 'Another man was awakened to the Lord this week at the mine.'

'I'm glad,' said Jenny. Rowland's faith had not yet won her, though to live with him and not be touched by it was impossible. Nor would she ever do anything to hinder or oppose him in it, not simply because she had no wish to, but also because she knew quite well that if she were ever to face him with a choice between herself and his God, he would, however regretfully, put her aside. He loved her completely, but she would never be first in his heart. That was something

288

she had accepted from the start, loving him as she did.

It was Joe who came into sight first, cheerful from having made a good sale, the dog running at his heels. Rowland went to meet him. 'I'm thankful to see you safe,' he said.

'Aye,' said Joe. A faint shadow passed over his face. 'I was never sure of it till it was all over. Has Jenny told you the verdict?'

'A fine, she said.'

'Aye. One shilling, and bound over for a year. George Lowes stood surety for me, and your cousin.'

'The same for all of you?'

Joe nodded.

There was a little silence.

'What's up with you, man?' asked Joe. 'Anyone would think you weren't best pleased.'

'I was thinking, that's all: five pounds for poaching a moor hen, one shilling for near killing a man and half blinding another ...'

'Why, I see,' said Joe, suddenly belligerent, 'I got off too light for you! You'd sooner they'd have had me transported – or hanged, maybe?'

Jenny, her arm through Rowland's, studied his face. It had a sombre, thoughtful look, and she even found herself wondering if Joe was right. Then her husband relaxed, and grinned. 'Why no, for then who would bring game home for the pot? I'm no use with a fowling piece. But all the same – do you think it just that a moor hen should be of more value in the eyes of the law than a man?'

'Why, we all know the rich man's game is sacred!' said Joe. He turned to look across at the dark slopes of Black Hill and Chapel Fell, and then on to Harthope, glimpsed through the trees. 'The Bishop thinks he owns this dale, and so do the Beaumonts, but they don't, not any of them, whatever the law may say. If anyone owns it, it's us. We know every nook and cranny, every blade of grass, we know the earth and the rock, we know how to seek out lead and silver, how to make things grow, we know its ways and its moods. We know it like we know our own bodies, better perhaps. We are part of it, and it's part of us, for it gives us life and it kills us and it's in our very breath and our blood.'

There was a long silence. Joe looked faintly embarrassed, as if taken by surprise at his own outburst. It was clearly a relief to him when Tommy came running to them out of the shadows, full of happy chatter. Joe put an arm about his brother and the four of them went together into the house and closed the door on the night.